Chronicles of Borea

Book III

The Making of a Bard

Siciliana

Second Edition

Joseph E. Koob II

Illustrations and Cover by Robert Haselier

The Chronicles of Borea

Fantasy Series

Book I – The Making of a Bard – Preludio

Book II – The Making of a Bard – Gigue

Book III – The Making of a Bard – Siciliana

Book IV – The Making of a Bard – Ciaccona

Book V – IXUS – Corrente

Book VI – Civil War Threatens –Tempo di Borea

Book VII – The Great War – Grande Finale

NEW: The Hunter's Mark – Novella

ISBN: 979-8-9884799-3-2

Sub-Titles

Preludio (Prelude) – short introductory piece of music, improvisatory in style, usually begins a work of several movements

Gigue (Giga, Jig) – a lively dance often serving as the final movement of a suite of dances in the Baroque period

Siciliana (Siciliano) – Baroque Dance/movement in an instrumental work in a slow $^6_8$ or $^{12}_8$ time with lilting rhythms, that resembles a slow jig or tarantella, characterized by dotted rhythms and usually in a minor key. It can elicit a pastoral mood.

Ciaccona (Chaconne) – series of variations over a ground bass (short, repetitive bass line) that sets the harmony

Corrente (Courante) – triple meter dance, often found in the Baroque suite

Tempo Di Borea (Bourree') – lively dance in duple meter with an upbeat quarter note

Grande Finale (Finale) – ending section or movement of a larger work – sonata, suite, etc.; often with thematic material from other movements and related in Key to the whole

The book sub-titles reflect the musical emphasis in the series. Taken from the Baroque period, all except the Finale are found in J.S. Bach's *Three Sonatas and Three Partitas for Solo Violin. The use of the "Grande Finale" can be found in Bach's Cantata #207*

The Chronicles of Borea

Drawn by fate onto paths unforeseen, **Jared, Thistle**, and **Ge-or** find that there are many hurdles to overcome as they grow in their chosen professions – Bard, Wizardess, Warrior. Through **Music, Magic**, and **Might** these three must learn to understand the most fundamental truths about themselves and the professions they have entered.

Music

Jared took the little melody and began to twist it as only he could, blending the old with the new until he was playing an intricate weave of the melody amongst itself, supported by the most ethereal harmonies he had ever played... Slowly, inexorably, he increased the tension as the music peaked, using the foundation of harmony and added tones to reach a point where there was nothing else to do but suddenly release it all in a cascade, as if he had opened a door to let in a morn's brilliant sunshine.

Magic

"That sensation is your core energy – once you can focus it to your center and are able to release or not release it at will, you will have made tremendous progress… Thistle, once you are able to fully control your inner force, you can begin magical training. It is always about control..."

Might

With both feet planted firmly on solid ground, he wove an intricate pattern with his blade, cleaving through the weapons, guards, flesh, and sinew of the beasts as they came at him. If the destruction of life could be considered an art, a type of beauty, it was certainly represented in how Ge-or handled his sword...

Evil

A shadow deeper than the night emerged from the ditch. Rising like a wraith, the black-robed figure slid as quietly as death itself along the surface, searching, stopping… stooping low…

Acknowledgements

Much thanks to everyone who has influenced me over the years.

Thanks to: my wife, Lisa; my children, Nathan and Elise, and Pat, son-in-law, who have been readers throughout the development of this series and helped me in innumerable supportive ways with this project; Anne Duston, one of my regular readers; Carolyn K.; as well as other readers and friends. Special thanks to my good friend and expert editor, Steve Bridge, who set me on the path to righteousness early on in this process, and who has been instrumental in making the final editions so much better. Thanks also to Stephanie H. of SLL Editorial Services for her early editing; Phil Lang for his work on the cover; and Taylar Johnson of Cypress Services for her work on the Second Edition; and my cousin, Robert Haselier, for his wonderful illustrations and cover art.

Website: **chroniclesofborea.com**

Blog: **chroniclesofboreabooks.wordpress.com**

Contents

Map of Borea

Steppes
Great Desert
Moutanes
BEU MTNS
Aguamville
Anada
Noloth Swamp
BENDIR
BAARTH
ATHALIA
Panterra
Dagger Isle
EFSTED
BOREA
Timi Point
Corrente
Aelfric
Aube
THE HORN
BEZE RANGE
IXUS
XUR
Great Forest
Thiele
Perris
Brea
Menda
CUTTER
KINGS WALL
SONIX
Frist
N
E
S
W

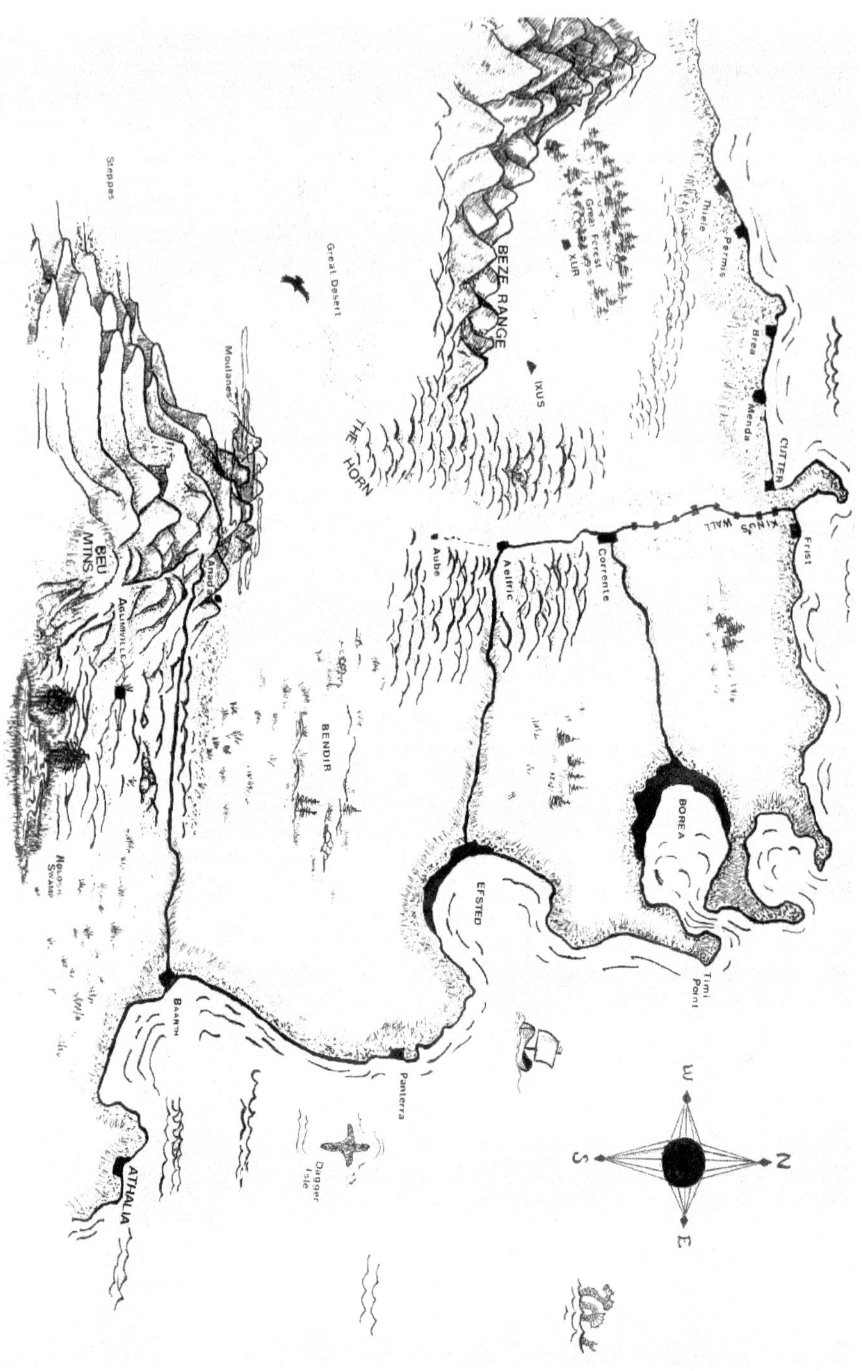

On the Road

Jared and Thistle stood close together. She was resting her head against his chest. He tried to breathe in her essence for the few moments they had left together. It was time to go, and he didn't want to release her, nor she him. They had only had two weeks – two weeks to get reacquainted, to take long walks together, to hold each other's hands, and on rare occasions to hold each other as they were doing now. It had been blissful.

His training started immediately; so besides spending time with Thistle, he had needed to make preparations for six months of being on the road. Leonis had recommended that Jared begin his Apprenticeship with a full year of minstrelsy, both to get acquainted with the breadth of the kingdom and to get to know its people. Performing, at least at the high level that he and his mentor would be expected to present, got one into many doors that would otherwise be closed to almost all others. There were two professions in Borea that consistently opened portals, figuratively, if not literally – Bards and clerics.

As an Apprentice Bard, Jared would be under the tutelage of either a Journeyman Bard, most likely, or a Bard. There were only seven from his class of more than a hundred that would be continuing on in their studies to become Bards. Of the others, another handful were apprenticing as researchers before going into their Masters work, as was Karenna. Simon-Nathan was now going to be taking his belated Apprenticeship, so that he could work with Karenna. By far, the majority who graduated from Bard Hall were finished with their education. They were returning to the family business, entering military service, or a few were moving on to the University for further study in other professions.

There were eighteen Journeymen Bards who were available to take on a new apprentice. These had the opportunity to request any of the recent graduates. Jared and the others who were continuing their work toward becoming Bards could choose their mentor from among those that had opted them. Jared had gotten six requests. He chose Elanar, who was now going out on his third and final attempt to finish his own Journeymanship, hopefully leading to his becoming a full Bard.

Jared had been surprised when he had received notification that Elanar had opted him. When they had spoken, the "almost elf" had been up-front: "You have the skills, Jared, or perhaps it is the demeanor, to get to know people readily. My people, the elves, are generally a quiet and meditative folk, which often comes across as aloofness. Though we love to sing and write poetry, we actually spend considerable amounts of time alone. This was how I was raised; and until those of us with mixed heritage were unceremoniously booted out of Moulanes, it was my life.

"I am nearly two hundred years old, my friend. I spent the first one hundred and fifty isolated in the elven enclave. I fully admit that when I came here, I felt completely out of place, and, well, I have to admit it, superior. We… No, I should say 'I,' for I shouldn't speak for a whole race. I put myself above others. I have changed, as you have noted even in the past few years, yet there is much anger still in me. It is hard for me to simply relax and enjoy this life, never to return to the place I grew to know and love in my idyllic youth.

"I have seen much of this world, and I know the mechanics of this profession inside and out. I was hoping that we could balance each other and learn from each of our strengths.

"I want to change, Jared; to change the things that have kept me so distant from others. I want to learn from you. And, I hope this does not come from any arrogance; but I feel there is much I can teach you as well – not only about music and wandering, also about the elves. I would like to help you understand something of that part of your heritage, though you did not grow up in the midst of it as I did."

It had not been a difficult decision for Jared. The other Journeyman Bards who had requested him were young and vibrant, full of music and life and the joy of being on the road; however, in many ways, Elanar was already his friend. What he had said rang true for Jared. He longed to know more about the elven side of his heritage, and he instinctively knew that there were many other things that Elanar could teach him. So today, in less than a minute, he would be trotting down the main avenue in Borea toward the city gates, starting a new adventure. He was excited, yet sad.

He drew Thistle closer and leaned down to kiss her goodbye. Their kiss lingered for a long moment. Jared felt an exquisite tingle run up and down his spine. He pushed back from the embrace. "I have to go, my love." He reached up and brushed a wisp of hair from her face.

"Oh, Jared." She smiled at him, and one tear rolled down her cheek.

"I know… Yuletide? We will be able to be together."

"Be safe, my love," she said softly.

He released her completely, then took two steps over to where a palace page held his mount. Swinging easily into the saddle, he waved and smiled broadly. Soon, soon enough, he thought, and they would be together forever. Life was good.

***

Jared met up with Elanar at Bard Hall. The two rode easily westward until they passed through the city's main gates, swinging south at the first junction. Their first stop was the seaside village of Finar, on the outskirts of the capital along the main commerce route. There they would entertain at the local tavern. This would be his life for the next six months.

Once on the main road south, Jared spurred his stallion into a gallop. Elanar followed. For a half a league they rode swiftly, letting the wind blow their hair back, relishing the feeling of freedom. Finally, they slowed to an easy trot, and each settled into his own musings.

Having finished his preliminary studies at Bard Hall, Jared was both excited and apprehensive about this new phase of his education. He knew Elanar was well-versed and knowledgeable about all the ins and outs of minstreling or "Barding." Jared was confident about his own performing ability, yet he knew he had a great deal to discover. As they had learned in Lore, being a Bard consisted of a great deal more than simply being a fine musician and a competent weapons-man.

Bards were first and foremost observers. He was expected to gather information, and not only compile what was freely offered. He was to learn to elicit it in many different ways. Ale and spirits were great tongue-looseners; however, he had also learned that their music, if used judiciously, could serve as a catalyst for the exchange of ideas. The right tune at the right time could elicit laughter and spontaneity, another might serve to calm and relax, and yet another to rile or create a tension that might lead to some other development. A change in demeanor could tell a tale in and of itself. Not only were they expected to listen, but to judge subtle changes: from expressions, to gestures, to more dramatic reactions in the people they encountered and engaged.

They were also the key disseminators of information throughout the kingdom and beyond. If the king, a mage, or a cleric wanted something spread to the far reaches of Borea, they let the Bards and their Apprentices and Journeymen know. If a secret needed to be given to a single key player, many times it fell to the Bards to pass it on. They were the trusted purveyors of important, and oft clandestine, information. They were also expected to perform ballads that told tales of the great events of the kingdom, to be storytellers; and

11

some were tasked to create epic romances for those who simply wanted a good lively tale.

There was much more that he would learn over the years to come. Jared could be an apprentice for four, five, six or more years. During that time, he would have a myriad of assignments and experiences. He would learn to help where help was needed; fight when there was no other choice or when he was called upon to engage an enemy; and more importantly, he would be expected to build relationships and trust, wherever he went. It was Elanar's responsibility to guide his young tyro through this maze of duties and to encourage him to grow in the process.

Music was the means to all. Each place they went they would be expected to perform. It was the music that would open doors for them, and often provide them the means to accomplish their other tasks. As Grandmaster Leonis had told him several times, he could move people with his playing. Now he had to learn how that ability could be manipulated and focused for a purpose. These first months he and Elanar would travel down the coast; then they would swing back north using a different route, visiting select communities in their path. Sometimes they would be the center of attraction at a grand court gala held by a local earl or duke. More frequently, they would be the entertainment at a local festival, tavern, market, or gathering place – wherever the people of a scattered community might get together.

Down the coast, they would mostly hit the larger towns, manors, and estates found along the main southern road. After leaving Efsted, as they continued south bordering the vast Bendir plains, the towns and estates of this more agrarian part of the kingdom would be much further apart. They would often earn their keep by performing and entertaining in taverns along the route.

Jared was surprised to learn just how lightly Bards travelled. Besides his lute, portative harp, some clothes, and his weapons, he carried only a few necessities for daily life. All else was gleaned from the populace along the way. At first, he speculated that they might have a frugal existence; however, Elanar assured him that for the most part they would be enthusiastically received and heaped with largess. Unlike minstrels, jongleurs, and performing troupes who performed for alms and handouts and oft camped outside the communities they performed in, Bards and their apprentices and journeyman, or 'Bardlings' as they were known by the locals, were the elite. A Bard or Journeyman Bard and his apprentice meant information, celebration, and the best of music, ballads, and epics. Unless things were dire indeed, even the lowliest village would bring forth its best for the visitors.

The past two weeks of preparation and goodbyes had been joyous and difficult. Unfortunately, Karenna and he had simply seemed to drift apart following his decision not to be a part of Simon-Nathan's plan for the three of them do their Apprenticeships together. He had met with his friends several times, including final rounds of ale at the Green Horse tavern two days before they all were to leave. It had been friendly, yet there had been a bit of stiffness to their camaraderie. As they parted company, he had gotten a buss on the cheek from Karenna and a brief hug from Simon-Nathan. He had wished them both well as they set out for the northern seacoast.

He was deeply sad that his relationship with Karenna had come to this pass; yet when he really thought about it, this was probably as easy a parting as there could have been. As early as the beginning of their fourth year, they had both begun to worry about what would happen between them. Neither one of them could conceive of a way that things would work out for the best. This way, he still cared about her, and he believed that she still cared about him; but the physical relationship was over.

They had shared a great deal in many ways. Without Karenna and his roommate, he did not think he would have survived his years at Bard Hall. He also knew that Simon-Nathan would help her get over him. He was the best friend they both had. Like his father, he knew how to treat people. Jared also knew that as devoted as they were to their studies, they would soon be immersed in their master's field project, the center of their Apprenticeship. The difficulties surrounding Jared's "betrayal to the plan" would be forgotten.

His brief time with Thistle following graduation had been something else entirely. It was almost as if they had gone back to that day when she and Sart had left him at the gate to Bard Hall. Their innocent and shy connection had resumed as if they had not had four years of intense learning and experiences in between. They had learned to be together all over again.

He had relished the light caresses, brief hugs, and occasional suggestive kisses. Without really speaking of it, they had agreed to take it slowly. It was one of the things that Meligance had in a way asked of him when she had taken him aside after graduation. She had said, "Be kind, be gentle. She is still learning and growing. Trust her to let you know what she is capable of handling." Jared did not think he could be any other way with Thistle. Somehow, he felt he should take care of her, though he knew that she had incredible power deep within.

Yet, how dissimilar their days together had been, too. There *was* something different about Thistle. From the start of their renewed relationship, she tried to explain that it had to do with her inner power -- if she kept it under control, it could add to their intimacy. He felt alive and vibrant, energized in some way, when he was with her, and especially when they were touching.

Thistle had told Jared that she had much to learn. Meligance hoped to see her apprentice out into the world for some "real-life" experiences as soon as feasible, yet she wanted Thistle to spend until the Yule learning new things and experimenting with her power and control. After that, she would reassess whether her star was ready to be on her own.

Jared smiled to himself as he rode. He had not realized how much he had yearned to be on the open highway. Bard Hall and his studies had been an incredible, often intense experience; but he was not one to spend his life in books as were Simon-Nathan and Karenna. This was life! He looked over at Elanar and grinned. Then he spurred his horse ahead again and simply enjoyed the feeling of the ride.

Expanding One's Horizons

"You are truly ready, Thistle," Meligance said. "The trials I recently put you through tell me that you have reached a solid Level Four control. Whilst I could send you out there," she gestured with her hand to indicate the world at large, "there are a few more things for you to learn. I will touch on these before I let you test the waters."

Thistle nodded expectantly. Meligance had already told her how pleased she was with the remarkable progress she had made over the past four years. It was why she had been willing to allow her to spend so much time with Jared the past two weeks. She was ready in one sense, but she also knew that her education as a Wizardess had only begun.

"Today we will start working on many of the fringe aspects of magic -- things that you have touched on in your practice, yet not refined. Over the next months we will also begin Level Five uses of energy: conjurings, connecting with other planes, and perhaps the most difficult form of our art – true creation from pure energy.

"First, I want you to go back to interacting with the world around you. Often the simplest and the most effective things we can do are basic manipulations of what is available to us close to hand. As you know, you can affect many things with energy, sometimes with a nudge here or there. Now is the time for you to experiment with that.

"Thistle, I will be busy for long periods of time this summer going about the kingdom's business. There is much Sart and I must do to ensure our network of helpers are well-placed and effective in their positions. As you know, we both keep spies and assistants throughout the kingdom and beyond to assist in our work and, more importantly, to provide information on a regular basis. For now, I give you a free hand in seeing and experimenting with the many ways you can affect all that is around you.

"Try anything you can think of, but always keep in mind that what you do affects others. Simple things may be fun at the time, yet have enormous consequences down the road. So, though you may think it is great fun to tweak a fop's ear, or give him an uncontrollable itch in an awkward place, it can come back to haunt you. Done at the wrong place and at the wrong time, it may even cause the beginning of a war. Everything we do as magic-users has a consequence. Think things through. Don't just do – plan, analyze, try out, observe, learn.

"Start today by spending time downstairs observing the many forms of tricks, illusions, sleights-of-hand, and so forth that the trainees practice. You can learn much from them. And though you have a hundred times the control, power, and skill that any one of them has, they are becoming adept at a singular focus.

"Take the illusionist as an example. Watch…"

Meligance drew her hand across the table in front of her. Instantly, two real-looking otters emerged from the ether and scrambled across the table, scattering papers as they went. With a wave of her hand, they disappeared when they got to the end.

Thistle's eyebrows rose. She had certainly done many illusions or combined illusionary tricks with other magic in her practices, but this was at another level altogether. The otters had looked real, acted real; and Meligance had even affected the environment so that it responded to the illusion, or somehow was able to have the illusion actually impact the environment. That, she knew, took control, planning, and concentration. She also knew it would be a fun thing to experiment with.

"So, my young Wizardess, I see you recognize the degree to which a thing can be taken. An itch is not just an itch if it serves some higher purpose. It must be perfect to serve the purpose for which it has been created. Thus, is it with all the things you will try. I trust your intelligence and judgment, Thistle. You are quite young and inexperienced, yet it is time to see what all you have learned can be used for.

"Do have some fun with this; however, please, always think things through. Wander about the palace and town. Take Alicia with you; she can help give you feedback and may even have some unique input, suggestions, and council. She is a bright girl. I am glad that you have become close with her. It is important for us to develop those friendships we may. Too oft, as you have noted, people pull away from us. It is one aspect of the power we wield – people fear it, and hence, fear us.

"By the Yule, if you have progressed as I think you will, there may be a task you can help Sart and me with. And perhaps, though I will need to speak to Leonis about this, your young Jared may be able to be a part of it as well."

"Truly?"

"Aye. The kingdom and its woes do not wait for us, I am afraid. There is much to do, and I will be forced to throw you into the mix sooner than later.

"Go. I will call you in intermittently to discuss your experiences. For the most part, Thistle, from now on I am now simply your guide. Much of the rest of your education will be from experience. It is, after all, the best teacher. In the late fall we will begin your Level Five work. For that, I will direct you for a pace again. Keep in mind, that, too, is highly individual; and I can only offer insight from my own work."

"Thank you, mum. Thank you for everything. I can't say that this has been easy, and I remember you telling me how hard it would be. If not for your care and… and demands, I would not be where I am today. I am extremely appreciative."

Meligance nodded, and Thistle could have sworn she blushed a bit. Her mentor waved her away. "It has been my greatest pleasure. Truly."

Thistle didn't see the smile and the single tear that Meligance shed, for she was already walking down the hallway, away from her mentor's studio, many floors below.

A Long Wait

Ge-or and Stradryk had decided to ride to the seacoast city of Baarth to spend the summer months. There, though the weather was still considerably warmer than the northern climes, refreshing ocean breezes tempered the heat.

They were able to find enough odd jobs providing protection for merchants and nobles that they could hole up in a respectable house they rented near the busy port. However, the longer they stayed in one place, an underlying sense of ill ease began to affect both of them. By mid-summer, Ge-or had reached his limit. He signed on to a cumbersome merchant vessel set to sail up the coast and back. At least he would be moving, albeit still in a restricted environment. He would enjoy the familiar feel of a deck moving beneath his feet. Fishing had been a major part of Thiele's livelihood. He had always enjoyed the freedom he felt when riding the waves far offshore.

On the other hand, Stradryk had no desire to set foot in a boat. He was as brave as any; yet the idea of heading out into that vast watery wasteland, not able to keep his feet to the ground, held no sway with him. He stayed behind and was content to scratch his itch for something different by signing on as protection for a mining party headed west. It was likely to be boring; but he, too, would be moving, and he would get a change of scenery in the bargain. Other than the occasional band of thieves, there was little danger on the southern routes.

Ge-or hadn't been on a ship since he had left Thiele. It was exhilarating to stand in the prow and feel the wind blowing in his hair. Though his duties were simply to protect the vessel should pirates dare to attack, he pitched in with the everyday business of every seafaring sailing vessel – from setting rigging to swabbing the decks. It was a good tonic. The trip took nearly two months, since they stopped at numerous villages' docks up and down the coast as far north as Efsted. Ge-or enjoyed the hard work and camaraderie of the sailors.

He also got to know the two sea-elves that served as pilot and navigator for the vessel. He had heard of the diminutive race in tales told by Bards; however, the fair-skinned "little people" did not like colder climes. Except in the summer months, only a few would pilot craft that far to the north; and they were almost never seen west of the Borean capital

He found they were a highly intelligent and likeable people. Nolo and Faldo were often busy piloting their craft; nevertheless, they enjoyed spending what time they could with the crew. Ge-or got to know them well.

The sea elves were quite small, especially stacking up next to Ge-or's height and bulk. Nolo barely reached four feet. Faldo was even smaller, not more than three-nine. Slender of build, quick in movement, and even faster to smile, they added a different dimension to the whole sailing adventure.

Ge-or loved to watch them at work. Their prescribed jobs were at the helm, yet the two often would assist the crew in changing sails, acting as lookouts, and helping mend canvas, rigging, and ropes. They could scramble up and down the masts and yardarms better than any, and they both seemed to love all aspects of working with the ship.

It was over rum one night that they told Ge-or a bit about their heritage. Nolo was especially talkative that evening: "Truthfully, much of our background is lost. Our lore relates that the first of our kind came across the sea from far to the east, at the same time or soon after the high elves. Some suspect that we were simply seafaring kin of the first elves in Borea, and that when we came to this land our paths diverged. On the other hand, perhaps we came from elsewhere to these shores. None of our sea-borne still live. We are what we are."

"And proud of it," said Faldo, who was several sheets to the wind. Having gotten off duty an hour before, he had enthusiastically applied himself to the evening's rum. He spat into the spittoon set to the side of the table. He was one who partook of the strange "tabacca weed," that Ge-or had only recently encountered much usage of on this southern quest. The plant was grown in fields stretching north and west from Panterra, and many a sailor and farmer seemed to use the stuff. When they first met, he had seen Stradryk putting it in a pipe, lighting it, and "smoking." The sea-elf used it in another strange way altogether, preferring to place a wad of the dried plant between his lip and gum. The result was a large quantity of brownish spit, which Ge-or thought was quite disgusting; but each to his own. Nolo occasionally indulged in a pipe himself.

"High elves!" Faldo spat again. "Personally, I don't think we're related. Locked up in that enclave of theirs and not letting anyone in for years and years; something wrong with that."

Nolo smiled. "He gets a bit rowdy when he's in his cups. Yet, I agree with him. I also believe we are a separate race altogether. We were likely hired to bring the high elves across the seas. When they got here, some of our ancestors decided to stay. The only similarities we have with them are the slightly pointy ears and our sunny dispositions. Hah!" He grinned broadly, took a long draught of his rum, and pointed at Ge-or's head. "Like yours. Thankfully, you do not appear to have inherited the haughtiness of our cousins."

Ge-or was about to ask a question when Nolo went on. "You see we have roundish faces. Makes us look plump, though most of us are not. Or, well, I should say we don't tend toward being overweight, just the opposite actually. And most of us have red hair. Ever seen an elf…"

"A high elf," Faldo squeaked, sticking his nose in the air.

"…with red hair? Light blond the younger elves, then white after a few hundred years. Plus, we're different in other ways. They used to like the sea, yet were never keen on sailing, like we are. They also live longer than we do; yet, we are certainly long-lived compared to humans. We don't hole ourselves away from the rest of the world either. To tell you the truth, the wise of our race do live extraordinarily long lives, almost as long as the high elves. Probably because they don't get in situations where they get hurt or killed. Most of us sea-elves tend to lead quite active lives. It's in our blood – the sea and ships, I mean.

"Who really knows the truth of Borea and her peoples? Maybe the eldest of the eldest in Moulanes; but there are whispers that they are reaching their time on this earth, too."

"That's what I wanted to ask about," Ge-or said. "If you came from the far east, across the ocean, have you been back? What is there?"

"Couldn't say what was there or what is there now," Nolo said. "It's been lost over time in our lore. We've never gotten back across that wide expanse of sea. Or leastways, if we have, we don't know about it." He cleared his throat and stared at the bottom of his mug.

A moment later, a loud snore from Faldo drew his gaze and he continued. "Every hundred years or so some youngster tries. Gets a crew together, builds a fine ship, and takes off for the east. If they make it to… to whatever is across the ocean, they never come back.

"We have had a few return from such adventures. Their tales are of horrendous seas, tricky currents, and dire ocean monsters. They went on for hundreds of leagues and finally turned back. The currents, weather, and simply the length of the voyage worked against them. We either no longer know the route, the quirks of that vast ocean, or it is impossible to go back whence we originally came." His voice trailed off. After a second, he perked up again. "I had a yen to sail east when I was a pup; my sire discouraged it, and, well, it takes money to build a ship and raise a crew."

"Do the high elves speak of the lands whence they came? Is there anything in their lore that you might have knowledge of?"

"Green pastures, rolling hills, a pastoral heaven by all accounts, or so I've heard tell. Never spoke to one myself. Why then did they leave an ideal place, and why would we have taken them? If you read history and lore, you'll find this and that about "The Golden Age," or the "Forgotten Country," "Heaven's Gate," this era or that time, and so on.

"There is always strife. No matter where you are, something isn't quite perfect. Different peoples, or even the same people, find reasons to wage war with each other, to disagree about something. Somebody always wants more.

"We have our... well, we had, Mangor, after that Kan, and now, the residue of their malevolence. Before that we had other evils to deal with in this world, or so our history says. The splitting of the Heart of the World did not create evil. Mayhap, it changed the balance. Even if you were to put the Diamond and the Star back together, would all evil be gone forever? I think not. Wickedness is a choice we all can make, else why was Mangor as he was?"

Ge-or sat up when Nolo mentioned the stone that he and others had spent a summer searching for references to, with Sart. Nolo had mentioned something that he wasn't sure Sart even knew. "The Diamond and the Star?" he queried the sea-elf.

"Aye, the two halves – well, not halves in size, but the two pieces of the Heart of the World. That's the great stone that the dwarves dug up and Mangor got his hands on and split apart."

"You know of these stones?"

"Oh, aye. It is a big part of our history and lore. We had the Star for many years, entrusted to us after the defeat of Mangor for our part in his downfall. It was lost when a ship of ours went down on the way to Borea. It is a blemish on our race. It was... nay, still is, our joy and our shame."

"It is simply called, 'the Star'?"

"Nay. It is truly named 'the Star of Galatea,' or 'the Blue Star,' and its compliment, 'the Black Diamond,' or, if you will, 'the Black Diamond of Mangor.'"

"Is there any lore as to where they are now?"

"Aye. A good bit, actually. The Black Diamond was given over to the high elves. After long caring for it, they could not abide its malevolence within their realm anymore, so they gave it to the kingdom for safekeeping. While en route to Borea, supposedly in the hands of a trusted elven prince and advisor to the king, it was taken."

"By?"

"Kan, of course, the prince and advisor who was supposed to deliver it. Too late did the kingdom realize that the Black Diamond corrupts all within its influence, which appears to be a significant range – certainly a hundred feet or more in circumference around it. I suppose, to give the poor fellow credit, he had it far too long on his ride from Moulanes north. It swayed him."

"And after that?"

"Lost? Destroyed? No one knows. Kan had it when he was destroyed from within. What has happened to it since is not known; some have speculated it was buried when his fortress was destroyed."

"And the Star of Galatea? Where is it now?"

"Like I said, it was entrusted to us after Mangor was destroyed. It was lost off the Borean coast, near Timi Point. To my knowledge it has never been recovered. The waters there are treacherous; it would be death to search there...

"I am not the person to ask. Any sea-elf knows what I just told you. Our lore-masters perhaps could tell you more. Why the interest?"

"I have a friend, a cleric. He seeks knowledge of such. He deems it important to the kingdom. Who would be best for him to speak to?"

"Tammero is our greatest historian, and one of the wisest and eldest of our kin. He abides near Panterra on the coast; but he is frail, and his mind comes and goes. I would warrant, though, that all he knows has been written down by our scribes. He himself was a prolific writer, and he still dictates to his apprentices when he is able."

"I am indebted to you, Nolo. My friend, Sart, will find this of much interest. He did not even have a name for these stones."

"We are not against sharing our lore with others. It is rare that anyone takes any interest. We are a small folk and few. Unless one needs a ship or our expertise, we stay out from underfoot – literally!" He smiled.

Ge-or laughed. "Well, you are a remarkable folk as well."

Nolo smiled to acknowledge Ge-or's compliment. "Come. Let us go on deck. My shift starts anon, and I could use the sea breeze to wake me."

"Aye. I will stand with you awhile. It is a pleasant eve."

Ge-or resolved that once they returned to Baarth, he would send a missive to Sart.

Finar was what Jared always thought of as a "crossroads village." Situated to the east of the southern road that ran along the coast, the small town was home to twenty or so hearty fishing families. Its tavern, set on the western edge of the community, served as a gathering place for everyone within a one to five league radius, and often beyond: farmers, craftsmen, and any travelers coming and going from the capital.

With its proximity to the capital, the Flying Griffin was a huge establishment by Jared's standards. The main room was akin to a large auditorium or arena. With its high ceilings, tiered seating on two sides, and dozens of booths and tables, it could easily hold several hundred people. Elanar assured Jared that there would be that many and more crammed in that evening. Anyone from the local area who could, would be there, including those who lived on the edge of the southern part of the walled city of Borea. Added to that would be the usual steady flow of travelers north and south.

When they arrived, the innkeeper, his wife, and the large staff enthusiastically greeted them. Ushered inside, their horses taken to the stables to be groomed and fed, Elanar and Jared were given a late lunch. After, they were shown to quite nice (by adventuring standards), large accommodations, a two-room suite set at the head of the stairs. Tavern owners loved Bards. Their clientele, even in remote places, doubled, tripled, and sometimes quadrupled for the time the elite musicians were there; and they were always disappointed when they left. Elanar assured Jared that they would earn their keep.

"You need to get some rest, friend. It is going to be a long night. We will be playing, telling tales and jokes, and relating news from dinner time through the wee hours. If not performing together, we mingle. This is both expected by the people in attendance, and it is part of our commission from The Hall – to listen, learn, and gather information.

"We also need to partake of drink, not just politely, but heartily with anyone and everyone. All night, if we don't already have one in our hand, we will find a mug of ale, rum, or other libation thrust into our hands when we aren't busy playing. The innkeepers are well-acquainted with the necessity of providing us with vastly watered-down mugs, so we can remain on our feet and cognizant throughout the evening. Still, we must be careful. Not infrequently an overly enthusiastic patron will press a stiff drink into our hands. The technique when that happens is to take one draught, then make every effort to move off to another part of the room, setting the offending mug down somewhere in the process. The real key is to always try to have a doctored mug in your hand when wandering about the room."

Elanar slapped Jared on the back. "You have a lot to learn, and quickly. Watch me; I will let you know as much as I can as we work these first few establishments. You will catch on quickly."

Before they settled down in their beds to rest, they went over the plan for the evening. The protocol varied from establishment to establishment, as differing clientele required differing approaches. At a large local tavern like this, so close to the capital and along a main road, the locals and itinerants would be fairly sophisticated, so pretty much anything would work. If they were performing at a manor or local lord's castle, it often was a mixed bag -- the owner might dictate in some ways what genres they would focus on. At the small villages and taverns they would cater to on their way back through farming communities and byroads set in from the coast, popular tunes and ballads would be the usual fare.

Tonight, they would start with popular tunes, to serve as background music as clientele began to show up for dinner. Jared and Elanar would alternate playing on the raised platform set in the center of the large room. "Feel free to improvise on current tunes and old favorites, Jared. Keep everything light and uncomplicated – simple harmonies. You can even improvise; though oft you will be asked to play this tune or that song."

"When a large crowd has gathered, I will take the stage and mix news, stories, and jokes while people eat and settled in for the evening. For the first month on the road, I want you to get a feel for how all of this can be woven together in such a way that it keeps people's attention. While I am doing this, your task will be to wander about and greet people. Probe for local gossip and other tidbits of information, particularly from wanderers and merchants. You will be good at that, I warrant. So just be yourself."

Jared had learned in Bard Lore that this was a key component of a Bard's work. It set the stage for not only how the evening would pan out performance-wise, but also for the dissemination and gathering of information. If handled correctly, judiciously, and with subtlety, it could make the rest of their job and evening far less complicated.

In kind, Elanar wanted to watch Jared's style as he "worked the bar." He had no doubt that with his easy manner and friendly approach, his apprentice would quickly draw people out and get them to relax and talk. It was the one area that Elanar had so many concerns with on his previous apprentice and journeyman treks.

"After everyone has gotten well into their cups, we will both go on stage and play together, alternating requests with ballads, songs, and even epic tales. After a few hours, people will start to quiet down, leave, or go to their rooms, even doze off. That's when I want you to try your more intricate improvisations of the old music blended with the new. If it works as I hope, this type of ethereal, peaceful music will help bring the night to a peaceful ending."

"You don't think it will be too esoteric for the locals and tavern folk?" Jared asked.

"Nay. You can work it as you will if you think it is getting too heavy. Go with the sense of the room. If you feel a need to lighten things up or alter what you are playing, do so. In a short time, you will learn what works with one type of crowd or another."

Elsewise, they both needed to be attuned to vary the master plan at any time. A single loud patron, a request from some dignitary on the road who had dropped in, or the overall tenor of the group could be indicative of a need to switch gears and try a different tack. Elanar explained that every group, regardless of size or place, had a personality of its own. It was wise to pay close attention to how that settled in for an evening. Bards attuned to the ebb and flow of that group persona could affect a change by playing a tune of one type, versus another. A rowdy, overly boisterous crowd that threatened to erupt into a brawl, could be calmed with the right melodies and harmonies, just as a morose bunch could be roused with a couple of energetic rounds, gavottes, or drinking songs.

Barding often came down to the finer aspects of what music was all about. A tune could be as influential as the most powerful potion or spell. Jared was at the beginning of his education of what those powers might be and how they could be used. Much of what he would study when he finished his Apprenticeship would be focused on Bard Lore – the true craft of their profession. Meanwhile, experience would be his primary teacher.

Jared was surprised when Elanar shook him awake. He had felt so energized when he had lain down that he did not think he could rest at all. Yet, he had easily dropped off and slept for several hours. It was time.

The evening and night went much as they had planned. Jared enjoyed the whole event. Afterward, he had to admit that by the time most of the patrons had left he was dead tired. He was truly amazed at Elanar's facility as a master of ceremonies, having originally thought the "almost elf" staid and aloof. Yet, his friend easily blended chatter about local news, the major stories out of the capital, jokes and barbs about this or that – particularly politics, princelings, and the powers-that-be, which were favorite topics – and little tales and asides. He had a quick wit and could pick up on what the crowd appeared to appreciate, then steer his efforts more in that direction.

In a way, Elanar surprised himself. Over his first tries at his Journeymanship, he had been more than competent at memorizing the material that went into the "news hour" presentations; but he had rarely connected with the audience. Now he seemed to be able to relax into the presentation, which in turn got the clientele involved with what he said and did.

Jared also enjoyed his part. He had always been easy with people, particularly the "regular folk," the type of people with whom he had grown up. He found that he could translate that into a relaxed approach to everyone from merchants, to local dignitaries, to the few highborn attending the evening's entertainment. He quickly picked up on what people wanted to talk about, learned what was important locally and regionally, and went with the flow of the clientele and their interests.

Elanar proved to be a competent and enthusiastic performer. During the long hours following dinner, the two of them played duets, took turns performing popular tunes and ballads on request, and led rousing community sings of drinking songs. Later, after most of the women and children had left, they played the popular ribald songs of the region.

As things began to quiet down considerably, Elanar let Jared take center stage while he wandered about the room talking with the few clients still able to hold a conversation. Starting with his lute and later switching to the portative harp, Jared improvised. The effect was amazing. For the first ten minutes, he was playing background music to low murmurs of conversation. But as people began to attend to what was happening and really listen to the music floating around them, all motion appeared to cease. Those remaining quietly focused on the ethereal, almost otherworldly glorious convergence of tones and harmonies hovering about the room. It was as if the tones interweaved, blending into each other as they hung in the air, never quite finishing before another equally delicious sound replaced it, and another and another. It was mesmerizing, beautiful, and moving. Of those still awake, there were few dry eyes when he finally finished – the last notes hanging in the air for what seemed like an eternity.

There was no applause. People got up and nodded or waved to Jared and Elanar as they paid their tabs and left.

***

It was far too early of the next day when Jared awoke Elanar with a cheerful, "C'mon, day's a-dawning and people are up and about."

"By-the-gods, Jared, it's still dark out, and we were up half the night. What's this about?"

"Lesson One, back to you, my friend. If you want to ken what I ken and learn to relate to people, you have to understand who they are and what they do. Come, *we* volunteered to help at the docks this morning. As you know, a boat came in last night. Everyone pitches in."

"Ayee-e-e," Elanar groaned. "What about breaking our fast?"

"Later, when the work is done. Let's go." Jared headed for the doorway.

"I've created a monster," Elanar moaned, swinging his legs to the side of the bed.

"Meet you downstairs," Jared said, with far too much enthusiasm.

Illusions, Tricks, and the Games People Play

Thistle spent the next week observing, querying students, and otherwise experimenting with the many aspects of "the craft" being illustrated by the apprentices in the Hall of Magic below Meligance's tower apartment. There was much to learn; but for Thistle, as Meligance had suggested, it was ultimately a matter of putting her mind to it and discovering how to use the power she could garner. Gathering and molding pure energy, she could use it to produce almost any end she wished.

She found Illusions required a mental focus and control that centered around fundamental imagery. This did take some personal energy to effect. Once she had a picture clearly in her mind, the creation and manipulation of the illusion was easy for her. She was surprised to find how little energy it actually took to affect one's perception. What was more difficult, and what she eventually would spend some time practicing, was creating an illusion that appeared to impact the immediate environs, as Meligance's otters had when they rustled the papers while running across her desk.

Thistle had great fun over the next few weeks practicing illusions and other "tricks" about the city. With Alicia watching to give her feedback, she created images that were as realistic in every way as she could make them: a runaway horse whose hooves thundered and scattered dirt aside, leaving imprints in the dust; a flock of chickens pecking at grain, clucking noisily, and losing feathers when they flapped excitedly; and even a small mouse scurrying along a rafter, dropping a piece of cheese when the merchant's wife screamed upon seeing it.

Even easier was her ability to manipulate what was already there. Generally, this took very little energy. Some of the mages referred to it as "mind control." Thistle understood the deeper mechanics of using energy. Thus, she could achieve a much finer control than they could. Moving an object across the table took many of the young apprentices in the Hall of Magic incredible focus and concentration, as they used their "minds" to move a piece of chalk or button. Thistle simply connected with the energy of the object, using her own energy. She could then easily move books, bricks, or even a wall should she desire to; yet larger and heavier objects did take more personal energy.

The same basic concept applied to tweaking a person's cheek, causing a burning sensation upon a fat merchant's bottom, or giving someone a toe twitch. She and Alicia had even more fun "playing" with things, animals, and occasionally people about the city. She was careful and abided Meligance's caution about the potential effects of magic. She tried to think through all possible results before doing the simplest of tricks. Even so, she learned quickly that the most innocent gesture could have more consequences than she envisioned.

Upon one occasion at a local tavern, a mug of ale spilt upon the tunic of a haughty dandy of the court, which led to much more than she had imagined. From Thistle's perspective, the fop had been all too full of himself, and he was treating the waiting staff abominably. Her nudge of the mug caused him to jump up and blame the closest serving wench, though she was at least five paces away when the "accident" happened. Thistle had to do some damage control by stepping in and assuring the fellow that it was a momentary loss of control of her powers, which she further demonstrated by cleaning the man's tunic with a flick of her hand, following that up by "accidentally" causing him a nose bleed. He was more than glad to leave her presence. The happy result was that he spread the word about the court that Meligance's apprentice was out-of-control. Thereafter, the dandies and fops avoided her even more.

A bit more difficult, because she had to garner a good bit more energy, was creating force fields or other types of barriers. These, she knew, could be useful in combat. She was smart enough not to try them out in public areas in the city. Instead, she did amuse herself with various escapades several times in the castle. Once, she set up a barrier across a hallway that led to one of the common relieving chambers used by those waiting for an audience with the king's ministers. She and Alicia sat on a balcony high above and observed the fun for a couple of hours. Fortunately, there were no accidents. Those who ran into the invisible barrier eventually had to give up in frustration and walk several hundred paces to the next nearest facility.

Another time, she placed a three-foot-high barrier in the path to the nearest dining area. Thistle was fascinated to observe those who would figure out that they could climb over it and those who decided to take the long way around. She rewarded the more entrepreneurial climbers with a lavender (her favorite color) ribbon tied around their ankle. She often wondered how long it took them to discover it.

Thistle also spoke at some length to those who worked with charms, herbs, potions, alchemical devices and concoctions, and so forth. They were fascinating areas; yet for the most part they were so far from true magic that she didn't wish to spend the time learning such things. That was more Sart's area, anyway. Fundamentally, magic was about manipulating energy, though only the best mages understood even that much. Certainly, there was energy at work in all they accomplished; but the alchemists, charmers, and herbalists often did not understand the root of what they were doing, what was happening. Thistle resolved to stay focused on what she could do using power gleaned from the world about her.

Levitation, flying, and teleportation were areas that truly fascinated her. However, there was little she could glean from the few students who were delving into them. For the most part, they also used the concept of "mind over matter" to achieve their limited results. In one sense, Thistle had already discovered and used teleportation when she worked with Blinkie, the original ball of purple energy Meligance had her begin her magical work with. Now, she wanted to do more work with this use of energy, because she still hadn't figured out quite how the energy worked when she teleported from the hall to Meligance's chambers and vice-versa.

Thistle had never tried personal levitation specifically, yet the concept was no different than that of raising or lowering a ball or a stool. She quickly mastered the ability to do this herself,; and then, with great fun, to do it to and with Alicia. They were careful, as Thistle did not want to endanger her handmaiden in any way; so they mostly limited their levitating to their apartments. Sometimes they would play games with the board, pieces, and themselves floating above Thistle's bed. It lent an air of both the mysterious and playfulness to the proceedings.

Magical "flying" was a combination of levitation with some propulsive force in one direction or another. Meligance had a good laugh when Alicia asked Thistle to inquire as to whether witches could indeed fly on broomsticks.

"Nay, not that I have ever seen," the Wizardess had answered. "Most witches do not even have the ability or magical knowledge to levitate. The few who do, if they are smart, use it only if exigency demands. It is one of those powers that fascinate, yet frighten people, even people who should understand better, like princes and kings. I have rarely used the skill myself, and mostly to get myself or others out of a dire situation. As in all wives' tales, there is some truth to the belief. Probably some village witch, figuring out enough of magic to levitate, did so one eve with her wand or staff to hand. Her silhouette was likely seen against the rising full moon. Thus, do legends and myths begin.

"Which of course, Thistle, gives one pause to think again of consequences. Flittering about the sky may be fun; but soon you will have a whole host of people thinking there are ghosts, witches, vampires, or worse about. Unfortunately, the possibility exists that an innocent person, somewhere, will get roasted on a stake, just to be certain that the curse has been taken care of.

"Do practice it in private. It is a useful skill to possess, and one you will need to be able to use in an instant should you, or a person of import to you, fall off a cliff, or perhaps need a way off of one safely."

***

The whole concept of teleportation occupied Thistle for several months. Learning how to transport a sphere of energy had been natural to her, so natural that it was simply a matter of envisioning the energy folding in on itself and sending it through the ether to bring it forth anew in a different locale. Accomplishing the same with a solid object, and from there to a living being, was something else entirely.

Thistle knew she had done both of these "tricks" before. Her first day at the palace, she had inadvertently made a coin disappear and somehow appear in Meligance's presence. Plus, every time she visited her mistress, she had to teleport up and back. She knew it was possible, what she didn't know was the process. One day, after repeated attempts to actually try the coin trick again, she asked Meligance.

"I was wondering when you would come to this, Thistle. It is an interesting technique, is it not?"

"I have not figured out how it happens. Nor am I able to reproduce it."

"What do you think happens?"

"I do not ken."

"Ah, but you do. What *must* happen?"

"Well, I know that energy passes through the ether, and, as we have discussed, at either a tremendous speed or instantaneously; so, I would guess there is a transformation of some sort to an object's energy?"

"Go on, Thistle. Think it through. You are on the right path."

"Strangely, I do not feel, at least when I transport from here to the Hall or back, that there is any transformation. It is like I am 'between' for the briefest of instants, and then I am there."

"Yes."

She started to sense the truth. "The coin, myself, all objects and things are already energy!"

"And?"

"The ether is mostly space. Everything is mostly space. So somehow the energy that I am, which is full of space as well, moves through the energy of the walls and air, which is also mostly space, without colliding or interacting."

"Exactly; so now you have to perceive how to accomplish this yourself. What happens here, at the spot near the wall where you arrive and depart each time, is that I have created a space, or better put, facilitated that area for such a thing to happen. Thus, not only can you come here; so can Sart, or anyone who has the understanding that it is possible. However, it would be foolish of me to set the stage for anyone at all to enter my studio at will; so there are blocks in place. In a sense, it is tuned like a lute string – to only allow those I will to enter. Of course, I shut the whole thing down when I am not here."

Thistle smiled; she was starting to see the way of it.

"So, you have the knowledge, figure it out from there." Meligance smiled back. "Good! This is an area I have wanted you to explore and develop. It is time."

***

Thistle, with Alicia often along, went about the palace and city practicing a wide range of skills. She found that she could easily spend an entire day using her power to correct or right things: one time it might be helping an overly-laden workman lighten his load; another, she might stop a brawl from developing or cause one to wind down by tweaking things in one direction or another. She could stop a cheat; protect someone from a thief; help a child chasing a ball into the street avoid a thundering horse; prevent a boiling vat from overturning; and so on.

After a day when she and Alicia had gone about the city looking for opportunities to help, and finding more than enough, she threw herself onto her plush sofa when they had returned to her chambers. "It's too much, Alicia. I want to help everyone, yet I can't. What should I do?"

Her handmaid had begun to question the direction their sojourns had started to take as well. They had somehow fallen into a singular purpose, which was only marginally focused on learning more about the use of magic, and more about using it to help people. "I think you should ask Meligance, Thistle. It is nice helping others with their daily struggles; nevertheless, is that what all your study and work has been for? Isn't your purpose supposed to be bigger than this? More grandiose?"

Thistle sat up at that, pushed her handmaiden on her shoulder, and laughed. "Oh, Alicia, I have created a monster. Where did you learn such a big word as 'grandiose'?"

"Sorry, mum. You said I should read as much as I could to… to learn."

"No, really, I'm kidding, Alicia. I think it is wonderful that you have learned so much and so rapidly. You are right; I should talk this over with Meligance. I feel driven to help others, yet also I feel like I am losing my true focus. I haven't practiced anything to do with teleportation in a fortnight."

***

Meligance smiled wistfully when Thistle related what she had been doing and why. "Truly Thistle, it is a good that you want to help others, to alleviate concerns and discomfort and so on; but Alicia is right as well. You are being groomed for much bigger things.

"One thing that is hard to learn – Sart, who is fundamentally a helper and healer, knows this, too – is that the world will wag as it will whether we interfere or not. You may save a beggar a knock on the head, or help prevent a crime; nevertheless, these things will happen and happen and happen. There is certainly nothing wrong with taking an occasion that presents itself and making it better; however, now that you are comfortable with manipulating things in the environment, it is time to focus on deeper things. Things that may make a difference to potentially saving hundreds and thousands of lives."

Thistle was considerably relieved at her mentor's words. She had been feeling the burden of the world on her shoulders; and though she would eventually bear it in other ways, likely much more dangerous ways, she didn't have to feel responsible for everything.

"Have you solved the teleportation puzzle?"

"Nay, mum, I am… well, I was progressing until I went on this mission to save everyone. I believe, based on what I have been working on, that there is imagery involved, mental strength, focus, and belief or certainty in one's ability."

"Good! You are on the right track. Continue to work through this. I want it to be your focus for the next month. I will be away. When I return, we should talk at some length about the mind and what powers it has; and perhaps it is time you had a chat with Sart about the whole concept of beliefs."

"Ah, milady, would it be inappropriate to ask what you might be doing. It seems I will need to take on some of your mantle of responsibility soon enough. Should I not know more about your… doings??

Meligance laughed, "A good point, Thistle. You have caught me up in my own tendency to keep things to myself. It is, unfortunately at times, how I and Sart, and many others of similar professions and responsibilities must be. We keep much to ourselves for our own and the kingdom's preservation.

"To answer your question, because you do indeed need to learn these things as well, is that I occasionally must go on quests myself. This is a small matter, more of a jaunt then a quest, which might yield some useful material for when we must begin training other mages. A well-respected wizard, who died over a hundred years ago, left behind a plethora of magical tomes and even perhaps some useful artifacts, in the cellars of his old manor. So, I go west with a small party to root out what we can find.

"Remind me to talk of this longer at another time. Now, go and keep up what you are doing. I will see you when I return."

***

It was only a few days after her mentor had returned, when Thistle barged into Meligance's studio (as if that were possible without the Wizardess's permission or knowledge), having run all the way from her apartment upon awakening. "Mum, he's gone."

"I assume by 'him' you are referring to your ovietti, Yolk?"

"Yes, mum, ah… I'm sorry for coming unannounced. I was so upset when I woke this morning and he wasn't there on my stomach as he usually is. I didn't know what else to do. I have grown so used to him being with me that it is like he is a part of me."

"I know you don't think so at this time, Thistle, but this is a good thing. It means he feels you are ready, capable, put it how you will. He senses that you are confident and powerful enough to do all that you do on your own. Your personal power has grown to the extent that he understands you are ready."

"I…"

"Do not worry. He will return. My ovietti, Pan, began leaving me around the same time, relevant to my training and growth. He always came back at times when I needed him the most. Remember, he only enhances your own inner power. Once Pan began to leave, it appeared that he was confident with what I could do.

"I imagine your next question will be, 'Where did he go?' That I cannot answer. Perhaps with others of his kind for a space. They must reproduce in some way, and for most creatures that takes two." Meligance's eyes twinkled.

"I miss him."

"I understand, Thistle. I had to learn to accept Pan's leaving, too. It will happen more and more as you grow as a magic user. He is trying to tell you that you can do all that you have done and more without him. He is allowing you to learn and grow even more. In a way, I think he is challenging you."

"Yes, mum."

"Go, my child. Keep at your work. Trust that your friend knows what is best for you. He will return when you need him. Be assured of that."

Later, Thistle remembered that it had been awhile since Meligance had referred to her as "my child." It felt good, and she smiled for the first time that day.

Not so Noble

After the first week of performing in the large taverns close to the capital, Elanar and Jared worked their way down the coast, spending most of their time in small- to medium-sized fishing villages, with an occasional manor performance for some lord and lady fit in along the way. They fell into an easy routine, though the nights were long and the only breaks they had were when they camped out or arrived late enough in the evening that the festivities weren't planned until the following night.

These were some of the few times Thistle could send him an orb, and they would have time to converse for a blessed half hour. Often he was unable to talk because he was performing, eating, or asleep. The best times were when he was in the stable near his stallion of an eve. They tried to time that; but often that was just hit and miss, too.

By the end of the first month, they neared the outskirts of Efsted, a large coastal city whose duchy encompassed an enormous area to the west and south. Elanar wanted to spend a few days playing in the outlying taverns before heading into the walled city, whose ruler was, by all accounts, a pompous and demanding character. He also wanted to give Jared his first opportunity to handle the news hour.

Jared's insistence that he and Elanar make an effort at every stop to pitch in and help out, whether it was with the fisherman, the local markets, the farmers, or wherever they could make a difference, was first greeted with reluctance, then resignation, and finally a grudging enthusiasm from the Journeyman Bard. Over the course of the time en route, Elanar's awkwardness among the common folk began to ease; and he saw that sharing in people's work, sweat, and everyday life brought him an understanding that he had never had before. It provided the added benefit that the two of them stayed in decent shape physically. They tried to fit in an occasional sparring practice with swords and knives, yet their evenings were so demanding that they could not keep up a regular schedule of exercise.

As a result of spending considerably more time among the general population, Elanar began to feel much more at ease when he roamed the taverns talking with the local clientele. He could share in the area's news and humor on a grassroots level, greet people he had just been rubbing elbows with on the dock or in a field, and even flirt with maidens he had met over a hearty lunch or while helping drive sheep or cattle to pasture. This also led to an even greater ease on stage, where he could share stories from one village to the next or tell a joke or tale about one family that had offshoots related to a marriage or relationship in the next village along the way.

Jared, too, felt he had learned a great deal, though he was quite nervous about making his debut on stage without an instrument in hand. He spent several days trying to work up a routine. He even practiced awkwardly during the late afternoons with Elanar giving him pointers. He had a good memory, so knowing what to say and building a repertoire that flowed from point to point was not difficult for him. Jared was more worried about feeling at ease in the spotlight. This was a completely different medium than getting in front of a group and presenting oneself as an accomplished musician. There, the instrument gave him a type of barrier or protection that wouldn't be available when doing the news.

Finally, after several days of practice trials, Jared was incredibly frustrated; and even Elanar admitted he wasn't ready. Then, Jared had an idea. "Hold a minute," he said, stepping down from the stage and rushing upstairs to their room. A few minutes later, he returned with his lute in hand. He stepped back up onto the stage and sat on the high stool situated in the center.

He started his routine again. Only this time, he punctuated the news tidbits, his jokes and jibes, stories, and so on, with strummed chords, or short bursts from a popular song that in some way related to what he was talking about. Elanar watched in fascination as he saw Jared's awkwardness began to dissipate and more than a tad of comfort enter his presentation. The longer he went, the more relaxed he became. By the end, he was actually enjoying himself.

Elanar clapped his friend on the back. "It is different, Jared, I have to admit; but it works for you. I'm not sure I have the improvisational facility to make such quick judgments on an instrument as you can; still, I like it. Give it a try tonight and we'll see how it goes. You may have found your niche, my friend."

That night there were a few awkward moments as Jared got through his initial nervousness and settled into the presentation, yet overall it was quite the success. He had a knack for choosing the right chord or chord progression to emphasize a dramatic, humorous, or poignant remark or story. He could also pluck the opening to just the right political or ribald tune at the most theatrical point in a tale to punctuate a point. He felt much better having the instrument in hand. It might have been a crutch at first, but his improvisational facility changed that quickly into a remarkable asset.

For the next three nights following, Jared relaxed more and more into the whole process. By the last night before they were to enter Efsted, he was being roundly congratulated; and he received many a pat on the back after his presentation. He tried using both the lute and his portative harp. Depending on the story or anecdote, he could emphasize things in slightly different ways with each. The lute, however, provided a bit more flexibility. After a while, he got to keeping both instruments close to hand. If he was inspired to shift gears, he would lay one down while continuing to talk and pick the other up.

***

Elanar tried to warn Jared of what they would face within the walls of Efsted and the duke's "Palace of Magnificence." Duke Edgar was more than pompous; he was, if one believed the gossip outside the walls of the city in all the local taverns, a pretender to the throne. He called himself "King of Efsted and Duke of Muir." Muir was the massive estate that he had inherited when he married the Duke of Muir's widow. Unfortunately, the poor duchess had suddenly taken ill and died a short time after their grand wedding.

Now remarried to another rich widow, he expected all his subjects to refer to him as "King" and his wife as "Queen". If someone managed to forget, which was rather unlikely, they would find themselves headless and their lands, titles, and/or goods confiscated. Elanar told Jared that to avoid potential ill will and conflict, the Bards had taken to calling the duke, "Your Eminence," "Your Grace," or simply, "Sire," as it was unlawful in Borea to call anyone except the King in Borea, "King."

The truth was, Edgar was the bastard son of the previous Duke of Efsted and only had come to power because his father had no other sons or daughters to lay claim to his title. His royal lineage, therefore, was tainted in the first place.

They had to plan their performance carefully. His Grace did not tend to abide frivolity. Any news hour comparable to the informal stagings they did everywhere else would be insulting to his ostensibly refined taste. They would be expected to perform proper programs of old music, including motets, chansons, madrigals – none of the ribald variety – and so on. Two hours or more of background music was required before and during dinner. A concert would follow, with a closing section of contrapuntal works that "would soothe the senses and prepare the royal blood for bed."

Still, Elanar planned to leave one part of their program intact – Jared's improvisations in the old-new style at the end of the evening. Since he predominantly used the interweaving melodic form of the old music with some of the more fundamental harmonies of the new, he felt that it was unlikely that the duke had enough of an ear to notice the difference.

As Jared found out rather quickly, the fellow had no ear at all. He would interrupt their introductory music, and even the concert itself, with a loud roar of, "Play me, 'The Little Lass is Smiling,'" or some other popular tune. They would then have to take a diversion until he waved his hand and settled back into his drunken conversations with his fellow nobles, completely ignoring the program at hand.

***

When Jared and Elanar were taken to their quarters, they were rather unceremoniously led to a remote section of the castle in front of a dilapidated wooden door with one of the three hinges barely holding onto anything at all. Opening the creaky panel, they stared into what could only be described as a cubbyhole with two cots, a bucket for essentials, and a chipped wash basin set on the floor. There was no window, which was probably lucky because there was no fireplace, no chairs, and barely enough room for them and their belongings.

Jared looked at Elanar; his partner looked back and shrugged. "I tried to warn you. I played here once before, and it was bad; this is verging on unacceptable. Bards are to be treated with respect. It is an unwritten code. This turd tends to treat anyone who represents the king and Borea with less than appropriate deference."

"By-the-gods, Elanar, we had better quarters in the lowliest of taverns. Our tent is more comfortable than this… this hole in the wall. This is outrageous. Why do we come here?"

"Because the king desires information, which you will soon discover is hard to come by in this den of intrigue. Everything is whispered here; they are all too afraid of the duke to speak out. That is why we spent more time outside the gates than I normally would have. The villagers there can speak their minds, at least to a point. In here… well, there are spies everywhere; so watch what you say and what you ask. Pay attention and glean what you can."

Elanar sat down on the edge of one of the beds, looking at the dust covered sheets with some disgust. "Well, at least we know that no one has slept here in a while. I will speak with the steward tomorrow, but it may not do any good."

"We have a week here," Jared moaned, plopping down on the bed opposite, a cloud of dust poofing up into the air as he did so. "By-the-gods, I am tired. I do not think I will have any trouble sleeping, even here."

"On the bright side," Elanar said, "there is nothing to do during the day except wander around where we may, so you can sleep late. Be prepared, for there will be many places about the palace that will be off limits. This so-called king is always extremely wary of spies, which you must admit, in some sense, we are. Your best bet for information will be the kitchen, work quarters, stables, and so forth, even there you will find hesitation to talk openly. The nobles will be tight-lipped. For the most part, they will ignore us completely, even if we ask them a direct question."

"What do we do for food? We have had nothing since we arrived, in spite of the grand dinner that was largely wasted in front of us."

"Don't expect a maid or servant to show up on the morrow. We go to the kitchen and scrounge. The staff there will treat you well, in spite of their lord's indifference to Bardlings. By the way, do we have any of that cheese and stale bread from the morn?"

"A bit. Shall we share?" Jared began rummaging in his backpack. "I'll head down when I wake and bring something back. I expect I'll be up before you."

Elanar nodded. "You can bet on that."

Things got even more bizarre over the next few days.

Elanar didn't have much luck with the steward; however, Jared, who always seemed to have a way with women, managed to talk to the head of the chambermaids, a Mistress Julia. Luckily, she appeared to have some sort of clandestine relationship going on with the steward; so he, somewhat reluctantly, Jared was told later, moved them to a small suite of rooms in a better part of the castle. Far from luxurious, at least these had some basic comforts, including clean sheets – compliments of Mistress Julia – a chambermaid to look after them, and a fireplace and small window in the living area.

It was late in the afternoon of their third day as they were preparing their "battle order" for the evening, when they received a knock on the door. Jared rose to answer it, waving at Elanar to stay seated. When he opened the door, he saw an older man dressed in noble, though not ostentatious, clothing. The man had a deep frown on his face. Jared recognized him as the earl of something or other. He had been seated far to the side at the main table during their performances.

Jared bowed slightly at the waist and said, "Sir?"

"May I come in? Please? I have something of import to ask of you." He looked nervously over both his shoulders, up and down the corridor outside, before stepping ahead.

"Of course, unfortunately you will find our accommodations are not suited for royal guests."

When he was inside and the door closed, he looked first at Elanar, then at Jared. "Edgar," the earl said the name of the duke with obvious disgust, "has plans for…" He stopped, wiping his brow with a pocket handkerchief.

Elanar raised his eyebrows; then when Jared looked over at him, he shrugged his shoulders, and began to get up.

"Please stay seated, Elanar. I am not such a fop or flunky that I need others to rise and bow to feel good about myself. I would ask a boon of you both. It is a matter of grave import to myself and… and to my family."

Elanar rose anyway. He bowed as Jared had done, offering the earl his chair with a wave of his hand.

"Nay, I'll stand. I am too worried and tense to sit. Well, here it is… I am the Earl of Saffra, west edge of the province of Efsted." He looked back and forth to Elanar and Jared. "Otal, my name is Otal. My daughter, Jennie, nigh on fifteen years old, is a handmaiden to Edgar's queen. He…"

The earl flushed red, wiped his hand across his face, and did sit down heavily in the chair that Elanar had proffered. "I am sorry, our duke," again, his disgust showed in his pronouncement of the word, "takes women, young girls, as he wills, and… and he has for some time been looking to my daughter." He buried his head in his hands and began to sob.

"She is only fourteen?" Jared asked incredulously, for he figured the duke to be well into his fifties.

Otal raised his head, and now there was a dagger look in his eyes. "Aye, and he would have had her before now if the Queen had not put him off. She will not prevail for much longer. I would… I need to get her from this place, and there is no other way than help from without. I do not fear for my own life; I…" A choking sound interrupted his words, tears forming in his eyes. "I do not know where else to turn."

"Earl of Saffra? That title is familiar to me. You are married to the Countess of Kent, cousin to the king, the true King?" Elanar asked.

"Aye, Jennie is our only child. I cannot bear to think… to think…" He broke down, sobbing, covering his face with his hands.

Elanar signaled Jared to wait. Then he paced for a minute while pondering what the earl had said. Finally, taking a step closer to the earl, he had an intense, focused look on his face. Otal looked up at him. "You ken how difficult a thing it is that you ask, and how grave a situation it will be if we help you?" Elanar said. Otal nodded; he choked back another sob.

"There is nothing we could do in most circumstances, because we are de facto representatives of the crown. Our hands would be tied, no matter how much we desired to help. This is different, and far more serious, because it has far-reaching political overtones. You are kin by marriage to the king, and your daughter kin to his majesty by blood. This is another thing altogether."

Elanar knelt in front of the earl and took his left hand in his. "Jared and I will need to think on this and discuss it at some length. There is a delicate political balance at stake here. We have to be prudent; though I do believe this is something that the king would expect us to act upon. I am sure of it.

"We are due at court. Can you come again tomorrow? Late morning?"

"We can meet, yet to come here twice would be too dangerous. He has eyes everywhere. Once, and I can brush it off as a special request for the evening's entertainment."

"What about in the court anteroom? Let's say at noon, before audiences begin?"

"Aye, that would be good. I might be able to bring my daughter. It would be best for you to meet her and her to meet you. She is so very young…" Another choked-off sob, but a moment later Otal got a hold of himself. He stood quickly and moved toward the door. "Noon, on the morrow. By-the-gods, thank you."

Jared and Elanar stared after him. Finally Elanar turned toward Jared, "Come, we must be off. Duty calls. Let us talk this over after we are done this eve."

Moving from Place to Place

It didn't take Thistle long to reproduce the "trick" of making a coin disappear. Using her focus and imagery techniques she could easily make any small object disappear and reappear in another place, at least within her line of sight. She didn't want to try anything big or send something out of her sight until she understood the process, and therein was her dilemma.

While she could do these neat little tricks, she did not know what it was she was doing. For several hours a day for a week, she stood in front of the full-length mirror in her room. She practiced making coins move from place to place, one hand to another, or from her to Alli, trying to analyze what was happening. She finally understood a key point: the energy that created the transition came from herself. It was not the same energy that she drew upon to create a ball of fire, lightning bolt, or to set up an invisible barrier; all that came from without. When she moved a small object, she could feel the slightest tingle within. After an hour or more of practice, she would begin to feel drained.

To prove this further, she spent several days sending larger and larger objects from one place to another. She kept her work confined to a space where she could have absolute control. She either practiced in her rooms or in Alli's. From this work, she determined that teleporting an object from point A to point B required not only her energy or personal power, but that the effort or expenditure of energy was directly proportional to the size and, interestingly enough, the distance that she sent the object. Thus, a chair was harder to move than a small vase, yet easier than a chest of drawers; and moving a chair from one side of a room to another, more difficult than moving it a foot or two. However, it was much easier to teleport an object with her personal energy than to move a like object physically.

As she began to move the larger objects about, she also noticed that at the moment she applied her energy there appeared to be a shimmering to the object just before the "spell" worked, or an instant before it moved. Alli, surprisingly, was able to see this effect as well.

Encouraged that she was starting to understand the finer aspects of the process, Thistle began teleporting objects from her room to Alli's and back – small at first and then larger by the end of the second week. With this work, she was able to answer one of the concerns she had considered from the outset – what happens if you try to teleport an object into a space that is filled or partially filled with another object? In other words, could she move a chair into a desk and end up with a bizarre combination of the two as a result; or worse yet, could she teleport an object into a living person and hurt or kill them.

The truth, it turned out, was that neither of these dire scenarios was possible, or at least not possible without facilitating some other aspect to "the move." Teleportation was incompatible with two objects occupying the same space. The exact reasoning was for the time being beyond her ken; yet she discovered that if she transported a chair partially into a desk because she missed her imagery slightly, the transported object would be "ejected" into an open space nearby. *Or*, if there were no open space, the object would not move from its original location. Thus she also understood she would not be able to use teleportation as a weapon – that is, unless she dropped a desk from above onto someone or something.

This discovery was a great relief to Thistle, as she had pondered the problem over and over in her head. Now that she understood the fundamental aspects of the energy she used, she felt more confident about the method. She was anxious to try teleporting herself, but she wanted to talk with Meligance about her discoveries. There was no sense in hurting herself before she received confirmation that she indeed had discovered the key idea behind the process.

To the Brink

Jared and Elanar didn't get any rest that night. They stayed up hashing out every aspect of the dilemma that had just presented itself in the form of a worried earl, his daughter, and a bastard duke whose ego was only overshadowed by his greed and lust. On the one hand, Otal was right – his daughter was in danger from a dishonorable man. It was their duty as Bards, or Bards-in-training, to do something about it, to find a solution. On the other hand, the duke was a very powerful force in the kingdom; and though he only provided token men-at-arms for the king's army, he kept this whole southern duchy in sway. He could field a strong army for or against his sovereign. Ostensibly, his loyalty was to the king; yet there was little doubt that if the old king died, he would make a move for the throne. The young crown prince might have trouble holding onto his sovereignty.

If Jared and Elanar helped the earl and were somehow able to spirit the girl from the castle to safety, their actions would, at the least, cause a dissolution of relations between the northern and central provinces of the empire, and at worse could start a war. This could have far-reaching effects, including a disruption to major trade routes north and south. Yet, the young lass was a relation to the king; and his majesty was a stickler about traditions, family, and honor.

Their one hope was that somehow they could find a way to get the girl out of the castle and across the northern border of the duke's lands, less than a league away, without anyone knowing they were involved. In truth, they represented the king, and anything they did would be reflected as such. If they accomplished this, the earl's life would be in danger. The duke would suspect it was Otal behind the plan, and whoever managed to secret the girl away would never be able to return to the Duchy.

They realized they had too little information to formulate any potentially successful plan. They needed to know who could be trusted. Who might be willing to escort the maiden and stay with her – a maid, courtier, or relative? Was the earl willing to take the risks involved? He would certainly lose his earldom and lands. And his whole family would be in danger once the girl did not return.

Even if they used a logical excuse to buy time – for example, a visit to a sick relative to get her out – the truth eventually would come out. The girl might be safe; unfortunately, others would be in danger. Depending on the duke's suspicions and reaction, this could affect anyone even remotely related to her family and all those concerned with her escape.

Deciding they would try to get the earl aside for a long chat, they set out for the anteroom ten minutes before the noon hour.

The room was surprisingly empty when they arrived. Typically, there would be dozens of courtiers, merchants, lesser nobles, and the like standing about hoping someone would hear their case. Elanar was immediately suspicious. He gestured for Jared to follow him to the side of the chamber, close to one of the two doors leading toward the outside. He wisely wanted to have an escape option should they be put in an indefensible position.

They were only halfway across the large space, when from archways on the other side poured a contingent of the duke's guards, dressed in their gaudy "royal" purple tunics. From a doorway that led into the throne room Otal emerged, prodded ahead at the point of the Master-at-Arms' sword. They were followed by the duke and his entourage of fops. Two of these drew a young girl into the room, grasping her under her arms.

Backing slightly and moving closer together, Elanar and Jared prepared for the worst. They were only armed with their customary utility daggers – thin, medium blades that everyone carried for eating and other everyday tasks. Though they kept these honed to a keen edge, they were hardly a match for several dozen men armed with swords. What they were immediately concerned about, however, was that the earl had already been found out. And without having made any decision yeah or nay to help the earl, they were already being seen as accomplices.

The heavyset, ruddy duke of Efsted took a few steps forward toward the center of the room, pointed with his chubby fingers at Otal and roared, "Traitor!" He looked toward his Master-at-Arms and gestured with his hand across his throat.

To Elanar's and Jared's horror, the man immediately stabbed the earl from behind, under his shoulder blade, the point coming out on the other side. Otal gasped, his hands coming up to the sword-point. He staggered forward and fell to his knees. His daughter screamed and tried to wrench herself free, but she was forced to stand and watch. A red splotch widened on her father's tunic as he knelt there, glaring with hatred at the duke. A second later, Otal's eyes fluttered twice, glazed over, and he fell forward onto the hard granite floor. The girl screamed again.

"Arrest them!" The duke roared out, pointing toward Elanar and Jared. The Master-at-Arms and some of his men rushed forward, weapons to the fore.

Elanar whispered to Jared as he drew his dagger, "Follow my lead."

Jared drew his utility dagger. He figured that any question of whether they were truly involved in this debacle and the relevance to the kingdom's politics were pretty much moot. Their lives were at stake within the walls of this insane "monarch's" domain. Whether they willed it or not, they were on a field of battle.

One of the soldiers, a tall fellow with long legs, outpaced the others and reached Elanar first. He lowered his sword toward the elf's chest as he came up. The Master-at-Arms was only a couple of paces behind coming toward Jared.

Elanar used much the same maneuver Jared had when he had been assaulted outside the tavern standing for Thistle's honor. The soldier was armored in chain and wore heavy gauntlets, so Elanar did not attack to harm, which would have been a challenge with the small blade anyway. Using his dagger, he twisted the rapier from the man's grip, grabbed the handle with his other hand, and placed a knee in the fellow's crotch. While the man doubled over, Elanar stepped back and switched hands with the two blades, facing the rest of the advance.

Jared met the considerably more adept swords-master with a parry, and then another. The man was quick. But, as were most who were trained formally and had not seen many real melees, he was not creative. After one more parry, Jared stepped into the resultant opening, flicked his wrist so that it slid from a parry into a strike, and made a cut at his sword hand. Thankfully, the Master-at-Arms was unarmored and not wearing any gauntlets or gloves. The blade slid across his knuckles, cutting to the bone. He shrieked, opened his hand, and let the blade fall. Jared caught it before it hit the ground.

Now properly armed, Elanar and Jared moved forward into the oncoming solders, rather than doing what everyone had expected, which would have been to retreat. This proved to be the one thing that saved them from a skewering from behind. The doorway to which they had been moving initially opened, and men with pikes entered the room from that quarter. The situation looked desperate in spite of the fact that their skills were obviously far superior to any of the men they were facing. They could be overwhelmed by the numbers in only a few moments.

Elanar, however, continued to move quickly to the side. He engaged the first soldier he came to, felling him with a heavy strike to the side of his head with the hilt of the rapier. The chainmail byrnie the man wore did little to stifle the blow, and the fellow hit the floor a second later. This left the elf an opening to the right. Jared, sensing his plan, followed directly behind, wary of any soldiers that might close in on Elanar's flank or back. The other men hesitated to advance further, after having seen their leader disarmed so easily by the lithe half-elf, and two of their fellows felled by the obviously well-trained Journeyman Bard.

Sword pointed ahead, Elanar waved it menacingly in the face of the next guard he came to. The fellow almost tripped over himself in his haste to back up. This left a clear path to the duke. Elanar was upon him in two strides, the rapier point held steadily under the triple chin of the enraged ruler.

"Stand them down or die!" Elanar shouted, pressing the sharp point into the duke's neck.

A hand wave from the duke and the guards lowered their weapons and took a step back. Elanar eased the blade a bit, at which point the duke turned toward him and raged, "How dare you attack me. You affront me and the crown. I will have you drawn and quartered. I…"

Elanar interrupted him by pressing the blade back into his throat. "Which crown might that be that we affront? The pretender's crown that you wear defying the true king; or do you think we have defied our guild, our oaths, and therefore *the* king in this way?

"What I know is that you have defied and defiled the king and this country with your greed, your pomposity, and your perversity. We are here to uphold the ideals and values of Bard Hall, of which the first is Honor. On your knees!" Elanar pressed the point slightly inward. The duke, with no succor at hand from the others in the room, was forced to fall to his knees.

"Behold your fine ruler," Elanar spat out, turning as he did so to face the large group now huddled more or less in a mass at the far side of the room. Jared stood at his side, twirling the "borrowed" rapier in his hand, as if to challenge any to approach while his partner spoke. "Hear me, for I speak for Bard Hall. The honor and rights of a young lady and her family will be righted this day. Would that I were able to correct other wrongs that have befallen the people of this duchy, but that I leave to the people and to the true king in Borea to decide."

Either not wanting to believe that he was in an impossible position, or so arrogant that he truly believed he would prevail, the duke interrupted Elanar again. "The king will not dare to attack me. My army is as great as his. He would destroy himself in such a pursuit. I…" He tried to rise, however, a slight renewal of pressure with the blade tip from Elanar caused him to sink back, glaring sideways at the elf. "I will roast the two of you and destroy your precious Hall of Bards."

"You think your army is greater than the king's," Elanar scoffed. "Have you not seen what happened here? Your finest sword disarmed by a lad with a kitchen knife – an Apprentice Bard on his first month out of school? And two of your personal guard also easily disarmed by a Journeyman Bard. This rabble army of yours wouldn't stand up against a regiment of the king's foot, not even against a single company.

"Come, Jared, let us show them some actual sword play." Elanar drew the blade away from the duke's neck and took a half step toward the group of courtiers, soldiers, and others. Jared raised his blade as if to follow. The mass of men drew even closer together and further back at the gesture.

"Hah, you see, Duke, they fear the two of us, neither yet even a Bard.

"Ah, there… Down... Now stay where you are, or I will skewer you here and now." The duke had tried to rise yet again. Elanar brought the sword back around to hover it near the duke's neck where a spot of blood now oozed.

Edgar sank back to his knees, glaring at Elanar.

"Friends of the court, soldiers of the duchy." Elanar turned, but kept the tip of the blade hovering near the duke's neck. "Hear me. My apprentice and I are going to leave this palace, these grounds, and this duchy traveling north. We will take with us this lass, her immediate and extended family, and the body of Otal, the brave Earl of Saffra. His only wish was to preserve his daughter's honor, and he shall be honored in turn.

"As a cousin to the king, Lady Saffra and her daughter will be sent to the court in Borea. This matter will be dealt with formally and appropriately. Unless, of course, some action were to happen here that would mitigate the difficulties that this event has caused. In either case, I assure you that there will be consequences.

"Following our successful departure from this duchy across the border, we will place the family in competent hands to transport them to the Borean palace, where they will find welcome and succor. Once they are in safe hands," he pointed his dagger hand at Jared, "we will then turn back and continue our travels through this duchy and on to the south as is our directive from our Hall.

"Now, listen well!" Elanar raised his voice and swept the sword blade up and through the air with a swish, bringing it forward to point at the crowd before him. "I declare here and now, no Bard, Apprentice Bard, or Journeyman

Bard will play this palace until such time as this issue is resolved. Jared and I will play the villages and taverns along the coast road. When we return along the western road passing through this Duchy, if in *any way*," Elanar almost shouted the two words, "we are molested or barred or attacked, the wrath of Bard Hall and the Kingdom of Borea will befall this entire province.

"Now, you and you." Elanar pointed with the rapier at two guardsmen, who by their livery appeared to be Sergeants-at-Arms. "Put together an escort for the Saffras, with a wagon for their belongings and a coach for the women. Treat the earl's body with respect, and have his wagon follow at a respectable distance when they depart northward. You two," he now pointed at two of the fops who had entered with the duke, "gather my partner's and my belongings from our rooms and bring them here; then see that our horses are saddled. Let us know when the Saffras are ready to depart." He tilted the blade back close to Edgar's neck. "We will wait here until all is accomplished."

Yet, Edgar still had not understood Elanar's resolve. He raised his voice angrily, "Do not move, any of you, or I will…" Elanar drew up his hand and brought the hilt of the sword smashing into the side of the duke's head. The fat man exhaled heavily and sank to the floor.

***

"Do you think they will take matters into their own hands?" Jared asked as they rode northward, right behind the coach bearing the grieving widow and her daughter.

"If they have any sense, they will do something. He is such a pompous, arrogant ass that he will behead two dozen of them for watching him be humiliated. They must know that. I would guess he is already in irons, or perhaps, already dead. Unfortunately, this province has been under his rule for so long that it may take some sorting out before a strong and, hopefully, equitable ruler is in place. Perhaps our king will see to that. He is getting on in years; yet his mind is sound, and he has always had a good heart. He will see to the Saffras. My bet is that he will send a strong contingent to Efsted immediately upon hearing our news."

"Aye, and there might be the rub. How will the king see what we have done, and what will be the political fallout? We were right to do what we did, but will anyone else see it that way? You were amazing, Elanar. I hope that the king and Leonis see things as you have. Personally, I see no fault in anything that you have done."

"Hah! Well I guess I did learn a few things in the hundred and fifty years I spent in Moulanes. In many ways the elves are wise, in others…" His voice trailed off.

"You are a born leader, my friend. I think we make a good pairing."

"As do I, friend."

Inner Strength

"Tell me." Meligance could see that her star pupil was excited.

"It's all about vibrations – frequencies of energy," Thistle gushed.

"Indeed, it is. Good. Very good, Thistle. And what else?"

"About using my own power. I cannot use the power of the ether, at least not yet."

"Good. Describe what you have been doing and what you think happens."

"I have only moved and teleported inanimate objects so far, mum; nevertheless, I feel fairly confident now that I can progress to living things. Moving something from one place to another is simple. I just apply some force to it. If it is enough, it will move as if I was pushing it. Vibrations come into play when I teleport an object from one place to another."

"Yes, and what do you mean by vibrations?"

"When I go deep within, I sense that an object, or myself for that matter, is vibrating; or perhaps "moving rapidly" is more accurate. Whatever we are, the things we are composed of at a finite level move constantly. If one adjusts the vibrations of an object, or the frequency of that movement ever so slightly, one can move one thing through another.

"I think, though it is basically speculation on my part, that all things in our world, on this plane of existence at least, have the same or similar vibrations. It is how we are able to perceive each other and interact with other things – objects and so forth. Other planes of existence have fundamentally different vibrations. Thus, to move an object through another object on this plane, I have to shift the object's vibrations. Perhaps I am moving it temporarily into another plane of existence?"

"Excellent. Exactly so. Do you know what this portends?"

"I have discovered the route to other planes of existence?"

"Yes. Which, my young protégé, is something that few mages ever understand. Certainly, some dabble in the 'black arts;' but they do so through long and convoluted paths that they think open gates or portals to other planes for brief periods. You, Thistle, have discovered one of the great secrets of our profession, one that no mage can easily teach another.

"It is something that we all, myself and the few great mages I have worked with, had to learn on our own. Your insights always amaze me, young lady. You are truly gifted in the art, and you have the intelligence that the art requires for true understanding.”

Meligance paused, assessing her pupil. Finally, she asked, “So what happens at the end of this process?”

“When I shift the frequencies of an object, I can push or send it through the spaces of the ether to wherever I want it to go. When I have it where I want it, or perhaps better put, when I have visualized the destination correctly and moved the object there, I change the vibration back and it rematerializes.”

“What happens if there is another object in that space?”

Thistle answered without hesitation. “The vibrations of each object, if too closely aligned – for example two objects with the same or similar frequency – cannot occupy the same space. It will either pop out into open space or it will return to its point of origin. I haven’t tried teleporting something for long distances, other than when I send orbs to my family. That is different since I am sending pure energy through the ether.”

“Good. Yes, you have the gist of it. Experiment more with this, and you will better understand how your energy affects it all. Now, tell me what you have discovered relevant to using your own personal power versus the power of the ether.”

“It seems,” Thistle said frowning slightly, “that teleportation is capable only if one uses one’s personal power to manipulate what you want to move. So far I have not been able to bring the energy of the ether to bear… perhaps it could be feasible in some part of the process; yet I have not discovered how. For this reason, teleporting is draining – to move a large object takes more effort than a small object. I would warrant that to move my body could be difficult and draining as well.”

“Yes, all truths, Thistle. The ability to teleport something is directly proportional to mass and…”

“Distance!” Thistle jumped in. “Yes, I know. It is as if I am physically pushing it along through an empty space. Even though I am focused on the energy of it, there is still the mass, and perhaps some type of resistance?”

“Yes, resistance is a good way to put it. At the most basic level, all energy affects all other energy. When you shift planes, you still encounter a type of resistance in the other plane. It is difficult, maybe impossible, to actually visualize or experience two planes at once. Sometimes it feels as if we are between planes, or in a type of ethereal plane that has little true substance. Also, some planes are so close vibrationally to this plane that they almost overlap in some ways. Therefore, we are still capable of interacting physically in those planes. Remember, we are limited in our abilities and what we can understand the further afield we go, as I have oft warned you.

"Yes, mum, 'control'."

"Yes, 'control.' So, you are ready to try this with living beings."

"I thought I might start with a plant, and after that, perhaps, a mouse, squirrel, other small animal, though I am loath to hurt a creature should I fail."

"You seem to understand the principles, so I do not think you shall fail. Show me what you have done."

Thistle demonstrated what she had been practicing; and afterward, Meligance sent her young mage off to take her art to the next level. She knew it was a huge step for one so young, yet the girl was as steady and sure as she had ever been in her development at this stage. Thistle had touched on the most powerful, and what could be in the wrong hands, the darkest magic of all. The next months would make or break her. Yet, it was something she would have to go through on her own.

The White Wizardess sighed and looked out the window. She had been through the same journey many years before, when she was a decade older than this wisp of a girl. The gods willing, she would come out the other side of all of this.

It was time, Meligance knew, that she must bend her mind and will to other things – including, most reluctantly, taking on other less talented, potentially useful apprentices. News from the west was increasingly ominous. They would be needed soon enough.

Dry Land; Then Back to the Swamps

The day Ge-or's ship pulled into Efsted was only three days following Jared's departure northward. It turned out the docks and town were in an uproar. The duke had been overthrown, and it was rumored that he had been slain. There were factions of nobles claiming this or that guild or part of town as theirs. No one seemed to have any true authority. Nolo and Faldo were content to quickly unload their cargo and reload with the preset goods due to be taken to Panterra and Baarth. With all hands working from dawn to dusk and beyond, they were off again within two days.

They had only two planned stops on their way back south, so Ge-or simply enjoyed the seafaring life as they set sail further from land to avoid the busier coastal sea lanes.

Two days out from Panterra, they were spotted by a vessel as they passed to the west of Dagger Isle, a rocky cave-infested refuge for pirates.

When the ship was sighted, Faldo set to cursing vociferously, while Nolo steered westward toward the Borean coast. He had hoped to avoid such a turn of events, as the open sea was a much preferable route south due to the currents this time of year. Unfortunately, it was also when pirates were most active.

The merchant ship was heavily loaded, and it was bulky and slow even when empty. It took the pirate clipper only two hours to draw near. Ge-or, two other hired hands, and all the seamen were armed for repelling boarders. Ge-or stood amidships with his longbow in hand and looked for a target as the pirates came even closer. Nolo looked over at him quizzically from his place at the wheel, as if to say, "You expect to hit something with that from one moving boat to another?"

Ge-or grinned and waved the tip of his bow at the sea-elf. His father had not neglected this aspect of their education either. He and his brother had spent many a day in the summer riding the waves and learning to shoot from a rocking platform. He had even learned to shoot some of the larger trevally during months when they were feeding closer to shore. That had taken real skill, as they had not only to deal with the movement of the boat, but also the adjustment that needed to be made because of the water refraction, as well as the movement and speed of the fish.

When the other boat was about a hundred paces out and closing fast, Ge-or set himself -- his legs spread wide to get rooted to the deck, with his knees flexible to the roll of the waves. Drawing back slowly, he brought the bow up to his eye. Finishing the smooth motion as the boat came alongside and only forty paces off, he anchored his sight on a pirate standing in the crow's nest and released his arrow. The shaft flew true. The pirate, goose feather protruding from his chest, fell into the sea from his perch.

Nocking another arrow, Ge-or set his aim again. This time he sent a shaft into the throat of the man at the helm. The pirate fell backward onto the deck, blood spurting from the wound. As a result, the wheel of the clipper spun around, causing the craft to suddenly veer away. They could see pirates scrambling to the wheel and about the deck, while the boat spun almost completely about before they had it under control.

Ge-or and the rest of the merchant seaman stood watching as a hasty counsel appeared to be held near the prow of the pirate boat. Then, after considerable gesticulating, a large man took the helm and steered the boat away. It appeared that quickly overwhelming a sparsely armed merchant vessel was one thing, but losing good men before the pirates were fully engaged was another altogether.

Nolo and Faldo broke out the good aged rum that evening to celebrate Ge-or's archery prowess. They had no further incidents on their way south.

By the time Ge-or was back in Baarth, Stradryk had also returned from his mining venture. Ge-or wrote Sart a long note about his conversation with Nolo before he left Baarth. He sent it via a reliable, expensive courier, attached to a merchant caravan heading north. He also told the cleric about his and Stradryk's current quest, and that they hoped they would be able to connect with him when they returned in the winter or spring to Aelfric.

It was just past midsummer, and their thoughts were turning toward the mountains and the pass south to Aglimiville. They hung around the city for three more weeks doing short protection stints for merchants, moneylenders, and various nobles. Finally, though it would be slow going, they saddled up with a merchant heading west and south to the swamp town. They could earn a bit more money en route, and they would be on the road together once again.

The first hint of fall was in the hills as they pushed slowly upward. It was a long slow trek with the mules and wagons heading up through the hills to the mountain pass and thence south and down into the edges of the swampland. Another month had passed when they finally saw the lights of the village of Aglimiville. Collecting their due from the merchant, they spurred their horses ahead.

Ge-or wasn't sure how the Aglimi communicated with each other, yet they seemed to have an efficient system. Ooglu showed up three days after they arrived. After a short discussion with their Aglimi guide, they set a date a week later to begin their trek. Ooglu wanted to take them deeper into the swamps where his people rarely went. It was rumored that the fire lizards frequented a large rocky crag sticking up out of the morass. There it was believed they bred and raised their young. It would take them a month to reach, and there would be increased risk because Ooglu was not familiar with the pathways that deep into the swamp.

Having learned the previous year that Ooglu insisted they travel light, Ge-or and Stradryk sold much of their traveling gear and their horses and mules. It would be costly to purchase what they needed once they returned; nonetheless, they got a good price, and the moneylender they placed their gold with assured them that even over a few months' time they would gain some value to their investment. The whole town was centered on trading. The flow of money and goods from hand to hand created a spiraling economy that tended to be highly profitable for anyone with cash. The bankers had learned to translate that into top interest rates for their clients, as it gave them the capital to move more goods.

Two days after the fall solstice they slid into the waters and followed their guide to the south and east.

Into Darkness

Within a few days of returning to her practicing, Thistle jumped from teleporting plants, insects, and small animals to "hopping" about her own chambers. Initially, she did not allow Alicia to either observe or take part in these experiments; but as her confidence grew, she finally consented to have her present.

After witnessing Thistle's leaps from place to place, Alicia asked her to do it to her. Thistle hesitated; she did not want to put the girl at risk, and though she felt confident in what she was doing, this was altogether a different thing. She guessed that the energy drain would be significant. Working with a vibrational energy she was completely familiar with (her own body) was considerably different from having that kind of deep sense of another. She decided to wait until she could meet with Meligance again before trying an experiment with another person.

Alicia was disappointed; however, she also knew her mistress had learned, sometimes through difficult experiences, that absolute control, or as near to that as possible, was needed to ensure a successful outcome with magic.

Meanwhile, Thistle began to use Alicia as a witness to her increasingly longer and more diverse teleportations. First, she tried moving from her own chambers to Alicia's. She found that this proved to be no more difficult than moving about her own room. Her chambermaid would squeak excitedly when she appeared, "I see you; I see you."

Thistle also had Alicia give her detailed reports of what she actually witnessed, both as she began the movement and when she re-appeared somewhere else. What she related matched Thistle's experiences while teleporting inanimate objects, plants, and animals. These accounts supported the young Wizardess's understanding of the whole process: "I see a shimmering, or it is like you are moving suddenly really rapidly, back and forth in one spot for a few seconds. Suddenly you're gone, and in another a second you appear somewhere else." Alicia always shook her head sideways when she described the phenomena, as if she couldn't believe what she was seeing.

"It is strange, Thistle. When you reappear, which always surprises me, it is like I see a blur of lights, or maybe shades of light; and then you're at the new place. I keep wanting to reach out and touch you to make sure you are you. I mean, that you are real. You always are. When you go from one room to another, like to my chambers, I am always so surprised that all I notice is you are suddenly there, as if you had always been there but I couldn't see you."

Alicia's responses gave Thistle another idea. She began experimenting with invisibility. Using the same shift of energy that she used to teleport, without the imagery or "push" to another location, she was able to, in essence, dissolve into the ether, yet remain in the same location. It took her awhile to figure out the focus she needed to maintain her senses within the real world, while she was physically occupying space in another plane or a place "between" planes. She also discovered that she could turn her senses more toward the plane or place she felt she was in physically. Then she could observe, at least partially, what that dimension was like.

She discovered that the slight shift needed to become invisible in her own plane led her into an ethereal and nebulous space that appeared to be an effusion of shades of grays and other muted, pastel-like colors. There did not seem to be any form of life or true substance to this other world. She also discovered that she could easily create the same energy shift in other objects, and she finally did consent to try the slight vibrational shift required for invisibility with Alicia.

Her first attempts at making her handmaiden invisible they practiced in their rooms. The effort was easy for Thistle, and soon they had a great deal of fun with it. They could play a variation on the children's game "lose you-find you" while invisible, because they found out that moving about while not being seen in the real world was feasible. However, as soon as they tried to manipulate any object in their world the effect would be broken, and they would reappear.

Whatever they were wearing, held in their hands, or about their person, basically, whatever Thistle included in the spell effect, went with them, and thus could be taken from place to place. Again, it was as if they had shifted to another dimension; though, "wherever" they were, they could still see their world. Thistle guessed that the vibrational shift was enough to make them invisible, but not enough to be fully in another dimension.

This whole area of experimentation puzzled Thistle, so she spent more and more time practicing and trying to understand the full ramifications of what was possible while invisible. She wanted to understand what the limits were to invisibility and teleportation. While she knew that what she did to accomplish temporary invisibility was similar in action to teleporting, it lacked the imagery for moving to another place and the force required to move one's energy there.

Thus, while it made some sense that she should be able to pass through a wall while invisible, that did not work. She surmised that the vibrational shift was not different enough for her energy to pass through another form on the same plane.

She also figured out why trying to manipulate something in their world while invisible broke the vibrational shift. The reason was simple – in order to use an object in a given dimension or plane, one had to be fully in that world.

The invisibility work was far less draining on Thistle's personal energy than teleporting. This was because the actual physical movement from place to place while invisible was made by walking, as one normally would; yet you were actually walking while shifted out of plane. When Thistle made both herself and Alicia invisible at the same time, they could move together or apart within whatever space they were confined to – like a room or set of rooms. However, they could not open a door, or move through a solid object, without a further shift of frequency or a shift back to their own plane. When the shift of vibrations reached the stage where she could move through a solid object in their world, self-propulsion, or the ability to walk in their world, was lost. She could move about in the new dimension, yet she was reluctant to try that to any degree because she did not know how that might impact her returning to her own world.

She discovered that she could energy-shift the vibrations of part of a solid wall or other object so that she and Alicia could pass through it. This was something different from teleportation – as she was in essence moving the wall out of the way by changing its vibration. Since their energy remained in this plane, they could physically move about as they wished, and therefore, through the wall.

Thistle did delve into, in ever more depth, her ability to move into and out of other planes by shifting her vibrations. Initially, she stayed "close to home" by not making any dramatic changes to her natural frequency. Eventually, she began to push the window a bit further each day.

Most of the worlds or planes she touched upon with her experiments were shadowy places where she could discern little that was concrete. Sometimes, there was a mesmerizing cascade of ethereal colors and shifting lights; but nothing seemed whole in these places, at least not to her senses. She never felt threatened, nor that she was in the presence of any living being, or at least not living in any sense that she could ken.

Thistle wondered whether her inability to fully engage in these worlds or planes was due to her own limited perceptions and expectations. She reasoned that they might be so different from what she was familiar with that her senses could not discern shapes, things, or even life-forms that might exist in them.

One day, after repeated excursions into planes she had explored before, she went more boldly into another plane that she had bordered on several times, by making a more intense incremental shift to her vibrations. She suddenly found herself in an inferno of colors, accompanied by a tremendous sense of heat. She tried to orient in the world while battling the waves of increasingly painful visual and physical stimuli. Within a short time, Thistle was sensing that she was holding back forces that could easily hurt or kill her if she let go of her control. She quickly moved back to the next adjoining world. The cacophony of sight, heat, and she only just realized, sound, abated almost instantly.

Though the plane she was now in was soothing and calm, she felt herself quaking as if she had been standing in the midst of a frozen sea, so she shifted quickly back to her own world. She stood shaking uncontrollably for a long time, trying to regain her composure. When she was finally under complete control, she found that she had been clutching the bed post for support with so much strength and for such an extended effort that her hand hurt.

She moved to the side of her bed, sat down, and went within to try to remember all the details of what had happened. She knew Meligance would want a thorough explanation of what she had done, what she had been through, and how she had handled it.

The experience was seared in her memory. The world she had briefly visited was alive with colors: vivid reds and oranges, the deepest blacks and mottled grays, screaming yellows that burst forth out of the swirling mass – almost as if fear, anger, and hate ruled there. And amongst the colors, flitting in and out of her vision, she thought she saw figures – contorted creatures that were twisted by the place itself, twisted by the emotions and pain she had sensed.

She opened her eyes when she remembered the intense sensation of heat and looked and felt about her body to see if she had been injured in any way. She found no overt sign of having been burnt or even reddened by what she had felt; she did notice that her gown and undergarments were drenched with sweat. She could hardly believe that she did not have some serious burns on her. She wondered if her instinct to battle with her own energy what she was sensing had protected her, at least from the worst of what she was encountering.

What she began to understand was that she could, if she desired, change her vibrational frequency enough to fully immerse herself in another world; and that some of these planes were similar enough to Earth, Gaia, that physically and sensually she could interact in them and with whatever abided there. She also realized that without tremendous focus and control a venture like that could be dangerous, maybe fatal. Some part of the experience screamed at her: "You can be seriously injured or even slain in other worlds or dimensions." It definitely frightened her. She would be ever more cautious in the future.

It was a long time before she moved from where she was, took off her clothes, and sent a sphere to Alicia so she could have a bath. She still felt shaken, yet she had a sense of what she had just experienced. She not only wanted to ask Meligance about this, but to also quiz Sart as soon as he returned.

Over the next two weeks, she touched on this same plane and several others that were equally frightening – only briefly and with great caution. During her excursions, she was able to discern more and more about each of the worlds. She found them very disturbing. It took her some time to figure out the reason. Though she feared the visual and physical manifestation of each of these realms, it was the barrage of negative feelings she got when she was within them that made her uncomfortable and afraid. It seemed that the essence of these realms was based in fear and dominance. The creatures she saw briefly flitting about at the far reaches of her vision felt like they exuded hate – towards her and towards themselves.

Yet there was also something that was almost tempting about these realms, as if they called to her to explore them further, to enter them fully and experience all that they had to offer. She felt that urge more strongly each time she connected to them. Yet she remained fundamentally repulsed by what she felt emotionally assailing her; thus, the temptation was easy to overcome.

Finally, she decided she had experienced enough negativity; so she returned to exploring more benign, peaceful realms as she continued her work with invisibility and teleportation.

The Power of Music

Elanar and Jared were back on the road south in only a week's time. They had led the small entourage of the earl's wife, daughter, and a few others north until they crossed the border. After they had passed their charges off to a contingent of the king's cavalry, they headed back to their duties as Elanar had proposed they would.

Thereafter, they received daily updates on the doings in Efsted. The couriers north and south along the main routes had doubled since they had, in a sense, created the coup that toppled the duke. When they were able to separate truth from rumors, they found out that Edgar had initially been put in his own dungeon. Within a couple of days, one or more of the pretenders to his duchy had murdered him. At least three of these nobles also died within the next few days. Chaos briefly ensued, as no one looked able to control the duke's soldiers or the city. It was only after a regiment of the king's army marched into Efsted and surrounded the palace that some semblance of order was restored.

A day after the arrival of the troops, a young general had arrived and taken over the position of interim ruler of the province. The king's proclamation that gave him complete power to restore order "by whatever means" was read at every street corner, tavern, and hamlet square in the duchy. Within a month he was to recommend to the king an older, more sensible noble to replace the duke – title to be determined based on his lineage, marriage, and ability.

Staying clear of these happenings, Elanar and Jared continued southward for the next month, spending a week in Panterra and its surrounds before heading further south along the coast toward Baarth. Mostly, they spent their time hopping from one village or crossroads tavern to another, gathering what information they could along the way. It was overall a busy, yet enjoyable time for both of them. Except for a few minor disturbances, not unheard of when people were in their cups, nothing further of note disrupted their travels. During this time, they received several important messages from the north.

The first, arriving by special courier came from the king's magistrate. It ordered a Merit of the Empire for Elanar and a Star of Borea for Jared, "For their efforts to save the king's relatives from a dire situation and for Exceptional Duty to the Empire." The Merit of the Empire was the highest honor given to those in service to the king, and the Star was its second.

Jared slapped Elanar heartily on the back after they had been read the formal notice brought by the king's messenger. "Hah, well there you have it, friend. Our worries have been for naught. You did the right thing. As I said, you were brilliant." What he didn't tell Elanar was that he had sent a long missive to Leonis asking him to recommend his partner for an award. In it, he had detailed the whole episode at the duke's palace, emphasizing Elanar's role. He was quite surprised that he had received an award as well; he had not mentioned his role in the whole affair at all.

Of course, he didn't know that Elanar had also sent a notice, more formally, to Leonis explaining both their roles and the reasons for the decisions they made and the actions they had taken. It was part of their duties to do so; nevertheless, he had emphasized Jared's importance to the success of what they had done.

The second notice came by regular courier, and it was addressed to Jared. It was a letter from Sart telling him of Ge-or's travels and alerting him that he might be able to catch his brother in Baarth before he and Stradryk left for the west. He also indicated that he had sent a note to Ge-or to try to get him to delay leaving the port city for the swamplands.

Still, Jared and Elanar were on a planned route. They could deviate slightly, yet they rarely did, because the villages all knew the general routine of the wandering musicians and troupes of entertainers. They expected the entertainers to show up for their special occasions. It was not uncommon for many of the smaller hamlets and towns to delay weddings and other festivities for when a Bard or Journeyman Bard would be in town. Bards were considered to be good luck, and of course the quality of the musical performance was raised considerably for the galas that followed the ceremonies.

As they continued their general routine from one village to the next, one thing that Jared began to get more of a feel for was the power that music had to sway people. It wasn't just about affecting moods, either, though that was one important aspect of what they did on a daily basis. He learned the basis of the concept from Elanar, but his partner was a bit stilted in how he implemented it. If Elanar wanted to alter what was happening in the room in some way, he tended to sing a set repertoire of songs and melodies.

Jared discovered that, with his skill at improvisation, he could affect things even more surreptitiously by inserting fragments of melodies, or a series of soothing chords, and sometimes even a hint of another tune beneath the surface of whatever he was doing. So, while the crowd might be rowdy and calling for ribald drinking songs, Jared could add an element of calm and sedateness by changing the harmonization underneath the tunes through the playing of a soothing harmonic chord progression or by adding an underlying counterpoint in the bass that spoke to a more serene and peaceful temperament.

The more he performed, the more he experimented with this influential aspect of the music. He was surprised and pleased at how much he could affect things. When Elanar was prowling the room, drawing people into conversations designed to elicit information and the doings in the region, he would work to create an atmosphere that helped put people at ease and also helped them to loosen their tongues.

He found that he could even mitigate a potential brawl on the far side of a room by adding a certain thread of music to the song he was performing for the general audience. And oft, as sometimes they performed long into the night and were up early and riding to the next town, he would decide upon a time to call it a night. Then he would play the right tunes to have the entire remaining population of the tavern nodding asleep within minutes.

One day when they were once again in the saddle trotting at a leisurely pace further south, Elanar called him on what he was doing. "You have been putting our clientele to sleep?"

Jared grinned. "Aye, but only when we have a long day on the morrow."

"I am not complaining. I find it amusing. You seem to have a knack for affecting people with your music. What else have you discovered along similar lines? Sometimes, I sense that you are doing much more with a tune than simply accompanying a rousing group sing."

"A good bit actually, as you probably have noticed, for you have a keen ear, my friend."

"True, yet I don't have the easy facility you do to add things and change things on a whim. This is advanced training you are delving into. It is what you will study when you return to Bard Hall following your Apprenticeship, and again when your Journeymanship is done. It is a fundamental teaching of the Lore of the Bards -- 'The Power of Music.'"

"Am I doing wrong, by trying things out now?"

"Oh, nay, think not that. To have this as a natural gift is one of the things that separates those who are good, even high-quality musicians, like myself, and well, someone like you."

"I think you don't give yourself due credit, Elanar."

"Nay, Jared, I know my limitations. Though you have taught me to be more creative and spontaneous with my blade, I will never have that knack with music. It is truly a gift that you have. I am not ambitious in that sense, my friend. I only wish, in some way, to get past the pain of my past and to become the best 'almost elf' I can be."

Jared raised his eyebrows when he heard Elanar say that epithet. He had used it himself in his head enough times, yet he didn't know the "almost elves" knew people called them that. It was rarely said aloud, and certainly never in their presence.

"Aye, we have heard such whispered about. It was a source of much anger for us; thanks to you, I have come to think of it in a better light, though it still hurts in some ways. In many other ways, I am beginning to realize that it is a blessing. I am learning to be proud of my heritage, from all sides, I hope.

"The elves are dying, Jared. I believe, as I have it heard it oft said, that their insistence of pure breeding is their doom. I do not think there has been a birth, or so rumor has it, in Moulanes since I and the others like me were born. And a pure birth? Well, it may be centuries before that when the last of those occurred.

"We… ah, they have always been slow to procreate. It is something that probably has to do with being so long-lived – in what way that changes the body and how it functions. It may even affect you, and your lass, my friend. Half-elven as you are, it is in your blood; and you take after elves more than most mixed breeds."

"Aye, I… well, we know this and have spoke of it. As a mage, she will have difficulty conceiving as well. We are mostly resigned to it."

"That may be for the best. Magic is potent in many ways, and not all of them controllable. I understand that it can be a sad thing. I wish you well."

"Have you a girl, Elanar? Wife?" Jared had never asked; he was reluctant to pry into Elanar's personal life. He had always waited for him to offer bits and pieces of his heritage, but now it appeared the opportunity was appropriate.

His friend's face darkened. "Once, in Moulanes, I was in love. She was pure-bred and much older. Her father… he disapproved. Not long after that, we were sent packing. I still think of her. She was beautiful… austere, in a heavenly sort of way. We were close, as friends. I always wished it could have been more. I never knew whether she felt anything similar towards me." He bowed his head. After a moment, he shook it and smiled over at Jared.

"Have you ever tried to reach her?"

"Nay. The doors are closed to those like me. To all, really. No one may enter who is not a pure elf, not without permission; and that is difficult, nigh unto impossible, to gain. Not even the Bendir Slivs, who are also not pure-bred and have isolated themselves from outside marriage for many centuries, are allowed within the enclave anymore. The 'high' elves keep to themselves in their mountain fortress and shut out all that might disturb their peace.

"It was a miracle that the elves sallied forth to help the dwarves during the Qa-ryk wars. Yet they had no love for Kan – he who betrayed their trust – nor for the beasts he bred. Even then, they did not let many into their enclave. Your father, Manfred, was one of the few they allowed up to the gates. You know the story?"

"He spoke briefly of it, and I have heard other tales since I left Thiele."

"There was great grief in Moulanes when your mother chose to go with him. Her brother would have killed your father except for the debt he owed. He believed he had paid his honor due with the blade; however, Lililia had other ideas. She truly loved your father. He was a handsome and fearless fighter."

"You knew him?"

"Of him. I saw him several times from afar. I never met him face-to-face. We fought the same beasts in the same battles."

"I didn't know you had been Qa-ryk battle-tested."

"In a way; I was an archer. I never faced them with a blade; and knowing what I know now from you, I may not have survived. You learned from a true master, Jared. A man who had fought and survived the worst of those days. He truly was a hero. It is not surprising that your mother fell in love with him when she tended his wounds."

"I miss him."

"I am sorry. I did not mean to make you sad."

"Nay, it is all right. I would remember him. He was a stern man and demanding, but he also was a caring and loving father. I remember my mother used to sit and watch us working out. We were still young. I miss her, too. It is through my memories that I hold them in my heart."

"You are wise, my friend. It is only recently that I would allow myself to think back on my days in Moulanes with Elisia. She will always be a part of me." Elanar took a deep breath. "That part of my life is past, and I accept that now. Now back to your question… Until recently I have been far too arrogant to allow myself the pleasure of human companionship, except for short-lived trysts. You have taught me that that, too, is a foolish thing. These days my eyes are more open. We shall see what we shall see. Hah!" He slapped Jared on the back and then spurred his horse ahead. Jared followed him at a canter.

Jared thought about their conversation for a long time. He was particularly interested in what Elanar had said about the power of music – particularly that it would be an important part of his studies in the future. In some ways, he had believed that what he had been doing was simply pure fun and games. Now, he realized that it was a much more serious pursuit. Yet, Elanar said it was fine to continue what he had been doing. He realized he had barely touched on what he could learn if he set his mind, ear, and fingers to the task.

Water, Water, Everywhere

The month-long trek to Mount Taa-glimi, the "place of all creatures," was arduous. Though Stradryk and Ge-or had braced themselves for the heat and wet, having the previous winter's venture to serve them as mental and emotional preparation, it was uncomfortable at best and almost unbearable much of the time. They had left earlier in the fall than any expedition would typically head out into the swamps. This was mainly because Ooglu felt they would have a better chance when fire lizards bred.

After three difficult weeks, they could see a mass of rock rising from the morass. It was a lone sentinel of rock, a monolith, that overlooked the rot of the deep swamp. When they finally approached its broad base, they could see that there was a jumble of huge boulders at its foot, as if a giant had stood at the flat-topped peak hurling stones down about the sides until nothing remained above except walls of solid granite.

When they began to climb, they found that the side was pock-marked with numerous crevices, caves, and overhangs, continuing up the steep sides as far as they could see. As mountains go, it was not large, really a massive hill; however, it looked huge, sitting as it was in the midst of the low-lying swamplands. Once they had climbed above the canopy, it was a strange sight to behold the gray-black mass stretching further upward, set in a sea of green, browns, and yellows.

The first night they made camp in a deep hollow that, if it had been inhabited by some creature, appeared to have been left some time before. Ooglu was noticeably uncomfortable on dry land. He kept insisting that dangerous creatures inhabited the island, and he should remain with them just in case. Stradryk and Ge-or could not have cared less about almost any danger; they wanted to sleep in a dry bed, not suspended above the tepid waters of the swamp, afraid to move lest they start their hammock swinging. Finally, they compromised. Ooglu fixed himself a position in a tree above the waters below their location. They all settled in for what turned out to be a raucous night.

They got little sleep. It was indeed mating season, and creatures all about them were calling in a wide variety of voices – screeches, howls, chirps, grunts, and growls. Ge-or often heard scrabblings and scrapings on the rocks outside their den; so he stayed sitting upright, his back to the wall and his bow and short sword close to hand. He managed a bit of sleep; but when the sun finally began to peek over the trees to the east, both he and Stradryk looked much like a pair of bedraggled muskrats sitting on a sun-drenched rock. They were not enthused when Ooglu told them how peacefully he had slept in his tree.

The next three weeks they spent hunting the elusive fire lizards. The terrain on the rocky crag was difficult to maneuver on. They found they spent more than half their time circling the immense structure, seeking out glimpses of the beasts or trying to locate their lairs. Their progress was frustratingly slow, regardless of the approach they took.

Beyond being able to move much faster in the knee to chest-deep fetid waters that circled the mountain of stone, Ooglu was as much at a loss as to how to hunt the beasts as they were. He had told them that even their eldest of his people had no memories of having successfully hunted the dragon-like creatures.

In the long hours they spent each day looking for the wily beasts, they did occasionally get a glimpse of one slipping about the rocky face of the mountain or skimming across the waters of the swamp at fast speeds. The fire lizards had a webbed foot; and their agility and speed were such that, when at their fastest, they could run across the top of the swamp. They were able to literally walk on water. Yet, they often would dive in and elude their pursuers almost as rapidly by swimming.

Over the course of the weeks they spent in pursuit, they got a fair mind's-eye picture of the beasts. They looked much like ordinary lizards – slim and long, with pronounced snouts filled with small, extremely sharp teeth. They sported long, dangerous-looking tails that they whipped back and forth in the water when diving and swimming away. Their skin was a mottled green with hints of brown and yellow, the perfect colors to blend into the morass. Their feet were wide with two to three-inch-long claws and webbing between each of the toes. Most surprisingly, they were huge. Ge-or estimated that the few they had gotten good looks at weighed twice or thrice that of a good-sized man, and they were easily eight to twelve feet in length.

Only once during those first weeks did they get close enough for Ge-or to have an opportunity at bringing one down. They had chanced to come at the creature from three sides. Ge-or, standing ankle deep in water, found himself staring into the maw of the beast as it perched on a large rock looking down at him. The fire lizard had appeared suddenly, likely chased from one side or the other by either Ooglu or Stradryk. It paused long enough on the boulder for Ge-or to nock an arrow and draw a bead on its open mouth. He released in one smooth motion as the bow came up to his eye. The arrow flew true, but to Ge-or's amazement the lizard snapped it out of the air as if it was a fly coming toward it. The fine birchwood shaft snapped in two as it closed its jaws.

In the space of time that Ge-or had between releasing the arrow and seeing its fate, he had, from long practice, instinctively set another arrow to string and brought the bow up again. The lizard was beginning to turn to make a dash past him into the swamp when he released the second shaft. It, too, flew to its mark, right behind the front shoulder of the beast. The point struck home in the crease of the left shoulder, the shaft splintered, and the lizard raced away as if nothing had happened. Ge-or found the shattered shaft and razor-sharp point lying on the rocks a few minutes later, no blood on any part of the arrow. The attack had not even penetrated the armored skin of the fire lizard.

That evening they sat in camp and discussed options. Ge-or did not see any way to successfully bring the beasts down without getting one to stand still for a period of time in a nearly perfect position so that he could shoot an arrow into its maw or underbelly. Since this day's hunt was the only time they had ever seen one stopped in one place long enough for them to get a shot off, he was not overly optimistic about achieving such an ideal set-up. Having hunted many creatures in many different ways, Ge-or's thoughts turned to finding a way to trap the lizards.

After a long discussion, with Ooglu's valuable input in regard to materials available, they decided to try several other approaches. First, Ge-or nixed the idea of attempting to lure the creatures into a baited trap. They were so fast that they likely had no difficulty catching the fish and small animals that were their staple foods. While he knew they could probably build traps that would hold the beasts, he didn't see them being tempted by a tied-up marmoset or pile of dead fish.

What they finally settled on was a dual approach. The fibrous leaves of the long grass that Ooglu wove together for slow cooking utensils were quite strong, resilient to stretching or shrinking when wet, and were in abundance this far to the south. In fact, the plants here produced four- to eight-foot leaves that would be ideal for making nets.

For the next three weeks, they settled in and harvested piles of the leaves while Ooglu, who could deftly weave the fronds together, sat half in and half out of the water near their cave, quickly creating the designs Ge-or detailed to him.

When they were done, they had produced six throwing nets – large circular expanses with stones tied around the perimeter of the circle – that could be tossed as far as twenty paces or more over a target, hopefully trapping it underneath. They had also put together several long rectangular nets, six feet high and thirty to fifty feet in length, that they hoped to put in strategic locations to funnel the beasts in one direction or another.

It was nearing Yuletide, Ge-or figured, when they were ready to experiment with their handiwork. Breeding season was long past, but the lizards still were quite mobile. Ge-or had spent many an early morning and evening trying to see whether they had any regular patterns to their days. It had been frustrating. They did not appear to have a seasonal routine, as did deer, boar, and other game he had hunted. He guessed that might be because in the swamp little changed except for the length of the days and nights. This far to the south, even that variance appeared to be less. The only thing that he could count on was that nearing the full moon and in the first days of the moon's waning, the beasts were more active.

Setting up the blocking nets and each taking a throwing net, the trio of hunters set out to try their luck.

Return

It was mid-fall before Meligance finally returned to the Borean palace and her prize pupil. Though she had regretted the long absence, she had known that this was a time Thistle needed to be alone to delve into the areas of magic that only the great mages had an inkling of understanding. There was no way to coddle this type of learning. She would survive and learn what control she could of these types of realms, or she would be broken by it.

When she had sent Yolk out to choose an apprentice, Meligance had at first been confused and disappointed by the creature's choice. The girl she had scryed showed no true signs of having a particularly potent gift. She had been a wisp of a thing soon to be married to a farmer and trapper. She should have known to trust the little fellow. When Meligance had finally connected with Thistle one night, a long time before the events that had brought the girl to Kan's Altar and eventually to the Borean capital, she had sensed the strength buried deep within her. Unlike her own gift, which she had felt early in her life, this girl's had been buried very deep. She had never dreamed she would progress so rapidly.

If Thistle had done well these past months, and Meligance had received no word to indicate that anything untoward had transpired with her pupil; then she would be ready to be sent out for her most important training – experience in the field. She could think of no one better suited to that task than Sart. The boisterous monk was an adventurer at heart. He was always involved in some quest or another, ever seeking the most important information the kingdom would need for what they would soon have to face coming from the west.

Well, it was time. She sent a sphere to summon the girl. It was amusing. Meligance had long ago believed she was beyond being nervous about virtually anything. Now, she felt like she was being pricked by a thousand needles. Oh, well, she thought, this is a first for me as well.

***

Jared and Elanar reached Baarth by early fall. When he discovered that Ge-or had already left for the west and south, the two took a much-needed break from their official duties to see part of the world, taking ship to visit the large seaside town of Athalia. Situated on the far eastern side of the Great Swamp, the large village was the last human and sea-elven community heading south. According to the sea-elves, who had sailed as far as any, the low lands and coastal marshes extended on interminably.

Although there was no key political reason for them to travel so far to the south to this lonely and remote village, it was considered the ancestral home of the sea-elves; and both Jared and Elanar felt it would be good to mix with the inhabitants for a brief period. They found their week there to be one of their most enjoyable stays. The sea-elves, by a slight margin the majority of the population, were kind, generous, and most appreciative of Jared and Elanar's willingness to play short programs every evening. Even more rewarding was that they could go to bed early during their sojourn, so that they managed to get full nights' sleeps for the duration of their stay in the town.

Reluctantly waving goodbye to their new friends, they set sail again for Baarth, and from there took less travelled roads inland through range and farmlands while skirting the Bendir plains, home to the Sliv elves. Since no one other than the Slivs were allowed into the plains unless doing commerce with them, they performed at small hamlets and wayfaring inns along the edge of their domain.

When they once again reached Efsted via their circuitous route, it was mid-fall. Having some flexibility in their path back to the capital, Elanar chose to take a road that cut diagonally north and west across the province, coming finally to the king's bastion at Corrente. From there, they would head back toward the capital, hopefully arriving for the Yuletide.

By this time, they had settled into a pattern that worked well for both. Elanar had warmed to the general populace, and Jared was beginning to enjoy all facets of their presentations and performances. Jared particularly liked the final hour or so when he could improvise freely and twist the melodies and harmonies this way or that to suit his mood and purpose. They had few concerns and were generally warmly welcomed by all. Small hamlet or large village, they were often offered the best accommodations and board. It was a pleasant time, though as the weather began to get cooler, Jared's thoughts turned more and more toward Thistle. He longed to see her, hold her, and, since at long last their waiting was past, to be with her.

He was also anxious to see his friends. Karenna and Simon-Nathan had sent a few notes that had eventually caught up with him on their travels. They had been enjoying their work. In his last missive Simon-Nathan had sent word that Jared and Thistle were invited to his father's for the Yule and that there was much important news to share.

***

Thistle arrived below Meligance's tower anxious and excited about all she had accomplished. This had been the longest time she had been without her mentor since she had come to Borea. She had understood that this was her time to flex her own wings a bit. Alicia had helped where she could with her mistress' work; but for the most part everything she had been doing, especially the last month or so, had been of necessity lonely, difficult work.

***

Meligance was sitting upright on the edge of her chair. She felt uncomfortable. Yet, in spite of being aware of her angst, she could not completely relax. She noted immediately that Thistle looked much the same when she approached her table. The next few minutes would tell her more.

"Tell me what you have been working on." It was more a request than a demand, which surprised Thistle a bit. She wasn't sure, yet she felt that her oft-stoic mentor was anxious about something. Still, she had done and seen so much over the past months that she skipped over the notice of the slight change in her mentor's approach.

"It has been quite interesting, mum… As we discussed, I continued my work in understanding and practicing teleportation. I find this both physically and emotionally demanding. I have tried to study and focus on all facets of the process from the inception through the move to the new position. Though it can happen quickly, depending on the effort I expend, it is not as fast as when I send Blinkie, ah, pure energy through the ether. To move my mass through the ether takes effort. The harder and faster I 'push' myself to my destination, the more personal energy I expend."

"Good. It is wise to ponder all aspects of your power and abilities, Thistle. It helps you maintain control in the worst possible circumstances. Have you tried teleporting other living things? Plants? Animals? Your chambermaid?"

"Plants and small animals, yes. Larger animals and Alicia or another person, no. I am still reluctant to try this without some guidance. When I teleport myself from one point to another, it is draining. I have hypothesized that doing this with another person of like or greater mass will be even more strenuous, as they are outside of my own mass and control."

"You are right to be cautious. Teleportation is an oft-misused skill in our profession. Relatively minor mages can learn the basics, and thus ken how to make the shift without fully understanding the process or import. They thrill others by moving things about a room, yet they rarely ken what they are truly doing. If they attempt moving others, the result is often quite disastrous. Without knowledge and control, it can kill. In the hands of an incompetent, it can destroy one's own magic. Never take this ability lightly; use it, even if just for yourself, only in an exigency. Keep in mind that competent mages, like Aberon, also use this ability effectively in many ways.

"That all being said, I believe you are ready. If your maid is willing, try it out with her and perhaps a few times with some larger masses, alive or not. Be conscious of your limits. Each new attempt will bring you more knowledge, so build from where you are now. Also understand that this ability is highly limited, because we almost exclusively use our own personal power. I have never tried to teleport more than a few – two or three others – and that is quite draining. It is not something to do if you anticipate needing your energy for anything else for even days thereafter. It is something that Yolk can help you with, as he will enhance your personal energy. Keep in mind that his ability is limited as well. You could hurt him as easily as yourself should you attempt too much."

When Meligance paused, Thistle asked a question she had been pondering for some time.

"Do you think it feasible to somehow incorporate energy from without in the process?"

"Perhaps," Meligance answered, "however, I have not found that path yet. If you do, then let us talk of it again. It would certainly be useful on occasion... What else?"

"I have been, by twisting the teleportation concept slightly, experimenting with invisibility. I found out that the ability to make myself and other objects invisible is similar to the vibrational shift of energy in part of the teleportation process."

Meligance nodded. She had come to the critical point. Had she gone further?

"And?"

"I think I have connected with other worlds or realms as a result. Realms that, from, or perhaps more accurately within a certain perspective, are parallel with ours – only a slight shift of energy away. When I change my vibrational frequency, I feel I am in essence travelling to another realm. I believe I am part of another plane for a brief instance during teleportation or for as long as I maintain the shift. The same is true when I become invisible. I simply shift out of this plane by changing my vibrations for the duration of the energy shift.

"It is like… well, something Jared explained to me about the new music that is all the rage. He said that one can make the music more interesting by shifting out of one key into another, either briefly or for longer periods. He called it 'modulation.'"

"Indeed. It is a good analogy… What have you discovered of these other realms or planes?"

"At first, I did relatively innocuous shifts from this plane to another closely aligned vibrationally; then I shifted to others that were also close in this sense. Alicia sometimes watched me, and when I only made a slight shift, she said she could still see part of me, a 'ghost-like' version of me. She certainly knew where I was in the room because I would quiz her afterwards.

"When I tried more pronounced shifts, still staying in a sense close to home, I disappeared completely. That is when I felt like I was inside another world. Though I wasn't actually physically manipulating anything in that world, I could sometimes sense shapes, see colors and shades, and even felt that there were objects and beings all about me. If I made an effort, I think I would have been able to fully enter that world and become physically involved with it…

"I do have a question, mum."

"Yes?"

"Can one move about in other planes, other worlds? And… and if one does, is the distance relative to our world? That is, if I return will I be a similar distance displaced from where I started in my room or…?"

"Good questions, Thistle. I am glad you are pondering these things. The broad answer is both 'No' and 'Yes.' Each plane is different, sometimes vastly different. Hence our laws, distances, and so forth, may not apply. You can only know by experimenting, and of course, then you take a chance. Control becomes suspect.

"One truth I can tell you from my own experiences in delving into other realms – when you are fully shifted into another plane you can interact in it, move about, and be affected by all that is part of that place, including other creatures. It can be extremely hazardous. Always use the utmost of caution, as you are doing.

"Anything else?"

Thistle hesitated, wondering how Meligance would react to the next bit; on the other hand, she was excited about all that she had discovered so she went on.

"One day I went further, shifting from the essentially benevolent-feeling world I had gone to first via a slight shift of frequency to another vibrational level next to it. I suddenly found myself in a horrible place... or it felt that way to me. It was confusing, initially; but after several attempts, I began to make some sense of what I was seeing and experiencing.

"It was a wildly colored world: deep reds, oranges, blacks, and occasionally vivid yellows. It was in constant motion. Oddly, I felt strong emotions coming at me: anger, wrath, and pain, all founded in a fear – a deep-rooted fear – that appeared to permeate all. It was really frightening. The first couple of times I found myself there, I shifted out as soon as I got myself reoriented. Later, when I stayed longer, I began to see more: shapes, creatures flitting in and out of my vision, and a… well, I would have to describe it as a pull."

"A pull?"

"A compulsion to go further in, to shift fully into that plane. I felt as if someone or something was calling to me. It was frightening, but also thrilling in a way. There was great power there. It felt like there was a separate cognizance that understood who I was and that I was there."

"What did you do?"

"I left. I could not stand the depressing pressure of the place for long. Though I felt the tug, the desire to move further in, the negativity threatened to overwhelm me. In spite of all the preparation I did before reentering those realms, I knew that if I gave in to that urge, I would have difficulty extricating myself."

"Those realms?"

"Oh, yes, I discovered several, perhaps more than several. However, I only shifted into a few of them. I could only stand to do so every other day, because the effect was quite draining emotionally. Some were darker and bleaker and more hopeless than others. I oft felt like I was protecting myself with my own energy when there." Thistle's voice trailed off, thinking again of the heaviness and fear she had felt exposed to during shifts. "What are these places?"

"You have touched on the Nine Planes."

"The Planes of Hell?"

"Yes, if you must. Some religious like to name them thus. They are simply other realms or worlds, parallel planes to this. And, as you have discovered, vastly different in make-up. Did you discover anything else?"

"Well, there is a curious thing, which I only began to think about today. For some reason, it came to me when I was practicing some basic energy work this morning."

"And that is?"

"Each negative plane adjoins a more neutral or maybe, better spoke, a more positive realm or plane. There was always a dramatic contrast between each of these parallel worlds. I would first shift to a vibrational level fairly close to mine and feel I was in a place of calmness, beauty, ethereal peace; then, with the next shift, I would find myself in one of these darker worlds. They seem to come in twos and are diametrically opposite of each other. Is this a valid perspective?"

"It is the truth as near as I can tell, for I have experienced these as well. Evil is balanced by Good, darkness by light, cold by heat, and so forth. It is the way of the universe. It is even a law of this land, I should think. There was ever a balance, or there was until the Heart of the World was split in twain."

"The stone Sart seeks?"

"Yes. Good, I am glad he has told you of it. We will speak more about that and his quest for knowledge about these types of things on another occasion. There is a key here to life that you have discovered, and it is worth pursuing a bit further. What I speak of is the notion that there is a duality in or to all things. We tend to think in terms of Good and Evil, yet one must take it beyond that. The real consideration, the true foundation of all things, is that there is always one thing opposing another or an opposite: white-black, hot-cold, strong-weak, and so on."

"Is there not also everything in-between, as a gray is between white and black?"

"A key point, to be sure; but it is the duality, I think, that sets everything apart. For example, would you ken cold if you did not have heat? Duality gives us a world to experience, even with its grays and off-shades. Yet, it is the blacks and whites that give us the true context of separation, or if you will, the striking contrasts – the more dramatic presentation of opposites.

"It is not an answer, Thistle." Meligance said when she saw the puzzled look on her pupil's face. "It is a 'ponderable' as Sart would say. So, ponder it. Such things can be life-long pursuits philosophically, even religiously. For now, let us return to the work at hand, my young Wizardess."

Thistle did not let the honorific pass. "Wizardess?"

"It is time, Thistle. I have taught you all that I may directly. And you have discovered much more on your own. A good teacher is merely a guide. Now your education will truly begin, because it is time to send you out into the world for your own adventures."

"I feel there is so much I do not ken yet, and you are far wiser than I, mum." Thistle bowed her head, suddenly feeling uneasy and alone.

"Wiser only because I have a vast experience I have learned from. Fear not, we will meet many more times for many years. I shall guide you further along your path as I may, unless you tire of an old woman's ramblings. We can learn from each other from here on. Truthfully, you have already taught me much that will help as you and I turn to training others, for that will be part of our task in the years ahead. The key difference will be in our relationship. You and I are now equals, Thistle.

"I know that may be hard to accept. In truth, you have made amazing progress and are at a point that took me almost two decades reach. You truly are a Wizardess, a White Wizardess of Borea."

Thistle was dumbfounded. A swirl of emotions swept through her whole body, not the least of which was that she felt far from adequate, and certainly not equal to her mentor. However, Meligance appeared completely serious. She tried to focus as *The* White Wizardess of Borea continued.

"Now that you have reached this important point in your development as a mage, I am afraid I must inform you that there are no ceremonies or pomp and circumstance to accompany your rite of passage – only my words and blessings. Come, give your mentor a hug and go celebrate with Alicia. You deserve a few days off. Also, see Sart, and after, come back to me. There are plans to be made." She smiled at Thistle; then she raised her hand to make one last point.

"Know this, Thistle, from this point on you are free to choose as you will. I will be a guide when you wish for one, and I will suggest paths for you to take; but truly, I consider us equals from henceforth. You are welcome to gainsay me or offer me advice any time you choose. I will learn from you as much as you will learn from me."

"I am humbled mum, and… and a bit afraid."

"Good. That is the way of wisdom."

Love Is in the Air

It was a cold and crisp late afternoon two days before Yuletide, when Jared and Elanar rode into Borea. Though they would have wished to simply get a good night and late morning's rest, they had been summoned several days before to make haste to the palace to receive their awards and gratitude from the king. It was a great honor, but they looked forward to neither the ceremonies nor putting up with the pomp of the court. It was required, so they stopped at Bard Hall, where they were met by several young students bearing new clothes to befit their rank. Then they were unceremoniously pointed to the hot baths where they did enjoy a long soak and scrubbing. It was particularly enjoyable since it had taken them two and a half days of hard riding to get back once they had received notice from the court.

Jared spent many of those hours thinking of Thistle, his friends, and of returning to Bard Hall, even if only for a short space before their next assignment. He found that he missed the hustle and bustle of the Hall, his friends, the structure of the classes – pretty much the whole experience. Yet, he knew that he had outgrown all of that and that his life had changed directions once again. He did worry a bit about seeing Karenna after this long time. The few notes he had received from her had been newsy, focusing mostly on her and Simon-Nathan's work together, with no indication of the deep and caring relationship she had shared with Jared for almost four years.

It was bordering on dinner hour when they were ushered quickly through the gates into the palace and thence, through a series of corridors, to a private anteroom awaiting the king's pleasure. They were filled in on what to do and say and told that this was a small ceremony specifically designed for the two of them, with only a small number of people in attendance including the Earl of Saffra's widow and daughter. Finally, there would be a feast for them and their friends following. They were also told that the king had previously dined and would not be attending the post-award festivities.

Everything went considerably better than they would have thought. King Alfred was a pleasant older man who waved away their coached gestures of deference. He motioned for them to sit in two plush chairs facing him at one end of the comfortably large room, whilst he asked this and that about their adventure. He was most interested in hearing about how they had managed to bring down "this thorn in my side" in so short a period of time, when he hadn't been able to deal with the problem of Duke Edgar for many years.

At first, there was no one else in the room except the requisite men-at-arms, two at each of the four doors, and the one minister, who stood politely to the side and behind the king. When King Alfred was satisfied with what he had learned from them, he motioned to the minister, who immediately brought his staff of office crashing into the floor thrice. Three of the four doors opened, and much to Jared's surprise, in walked Thistle with Sart, Meligance chatting amicably with Leonis, the Saffras, three of Elanar's "almost elf'" friends from Bard Hall, and most amazingly Simon-the-Elder, his wife Rachel, daughter Athena, Simon-Nathan, and Karenna and her family.

If it hadn't been for protocol, Jared would have leapt up and run to greet everyone. However, the king did rise, and the minister indicated with a wave of his hand for them to do so as well.

The king nodded to all as the gathered guests bowed to him. He moved his hand in an upward motion to allow them to straighten. When he began to speak, his voice was soft, but firm, accustomed to having people listen. "I appreciate all of you coming at this Yule-time at my request. It is not for me, that I had you come; it is to acknowledge with honor these two for doing the kingdom and myself a great service.

"Leonis…" The grandmaster took a step forward and again bowed slightly at the waist toward King Alfred. "It speaks to the high quality of your Hall and your students that they continue to live the ideals set forth in your charter. I am most appreciative." The king inclined his head, which was respectfully acknowledged by Leonis with another bow.

King Alfred continued, addressing them all. "I must apologize for the lack of ceremony and pomp; I have come to appreciate much less of that sort of tomfoolery. Hopefully, I will be able to offer more heartfelt thanks in return. Please gather closer whilst I say a few words to these fine young men. Leonis, you may take over from there."

The rest of the proceedings were a blur to Jared. King Alfred made some short comments before awarding them their medals. He handed Elanar a document that stated he was being offered a small manor grant to the north and west of the capitol. It was, as he said, a gesture; nevertheless, it was more than that, because with it Elanar was dubbed a lord of the realm with "all rights thereto appertaining."

Even more surprisingly, at a gesture from the king, Leonis stepped forward and anointed Elanar his Bardship, "by the authority of the Council of

Bards." Unabashedly, Elanar wept when he knelt before the king and the grandmaster, overwhelmed by this tremendous change to his fortunes.

King Alfred excused himself at that point, thanking everyone again for coming. The next half hour was a milling about of everyone welcoming the two wanderers back and congratulating them. Jared did not have any time alone with anyone; but he did manage a kiss to the cheek of all the ladies present, even Meligance, who was not above blushing slightly when the young and very handsome half-elf bent toward her.

At the dinner, Jared and Elanar were placed at the honored spots at the head of the long table. Everyone else was seated more or less according to rank. Thus Meligance, Leonis, and Sart were nearest to the two honorees, with Thistle seated next to Sart. Then came the Saffras and the two patriarchs of the two families present, Simon and Karenna's fathers, both notable men in their own communities, followed by wives, families, and finally all the others from Bard Hall ranked according to their tenure as students.

By royal standards it may not have been an elaborate feast; nevertheless, after ten courses and with piles of the most decadent looking pastries he had ever seen set before him, Jared was more than stuffed. He had felt obligated to try at least a smidgen of everything; the problem had been that it all tasted so wonderful that it was hard to stop with a taste. It all had been a dizzying, pleasant experience. Jared was glad when Meligance nodded to the head steward and the final plates were cleared.

Jared did manage a few moments with Thistle as they were led back through the maze of corridors and rooms to the entryway. She assured him that she would be arriving at Simon-the-Elder's house by noon on the morrow; and though he wished he could spend time with her that evening, he knew he was dreadfully tired. He barely remembered the goodbyes. At the end, he leapt up on his immaculately groomed horse, cared for by the palace stable-hands, for the ride to Simon-Nathan's house. Elanar, whom the merchant had begged to join them for the Yule, rode with him. The other elves politely declined the same offer, having duties at Bard Hall; however, Elanar was keen to follow and accepted the invitation graciously. All the others had come in carriages, so the two honored men followed the gilded caravan through the streets.

By the time they reached the large manor house near the center of town, they were all yawning their goodnights. Jared was nodding off in bed before he had the fleeting thought that he hadn't had any time to talk with Karenna or his former roommate. She had seemed happy, almost joyous, and Simon-Nathan had been beaming throughout the ceremony and dinner; so he took that as a good sign and drifted off contentedly.

He woke late and realized that the sun was already climbing high in the sky. Washing quickly, he scampered down the stairs hoping to find either Karenna or Simon-Nathan before Thistle arrived. He entered the drawing room virtually at a run, stopping in his tracks when he saw a small troop of women and young ladies gathered there. They were all cooing around Karenna, who stood in the center of the room on a small stool, posing in what appeared to be an elaborate white dress that seemed a bit over-flowery for the Yuletide. It hit Jared all at once. She was getting married and… and to Simon-Nathan.

Karenna saw him, waved, and blushed deeply. She shooed the women away, motioning only to Simon-Nathan's sister, Athena, to stay while she stepped down. She whispered something to Athena, who nodded back. Karenna took a tentative step toward her former lover. "Oh, Jared, I am so happy and… and so sorry that I didn't have any time to speak with you last night. It…"

He stepped forward and reached out with his hands and took hers. "Karenna, it… I am so happy for you. I knew of Simon-Nathan's affections for you. He always… It is he?" She nodded, smiling broadly then. She looked truly radiant. "He was always a gentleman, and we… we had something special for a long while."

"We did, but as you said we have all changed. This fall was the most fun I have had ever in my life. We truly are a pair… of scholars, I guess." She laughed the bubbling laughs he knew so well. Jared turned when he heard a voice from behind in the doorway.

"So, you know. I'm sorry, Jared." Simon-Nathan came to meet them. "We so desperately wanted to get you aside last night to tell you, yet protocol conspired against us. You are good with this?"

"More than good, old friend. This is a beautiful and wonderful thing. You two have always been the closest of friends; and there was always more than that there, even from the beginning. I sensed that. I am so happy for you, and I know Thistle will be as well."

"Will you stand with me this eve for our wedding? You are my best friend." Simon-Nathan took Karenna's hand and looked at Jared with tears in his eyes.

"I would be honored, but I have nothing to give you both. I… I feel at a loss."

"That you still consider us your friends is enough of a gift. We three, and now four, the gods willing," for Thistle's carriage had driven up in front of the main gate, and Simon-Nathan gestured in that direction, "have been the best of friends. We saw each other through a great deal. My guess is that there will be other trials ahead that will be much easier to weather if we remain close. Come, let us greet your lady."

Jared saw that Simon-Nathan had grown in many ways over the intervening months since graduation. His friend looked yet a bit taller, in good shape, and more than anything, self-confident and assured. This was indeed an interesting and joyous turn of events.

Simon-Nathan took Jared's arm briefly as they walked down the pathway toward the carriage. "I have given Thistle the room next to yours. I hope that suits."

***

The wedding turned out to be a monumental affair held at the largest cathedral in the city. Sart presided over the ceremony with permission of the Bishop of the Church. The building was over-flowing, as Simon-the-Elder was well-known and well-liked, being a generous man and one of the key merchants in the sprawling city. Athena and Karenna's sisters were lovely standing with her. Jared was joined by Karenna's brother and two other friends from Simon-Nathan's Master's History program at Bard Hall.

Following the rites, there was a great feast at one of Simon-the-Elder's largest warehouses. It was decked out for the occasion with so much festive regalia and pine boughs that it was almost impossible to tell it was normally used to store goods. It was a grand affair for all.

Jared had been told that there would be a follow-up celebration for their closest friends and family at the manor that evening. He took the advice and only nibbled politely at the mounds of food set on tables throughout the hall. He and Thistle enjoyed quite a few turns on the dance floor; and there were times that Jared felt as if he were literally floating slightly above the surface, so light was she on her feet. He also had a lovely dance with Karenna. At the end, she gave him a quick buss on the cheek and thanked him for everything. Though she had tears in her eyes, he knew it was simply remembrances of what had been and was no more – no regrets on either side.

It was late in the afternoon, as the party was winding down, when Jared noted Athena sitting in a corner of the hall with Elanar. They were deep in conversation. He mused a bit on that interesting sight. When he realized that he had seen them together quite a bit that day, including many dances, he truly began to wonder. Thistle came over at that moment and pulled him away,

"Let them be; they are happy together." She drew Jared around a corner, through a doorway, and out into the brisk winter air. She pulled his head down to hers and kissed him. This was not the light, chaste, suggestive kisses they had shared several times during the day. It was a deep kiss, desiring much more. He felt a strong tingle run up and down his spine, and he groaned. "Soon, tonight, my love. I will come," she whispered in his ear. She released him and pushed him back towards the door.

Jared noted with interest that Elanar had been invited to the evening festivities as well.

Too nervous and excited to eat much and not wanting to be inebriated this night, Jared nevertheless enjoyed the bliss of the get-together. He and Elanar were asked to perform, which they did graciously for a short while. Soon many others joined them, including Athena on the soprano recorder, Karenna on alto recorder, Simon-Nathan on the fiddle, Simon-the-Elder on the tenor recorder, and Rachel on the bass recorder as everyone celebrated with merry carols.

It was fashionably late, when a much-overdone carriage came to pick up the bride and groom to take them to the most elegant inn the city had to offer. The two promised they would return on the morrow for the Yuletide; but they had a week planned "somewhere a bit further south" before they once again took to the road to continue their Apprenticeships.

***

Jared hadn't been in his room more than two minutes when he heard a light tap on the door. He set his book aside. Reading was a habit he had started during the long hours before performances, if the ride from one venue to another had been short. Thistle slid quietly into the room. He had expected her to take some time before she came to him; and he was a bit non-plussed when he saw that she was still dressed in the elegant evening gown she had worn throughout the festivities, yet she had obviously kicked off her shoes in favor of bare feet.

She came to the edge of the bed as he made to get up, holding her hand palm outward to let him know she wished him to stay where he was. She sat at his feet, about as far from him as she could get on that side of the four-poster bed. "We need to talk, Jared."

He looked at her quizzically. She had never been shy about being close with him when they were alone together. She looked downright serious, not at all like she was in any sort of mood to be romantic.

"I know, my love." She placed her hand below his knee and began stroking his leg with her index finger. "This probably isn't what you imagined; still, it is important. Be patient a bit longer." She stopped the motion of her finger and drew her hand further down toward his ankle. "I have to tell you what it means... what it will mean to be with me... with a mage. You are far more experienced than I in many ways; however, there are things that will be different, far different for us because of who I am."

Jared waited. Thistle managed a slight upturning of her lips. "I have to explain to you what... what Meligance and I talked about for some length a few days ago. Then you will have to decide if this is what you truly want. If what I am and what that portends is something you can bear."

Thistle's cheeks reddened and she lowered her eyes. Bending at the waist, Jared stretched forward, taking one of her hands. "Thistle, I gave my heart to you long ago. That hasn't changed. I love you; I want to be with you. We have talked about what it means to be a mage, that you may not be able to bear children, that..."

"Enough!" Thistle said the word more strongly than she would have liked; she was uneasy and a bit fearful of how her love would react to what she had to tell him.

Jared sat back, dropping her hand, stunned at the force of her directive.

"Oh, Jared." Tears came to Thistle's eyes and began to trickle down her cheeks. "I'm sorry. I'm horribly nervous about this, and that was far more forceful than I meant it to be. Forgive me. Please, listen and … well, we will decide together. You know I love you, and I know you care deeply for me. Love may not be enough, if... if you can't accept me completely for who I am, for who I have become. Just give me time to get through this. Please."

He nodded, but did not reach out for her again. He waited.

"I am powerful, Jared – really powerful and quite dangerous." The tears stopped and Thistle straightened her back a bit. She was looking now directly into his eyes. He could see that there was a strength in her that he had not noted before, a resilience and a hooded power.

"It is hard to describe to someone who does not have natural magical ability, the energy I have within me and what energy I can command." Thistle was now staring at Jared intently, her hand clutching his ankle. "Jared, I could destroy this building, this whole block of buildings with the power that resides within my core, and… and I could destroy this city with the power I can draw to me. I'm not even sure Meligance fully understands the power I have tapped. Though she and I are much the same, in some ways I know I am fundamentally different. She has hinted at that on more than several occasions. For whatever reasons, I have been blessed, or cursed, with this innate ability. It is far more than even Sart was concerned about when we first met. Once I became aware of it, I have… I have developed it much faster than my mentor ever did, and faster than she would have believed possible.

"Jared, you need to understand this, because whether we are in bed together or simply living our lives together, it will always be there. It is not something I can walk away from or will away.

"I am here, right now, able to touch you, able to consider being one with you, because I have learned to control it to an extent where you and I will be safe."

"With that said, magic is, and you know Sart is fond of saying this, 'suspect.' Though I have learned a fine degree of control of my personal energy, and as a result, the ability to draw and control energy from without, it is never absolute. Please understand this, because it means that at all times," Thistle's grip on Jared's ankle tightened even more, "and I mean 'at all times,' even at the height of passion, there is a part of me that *must* remain in control. Else I could hurt or kill you and damage myself as well. Do you ken what I am saying?"

Jared knew he had not had time to fully process and understand what Thistle was telling him, but he nodded again. His mind was awhirl with what that might mean to them, to him, to her; and none of it felt quite right – not the rightness of giving oneself fully over to the experience of love and passion. Truthfully, he cared on one level what it all might mean to them; on another he didn't, because he loved her in spite of all this, or perhaps, because of it – it was who she was. He didn't know what to say, yet she seemed to want a response; so he said what was paramount in his mind. "You mean that you cannot fully give yourself over to the experience of our love?"

"Yes, Jared, that is what I mean. However, that isn't all of it." More tears came to her eyes. She brushed them away quickly. "I can love you, Jared – passionately, lovingly, with a full heart. I can do what all lovers do. I can experience the climax of passion, physically and emotionally; yet there will always be that tiny part of me that I have to hold back, keeping my full power in check. I know…"

Thistle stopped again and smiled, lovingly and mischievously, Jared thought. "Oh, Jared, you should have seen Meligance, the Great White Wizardess of Borea, talking to me about all of this. It was quite amusing because of her discomfort. It was difficult, and in some ways embarrassing, for her to speak of these things. I am the first she has taken on as an apprentice. Teachers learn as well, and I will not be the last. It was really awkward for her.

"Anyway, my power has uses, too. Have you noticed an energy throughout your body, a tingle up and down your spine sometimes when we have kissed, since we have been in physical contact again?"

Jared nodded, surprised that she would have noticed such a thing in him.

"That was me, Jared. My magic. I can…" She blushed. "I can… well, I guess 'enhance' might be the best word. I can enhance our experiences, our union as lovers, in many ways with my power. I let you feel a tiny mote of that today, because I wanted you to ken what I am now saying. Magic is useful on many levels. You and I can experience things that others might not even dream of. Meligance gave me a few hints, some insights. She also said, 'Do what you have done so well, my young mage, experiment, enjoy, have fun.'" Thistle reached out and brushed some of Jared's long brown hair back from his forehead. He felt a strong, and he had to admit, exciting, tingle, run from that spot throughout his body. He opened his eyes wide and tried desperately, and quite unsuccessfully, to keep his manhood from responding.

Thistle laughed lightly. "So, you see."

She got serious again. "Jared, understand this, it can add a great deal to our being together. It makes me different. It means that I have a power you do not have. If you feel uncomfortable at all with this, we should discuss it further. You need to know and accept that I have this power; *we* need to decide if you are willing to accept my ability to use it."

"It will not hurt me?"

"Not physically, not if I stay in control; that is always a hazard, as I have said. It is more an emotional effect that you need to understand. Will it bother you to be with someone who has these powers, powers that you don't have?"

"It does not feel of concern to me; I love you for who you are. If that means accepting your power, so be it. I can swallow my pride a bit. Plus," he winked at her, "I have some powers that you do not know about."

"Well, we shall see…There is one other thing, Jared."

"Yes?"

"It would be wise to go slowly, carefully, for a while, perhaps even a long while. I need to understand how all these… well, how all these new sensations I am going to experience will affect me so that I can maintain my control."

"Can we lay together?"

"Yes, tonight, if you will… It might be best to just touch each other – satisfy each other in that way this first time." Jared could see Thistle blush a deep red in the candlelight. "Then tomorrow… well, we shall see, shan't we?" She stood suddenly, pulled her gown off in one smooth motion, revealing lacy undergarments and a slim, fine, filled-out figure. She climbed into bed with Jared and touched him lightly on his chest. He drew her in towards him, and he floated into the exquisite softness of her arms and body for the first time.

The Dark Side of the Yule

This was definitely not his favorite time of the year. Aberon was especially unhappy because he had spent the last few days leading up to tonight's frivolity amidst the hustle, bustle, and joy-of-life of the season.

Now he was mixing among the great and not-so-great in the Grand Ballroom of the Borean Palace. Of course, he had had to change his appearance. No one would feel comfortable around him if he were himself. "Hah!"

He wondered why these overly-dressed, out-of-shape dandies, courtiers, and fat merchants milling about would find his true form – thin and sinewy – so distasteful. Perhaps, it was because it was such a contrast to their indulgent opulence. He had chosen the form of a corpulent, yet not overly so, merchant dressed in vivid greens and yellows, which spoke to this crowd of money, lots of money. They would have avoided him like the plague and disdained his company altogether if he had entered the palace as an ascetic monk in black robes. He probably would never have gotten in, even with his magicked invitation.

All disgust aside, this was the best place to gather information from drunken fops. Aberon had even spoken to the king's chief minister for a while. With a bit of magical tweaking, the fellow had been quite loquacious.

Most of his work here was done, and he would soon be free to go. Unfortunately, everyone seemed to want to talk with him, find out who he was and what he sold, and so forth. Many times, he could brush them aside with a quick aversion charm; but sometimes they got to him while his attention was directed elsewhere. Well, there was nothing for it; he wanted to meet with two others in this mass of people: the royal librarian, who could, and would with the right impetus, give him access to the deeper vaults; and the minister of the army, from whom he hoped he could pry out some information about what the kingdom's plans in the west might be for the next five or more years. Soon, if all went as he had prepared, he would be in a position to move to the top; then *he* would be directing the eastward expansion of the Qa-ryk hordes and the destruction of the empire.

He yet had work to do. Now that he had taken the time to develop the energy he had received when Kan's Altar had been destroyed, he was far more powerful than he had been before. That meddling cleric's plan had gone awry -- though Aberon had lost the stone, he had gained much, much more. Eventually, he would take care of that small problem, too. For now, it was still in the hands of the young Bardling, as benign a place as any for it to rest for the nonce.

The Three were now gathered in the Black Fortress protecting the Great One, the Great Druid. They were frightened enough of Aberon that they had joined forces. Aberon knew he wasn't quite ready to take on all of them at once. There were still things he wanted to put into play before he made that move.

He had consolidated his strength well this past year: Six and Seven were dead; Four and Five had capitulated without any resistance, wisely realizing they were outclassed. It had been amusing to see them grovel when they had heard about their brethren's' spit-roasting and dismemberment. Indeed, that had been an entertaining evening or two, much more so than the past three eves.

He could have sent either of his two new colleagues to do this menial chore; but he did not want them to ken what he was about, not yet. He wasn't going to trust them, not until he was the One. From that point on, his rule would be from fear and overwhelming power. Once he had gathered the information he sought, they *would* have something to fear – that is, if it led to what he was hoping to find.

Ah! The royal librarian! Off in the corner as might be expected. The man was incorrigibly dull. However, Aberon would use that to his advantage. He would engage him in some light banter and prod the fellow's ego a bit. This would result in his gaining access to the vaults he needed, far beneath where they now stood.

"Chief Librarian Pons?"
"Yes?"

New Directions

It was a week after the holiday season. Leonis had called Elanar and Jared to his office. They had both stayed at Simon-the-Elder's through the three festive days of Yule, but since had moved to private rooms in the graduate section of the Hall. Now they were spending the better part of their time being debriefed about their journey. It was time to find out what was in store for them for the New Year.

***

"Come in. Come in." Leonis' deep voice resounded through the heavy oaken door before Jared's knuckles actually made contact with the wood.

They were surprised when they entered. Sitting at the table in the meeting room were Sart, Thistle, and a heavy-limbed, dwarfish-looking man that Jared had never seen before.

"Welcome, welcome… You both know our esteemed cleric and our young Wizardess. This," Leonis nodded a slight bow to the stout man sitting to his right, "is Motuk, a friend and companion to Sart on any number of missions and adventures. He is of import to what we plan today.

"So, shall we get down to it? Sart?"

The cleric stood, nodded to all, and for a person as bulky as he, bowed gracefully toward Thistle. "I have asked Grandmaster Leonis to grant me the boon of your service for a period. There are things I must accomplish over the next months that require both finesse and, quite possibly, power applied judiciously in the right places – in other words, there may be some fighting involved, or at least some persuasion." He smiled.

Jared looked with surprise and elation over at Thistle. He could see a twinkle in her eyes. He inferred that she must have known of this for at least a short space of time; however, they had not been able to spend any time together the past few days. Meligance had called her back to the palace following the Yuletide days of celebration. He had worried more and more as the days passed that they would once again be apart for a long time whilst he returned to the road with his minstrel duties.

"For some of you, this will be your first true adventure coming out of training; so we will be cautious and take things as they may. Though there are things I wish to accomplish, of paramount consideration and part of the reason for this, is to provide you, Jared, Wizardess, and to a certain extent Elanar, with experience. It won't be long before we call upon all of you for more involved

95

and dangerous missions relevant to the safety of the kingdom and all that portends.

"To get to the point – in a fortnight we will meet here and thence southward to Efsted. Weather permitting, we will catch a boat there that can take us to Panterra. From there, I do not fully know our route. It will partially depend on our successes to that point. Eventually, I do hope to meet up with Elanar and several of his brethren.

"Elanar, you will remain here in Borea at the Hall for now. Leonis has plans relevant to your further education and indoctrination as a full Bard. I will send a courier north when we leave Panterra. Then you and your fellows must make as good a time as you may to catch us up in the western border town of Aube.

"From there, the plan will be for all of us to ride into the foothills and mountains. There is an old dilapidated manor above a now-empty village that once served as a gathering place and wayside trading post for the gnomes, dwarves, and those who would deal with them for their ore. It was a wealthy center. There may be places of interest to explore around or beneath the ruins. Hopefully, if my projected timetable works out, we can meet up near the beginning of summer. After we explore that vicinity… well, I have not planned further.

"Following this brief meeting, Motuk will guide you as to what types of gear, weaponry, clothing, and so on will be recommended for our adventuring. We will purchase food along much of the route; nonetheless, at times we will stock up when we know we will be camping. All the gear we need for tenting and cooking is already gathered. We will be comfortable as we may, when we do not have taverns or inns to rest in.

"Jared and Elanar, you are to meet with the weapons master and minstrel master for further instructions regarding this quest.

"Thistle," Sart again nodded a bow toward her, "you will meet this week with Meligance.

"For everything else, Motuk should be able to address most of your questions; if you need to see me, I will be at the palace."

Sart bowed toward all. He gestured for Motuk to stand; then he and Leonis exited the room together.

Following the meeting with Motuk, Jared pulled Thistle aside into an alcove as they walked down the main corridor of Bard Hall. "You knew of this, Thistle?"

She stood on her toes and gave him a light kiss. "It has been in the works for a while, but Sart and Meligance hadn't settled on whether you and Elanar would be involved until yesterday."

"I am overjoyed," Jared said, picking her up by the waist and swinging her in a full circle, before setting her back on her feet. "I can't believe we will be able to be together. I was so worried I would have to leave you until the summer."

"I think Meligance pushed Sart and Leonis to include you, because… well, she cares about me." Thistle smiled that sly smile of hers.

Thistle's smile reminded Jared of…? "Meligance," it finally came to him as she continued. "Plus, she wants me out in the world getting experience. She has further decided to take on several other promising young mages as apprentices. Eventually, I will be called upon to take part in training others as well. For now, we can be on the road together."

"It feels like we are starting back where we left off when we came to Borea over four years ago."

"In a way, still, we have both changed. Please understand, my love, that I have changed dramatically. What I said to you the other day is the truth. I have immense powers at my fingertips. I hope you understand that, because it does change things...

"For one," she reached out and took Jared's hand, entwining her fingers in his, "don't be gallant or foolish trying to protect me. I can protect myself. Use your head first. Look to me if there is time, before trying to be brave for my sake or for anyone else's for that matter."

She pushed him out at arm's length while maintaining her hand in his. She added even more seriously, "It may be hard, Jared; there are times when you will have to trust me completely. Times when I will direct you, command you and others, even Sart. An instant may be all you have to obey me. If you hesitate or try to question me, someone might be hurt or killed."

Jared stared into her incredible green eyes. He knew she was right; he also knew that what she was warning him about would be difficult for him to accept fully. He naturally felt protective of her.

"I will try, Thistle…," he answered hesitatingly. "I know we have changed, my love. I have changed, and I have learned many things as well. It will take me awhile to get used to… well, the new you. I will try to do as you say, but sometimes it may be difficult for me, I think this will be a learning experience for both of us, in ways that perhaps Sart and Meligance haven't imagined."

"Perhaps, yet they are both wise in many ways we don't ken as well. This may be precisely what they hope to happen – that we will learn from and about each other. I imagine there was a time that they went through much of what we will experience on this quest." She paused for a moment. "Are you excited, Jared?"

"More than excited, my love. I think it is a wonderful opportunity for us. We will get the chance to know each other again and to explore new things as well."

"I expect that Sart and Meligance had many a conversation about what experiences we should have."

"I would bet on it," Jared grinned.

***

They were all sitting around a modest campfire, heads downcast, discouraged. Even Ooglu, who almost universally was forward-looking and positive, appeared to be dragging. For the past five weeks they had tried and tried again with the nets, enclosures, anything they could think of; the beasts were just too fast and wily.

Ge-or had one of their nets in his lap and was absentmindedly fingering the material. Stradryk looked at him, shrugged, and said, "Perhaps we need to make them even bigger."

Ge-or smiled and shook his head. "Nay, friend, it is not the nets. We are at fault. We are no match for these creatures. I have hunted many a cunning beast in the north country, yet I have never seen anything like these. You can't track them because they run on water. You can't outrun them because they are faster than the fastest cat I have ever seen. They run like the tiny lizards we see in trees, but they are nearly as big as a small horse. Their nests are out of reach, and we cannot out-craft them, either." Ge-or pointed with his head up to the heights above them, a place even the most daring of gnomes, reputedly the best climbers in Borea, would hesitate to climb. "Plus, to add insult to our already obviously limited abilities regarding these creatures, the three shots I have had at them haven't even penetrated their hides. I am at a loss."

"Did any of your kin ever capture or kill any of these things?" Stradryk asked Ooglu. Though he already knew the answer, he had never actually asked the question directly.

"None in memory and we have good memories. I have heard of hunts, a very few like yours, where an Aglimi leads a band into the swamps after the beasts. However, there is no mention in our lore of anyone having taken one. I do not know. It is why I hesitated to take on this task, yet a matter of honor is something my kin understand well. I am sorry I have no more ideas on this."

"It is not your fault, Ooglu. You have done all you promised and more."

"Should I begin our supper? I have some nice fish for stewing, marsh tubers, herbs. Or do you wish to try once more at dusk?"

"Nay, we are done for this day. I am pondering whether it is worthwhile to continue this folly further. What do you think, Stradryk?"

"I am well tired of water, bugs, and muck, I'll warrant you that. And I don't like giving up on any quest. We still need some form of protection if we go after this fire beast, this red dragon, of yours, Ge-or."

"Aye... I..." Ge-or stopped suddenly, watching Ooglu as he took out the "pots" he had woven from the swamp grass several months ago in the early stages of their journey. The long leaves of the plant were a type of grass, which he had woven into a double layered tight interlace that held water, and could be used to steep stews and broths over a low fire. It was the same material from which they had woven their nets.

Ge-or stood, reached out and gestured for Ooglu to hand him one of the pots. Once he had it in hand, he turned it over and over examining the mesh, the tight-weave, and the quality of the material which had been used many dozens of times over cooking fires. It looked darkened on the bottom, but there was no other form of deterioration at all. It appeared as if it could be used another hundred times.

"Ooglu, tell me about this grass."

"Viclava, the cooking weed?"

"Yes. What are its properties?"

"Properties?"

"How does it work? How can you cook with it time and again without damaging it? How long does it last? How long will it hold water, stay damp? Things like that."

"Ah, I see... well, to us it is a weed. It grows everywhere in the swamp, most prolifically here in the deep swamp. It is a bother, yet one with many uses. It has tight... fibers, I think you call them. They are 'abiglagrati,' ah, they absorb water..."

"Porous?"

"Yes, just so. It is why they are useful for cooking. You have noticed I only cook things that are wet or moist in these pots I made: stews, soups, and the like. It is because the water taken into the leaves helps prevent them from burning. If I tried to cook a fish or meat with no water, they would burn like any other plant, albeit much slower. Did you notice that I always dip them in water before I begin to cook with them?"

Ge-or nodded. He was thinking quickly. Stradryk had also now caught his drift. "What if I made clothes of these, like a type of armor. Would these repel heat when wet? How long do you think it would remain wet if being worn?"

"Armor of grass? Instead of fire-lizard skin?"

"Exactly. Is it possible, Ooglu?"

"I don't know why it wouldn't be if it were woven in an appropriate form. Would it not chafe and itch your pale skins?"

"Not if worn on top of other clothing or leather. How often would it need to be soaked to be effective in such a way?"

"I can use a pot I have dipped in the morning again in the evening without re-dipping it. At least a day I would think."

"I think we may have found our fire armor," Ge-or said, his eyes shining.

"You really think this can work?" Stradryk asked, reaching out to take the bowl from Ge-or. He turned it over and over in his hands, examining it closely. "Will it provide enough protection?"

"Nothing will provide all the protection we need, yet with the fire-resistant potion from Sart as part of the bargain, and making garments of these fronds and doubling or even tripling the thickness…? I think it might. Tomorrow,

100

let us get started. I want to see what we can create with different weaves, and how it would feel to wear it, before we fully abandon our quest for the lizards. I am as ready as you are to get out of this humidity and heat."

"This will satisfy your quest?"

"Aye, Ooglu. If it works, you can lead us out of here, and you can have your stones. I will be satisfied. Are you willing to knit enough of these grasses into as tight a weave as these bowls to make several suits of clothing to fit us both?"

"It is no problem. I can provide this much in two days time."

"Good. Once you have enough ready, we will work and sew it into a form to test it. After that, if all is well, we will take back sheets of this weave and have a tailor fashion us suits from it. Agreed?"

"It is a good solution. I will be able to return to my home early. I am pleased." Ooglu smiled and returned to making dinner.

***

It took the "swamp rats" three weeks of steady work before they were satisfied with the viclava suits they had made. There were still details that could be improved. They had worked with Ooglu on varying the weave, the size of the fronds used, the thickness, and so forth until they had produced a "cloth" that was tight, flexible, and strong. To prove his point, Ge-or wore the final version of the loose-fitting garment over his regular clothing for two full days. He even sparred with Stradryk with it on. It wasn't ideal, but he felt the design could be improved with a tailor's eye for fit. They had discovered that if you split a frond of the plant length-wise you could produce strong strands of the stuff that could be used as thread, given a large enough needle, which, of course, was an item that was part of any adventurer's kit – several of them in different sizes were essential for mending cloth, leather, and so on.

Ooglu taught them how to do a wide variety of weaves so that if the design needed adjustments, they would know what to do. They stayed an extra week while all three of them wove enough of the fabric to make clothing for four or five large men. They also split many of the leaves to make hundreds of yards of thread, which they wound on some sticks into a couple of large spools. They wanted to be sure they had enough for the tailor and some leftover should they need to make their own repairs; and since the fronds were largest and longest in the deep swamp, they packed up an extra bundle of loose leaves. At the last, they had to dry all of their handy work for several days on the rocks, as the bundles would have been too heavy to lug through the swamps if they were wet.

Ooglu created backpacks out of another type of waterproof leaf. With these, they were able to pack out their wares so that if they slipped and fell into the water (not an uncommon occurrence in the marshes), they wouldn't have the additional burden of wet frond cloth to carry. By midwinter, they were happily on their way out of the swamp. Ge-or and Stradryk wanted nothing more, ever, to do with such wet, hot, sweltering conditions. A cold mug of ale was the first thing they planned to purchase when they reached Aglimiville.

Thankfully, Ooglu had been savvy enough about even the deep swamp to keep them from any serious trouble. Aside from bugs, leeches, and other slimy things, they had avoided the more dangerous swamp creatures throughout their journey. On their return, they trusted him to find a path free of danger. The two fighters focused on carrying their loads, so they could make as good a time as possible.

They didn't converse much. However, Ooglu would always point out what they needed to know. Rarely did humans or their ilk spend much time in the swamps. Most often his treks were to lead botanists, herbalists, alchemists, clerics, and the like to a specific area where certain herbs, tubers, and other plant-life important to their professions could be easily obtained. The only ones who dared to take even these short treks were those who wanted to pick their own goods and obtain the freshest available.

It was unusual for anyone to want to go into the deep swamp. Those few who dared rarely stayed more than a week – typically, only enough time to gather whatever it was they had come for. These two had survived two long treks. They had complained, as all men will when stressed; but they had also been willing, even eager, to learn and accept what their Aglimi guide offered.

Still, as they neared their destination, the two adventurers could tell that their guide was anxious to return to his family and people. When it finally came time for goodbyes, Ooglu let them know that he was grateful for their willingness to accept the alternate solution to the quest, while still paying the agreed-upon fee. "You have been good men and true companions. If I can ever be of service to you, it would be my and my people's honor."

Stradryk and Ge-or bowed deeply toward their Aglimi guide. It was not without emotion that they said their goodbyes. The two extra emeralds they had included with the payment would be welcome by the Aglimi witchmen, and Ooglu's family's stature would raise a notch as a result of his effort. They were sad to see the oddly-built marshman dive back under the water to head home.

On the Road Again

They were two weeks from the capital on the road south. Sart pushed them during the day; nonetheless, they almost always stopped early in whichever town or wayside inn they encountered about the time the sun was setting. They had been well cared for by every establishment they had stayed at.

There were many reasons for their quality accommodations, which included, when available, a separate room for Thistle and Jared. Sart was well-known and well-liked in the region. He would hold clinic for a couple of hours at each of their stops, helping with common ailments and complaints. In addition, Jared, as a skilled musician, was always asked to play. And though he wasn't on duty, per se, he was willing to perform for an hour or so each evening.

It turned out that their high card was Thistle. On their second evening out, when they stopped at a large tavern habituated by many wealthy merchants who travelled the north-south coast road, Thistle signed the register for Sart, as he had been stopped by several fellow clerics at the door. It turned out that Thistle's royal Wizard's mark, an indication of her rank and stature in the mage community of Borea, got the innkeeper not only excited at having an "imperial and splendid" guest, but extremely nervous as well. Jared and Thistle received the most elegant of rooms, truly a suite complete with two servants, usually reserved for the wealthiest merchants. Sart and Motuk were shown into the next best chambers the innkeeper had to offer. From that point on, Sart insisted that Thistle sign them in.

Jared found the whole thing quite amusing; however, it also served, until he spent some time in the saddle thinking it through, as a bit of a thorn in his side. This was the type of thing that Thistle had expressly warned him about, yet far removed from a battle or emergency situation. She was, truly, a completely different person than the young, frightened girl he had first met in the hills above Thiele. She was confident and carried herself as if there was nothing in the world that could scare her. Her bearing spoke volumes to all who met her. She was cool and direct -- not demanding -- and she expected to be treated in certain ways.

Somehow, all of that came out even with her light, almost carefree, generous nature that put people at ease, despite who they knew her to be. Yet Jared sensed in her, especially when they were alone together or when they rode side-by-side holding hands and chatting about nothing of significance, that a good bit of the girl he had fallen for remained. Sometimes he had to remind himself that there was so much more to Thistle than he could even ken at this point. He knew he would learn a great deal more about who she was as a person and as a powerful mage during their trek.

Thistle, for her part, was quite enjoying herself. Though she missed her hand-maiden and the luxuries of the palace life she had gotten used to, she had grown up to a hard country life. So, even with the long rides, this was far easier than that. She had sent Alicia home for an extended visit: "a well-deserved respite from putting up with a mage's idiosyncrasies." Thistle missed her most in the evenings when they had fallen into the habit of chatting amiably while Alli brushed her mistress's hair.

Jared was patient with her – kind, gentle, yet strongly passionate when she needed him to be. When they were alone at night, they explored each other and the ways of magic. They were having so much fun that often they would spend most of the mornings dozing in the saddle.

Sart was pleased with how things were going. This undertaking had many purposes, some of which were directly important to the kingdom and the work he was doing; however, there were many other less obvious reasons he had chosen this particular group. He and Meligance had talked for many hours about what the right situation would be for the young Wizardess's first venture into the "real" world.

At first, they had not considered including the young Bardling; but eventually Sart had broached the idea with the White Wizardess. She had mused on it for several days and finally agreed that it would challenge the two in many ways. For better or worse, they would learn more about the individual qualities of both. They would also find out whether the relationship had staying power. The two young ones did not ken the import of their lives and skills to the kingdom.

Meligance and Sart knew how desperate things were becoming in the west. Following the destruction of Kan's Altar, the dark powers had shifted deeper to the west; and from all the reports they received, those powers were not only growing, they were focused more and more toward the destruction of everything west of the King's Wall. Here were two who could make a difference. First, however, they needed to get rooted in who they were, together or apart. This trip would be a factor in how that played out.

For now, things seemed to be going well for the pair. They obviously enjoyed being with each other. Though he was "of the cloth," Sart had had plenty of experiences in his youth; and, if pressed he would likely admit he wasn't against an occasional liaison even now—judiciously arranged, of course. One had needs, and he had always been of the mind that it was best if they were met, for otherwise they might distract you from more important work.

Sart had hoped that Ge-or would receive his message and be able to go on this adventure with them. It would be good to see the two brothers finally get together. One had to admire the older brother; he was persistent in his quest to retrieve the father's sword. The letter Sart had sent told Ge-or they hoped to be in Panterra by midwinter. Perhaps Ge-or would meet them there. Sart would not need the big fellow's sword until later in their quest, and more the better if Stradryk was with him.

The truth was that Sart didn't know what to expect in the hills west of Aube. The area southwest of Aelfric had been over-run during the first Qa-ryk War and hadn't been inhabited by humans for at least fifty years. Its heyday had been another fifty years before that. There was no telling what might greet them upon their arrival.

All Are Not Welcome

Early on the eve of their twenty-second day on their trek, the small party rode up to the gates of a monastery situated several leagues to the west of the walled city of Efsted. Sart had explained to the others that the enclave was the oldest maintained by the followers of the Cross. It had stood four hundred years. He knew that within its dungeons was a wealth of historical and religious tomes, manuscripts, and scrolls dating back several hundred years before that and more.

He had never tried to get in before. The clerics of the Cross were covetous of all things related to their religion and history. They were also not overly indulgent, generally, of priests from other persuasions; but Sart's need was pressing. He felt certain there would be documents within the monastery's vaults that would refer to the history of the Heart of the World, and more importantly, what had befallen the two halves of the stones upon the downfall of Mangor. He hoped that they would not be turned out altogether, as he did not relish the leagues-long trek back toward Efsted to find alternate lodging. Most monasteries have an open-door policy regarding wayfarers who come to their gates; Sart was hopeful they would be welcomed graciously.

Once Sart identified himself, the gatekeeper let them in. He seemed quite put out by the notion of accommodating four people for a week, one of them a powerful priest of another religion. Yet, he dutifully led them to the abbot's office anteroom. There he left them, muttering under his breath as he returned to his post.

They waited for over an hour for Abbot Michaels to show. By that time, Sart was mumbling under his breath and Thistle was fuming. To top that off, the head monk, when he finally did show, was none too friendly. He stonily said they were welcome to wayfarer rooms and board. However, when Sart explained their mission, he said they would not be allowed, under any circumstances, to visit the monastery's library.

By that time, Thistle had had enough. She was used to being treated with deference, and while she was most uncomfortable acting the part of a Wizardess of Borea, she was one. Perhaps the time had come to flaunt that a bit. Sart, who was standing to her right and front facing the Abbot, trying to find words to change the fellow's mind, saw her step forward and motion to him, indicating she wanted him to stand down. Curious as to how she might broach this concern, Sart nodded and bowed to the Wizardess as she passed.

Thistle took another step forward and appeared to grow taller as she spoke. "One minute, sir." Thistle purposely left off any honorific. "I think you mistake whom you are addressing. If this is the hospitality of a wealthy abbey of long tradition, I think perhaps it is time the king reconsidered your tax-free status as a refuge for those who are weary and seek sustenance herein. I, sir, am a White Wizardess of Borea, second only to Meligance, the Great White Wizardess, my mentor. I suggest you rethink our accommodations and this honest cleric's request."

The Abbot's eyes went wide. As he stumbled to his feet, he blanched to a pale white, then went red in the face. He could see in the young women's demeanor that she was what she claimed, and he would not have been a priest of any stature if he had not been able to sense the power within her. If he had been interested at all in paying attention to these four when he entered the room, he should have been able to notice her power signature immediately. "My lady," he bowed, perhaps lower than he had bowed since he was a simple priest. "I am sorry. Please forgive me. I will arrange for our best rooms and fare for all of you. You do us much honor in coming to our monastery. Please accept my humble apologies. I personally will see that your needs are served."

Thistle did not respond, only stared at him as if to say she was still not pleased.

Abbot Michaels swallowed hard, and though he was both astounded by her presence in his cloister and afraid because a powerful mage was now standing before him within the protective walls of the enclave, he remained adamant about the use of the library by outsiders. He also knew that she waited for an answer to their other request. He would have to say something. Finally, he took the vaunted position of his church, hoping she would not fry him on the spot.

"Unfortunately, milady, I cannot grant your other boon. It is a long-standing policy of this monastery and of all the monasteries of the Cross that we do not allow strangers access to our holy documents." He bowed low again, keeping his eyes fixed on hers, wondering at her temperament and how she might react to a bold declaration.

Thistle was still angry. "Cannot? Or will not, Friar Michaels? I…" As she spoke, Jared came up behind her. He reached out and touched her arm lightly, whispering in her ear, "Allow me. I can right this."

Thistle turned and looked at Jared; she noticed immediately that he seemed sure of himself. She said, "Abbot, please, if you will, listen to my companion. He may be able to give you good cause to alter your tradition this one time."

Jared stepped ahead and nodded a bow toward the Abbot. "Your reverence, please listen to what I have to say. I think you will find that our mission is honorable and best for all concerned. It has the safety of the kingdom as a primary foundation. Sart, the good cleric before you, seeks only historical information. He has no interest in disturbing your holy documents or even touching them. His, our, purpose is only to gather information that may help stem the tide of evil ever encroaching from the west…"

Jared continued for several minutes, detailing their particular interest in the library's holdings, and even pledging that they would not touch anything without specific permission. He also added that the Abbot could have as many acolytes, priests, or scholars as he desired, present during their search, so as to ensure that they did not step past their bounds.

What was amazing, and it was extremely subtle, though Thistle and Sart picked up on it almost immediately, was that Jared was in a sense singing what he was saying. There was a flow to his words that spoke to the ballads of old. His carefully chosen words and phrasing continued ever forward, with a sense of rhythmic unity throughout, yet with no true sense of time or beat. There was also the hint of a melody interwoven within the words that began to relax all within the room. At a given point, Jared seemed to add an urgency, a need, even a demand to the confluence of words and sounds. Later, when they all considered the experience, they would have said that it had been beautiful, moving, and powerful. It was as if he had sung a long song accompanied by his own inflections, tone, all blended with elements of the spoken word.

After he was finished, the Abbot stood, shook his head as if to clear it, and said, "You are a Bard." And he began to wonder why so powerful a party was visiting his monastery. He also questioned himself later whether he should have paid closer attention to the dwarf-man standing to the rear of the three.

Jared did not gainsay him, only waited.

"Young sir, you are persuasive. You have great talent, yet you also make sense. I will grant what you request. Be assured, my brethren will oversee all. Is that satisfactory to you, Wizardess, Sart of the Earth?"

Sart nodded a bow, thanking the cleric with the gesture.

Thistle also nodded, for the Abbot's eyes were on her.

***

"By-the-gods, Jared, that was amazing." Sart was sitting with the others in the ante chamber to their suite of rooms following an excellent dinner at the Abbot's table. The fellow was anxious to please, now that he knew Thistle's status. He had brought out his best mead and wine -- the monastery was famous for its cellars, as well. They were all nibbling on a truly extraordinary cheese made and aged deep below the ground in ancient grottos. It had been brought up as a final gift to accompany a well-aged port.

Thistle squeezed Jared's hand. "Yes, my love, that was truly wondrous. I did not know you had such a gift."

"I guess I do. According to Elanar, it comes to me naturally. I actually practice it all the time when I perform. Music can be very powerful, quite persuasive."

"Is this not considered an advanced skill, even for Bards of stature?" the usually quiet, even for a dwarf, Motuk asked, for he had been quite impressed as well.

"One learns it in Bard Lore, of which I had a smattering in my studies. It is predominantly learned after one's Apprenticeship and Journeymanship. Elanar and I talked of it on our journey together. I found the practice useful when we were tired or when things got... well, let us say 'difficult.' I could always twist things in the direction I wanted them by adding harmonies and underlying tunes to the melody or counterpoint I was playing, or by changing the rhythmic flow slightly, and so forth. It is truly fascinating to see a potential fight calm down by using the right notes and harmonies."

"There is great power in music, and it can be turned in many ways," Sart said, staring more intently at Jared. The boy had surprised him before, but this... this was something rare. Leonis and Meligance would want to know of it. What he didn't add, because he felt it was too soon, with little knowledge to back it up, was that the pendant Jared carried with him had perhaps come to him for just such a reason. Magical items often seem to have minds of their own and a tendency at the least to find an owner that suited their balance. Perhaps the gem had fulfilled, or partially fulfilled its purpose by saving this lad's life. If so, then it might eventually decide to move on to another or...? Sart would need to ponder more on this; the boy certainly had amazed him this day, and it might behoove Sart to pay more attention to the gem's influence. Perhaps it was aiding this new aptitude the young half-elf had shown this eve.

"You have much to learn, I would warrant, Jared. You are early on in your Apprenticeship, yet you obviously have a true talent in blending music for a deeper purpose. The masters at Bard Hall may address this sooner than later in your studies. They are oft willing to stretch their curriculum for those with a gift in a special area.

"Well, an interesting day, to be sure. Tomorrow we tackle the mundane task of sifting through old documents. It's not exciting, yet perhaps it will prove rewarding. I am tired and will to bed. Good night, all." With that, Sart rose and clapped Jared on the back. "Most enlightening, my son, and most enjoyable to watch, and," he added as an afterthought, "to listen to."

Thistle squeezed Jared's hand again. She had something special planned for the night as a celebration of his success with the Abbot.

On the Move

They spent six days in the depths of the library at the Efsted monastery working long hours by candlelight at first, and finally, frustrated with the heaviness of the place, by the bright light of Thistle's conjured orbs. Even Motuk, who knew enough of the old language to read titles on scrolls and tomes, helped with the search. Their stay had been uncomfortable because of the general attitude when they arrived and the continued "stiffness," as Sart described it, of their hosts. They had been well cared for and treated as royally as one might be at a monastery, but there was always an underlying tension when they mixed with the residents. They were anxious to complete their search and leave.

They had some success. Sart was able to glean some general information about the finding of the Heart of the World, the dwarves' and gnomes' possession of it, and then its taking by Mangor, fifteenth ruler of the Dragon lords of old. It was he who split the stone and became swayed by the dark half – the Black Diamond, as it was named.

After his defeat, both stones, the Blue Star and the Black Diamond, were mentioned here and there in various historical sources they found. That is until the Star was lost at sea as Sart had learned initially from Ge-or, and that Kan had absconded with the Diamond. He hoped to further understand that sequence of events when he spoke to the sea elves in Panterra. The other half, the dark half, though long-stored away protectively by the elves, was taken by Kan when it had been entrusted to him to transport it to Borea. Its history appeared to end with his defeat from within. No records they perused spoke of whether it had ever been found among the ruins of his castle.

After they left the monastery, their next primary destination was Panterra. Sart had written Tammero soon after he had received Ge-or's letter. Eventually, he had received a polite reply from one of the sea-elf historians saying that they would be happy to share their lore with the cleric; nevertheless, any communication with the elderly and infirm master historian would depend on his condition when they visited.

On the road again, they continued their leisurely pace further south. En route, they made short visits to several smaller monasteries. If all worked according to plan, they would have a week or more in Panterra to provision for their trek west. Sart wanted to head across the plains and finally north toward

Aube once the spring showers had lessened. Many of the smaller roads were not well maintained and would be a quagmire if they left sooner.

The first signs of spring in the south were blossoming when they finally rode into the seaside city, where they were warmly welcomed by the sea elves. Sart, Thistle, Jared, and Motuk spent almost two weeks talking with the local historians, delving through records, and waiting, hoping to get an audience with the elder statesman of the sea-elves.

***

Stradryk and Ge-or had never tasted anything quite as cool and refreshing as that first cold ale once they had emerged from the swamps. The heat had steadily increased over their last two weeks trekking back through the marshes. They were more than happy to climb onto dry land and bid their goodbyes and thanks to Ooglu. Though they couldn't shake hands, the three had spent enough time together that it was a sad parting. Ge-or honestly said he hoped that they would meet again, with the caveat that he wouldn't have to go "swamping it." Their Aglimi guide had finally slid back into the waters with a wave goodbye.

The two adventurers spent a full two weeks in Aglimiville regaining some of the weight they had lost and getting re-acclimated to living on solid ground. They relaxed, slept comfortably, and made up for months without drink and female companionship, for these types of entertainment were always available in areas where people gathered. They also paid the high prices for meat – beef, lamb, and pork which were all imported – at the local taverns. They had had their fill of fish, reptile, and other more exotic fare during their many weeks in the swamp.

Finally, with the heat and humidity getting uncomfortable enough in the town, they decided to begin their journey back north to Anada. There they planned to garner jobs on a caravan eastward to the coast to Baarth, where they figured they would spend the heat of the summer, then finally head north in the fall.

When they reached Anada, which was set in the hill above the southern plains and west of the easternmost vestiges of the Great Desert, they finally caught up to a missive from Sart – Ge-or and Stradryk read the note many times. It was late to catch Sart's party; the final caravans from Anada north to Aube along the edge of the desert had already departed. It would be early fall before any others braved the desert, and suicide to attempt the crossing alone.

Only the heavy caravans could carry enough water to make that trek; and even then, it was considered far too treacherous to attempt during the warm months because of the heat, dryness, and the chatts who were far more aggressive in the summer.

Friends,

I hope this finds you well and successful in your ventures. I am planning a long trek south to Panterra; after that, west and north to Aube. Your brother and others will be travelling with me. I hope you, Ge-or, or both of you, if Stradryk is willing, might catch us up either in Panterra (early spring), or Aube (early summer). From there we will travel west to an old manor site I wish to explore near Seston. Should you not be able to rendezvous with us during the summer, I will leave word at the Prancing Unicorn in Aube as to our further plans, with instructions on what to prepare for should you wish to find us. We will likely head further into the wilds at that point.

Your swords and experience would be most valuable as we head west. Hoping to see you soon.

Sart, Cleric of the Earth

Finally, they decided to follow their original plan. They would head to Baarth and spend the summer as they had the previous one, hiring out on odd jobs. In the early fall, they would wend their way back to Anada to try to hire on to one of the first caravans heading north. With luck, they could make the long haul in a month or less and seek Sart's party when they got to the border town.

Ge-or shook his head more than once over the note. He had longed to see Jared since he had found out he was alive. Yet whilst his brother was at Bard Hall, he had not had any occasion to head that far north and east. He had almost gone that way when he found himself far to the north while seeking Leona, but he had turned back south and west to continue his search. Now that an opportunity presented itself, he was forced to stay in the south until the weather began to turn.

He briefly considered a ship voyage north to Efsted, yet Stradryk was deathly afraid of leaving dry land. Ge-or felt he owed a debt to his friend for sticking with him for two rather uncomfortable winters trekking through the swamps. The reunion would have to wait.

Although Sart did finally get an audience with Tammero, the old elf was extremely frail, and his memories so faded that he was unable to offer anything to Sart regarding the loss of the Blue Star. It turned out that the records of the sea elves were clear as to when and where the ship bearing the gem sank, whilst bringing it north to Borea. All the sea captains they spoke to gave them the same information, describing Timi Point as one of the most dangerous stretches of water along the coast.

Nor did they believe there was any hope of salvage. It was one of the anomalies of the coastline and currents that ships heading north have to pass far to the east, until they are well clear of that point, and then turn in and come south to enter the Borean Bay. The rocky shoals near Timi bode ill for any vessel. It had been the worst of luck that an unexpected storm of such ferocity came up and drove the boat carrying the Star into the rocks on that fateful eve. The ship, all those aboard, and whatever was on her had been lost; and nothing had ever been recovered.

It was also unfortunate that although the event was recorded in detail in their lore, no one had thought to make a drawing of the gem or to describe it beyond, "a medium-sized, irregularly-shaped diamond with murky depths, sometimes with a hint of light blue within." It was not much to go on, for there were many uncut stones that could be described in this way. No one mentioned anything about the general shape, whether the edges were sharp or smooth, perhaps faceted in some way from the splitting, or how it may have fit into the larger stone before it was excised. The only other description stated: "It is often cool to the touch and on rare occasions seems to offer a soothing, healthful sensation to all within its scope of influence. Otherwise, no particular powers have been attributed to it, unlike its brother, the Black Diamond, which has oft been described as having a distinctly malevolent feel."

With the information they gleaned from the sea-elf historians, Sart was able to fill in most of the lore leading up to the loss of the Star. There were long lists of dwarf and gnome rulers who had guarded over the Heart of the World before Mangor stole it. There was no doubt that the elves had kept the Black Diamond safe for many long years, until it was to be sent into the care of men. It was never clear why the elves, dwarves, and gnomes had not sought to put the two pieces back together when it was in their possession, or if they had, any information as to why the attempt had failed. Thus, each source and list lamented that the world would always be riven into good and evil, evil and good, with the Black Stone having greater sway.

It was quite clear that, for whatever reason, the two halves had remained separated. The Black Diamond had been taken to Moulanes and the Blue Star kept in Panterra in the sea-elves' care. Finally, after many long years, the elves, weary of keeping the dark stone safe, had asked the new Borean King to take on the burden. He had agreed only if the Star would be in the empire's care as well.

King Unis had asked the elves to send it by strong escort to the village of Aube between the Bendir and Borean borders. There he planned to meet them with a strong force of soldiers to take the stone into the west where it was to be secreted in a stronghold far from civilization. Hopefully, that far away, it could not influence the kingdom for ill. A strong guard was to serve six-month terms at the deep vault that had been prepared for the stone, keeping all away. Before the two groups could meet, the elven mage, Kan, leader of the expedition from Moulanes to Aube, absconded with the stone. He killed two-thirds of his brethren, and then headed into the west.

Both stones had been lost to the kingdom within two months of each other.

Sart was disappointed that they had gotten limited further information about the Diamond, its splitting, and the fate of the two halves. Still, he felt he understood more than he had before. He was anxious to continue their trek, because he felt strongly that the witch-woman of the Bendir Slivs would be able to have relevant information about the Diamond, too.

***

Their group set out for Aube in the mid-spring after the worst of the rains had passed. Since he wanted to cross the great plains of Bendir instead of taking the long route north and west, they would have to have permission from the Slivs. He had had dealings with the Slivs a couple of other times; but because they were reluctant at any time to let wayfarers pass, he would need to request the boon again.

The darkness spreading eastward had caused all the races to be more careful. The Qa-ryk expansion had driven the Bendir enemies, the chatts, kin to the goblins and gzks, further eastward to the western edge of the plains. These creatures found horseflesh more than palatable. Thus, the Slivs spent considerable effort guarding their western border from raids by these desert-dwelling beasts.

The Slivs unfailingly protected all their borders, not just the west. Their horses were so prized that there were always some who thought they could make a profit by sneaking in and making off with a few. Almost none succeeded, yet there were always fools who seemed willing to risk their lives for a valuable prize like a plains-bred stallion.

Initially, Sart's small party headed for E-au, a trading center west and a bit south of Panterra. It was the primary arena for merchants and others to bargain for those horses the Slivs were willing to sell each year. Soon the road would be busy with anyone who wished to trade with the Sliv lords. For now, it was a quiet peaceful ride with only a few of the early, and generally wealthier, traders moving westward.

E-au was four days easy ride from Panterra. The wagon road led through rich farmlands and ranches where much of the kingdom's beef was raised. They rode into the trading center around mid-day and could see the vast grasslands stretching to the west, south, and north. The main building of the outpost was a large inn, with outbuildings built for the many traders who frequented the place during the spring, summer, and fall. Much of the trading complex was a series of interconnected stables, enclosures, and galley-ways for the animals. The trading arena, designed by the Slivs, was located at the far western edge. It was an open-fronted, low structure that was less likely to frighten the horses who were used to roaming freely over the great plains. The Sliv lords and maidens who came to the post with their herds preferred to stay out of sight in their tent cities amidst the grasses.

The trading center was just getting under way for the year and though there were a few horses in the enclosures, Sart guessed that these belonged to the merchants who had arrived for the high-priced early sales of the finest steeds. The Slivs typically kept the horses they were to sell out near their camp until a date had been agreed for a particular sale. Sart decided that they would spend the night at the White Stallion Inn. They would ride west at dawn to negotiate passage with the Sliv lords.

After settling into their rooms, they met at a large indoor emporium near the inn. The Sliv society was formal and tended toward rigidity in its customs. Sart knew the exchange of small, high-quality gifts, was expected. What they offered as an introduction to the negotiations for their passage across the plains did not have to have a high monetary value, but it was expected to be the best available. This building housed not only the manufactured goods that the Slivs traded for; more importantly, half of it was stuffed with the finest wines, preserved foodstuffs, silks, laces, and linens, cheeses, incenses, soaps, and the like. Sliv lords and ladies, typically quite well-off because of the prices they commanded for their steeds, liked to indulge their senses. Much of these goods would be bought by them for the credits they received at the horse sales.

Jared, Thistle, and Motuk wandered the aisles breathing in the mélange of smells while Sart selected some choice items. The cleric knew what he was about, both from long experience with indulging himself when he had the funds and opportunity, and because he had learned through ample association with the high-born and wealthy of Borea what top quality meant.

Generally speaking, clerics were not wealthy. They turned over whatever they gleaned from their adventures, if they were of the daring nature as Sart was, to their churches. However, Sart did much of his work for the kingdom under the guise of his church. The "Earth Birds" were less of a church in the usual sense, than a religion or belief system. They only had a couple of monasteries that served as centers for aiding large populations of people through their ministries. Unlike the more formal religions, they did not build churches or shrines in every hamlet and town. They relied on the good nature of their itinerant brethren to spread the peace of Gaia and to offer succor and healings about the country. Therefore, the brilliant silk scarves he chose, the two bottles of a fine Borean Red, and some rich and creamy wheels of goat cheese from the north, were paid out of the king's treasury.

***

At dawn the next day, they started westward from the horse-selling arena. Few people dared venture past the trading post. Sart was not worried about doing so; he had done this a number of times and knew the protocol. As a precaution, they had bundled their weapons on their baggage mules. Riding slowly, they kept to the main track leading to the Sliv camp, which was well defined by hoof prints. Sart carried a light blue silk banner set on a long pole to announce their purpose.

They had gone less than half a league when suddenly a dozen horsemen and horsewomen emerged from the tall grasses surrounding them. Though they all carried lances or bows, none of the weapons were held in a ready position. They were willing to parlay. A tall maiden addressed them. Her words were formal, yet not severe.

"Hail good cleric. What business have you with the Slivs?"

Sart motioned for his group to dismount. It was a gesture the Slivs expected – a type of deference to them that they were the better riders. He bowed to the Sliv maiden who was obviously in charge of this patrol. "Maiden, I am Sart, cleric of the Earth. We come to request permission to cross your lands. We are on a mission for Borea and there are time considerations that passage across the plains would ease. And, if she wishes it, I would speak with Nagama'a."

The maiden raised one eyebrow when she heard their high priestess's name. Few outsiders knew of her, and very few from without their society had ever met with her. She made a slight bow to Sart. "I am Elena, at your service. Please follow us to camp. You may ride."

Sart had explained this custom to the others as well. Given permission to ride, they had passed the first major obstacle. It is why he had mentioned their witch-woman's name. He knew it would raise more than eyebrows when they understood that he had been into the heart of their society before.

The camp was less than a half a league further to the west. Before long they could see the white peaks of the Slivs' large tents. Jared, Thistle, and Motuk, who had never been to the plains, nor seen one of the horse-people's camps, were astounded by the size and number of tents spread over a large area. Many of the bleached-hide structures were connected by canopied walkways. The camp looked almost deserted for they could see no more than several dozen people, including those who had escorted them and those watching over the herd of horses grazing to the west of the camp.

Elena led them to the largest of the tents, gesturing for them to unhorse. She lightly leapt from her saddle, waving to dismiss the younger blades with her. Taking a step toward the tent, she announced herself, "My lord." She bowed low and held the bow.

A moment later, a tall, dark-haired elf came to the opening. He gestured with his hand for them to enter. Elena straightened, indicating they should follow her.

Even having heard Sart's description of the Slivs' lifestyle, the inside of the tent was more opulent than any of them could have imagined. Luxurious rugs covered hides which in turn covered the matted grass and dirt; plush pillows, bolsters, and tapestries were about the walls and lying on the floor. An ornately carved, cushioned chair was set in the center facing the door. A brazier and several lamps hanging from above provided some light. As their eyes began to adjust to the lower light level, another, even taller elf came through one of the side flaps set in the tent wall. The Sliv Lord strode forward, gave a slight sign of recognition to Elena, who bowed. Finally, he gestured for all of them to sit on cushions whilst he moved in front of the chair.

He was thin and well-muscled – what Jared would have described as acrobatic. He had penetratingly dark eyes; and he was dressed, as all the Slivs, in humble cloths designed for riding horseback. His only accoutrement that might have designated his rank was a broad silver neck gorget that curled in a half moon high up on his chest and was affixed with a heavy chain.

"I am Rwen'a, leader of the Stallion clan. It is our honor this year to serve as the liaison to this post for our brethren in the trades. You have a request of us?"

Sart bowed from the waist as he sat, an awkward maneuver at best. Rwen'a gestured for him to rise. The elven leader sat, back rigid, maintaining a formal and powerful presence. Sart bowed again once he was standing.

"I am Sart, Cleric of the Earth. Please allow me to introduce to you, Thistle, White Wizardess of Borea, Jared, Apprentice Bard, and Motuk, stout dwarven-warrior." Each rose when they were introduced and bowed at the waist to Rwen'a.

They remained standing as Sart continued. "I have urgent business for the king, and we wish to pass through your lands." He gestured to Motuk who brought their gifts forward and laid them on the rug in front of the Sliv leader. "Gifts for the Sliv lord Rwen'a and the Stallion clan."

Rwen'a nodded his thanks.

Although Jared watched carefully during the introductions, he could see no reaction from Rwen'a to Thistle's title. Interesting, he thought.

"I would also like to meet with, should it be feasible, Nagama'a. She and I have shared moments of import together before. She sees much, and there are forces at play that she and I may find benefit to speak of."

Rwen'a didn't move at first. After a brief pause, he stood. "You will have your answer at dawn, Cleric of the Earth."

"Elena," he turned toward the maiden. She bowed again. See that they are comfortable." He nodded a bow toward Sart, and then toward Thistle; finally, he turned and disappeared behind the tent flap from where he had emerged minutes before.

"Come." Elena led them from the tent.

They were housed in another, similarly luxurious tent complex. It had enough rooms attached to the main chamber that they could each have separate sections to themselves. Several younger Sliv maidens and lads attended them. They brought water for bathing, making sure they were comfortable. After they had refreshed themselves, a meal comprised of a vast variety of meats, cheeses, fresh breads, fruits, and other delectable treats was offered. Stuffed and happy to take part in another Sliv tradition, they all retired to their compartments to rest during the heat of the day.

They had all re-gathered in the main room and were discussing what they had seen and experienced already, when Elena came back. This time, upon entering the tent, she bowed low at the waist toward each of them. "Rwen'a has requested you at his table for dinner. He has also instructed us to take you about the camp and introduce you to our ways and our horses, if you have an interest?"

Sart stood and bowed. "It would be an honor. Tu honora ea."

"Tu honora es," Elena bowed again.

The next few hours they spent under the tutelage of the Sliv maiden, who seemed to be in an uncomfortable role. She made every effort to be friendly and open, yet there was a stiffness about her mannerisms and in how she spoke. Still, the afternoon proved fascinating. They spent a good bit of the time watching the Slivs work with their horses. It was amazing to see how closely tied the elves were to the animals. When they rode, it was as if they became one with their steed; there was a fluidity and joy to their movements together – warrior and beast.

At one point, when they passed the corral where the Slivs had stabled their horses and mules, Elena stopped and cradled Jared's stallion's muzzle in her hands. "Breathwind," she said, "it is good to see you again, my friend. I am glad you have found a good master." She turned to Jared. "He is a fine stallion from our best herd. I knew him as a colt. I am pleased that you have cared for him so well. May I let him run with our horses for the night?"

Jared was surprised that this elf-maiden would have remembered a single colt, now grown to full stature. Simon-Nathan had indeed given him a princely gift if it was from this prized stock.

It was nearing full dark when Elena brought them back to their tent to prepare for dinner. Sart explained that this was a unique honor that even he had never been afforded. Slivs were shy and protective of their solitude. It was most unusual that they had been invited to dinner in a lord's tent.

The dinner was long and even more sumptuous than their lunch had been. Their host was extremely gracious, but also a bit uncomfortable having strangers and outsiders for dinner. He had asked several of the higher-ranking lords and maidens to attend. He included Elena, who seemed to have some status; yet she was seated far down from where her lord sat at the low-built "table," which was a raised platform of rectangular pillows with rugs laid atop before which they all sat cross-legged on other pillows. Interestingly to Jared, Thistle was placed at Rwen'a's right and Sart to his left, the places of highest honor.

Jared found himself seated next to Elena on the one hand and a young Sliv lord on the other. While he made an effort to talk with each, they both were obviously ill at ease with the situation. Jared was not sure whether it was the strangers present or the honor of dining with their clan leader that caused the two the most disquiet. Questions were politely asked and answered. The conversation was about the general topics – food, wines, weather, and so forth, and also about things all warriors talk about – weapons, the hunt, riding, and so on – yet it never felt quite comfortable to Jared. It was as if there was some current of unease present throughout the repast, even in Rwen'a's demeanor.

It was not until all were done and it was well into the night, that Rwen'a stood. "Word has come from Nagama'a and the Fleethoof clan. You are welcome. She appears to have anticipated your arrival here." The elven leader said this as if it were something easily accepted that their wise woman would know of such things. "There is some urgency to her request to see you, and you are to leave before dawn. Each of you will ride our stallions and mares. Haste is required, so it will be a long, hard ride with changes of horses along the way. All your belongings and animals will be brought along. I am honored to have been able to serve you." He bowed low and left the tent chamber.

***

Aberon was headed back into the west at long last. Though he would have wished things to have gone faster in the library's vaults, the king's collection was notoriously poorly arranged. It had taken him weeks to find what he was looking for. Once he had it, he read it, memorized what he needed; then he destroyed it. There was no sense in letting that meddling cleric find it. The fellow always seemed to have his nose in things that were far too close to home for Aberon's liking.

Meanwhile, he sent word to his own brethren to meet him in the west, near Kan's former fortress. There was work to do. It would take some time to set up. If all went well, he could finally accomplish what he needed to claim his final victory over his rivals. There was little enough information to go on even with what he had unearthed. Well, at least he knew what he was up against. It was unlikely that the item he sought had been disturbed.

Aberon sneered. This would be a bit of a trial for him as well – something to test his new powers before the druidic battle ahead. So be it. He liked these little challenges. If he found what he was looking for, it would be worth the effort.

Surprises all Around

They rode fast and hard, covering great swaths of prairie until their steeds tired. Then they were met by another contingent of Slivs with fresh mounts, and they continued on. Thrice they changed horses, until nearing sunset they saw a great expanse of white come up out of the sea of waving greens and browns in front of them. Jared wasn't sure how far they had ridden – the horses were swift and had tremendous strength and endurance. He knew they had covered many leagues and were deep within the Bendir plains.

As the sun disappeared, they rode into the edge of a massive camp. They were immediately taken to a large tent, provided water, and allowed to clean up briefly. Finally, they were led a long way into the center of the tents. Elena, the only elf to remain with them on the long ride from Rwen'a's camp at E-au, gestured for them to wait at the entrance to a deep blue, oval-shaped tent. It was the only colored tent they had seen. She paused at the tent flap, bowed, and waited.

A second later, a voice, strong and rough-edged, came from within. "Enter all."

Elena held the flap of the tent for the others. They followed Sart's lead. Elena stayed back; but the voice said, "Join us, Maiden. You are near enough of age to hear these things."

Once inside, they had to allow their eyes to become accustomed to the dimly lit interior. Only a small brazier, burning orange with coals, and a few candles near the back center of the chamber afforded any light. As their eyes adjusted, they could make out a raised platform covered with dark blue rugs. Upon this was set a large pile of pillows of different shapes and sizes in the shape of a chair. Sitting coiled up in a near ball on the top of the pillow-chair was the oldest person Jared had ever seen. The Eldest Witch, for that is how she called herself, of the Sliv nation was afforded the greatest stature of all her kin. She was considered the wisest in lore and in healing and was a seer of long-standing. Even the most powerful of the Sliv lords paid her deference. She was wizened with age, yet they could tell by her keen, penetrating eyes that she was far from being frail or addled.

Nagama'a motioned for all of them to approach the dais. When they were in a semi-circle in front of her, she swung her legs around agilely and motioned for Sart to approach. She laid her hand on his brow when he bowed in front of her. After her blessing, she put her hand under his chin and raised his head. She smiled broadly, chuckling as their eyes met. "I have looked forward to this day, my friend. It has been too long."

"Indeed. I am honored you have consented to see us."

"Posh. I have been waiting for you. There is need."

"For?"

"In a moment; allow me first to greet your fellows. You have graced us many-fold, my dear cleric. I have longed for this day for a score of years."

Sart stood aside. Nagama'a gestured for Motuk to come forward. She placed her hand on his brow. "Dwarf-kin and stalwart. Go with my blessings, child of the mountains. Ware travelling alone; life has many surprises." He bowed low, wondering about the warning; he stepped aside as Sart had done.

She gestured for Thistle, who also came forward and received the witch's blessing. Nagama'a surprised everyone by saying, "Welcome home, my great, great grand-daughter. I am filled with joy to meet you. Please come closer and give an old woman a hug." Thistle's mouth dropped open, as did Jared's; nevertheless, she did as she was directed.

Whilst in the grip of the old women's arms, the witch whispered something in her ear. After a long minute, Thistle gasped, straightened, and looked over at Jared. Then she began to cry. Sart went to her, wrapping her in his arms.

Jared wanted to go to Thistle, but Nagama'a put her hand out toward him waving for him to come to her. Confused at Thistle's response to the witch's words, he nonetheless stepped ahead and received her blessing as well. After she removed her hand from his forehead, she placed it on his breast. "I would like to hold it," she said.

Jared blinked. He had not thought of the pendant for a long time and only noticed it when he removed it to bathe. It always stayed around his neck on a strong leather thong, hidden beneath his tunic when he was on the road. He glanced at Sart; the cleric nodded.

Reaching behind his neck, he lifted the leather strip over his head and drew the stone up from under his garments. He carefully handed it to Nagama'a.

She took it and twirled it around her fingers. "It's been a long time since I have held you – you are needed, precious one." She held it up toward the light of the brazier and peered into its depths. "A long journey, I see. Well, the path lies ahead." Wistfully, it seemed to Jared, she handed the pendant back.

Nagama'a stood, announcing to all, "Come, there is work to do, and soon. Sart, we have an illness among the children, and it is deadly. I need your help and this young Bardling's as well." As she drew her robes about her tiny thin body, she directed each in turn. "Elena, take this maiden and prepare her for the Qua-a-tu. I will come later. Sart and Jared, you will come with me; I have all prepared. Motuk, rest. I will have need of your strength later. Come, we must hurry."

Jared's mind was awhirl. He wished to go with Thistle, for she looked like she was in shock and quite upset by what the witch woman had whispered to her. Sart, however, urged him to follow Nagama'a, telling him as they went that Thistle was in good hands. He assured him that he could be with her later, if needed. They were led through a maze-like passage, until they stopped in front of a long, low tent that stretched for as far as he could see in the dim light of the early evening.

Following the witch-woman inside, Jared could see why there was an urgency to Nagama'a's wishes. There were over fifty children of varying ages lying on tapestried pallets, stretching down the length of the connected tents. Each child had an attendant maiden kneeling nearby, bathing its head at regular intervals with cooling water. He could see the flushed, feverish faces and glazed eyes of the children nearest to where they had entered.

Sart immediately went to the closest and knelt, touching the young one's forehead and checking his pulse. He looked at Nagama'a. She nodded. "The Curse," was all she said.

Sart shook his head. "We do not have the power, wise one."

"He does." She pointed to Jared. "And he has the stone. It came to him. It was foretold. It is time."

Jared looked at Sart, over at the witch-woman, and then back to Sart. The cleric shrugged his shoulders, yet, oddly, he also nodded. Jared didn't know what she was attributing to him, but he knew he had no healing powers. Finally, he took the pendant from around his neck and held it out toward Nagama'a.

She did not take it. Instead, she gestured for him to put it back on his neck. "Come. You must start now, or they will all be lost." She took his hand and drew him past the line of pallets. Stopping halfway down the row, she pointed to a stool with an intricately-shaped wooden lyre standing next to it. "Play the healing music. It is here," she tapped his chest, "in your heart."

Jared wanted to protest that he had never studied anything to do with healing music and that he was not who she believed he was; however, she was insistent. She pressed the lyre into his hands. Reluctantly, he sat down, strummed the instrument to gain a feel for it, noticing that it had been perfectly tuned. He glanced up at Nagama'a, and she smiled. She tapped his chest again. "From the heart. The stone will vibrate with it when you have it right." She stepped back and waited for him to play.

Jared was at a loss, yet he was willing to try anything. These children were obviously very ill. He had no idea what "the Curse" was, nor what to play; so he started with the first tune that popped into his head. It was an ancient tune, often reprised in many ways throughout the ages. It had even been used several times in children's ditties. When he started the first strand, Nagama'a bowed to him; then she gestured to Sart to follow her. She left Jared to his own devices.

Warming to playing, Jared let himself flow into the music. He took the little melody and began to twist it as only he could, blending the old with the new until he was playing an intricate weave of the melody amongst itself, supported by the most ethereal harmonies he had ever played. As he drew the music in on itself, he wove another line of the melody into the tenor line, while at the same time inverting another strand of it in the lowest register. This he supported with a long slow harmonic progression that he drew from the roots of the tune. He blended the chord progression expertly with the several lines of melody that he now had woven together into a seamless flow. Slowly, inexorably, he increased the tension as the melodies peaked, using the foundation of the harmony and added tones to reach a point where there was nothing else to do except to suddenly release it all in a cascade, as if he had opened a door to let in a morn's brilliant sunshine.

It was at that moment that he felt a stirring on his chest. He could feel a throbbing sensation coming from the pendant as if it was singing to him. He sensed the melody of the stone, and he drew that into his melodic weave. He was off again, building the pattern once more, this time with even more of a drive upward and forward. Until once again a release was inevitable and the music burst forth, liberated of all boundaries.

He did not know how long he played. He did what came to him, following the pulse of the stone and of his heart. The two blended together, and the rise and fall of what he created went on and on as if it would never end. He didn't stop until he felt a hand gently touch his shoulder as the music came to a final resting cadence once more. He opened his eyes and was surprised to see that it was daylight. Sart was standing next to him looking extremely tired.

"Come. I should look to your hands."

Jared looked down and saw that his fingers on both his hands were bloody from playing. He nodded dumbly, set the lyre down, and stumbled after Sart back to their tent. He fell asleep while the cleric was tending to him.

He awoke much later in the day, he thought, as the light was fading. Sart was sleeping next to him. A Sliv maiden, perhaps it was Elena, gave him something to drink and he fell asleep once again.

It was another long while when he woke again, for it was now bright outside. He tried to push himself up, but he had almost no energy. This time Sart came with something for him to drink. Jared managed to ask, "Thistle?"

"She is well. Recovering. Soon you may see her. Here, drink this; you need to rest more."

Jared drank; as he fell asleep, he puzzled over Sart's words.

Some Questions Answered

The next time Jared woke up he felt considerably better. After doing a mental and visual check of himself, he found that the bandages that had been on his fingers had been removed. He pushed himself up and looked about. He was, he believed, in the tent where they had first gone upon finishing their long ride. No one was in the chamber. He shifted himself so that his back was up against a large soft cushion. At his movement, Elena came through a flap that led to an adjoining room. She smiled at him and came over. After bowing deeply, she said, "How do you feel?"

"Good. Very good, in fact. Where are the others?"

"Soon. Your cleric is about the camp seeing to others in need. Nagama'a will be here to speak with you soon. Please wait."

"My… my… Thistle?"

"Nagama'a will reveal all."

"You have cared for me?"

"I and others."

"Thank you."

"It is our honor; we are in your debt."

"The children?"

"The Curse is lifted."

"I am glad. How long have I been resting?"

"Near to two weeks."

"Two weeks?" Jared exclaimed, "How…?" He stopped when the tent flap opened again and Nagama'a slid into the room, smiling at him as she came over to his bed. She, too, bowed low when she approached. He made an effort to rise; but she laid her hand on his chest, kneeling next to him. She pivoted until she was seated, her legs crossed. "Not yet. The others will come here soon. You still need more rest. The healing music is quite powerful; still, it costs much in energy." She tapped his chest, paused, and said, "There are things to tell you before the others come. May I sit with you awhile?"

"Please. I am honored."

"The honor is mine. You have saved a generation of our people. We will always be in your debt."

"It is not owed."

"Still, it is given… Jared, there is something to tell you, something difficult." Nagama'a took Jared's left hand, holding it in her lap.

"First, know this, my youngling – you are a healer. Music has at its roots an incredible power to heal. It is for this reason I believe the stone has come to you. Of this, I can say no more, for it is not the right time or place. In time, you will be able to heal with much less of an expense of personal energy. For now, know that you have this gift. There will be other times when it will be called for. You will know when, follow your heart. Do what you did for us – play what speaks to you, and let all else happen as it will." She tapped his chest again. "Always from here." She smiled as she had when she had given him the pendant back on their meeting.

Nagama'a shifted her position slightly, so she was now looking directly into his eyes. "There is another healing that must be done… You are in love with the young Wizardess?"

"Yes, very much so… She is all right? She seemed upset by what you said to her that first eve."

"She needs you." Nagama'a looked into Jared's eyes. "She has been deeply hurt, perhaps more than you can understand. The only healing needed here is love. The rest is over."

"What?"

"A moment, please, young half-elf. This is hard, even for an old wizened one like me who has lived and loved through much." Nagama'a paused, trying to choose the right words.

"Listen carefully. Your woman, she was with child, Jared. It was damaged, badly damaged, and had to be taken, else it would have destroyed her from within. I am so sorry."

"A child? Gods, what have I done?"

"No!" Nagama'a fairly shouted at him, her dark eyes penetrating to his core. It was a command, not a statement. "There is no fault here. Take none on. You loved; these things happen. True love is never wrong.

"Jared, listen to me." She grabbed his arm with her two hands; her grip was strong, and she held him tightly. "She was never going to have a normal child. Never! Her power is too great, greater than I have seen in all my long years. Now, she will no longer have to worry about it. I am so sorry; that, also, was necessary." She kept his eyes locked on hers by force of will.

"Listen to me carefully. All women, whether they admit to it or not, have the deep need and desire to have a child. Sometimes they put that aside for other reasons; and it is a good choice for them because of circumstances, because of who they are or who they wish to become. For Thistle, it was not a choice.

Understand that though she knew the chances were slim that she would ever bear a child, the possibility, however remote, was there. Now, it is not. She is hurt, as I said, perhaps more than you ken."

Tears were streaming down Jared's cheeks. He reached out to Nagama'a, who took him into her arms. She realized she had been right, there was healing needed here as well. The two young ones would be whole together again. Their love was true, and that was what she had needed to know.

After a long moment, when the boy's crying subsided, she released him. "It is time for your Thistle to come in. Are you ready to see her?'

Jared swallowed hard and nodded.

"I will be close if you need me. Sart is close, also. Be together; it is the best healing there is."

As soon as Nagama'a left, Thistle came through the same flap of the tent. She paused in the doorway. Jared could see, even in the dim light, that she had been crying. Her cheeks were shiny with wet; but she looked fine otherwise, not ill like he thought she might. She looked at him, and he held out his arms. She ran across the space between them, and he pulled her down. They lay there together for a long, long time. No words were necessary.

It was several days later, when Jared was feeling almost back to normal, that he and Thistle asked to have an audience with Nagama'a with Sart present. The witch, back to her normal duties as seer and healer for the Fleethoof clan, set aside time for them in the mid-afternoon.

They all met in Nagama'a's tent. She preferred the soft darkness because her old eyes were sensitive to the light. The four sat in a circle. Thistle asked their host a question, "When we first met, wise one, you referred to me as your great, great grand-daughter. I do not understand."

"Perhaps I misspoke slightly. It is more likely that there should be several more 'greats' attached to that, or more than several, child. I am over six-hundred years old, ancient even for a Sliv elf; and it has been well over a hundred years since I had a child. I knew as soon as I saw you. Somewhere, and perhaps if you wish we could trace the lineage, you come from my stock. I know these things, see them with my power. If you could see me as I was when I was young, well, there are resemblances… or were," she smiled.

Jared, listening carefully to every word, suddenly drew a bit straighter... Her eyes! he noticed. For Nagama'a was one of the few he had ever seen who had the deep, incredible green of Thistle's eyes.

Nagama'a continued. "Many years ago, the Slivs were a more open society. As you may know, we are not true elves, or 'pure' as the elder race would speak of themselves. In the first age, we bred with humans. It has only been recently, the past several hundred years or so, that we started to tighten our borders and our society. This is still a point of some contention amongst the elders and the young lords." Nagama'a sniffed, as if she wished to say a good bit more about that bit of information.

"The Curse, the fever you witnessed in our young, comes, or at least so I believe, from a weakness due to our inbreeding. It only attacks once every fifty years or so, but it is devastating; and it kills many of our young from the ages of three to twelve. We have few enough children as it is, which is another part of our elven heritage. This time it was exceptionally bad.

"Jared," she turned toward him, "what you did was miraculous. You saved a whole generation of our people. Those fifty-two children were from all our clans – fifty-two children out of more than twenty-thousand tribal members over a ten-year span. The numbers become less each year. Last year, we had only four births in our whole society.

"With the elves, the elder race, I have heard it is worse. No births in over two hundred years. It comes, in part, from our arrogance. What use is long life, if there are none to survive us? Hah!" And with that, she fell silent.

Thistle bowed from the waist. "I am truly honored to have your blood, wise one."

"It is your power that I read, child. It is tied to mine; I can feel that. It was long-long ago, yet we are linked. It is good to know that there are those outside of the clans who survive me. It is I who am honored."

There was another long pause. Jared broke the silence. "Thistle and I would request a boon of your people and of Sart."

"If it is within my power, it is already granted."

"We would like to be married amongst the Slivs, with you and Sart presiding. Is it possible?"

This time it was Nagama'a and Sart who were surprised. The Sliv witch-woman stood up, beaming. She bowed low to both of them. "It would be the greatest honor for me and for my people. Will it be appropriate for your religion, Sart?"

"I can fit in anywhere," Sart winked. "It would be my true pleasure."

Jared added, "We are willing to follow whatever rites you wish. We had wanted to be married amongst our relatives and friends, but this seems to be the right place and time. It is our wish."

"So be it. Come, my good cleric, it looks like we have some planning to do."

The wedding took place a week later amidst tremendous fanfare. It looked as if the entire Sliv nation came – in truth it was probably only a tenth of their wide-spread populace. The festivities lasted for three days. The elder women of the Fleethoof clan, who had taken in Thistle as one of their own, produced a beautiful, intricately woven gown for Thistle, made of the finest linen. Every detail was seen to, as there was much for the clans to celebrate.

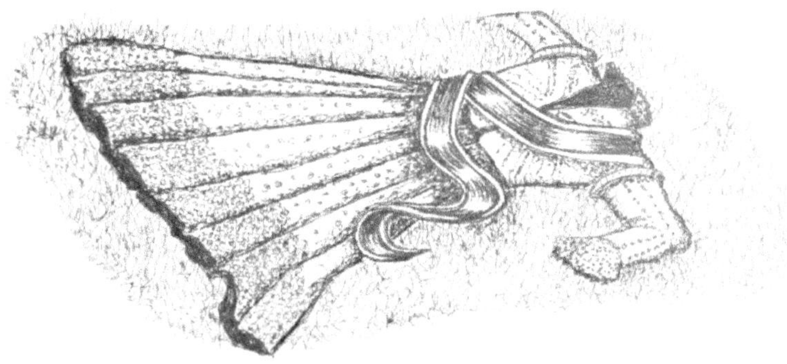

The young lovers were separated for the three days prior to the ceremony, but that turned out for the best. Jared, as was the Sliv custom, had to prove himself a warrior before he could take a bride. With his prowess at arms, he had excelled at all the tests except one, riding. For that, though he was certainly experienced and capable by human standards, they passed him with reservations. He promised that he would return at some point and receive appropriate training in horsemanship.

Thistle was fussed over, scrubbed a dozen times with different herbs and cleansing stones, oiled and re-oiled, and massaged. Then, when she believed she could get no more relaxed, she spent an evening and night in a sweat lodge with other young maidens, telling stories of men and giggling most of the night.

The ceremony, when it finally came as the sun set one bright spring evening, was simple and straightforward. Jared thought Thistle so incredibly beautiful that he almost choked on the few words he had to say. He could not keep his eyes off her. As a special honor, Jared was outfitted as a Sliv lord. He stood as tall and slender as any who had been married on the plains before him.

After a long and drawn out, extravagant banquet, the couple were led to their own tent. An honor guard of twelve Slivs was placed around the tent, set out at an appropriate distance, making sure they were not disturbed for a full day and night. They spent much of that time in each other's arms.

Back on the Road

With the summer heat beginning to bear down on the plains, once again the adventurers prepared to continue their trek. They were far behind their original schedule; and Sart was anxious to move ahead, though the delay had been necessary. They were sad to leave, but the life of the Slivs was nomadic. Already the clans were beginning to strike camp, and soon the herds would be moved to the east and north during the hottest months of the year. Elena and two young Sliv men were to accompany them west and north until they were in sight of Aube.

In a dawn ceremony, Nagama'a named all four "Sliv-friends." It was a rare honor that would allow them free passage through their lands and succor in any of the clan camps. Each also received an individual gift of thanks from the horse people. Jared was given an Anu – a flute-like instrument made from tightly woven, layered grasses that were treated with resins and oils until it was stronger and more resilient to the elements than wood. He was told that it took a century to make one of them. When played, it produced a hauntingly beautiful, ethereal sound that suited the type of music he liked to improvise. Motuk, Sart, and Thistle each received steeds of their choice. The sturdy, short dwarven-warrior chose a special breed of pony suited to his weight and height. Sart selected a broad-backed stallion named Strongflank that would do well on long treks with the large cleric on his back. Thistle picked a frisky young mare that came from the same lineage as Jared's Breathwind. She was named Wind-of-the-East; and being small for that breed, she suited Thistle's slight frame perfectly.

Finally, with all farewells said and after many hugs and tears, they set out following Elena's lead through the tall grasses. Before long, they were swallowed up in the sea of green and could see only occasional glimpses of the tallest tents when they looked back.

There was no set timetable. Sart, however, was anxious to move ahead. He had asked Nagama'a to send a rider north to Efsted to pass word on to Elanar. He hoped that they would all meet in Aube in about four weeks. By then, it would be nearing mid-summer; and though this was a bit later than he had planned to start their trek westward, he had built in enough flexibility that he hoped they would accomplish what they had set out to do.

Elena and two Sliv lads served as their hosts while in their country. Ample provisions of excellent quality had been packed to make their journey across the plains as comfortable as if they had remained with the main camp.

Each evening tents were raised in an amazingly short space of time. The Slivs had perfected a design that made the process of putting them up, as well as disassembling them into compact bundles, nearly effortless. These were much smaller versions than the clan tents; still, they were dry, roomy, and much more comfortable than anything they were used to.

There always seemed to some stiffness in the Slivs' manner, though the two boys were more relaxed than the staid Elena. Their culture was built upon so many traditions and protocols that it was difficult for them to completely relax with "outsiders." In spite of their awkwardness, they were gracious hosts. They enjoyed conversing on many subjects, especially weaponry, horses, hunting, and all that had to do with their life on the plains. Jared was particularly interested in learning as much as he could while in their company. He would spend part of the long day's ride getting instruction from Elena or one of the lads on horsemanship, shooting their short, curved bows from the back of a running horse, and learning how their long, thin, tapered Sliv-blades were used. It was at these times that he felt like even Elena could relax and show them her true personality, unmasked by the codes of behavior of her people.

They were into their second week of their journey from the main camp, when Jared pulled Sart aside during their ride to discuss with him a concern that he had been pondering for some time.

"Nagama'a knew the stone, Sart. It was as if she were handling a thing that she had handled before. It was as if she had met an old friend."

"I know. I have considered this at some length. She would not talk any more of it. I asked several times. The last time, she stared hard at me, cleared her throat, and said, 'It is not time for you to know.'"

"Aye, it is the same response I got. She knew of its power to heal, and she somehow felt it had 'come to me,' for some purpose. I got the feeling it wasn't necessarily for healing the Sliv children, either."

"Yes, I sensed that also. It seemed like this experience was a way to wake up the healing music in you – as if the healing itself were secondary – important, even critical to their people, but secondary to something much larger."

"Should we have pushed her more to understand what this is about?"

"Nay, she would not have budged. She is wise. Her strength, power as it is, is different than mine or, for that matter, Thistle's. She sees much. She has visions and kens a far broader perspective of the flux of this world than even Meligance. This is Nagama'a's gift.

"In some ways, she reminds me of Ordrake… Ah, yes, you haven't met him. He is an old friend and mentor of Meligance's. At any rate, Nagama'a also knows that if she meddles too much in the flow of things in the short run, it could spell disaster in the long. Her true gift is that she follows the patterns of what she sees, only influencing that which she has been told or 'gifted' to influence. Beyond that, though she has the sight and the power to do more, she lets be."

"She is amazing. Every time I was with her, I felt humbled."

"You are wise then, my young Bardling. I have felt the same way, though surprisingly she has oft asked my advice when I have spent time with her.

"Perhaps I should not tell you this, Jared, but you should know. She asked me about Thistle. What to do. She asked about your true feelings for her. It was a hard decision for her… and for me as well. She was correct in her assessment that Thistle would have died if she had tried to have the child. Yet, these decisions are not easy choices to make. Your wife has changed as a result, Jared, and so have you."

Jared nodded. He glanced back over his shoulder at Thistle. She saw him and waved and smiled. He waved back, turning back to Sart in order to respond to his statement. "Aye, in several ways." Jared fell silent. Sart, sensing that he needed some time, drew his horse ahead to speak with Elena.

Jared knew he and Thistle had both had changed, and in some ways for the better. They had taken this tragedy and drawn together more as a couple. Their joyful, intimate love for each other had solidified into something deeper and more spiritual. Each, also, felt a profound sense of loss, a loss of innocence in one sense, and a loss of possibilities. There was an emptiness or void in their lives where there had not been one before.

There were still times when he saw tears in Thistle's eyes and wetness on her cheeks. Sometimes he would wake, and she would be sleeping on his chest; his shirt would be damp with her tears. They had lost something precious as individuals and as a couple. Though it had only been a thought, a remote chance, now that it was gone, it was as if something or someone had taken a piece of their potential for happiness away from them.

Jared rode alone for a while. Something suddenly welled up in him; and he smiled, tossed his head like a horse enjoying his freedom, and galloped back to his love. He reached out, took her hand, and leaned over and gave her a lingering kiss. Thistle looked at him with a question in her eyes. He answered, "Because I love you."

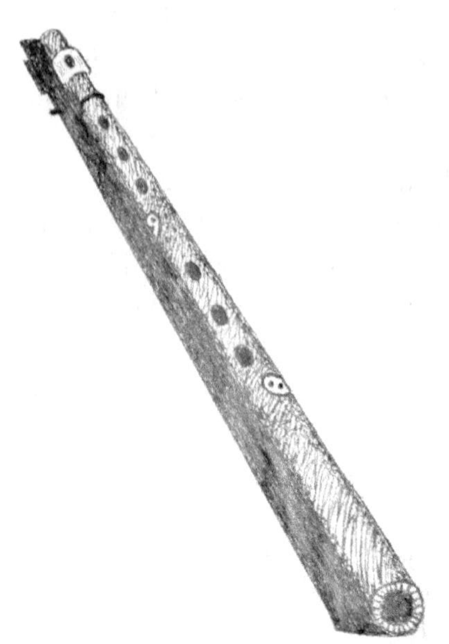

Goodbyes, Meetings, and Moving West

They were less than half a league from the gates of Aube when Elena and the two Slivs drew up. The three plains warriors were anxious to return to their clan, which was now moving steadily east and north to the summer forage grounds. It was time to say goodbye.

Even Elena released her rigid self-control for a minute when Sart pulled her into a big bear hug. She smiled, giggled, and tried to squirm her way out immediately; but the large cleric held on. After that, she kissed each of the others on the brow, bowing low in thanks for all their help. "The gods speed you on your quests," she said. Finally, she turned toward Sart and bowed even lower. "If you have need of some fine blades, I would be honored to accompany you and your companions. I have quests yet to fulfill outside our realm before my final elevation."

Sart bowed low in return. "Tu honora es."

"Tu honora ea," and with that she spun her horse around and kneed him into a gallop, followed closely by her companions. Within a minute, they had vanished into the tall grasses.

They arrived in Aube in the early afternoon and were met at the gates of the town by Elanar and his two elf-friends, Allin and Joelin. The three had arrived several days before, and according to Sart's instructions had garnered all they needed for their venture west. Sart was quite pleased that so much had already been prepared. Once they had settled into the Prancing Unicorn and had a good meal and a few ales, he called them together to plan the departure the next morn.

"We head west tomorrow into dangerous country. Robbers abound in the hills near Aube, hoping to descend on poorly-armed merchant caravans or weak mining parties. It is one of the reasons I have assembled this formidable group. We may also meet chatts in and about the site we hope to explore. They are more active this time of year. Aube and the Bendir plains mark the extent of their range north and east respectively.

"If you have not fought these creatures before, they are wily, quick, and have a deceptive strength. Like their cousins, the gzks and goblins, they attack in groups and use to advantage their claws, fangs, speed, as well as in numbers. Of these three societies with common ancestry, chatts are the deadliest. They use the desert terrain and their ability to shift directions in an instant to disconcert their prey. Unlike their common brethren, they will not be stopped by wounds that might easily disable or kill a man, goblin, or gzk. The desert environs have created a unique adaptation in them, in that their blood is thick and viscous. They will not bleed out from a deep wound, and they will continue fighting as long as they can move. It is best to ensure that one is down and unable to get back into the fight before ignoring it. Cut off its head, limbs, whatever you must do to immobilize it permanently. I have seen good men killed from behind by a chatt they thought out of the fighting. Be careful and watchful should we encounter them.

"I plan to start out tomorrow at dawn. We will be joined by one other at that time. He is quite large and fearsome looking; but he will accept all who are with me as friends, so fear him not. He is a remarkable scout and guide, as well as a stalwart fighter. He will add to our strength and ability to avoid ambushes and traps. I will introduce you to him when he arrives. Please welcome him warmly." Sart cleared his throat, then gestured toward Jared.

"I had hoped that Jared's brother, Ge-or, and his companion, a half-gzk named Stradryk, would have been able to join us on this part of our quest. They are both experienced and brave fighters. However, they have been in the south on their own quest, and my guess is that they did not finish until it was too late to cross the desert. With some luck, I hope they may join us for the last leg of our adventure once we return to Aube. I will leave word for them here as to our plans.

"Rest well and be prepared. Beginning tomorrow, we will set watches at night and ride ready for battle."

Jared and Thistle spent the eve with Elanar and his friends in the tavern's common room sipping final rums. They shared stories of their most recent adventures and studies, and generally spent the time becoming better acquainted. Jared had not spent much time with Joelin and Allin; and Thistle, who had met Elanar on several occasions, had not spent much time with any of them. Motuk joined them after a last conference with Sart. As it grew late, they all settled into a respectful silence brought on by their own musings of what lay ahead and the soothing nature of the strong drink.

It was not long before sunrise when there was a knock on Jared and Thistle's door. They had been up and preparing for the day and were surprised by the intrusion. When Jared opened the door, he saw Sart standing there looking a good bit embarrassed. "I am sorry to interrupt your preparations, but I need a word with you both. If I may?" He gestured inward.

Jared waved him into the spacious room situated on the third floor of the tavern. The Prancing Unicorn was a haven for merchant caravans: both those heading up from the south out from the long trek across the desert and those coming from the north and beginning their journey across the harsh sandy expanse. The wealthy tradesmen appreciated comfort and were willing to pay well for it. Luckily for them, this was the off-season, and good rooms had been readily available.

"Again, I am sorry to disturb; I would tell you both a bit more of our plans now that we will be travelling westward into dangerous country. I need to ask you, Thistle, an important question." Sart drew up one of the plush chairs near the bed where Jared and Thistle now perched on the edge.

"I mentioned bandits last eve, that is only half of the truth – part of our purpose is to deal forcibly with these outlaws. It is why I have gathered such a powerful group and would wish for even a few additional strong blades. Over the past few years, especially most recently, these diverse groups of robbers have begun to band together into a unique and deadly fighting force. Where once the caravans could be protected by hiring on a half-dozen quality fighters, they are now facing an increasingly large and murderous throng that numbers in the scores and sometimes hundreds. There appears to be someone at the helm – a central leader – who controls these marauders, and who exacts a tribute from all who travel south, north, or west from Aube.

"A few months back, the king set his third cousin to the task – a boy who was more enamored of wearing a uniform than learning to be a warrior. He made several limited attempts to force the issue, but the dandies he sent forth leading inexperienced troops met with disaster. He led the last expedition and managed to lose his life and half his troop in the venture. Thus, the merchants have been forced to pay large amounts for safe passage or hire on dozens of guards. It is reaching a crisis stage. The merchants are talking of avoiding the western routes altogether and taking the long seacoast passage through to the southern mountains and the swamps. Which, as you likely know, would take twice the time and mean a huge increase in the cost of goods and ores from those regions.

"This is where you come in, Thistle. Meligance has assured me you will be able to provide the cover and protection we will require to set a trap for these raiders. What I need to know is whether you feel you would be able to provide a magical cover or illusion for our entire group. It needs to be enough for us to appear as if we are a well-stocked supply party heading into the west to resupply miners active in the old dwarven digs. My hope is that the bandits will think us fair game and set an ambush, whilst we will have prepared a trap for them instead. Can you do this type of illusion, Wizardess? For an extended period?"

Thistle nodded.

"And also," Sart added, "would you be able to bring your powers to bear in battle when the time came? Have the strength left to fight?"

She nodded again. "Will I have to cloak us against any magical probing? That would be considerably more difficult to maintain for any length of time."

"Nay, I think not. There has been no mention in any of the reports of magic being used by the bandits."

"Good. And at night?"

"You can relax much of the imagery when we stop. We will camp in controlled sites with watches set. Plus, my friend, whom you will meet in a few minutes, will help keep the surrounding area free of spies."

"Good. That will make it easier. What you ask is not easy. Illusions come mostly from the inner power we mages control, and such power is limited. If I understand what you require, it should not be a concern. I will need to focus though, especially during the day; so it would be best for me to ride within a protective shield formed by our companions. If we are attacked, I can shed the illusion in an instant and respond. It is critical that all understand what that could mean."

"Which is?"

"They have to stay back and let me do what I do. I will need room. I can protect myself, and I need no heroics in that respect. If anyone charges the enemy, I cannot be as effective. Let the enemy come to us; then I can do what must be done with the least amount of effort."

"I understand. I have worked with mages before in similar situations."

"Good. Be sure the others understand, Sart." Thistle squeezed Jared's hand to make sure he understood what she was saying as well.

"Yes. Good, that is settled. Tonight, after our evening meal, I will openly discuss these plans. Our first day is on the open road, and we will not likely be bothered. Early on, there are few places to hide to set an ambush. The illusion will be necessary from the start. Once we edge into the hills, it is my hope that things will come to a head quickly." Sart stood and turned to leave. He paused, turning back. "This will be your first test, my child," he said. However, he was looking intently at Jared when he said it.

Not long thereafter, they were all gathered at the stables connected to the inn when a massive form seemed to slide out from the mistiness of the early dawn and slip quietly up behind Sart.

"Ah, here you are, my good fellow." The cleric turned and gave the hairy creature a hard swat on the shoulder. "Come, step forward so you can meet everyone."

Jared blinked several times, for what he saw was a grizzly bear-like form suddenly waver in his field of vision and slowly morph into a large, hairy man. While he watched, the bear-man lumbered forward rising from all fours to stand a full head and a half taller than Sart, who, at more than six feet, was tall himself.

Sart introduced the newcomer. "Meet my recent companion and friend, Niet. He is, as you may have noted, a shapeshifter, a lycanthrope. I rescued him several years ago when he was still quite young, a cub really. His mother had been killed, and he was being beset by goblins when I came upon him on one of my treks to the far west. Under my protection and that of others, he has grown into his full form. He has occasionally accompanied me on other short ventures.

"Please do not be afraid. He counts all my friends under his protection, and he is quite powerful – a proven and deadly fighter and an exemplary scout. He rarely speaks, yet kens much. He will be most active at night, helping to watch us as we rest, generally in bear form.

"Also, understand that he does not drink blood, fly, ravage the young, or any other old wives' and witches' tales. Lycanthropes are much like all meat-eaters; they eat other animals. He has by circumstance, and his own choice, attached himself to me. I find his company and strength comforting and his friendship precious. Since he has grown into his adult form, it is far too dangerous for him to dwell in more populated areas; so he has made the hills betwixt Aube and Aelfric his home.

"Come, let us be off. Tonight, I will tell you more of our plans."

***

Ge-or and Stradryk settled into the easy pace of the caravan. It would be a slow trek westward to Anada; nonetheless, it felt good to be on the move again. It was mid-summer; and the time they had spent in Baarth had been interesting, yet not exciting. Stradryk had hired out as a caravan guide back and forth to Panterra on several excursions; and Ge-or, who found the change a pleasant diversion, had spent much of the early summer on boats running up and down the coast. His prowess with a bow had spread amongst the merchant fleet, and he could command a high price for his protection services. If all went as planned, they would arrive in the southern border town late in the summer and hang about there until a caravan was willing to brave the early fall heat to make the desert crossing.

***

It has been awhile, Aberon thought, studying the rising pile of massive rocks in front of him. He reveled in the power of the place, it always frightened him a bit. There was much more here than his brethren knew, than he knew; but now he had a good notion from where at least some of that residual power came. It was what he had come to acquire.

He turned and waved for the others to follow him. He wondered if he had brought enough of them: three priests, two of these druids, who had pledged to him. The others were mere acolytes, with five young sorceresses – these had been chosen more to take care of their needs than to help in his quest. They each had power to hand if they needed it.

I will find out, won't I? He thought, as he stepped ahead onto the narrow path that led up to the entryway and thence down into the depths.

Fair Fight?

That evening after a hearty dinner prepared by Motuk, who was a decent cook of the trail variety – lots of good hot food, but not many frills – Sart drew them all together to fill them in on what he expected for the next few days. After he had detailed everyone's role and how he saw the whole scheme falling out, Elanar and the other elves were still skeptical. "You mean we're going to purposefully head into a trap, an ambush? Wouldn't it be far safer to attack them in the hills at their campsites?"

"Safer? Perhaps; however, it is unlikely that we would be able to surprise them or even find many of them. According to the intelligence I have received, they constantly move from campsite to campsite. My understanding, and this is as current as our information can be, is that they rove about in small bands until they spot a caravan or party worthy of their attention; then they come together for an ambush. Our goal is to get them to commit to a large-scale attack. Thus, the illusion that we are a well-stocked mining supply train, with just enough fighting power to entice their leader to bring forth many, if not most, of his retinue to waylay us. We will have a chance of crushing them in one blow, without having to waste time and effort chasing small cadres of them about the hills west of here."

"Still, it seems like we are walking into a volatile situation. I…"

Thistle stood up and raised her hand palm outward, cutting Allin off. "My good elf, I understand your trepidation; please allow me to demonstrate. The three of you," she nodded at the elves who were seated together, "go up to the crest above." Thistle pointed to a spot about seventy-five yards to their south that overlooked their campsite. "Then come back and tell me what you see."

Elanar led them up while Thistle waited patiently. Soon they returned. "It is beyond what I would have imagined, I'll warrant you that." Allin bowed low toward Thistle. "You have amazing control of your powers, milady."

"Tell the others."

"There is a separation, maybe fifty yards up, where what is real – what we see as we all see it now – suddenly changes as if one has walked through a veil. I noted it when we walked up, but it was much more pronounced when we returned. I truly could not believe my eyes when I walked through the illusion back to this… reality."

"And the illusion?"

"It is as Sart spoke. I saw a campsite, much as we have here; though there were twenty mules, not four; fifteen men – eight or nine of them looked to be fighters; five women – camp followers and cooks; and twenty steeds; plus, mounds of supplies in wagons." Allin chuckled. "Not to mention, wine tuns, beer casks, and several barrels of rum. The detail is astounding. Everyone is moving about as they would at any camp. Amazing!"

The other elves nodded at all that Allin said.

Sart stood and questioned Thistle. "I thought you were going to do only a general illusion, Wizardess?" He added the honorific to remind all of them that Thistle was much more powerful than her years would indicate.

"The illusion itself costs little in personal energy to bring into being. The power drain is not based so much on the size or depth of detail, but to the length of time I hold it. It takes energy to focus and control it. For all our sakes, I felt I may as well create something that could not be penetrated easily by keen eyes."

Sart shrugged his shoulders. "So be it. Does that assuage your concerns a bit more?"

Elanar and the others agreed. However, he did press one more issue, "Would it be too bold of me to ask what happens once the ambush is sprung on us, milady?"

Thistle smiled, "Not at all. Observe." She passed her hand slightly in front of her body, raised it to eye level, drawing her fingers in as she did so. An instant later, she flung her wrist and fingers outward and down toward the ground at Elanar's feet. A tiny spark, smaller than a firefly, flew from the space in front of her fingers and hit the ground, exploding in a brilliant, but contained array of red, orange, and white light. The ground erupted, sending a cloud of dirt knee high into the air. There was a muffled explosion as the cloud expanded. Everyone watching blinked and instinctively drew back.

Thistle looked toward Sart, smiling. "I hope that does not give us away, my good cleric." Sart shook his head, grinning at Thistle.

"Imagine that a thousand-fold," Thistle said. Smoothing her riding tunic front as if it were a fine gown, she sat back down, adding, "In those two gestures I eliminated the illusion and, if we had been in a true battle, sent a massive ball of fire into the ranks of those attacking us. If there are other concerns, for example, a ranged attack from bows or spears, I will deal with them as well. I can deflect these types of attacks easily."

"Which," Sart's voice boomed, "is why I have cautioned you several times already to stay close at the beginning of any action and to keep your heads down. We will maintain a defensive posture until our magic-user gives us word to attack. Use your shields and bows but maintain your position. Anything else?"

No one raised any further concerns.

Three days later, shortly after they moved into the hills, they were attacked along the broad cart path they followed. It was an ideal ambush location: high rocks on both sides of the road, a bend ahead that could be barricaded without being seen until one was upon it, and a relatively narrow entrance into the site between two cliff walls behind, hampering any retreat.

The robbers struck in force. First, they launched a missile attack, which as Thistle had suggested she would do, she brushed aside with a wave of her hand. All those around her instinctively either ducked or raised their shields to ward off the incoming shafts, though none of the missiles made it through her energy block. The arrows and spears clattered into the dirt at their feet. The young Wizardess followed with a wave of her hand in front of her body that encompassed all the elements of the bandits now emerging from the boulders on either side of the road to their fore. Starting on her left and expanding as her hand swept across, a massive swath of fire roiled toward the oncoming figures. Before they could react, beyond putting their hands up to protect themselves from the inferno, it rolled over them leaving all in its wake dead and charred.

Thistle turned her attention to the north. Within a second, she sent another expanding ball of flame in that direction. As the fireball exploded amongst the rocks, Thistle redirected her attention to the south, repeating the motions as she focused and guided the energy she controlled. She followed these attacks with a powerful bolt that she directed around the bend in front of them. When it struck something solid, it exploded. Sparks shot up above the boulders in every direction and these were followed by howls and screams from that quarter.

It was all over in less than two minutes. After Thistle's devastating attacks, Elanar, Motuk, and Jared spurred their horses about and rode back through the narrow canyon to check their rear. Any remaining bandits were already scrambling up and away from the ambush site. They managed to bring two of these down with their bows before they could get out of range.

Minutes later, after they had drawn together to assess the situation, they heard more screams to the west and a great growling roar of challenge. Niet was at work amongst the runners.

The next few hours were spent trying to determine from the remains the extent of the damage they had wrought to the bandits' continued ability to wage the intimidation warfare. The final body count was eighty-six. Two badly wounded robbers, who had been at the fringe of the explosions, were brought into camp from the ruins above.

Sart healed the worst of their burns and salved the rest. Afterward, with Niet hovering near, they were more than willing to answer questions.

They discovered that this attack had been formed by sixteen different small contingents of brigands, who had been gathered quickly by word of mouth. Unfortunately, Smash, the head of the "New Way" band of thieves, had not been present for the assault. According to the bandits, their leader rarely came out of hiding, and then only to divide the spoils of an engagement. These two, even under threat of Niet's fierce growl and Thistle's obvious power, couldn't tell them the location of his hideout. The only information they got out of them was that it was "out west" and that he moved a good bit.

When queried about how many more bands of outlaws were in the vicinity, the two could not give an accurate estimate either. "Biggest party I seen was this un," the one said; and the other nodded in agreement. Smash had runners he used to connect one band to another. Each cadre had one runner who was required to maintain close connections with two other groups so they could be brought together quickly. Thus, there was always plenty of overlap to ensure they could gather enough men together for a job.

Finally, Sart gave each of the bandits a utility knife, a silver piece, and an admonition to mend their ways or else he would send Niet after them. He set them on the road to Aube. In bear form, Niet dutifully ambled forward and took big sniffs of the two "to remember" who they were. They were more than happy to scamper eastward as fast as their legs could carry them. Sart guessed that they would walk all night and likely leave the vicinity of the border town as soon as they were able.

Sart had hoped that the leader of the raids would be caught in their counter-ambush. Still, he had not really believed they would get him that easily. Part of their further plans would be to ferret out what they could of other robber bands on their way to the manor at Seston, sending out patrols as time and opportunity provided.

That evening, Thistle was able to relax. There was no reason for her to continue the illusion. It was good not to have to keep part of herself separated, focused, and controlled. She smiled as she nestled into Jared's comforting embrace. It was funny how a demonstration of power changed peoples' perspective. The three elves had all been deferential since the fray. She didn't like the distancing her power caused, but sometimes it proved useful.

Place of Power

Although the overall distance was not great, it took them another week to reach the ruins of the outpost and manor. Each day when they set out to the west, Jared, Niet, and one of the elves would head out on a tangent north or south seeking additional robber factions amongst the rocky hills. The were-bear had an excellent nose. He could sniff out hidey holes set deep into the rocks. The bandits proved almost equally as wily. Over the course of the week, they managed to discover eight dens; only twice were the occupants in situ. Both times, the cornered men decided to put up a fight. Once they saw the great bear looming into view, those left alive surrendered at once.

Thistle cheerfully offered to do a mind cleansing on the bandits – a relatively easy trick using her inner power that Meligance had taught her one day. "It is useful in certain instances, child. Use it cautiously. We can't have half the world running around not knowing who they are. It is indeed tempting at times to use on those incorrigibles we oft have to deal with." Meligance had smiled with that slight upturning of her lips that Thistle knew meant she was both offering something light-heartedly in one sense, but also with serious substance as well.

Sart preferred to let these two go free, so they could spread the word that they would all be hunted down if they remained in the area.

As they drew close to their destination, they could see a large building in the distance, looking out over an expanse of lowlands surrounding it. The stone manor was set on a smooth-topped, round hillock that had at one time overlooked the verdant plain of a small valley. The inn, stables, and trading post had been built at the foot of the hill along the now abandoned trade route.

When they inhabited the Beze range, the dwarves and gnomes had found it fruitful to have an alternate trade route along the hills. This led south to the point of a ship-like spur that thrust into the yellowish-brown dunes of the Great Desert – the point was known as the "Horn." The route was no less dry than the main road south from Aube to Anada, and somewhat longer; however, the rocky hills afforded some protection from the hot winds and blowing sands that roiled across the desert from the west. When one finally reached the eastern edge of the Moulanes enclave northwest of Anada, there were a few streams that came off the mountains during the spring and fall that offered parched caravans a bit of relief.

With the range all but abandoned now, except for small groups of miners who braved the robbers and chatts to scrape more gold and gems from the deserted excavations, the route had closed down. Even though the Qa-ryks had withdrawn northward following their defeat, the gnomes and dwarves had no desire to return en masse to their old digs and homes. The memories of all they had lost during their flight were still too painful, and the threat of another Qa-ryk expansion south and east was omnipresent.

Once, the manor had stood as a symbol of the kingdom in the southwest. It had been considered a choice posting for a princeling or lord who wanted to make a name for himself in the "wilds." Those men were dead and long forgotten, and over the years the fine mansion and grounds had deteriorated from neglect. They could see its crumbling, dilapidated walls as they rode up the hill from the north.

"Stop!"

The command came from Thistle. Everyone immediately reined in their mounts and looked at her, then toward where she was staring. She had been leading the group by only a few yards, but something had caused her to rein back suddenly. Jared, who was to her right and slightly behind, could see that her eyes were fixed on the structure of the old manor house some two hundred paces in front of them. She pressed her right palm flat behind her back to indicate that they should wait. Slowly, she inched her horse forward. A minute later, her concentration on what lay ahead was interrupted by Sart.

"Hold there, Thistle." He rode up next to her as she reined in her mount. "I was wondering when you would notice. Come, let us all have a chat." He turned his horse to the east away from the mansion and after a few minutes dismounted. The others followed suit.

"You knew of this?" Thistle asked when she was standing on the ground with one hand holding her reins and her other placed on her hip. Her stance was wide, as if to challenge the cleric.

"I must confess, I did. It is the reason we are here. Please forgive my impertinence, Wizardess; it was important for me to see how soon you would notice the aura. I, myself, was not so sensitive and blundered ahead another hundred yards before I recognized the signs."

The others of the party had all drawn up around the two and were wondering what they were conversing about. Sart gestured toward Thistle, to give her the floor to explain.

She shook her head, trying to look annoyed at Sart, nevertheless, a smile eventually crossed her lips. He was a wily soul, after all; and this had not been something to test her skills, so much as his. She looked around at the group. "There is a strong magical aura or energy ahead. It does not seem dangerous or 'evil,' if you will. It feels more of a neutral force flowing from or about the manor. I called a halt because I felt it wise to explore this phenomenon by myself, in case there was any danger. I..." She looked over at Sart, "I do believe our dear leader has been here before and witnessed, or 'blundered upon' the same energy tingle that I picked up just now."

"Indeed, I was here," Sart said, bowing with a flourish toward Thistle. "Several years ago, I set out to explore this region, attaching myself to a mining party. We chose to stop in this area overnight; and as is my usual practice, I decided to explore the old ruins. I was amazed to find that there was a strong energy vibration all about the manor. As our young mage here was ready to do, I chose to explore it further. However, as I moved in toward the house itself, the aura increased greatly. I am no user of magic; and though I can sense these forms of energy more than most people, I did not wish to pursue the matter without a competent magic-user available. This is the first opportunity I have had to return. I thought," he again bowed low toward Thistle, offering a silent apology for not being open about the phenomena, "our Wizardess might identify this phenomenon much more readily than I."

"How close did you get?" she asked, choosing not to acknowledge his confession.

"Almost to the old steps, but no further. At that point, I could feel a distinct pulse of energy. It was, shall we say, uncomfortable."

"Wait here." Thistle turned to go, handing her reins to Jared.

"Thistle." Jared touched her shoulder lightly, concerned for her safety.

She turned back toward him and smiled, touching his face lightly with her hand. "I ken energy, Jared, and I won't take any unnecessary risks. It is as natural to me now, as pitches, harmony, and music are to you. Everyone, stay here, except you, my good cleric. Follow me at ten paces; stop if I signal. I will be focused ahead, so please obey instantly."

"Milady."

Jared was actually quite amazed by the way Thistle held herself and how she directed the cleric, not to mention Sart's deference to her command. She had changed, and he was slowly discovering how much.

Thistle strode confidently toward the old manor, stopping every twenty paces or so to reassess what she was sensing. As Sart had indicated, the aura increased with each step; and she could feel a steady pulse of energy as she approached the well-worn marble steps that led up toward the old entryway, now with only one partial pillar standing. Still, she felt no danger in or from the energy, so she pressed ahead.

By the time she stood in the entranceway, the pulse was strong enough that she waved to Sart to stay where he was. She felt the need to adjust her own energy vibrations so that this force flowed more easily about her. What Sart witnessed, since he was the only one who was close enough to see, was Thistle's form suddenly grow ethereal before his eyes. He was concerned at first; then he saw her wave and smile. An instant later, she disappeared into the manor proper.

Thistle had shifted her natural vibration rate slightly to make it easier to explore the energy she faced. In a true sense, she had stepped partially into another dimension or plane. She pushed her ethereal body ahead until she located the center of the energy. There she stood feeling the ebb and flow of the pulses, using her understanding of energy, power, and magic to ken what was happening there. Finally, she drew away and moved back toward the door of the manor and out. As she appeared in the doorway, Sart saw her once again solidify and step toward him.

"Come. I will explain when we get back to the others," she said. "We have both likely stayed long enough in this force field."

Thistle addressed them after they had drawn further away from the faintest effect of the flux. "From what I can discern, this place has become a vortex of power. Lines of force meet near the center of the old mansion and have created a powerful energy field. I felt about with my own threads of energy. It appears that this confluence occurred some years ago as the result of a shift of the foundation of this whole region. Perhaps caused by an earthquake or even a magical explosion?" She looked questioningly at Sart.

"The area is prone to shaking," he said. "I have been here when tremors have occurred. So that is certainly a possibility."

"For whatever reason, it has caused this power center to be focused here. I'm not sure how that knowledge may be of use or not."

"You sensed no control behind the energy – a wizard's mark or the like?" Sart asked.

"Nay, it is a completely natural occurrence. Nor is there any negative or positive aura; it is neutral in that respect."

"Anything else you can tell us?"

"There is enough power here that it might be used by those with the knowledge and skill to shift from one plane to another, or to bring something into this plane from another. How…"

Thistle thought of something else. She looked at Sart. "Do you not feel different, my good cleric?"

"I feel good…? Well, now that you mention it, I feel quite good, energized, as powerful as I have ever felt within."

"And I, as well. It is an energy that one can feed off, especially those who are in tune with their own energy. It is a fount that those who understand can use it to rejuvenate themselves."

"So, mages, sorcerers, priests?" Elanar queried.

"Perhaps all who stand near, though it would be dangerous for most to get any closer than Sart did. I had to shift slightly out of plane to stand in the center of the field of force myself. Overstaying one's time within such a vortex could be detrimental even to the gifted. Interestingly, it could also serve as a remarkable re-energizing point for those who wield different forms of power."

"Including Black Druids?" Jared asked.

"I would imagine, yes."

"This site could be dangerous if they found it and chose to control it."

"Just so," said Sart. "Which is why I felt the need to discover its nature. Meligance will find this of some import. It might be a place that the kingdom will find of interest once again."

"There is a drawback to gaining power in this way, thankfully," Thistle added. "It will only last until one uses their power. For this source to be of any use, one would have to stay within range – perhaps a day or two's ride."

Sart nodded; he motioned further down the hillside. "Let us set up camp in the valley, past the ruins of the old inn. On the morrow, we will explore the whole area further and see if there are any other influences from this phenomenon or any secondary vortexes associated with this one."

"Are such things common?" Thistle asked, gesturing toward the manor.

"Common? No. One does not oft find power sites like this about Gaia anymore – places where many lines of power converge. Energy lines were common lore amongst the old religions. Many of our churches were built above these ancient worship sites that were said to have been power centers where two or more energy lines intersected, sometimes creating vortices of power, like this one. Rarely, however, according to all the lore I have read, have there been sites of as much concentrated force as this. I would warrant that all of you would sense this power if you moved close to the portal of the manor."

Sart mused, "It was supposed that Mangor originally drew much of his personal power from a place similar to this. When the earth shifted and that source waned, he was brought down, in spite of all that he had become and drawn to him. Some claim there is a place of power in Moulanes, yet the elves do not speak of it." Sart looked toward Elanar and the other elves.

At that, Jared wondered whether the inclusion of Elanar and his fellows on this particular quest really had to do with their expertise with weapons. He sensed that Thistle was asking herself the same question. The cleric was ever wily in his method and purpose.

Hesitating a few seconds, Elanar shrugged his shoulders. "There are two energy vortices in Moulanes that I have knowledge of." Allin and Joelin nodded as he spoke. "They are sacred groves, used mainly by our own mages and healers. Most who live in Moulanes have only been on the fringe of these areas, the outer circles. The inner rings are considered taboo for all except for our wisest and eldest. From what our Wizardess has described, neither is of this magnitude. It is possible they are more powerful than I ken. They are most oft used as centers for rest, rejuvenation, and meditation."

Sart acknowledged the willingness of Elanar to speak of the elven site with a bow. It was rare for elves to divulge any of their secrets. Though it could have been out of malice toward his brethren for banning them from their enclave, the cleric did not sense that was at the root of why Elanar had spoken. Spreading his arms, he said, "Let us all rest well this eve. Till the morrow."

Manor Fed

The morrow came sooner than any of them expected when a long low growl from Niet woke them as dawn was broaching the skyline to the east. They were all quickly on their feet, peering into the darkness to the west, the direction in which the big bear stared intently. Elanar had been on the last watch; and he was crouched about ten yards to the left of Niet's massive form, also peering westward, his bow to hand, not drawn.

Thistle sat up and swung her legs around under her, while Jared spun off of their sleeping pad, drawing his short sword in one smooth motion from the scabbard set next to the bed. He also grabbed his bow and quiver as he came up. He could sense, though it was still too dark to see much, that Allin, Joelin, and Sart, sleeping back and to their right to give the two some privacy, were also moving. He wasn't sure where Motuk was; but he didn't seem to be in the immediate vicinity, which raised his sense of alarm.

Niet growled again and began to step forward. A hissed warning from Sart stopped him. Jared sidled sideways to his right, drawing Thistle up with him as he went. He wanted to connect with the others visually; so if an attack came, they would know exactly where their friends were. He had moved about five paces when he saw his companions sidling his way. He whispered to Allin, who was closest, "Short swords?"

It was a statement and a question. Before leaving Aube, they had discussed preferred weapons for the types of fighting they might encounter on the westward trek. Jared had strongly recommended they all bring the shorter, lighter, and more maneuverable blades. He had never fought chatts before, yet according to Sart they were cousins to the goblins of the caves and the gzks of the forests. He had fought these on a number of occasions in his youth on expeditions with his father and Ge-or. Long swords were an unwieldy choice for fighting the agile creatures. Sart had nodded his approval. The elves had insisted on bringing their long swords, too. Jared hoped they had the shorter blades to hand. He could now see that Allin had picked up the shorter blade. He could not see well enough to tell what weapons Joelin and Elanar had with them.

For several minutes they could see nothing more. Niet continued to growl at intervals to let them know that something was still out to the west of their camp. By the time they could make out flitting movements in the distance, they had all gathered in a semi-circle behind and between Elanar and the bear. Jared grimaced when he saw that Elanar now had his long sword in hand. He knew the elf was a superb swordsman, having won the long sword cup several times at Bard Hall; but Jared knew before Sart spoke what they were up against.

"Chatts," Sart whispered, spinning his mace in his right fist. "Watch and wait. It is better if we hold close and let them come at us… Thistle?"

"Behind you; I will be ready in a second."

Jared turned. He saw that his wife had started to climb a large boulder near the campfire. When she scrambled onto the top, she braced herself with her feet spread shoulder-width apart so that she could wield her magic over her companions' heads without having to worry about affecting them in any way. Raising her hand, she spoke one word, "Eliar."

A comet-like flame of white coruscating light flew from her outstretched hand and arched up into the sky several hundred feet. It expanded into a large ball and began to float very slowly downward. The intense sphere lit up the entire area as if it were daylight. Now they could see what lay to their fore.

There were hundreds of mottled yellow and brown chatts scampering in and out amongst the ruins of the trading post, and beyond that, around the manor. Sart realized immediately that there were several odd things about what they were seeing. First, chatts rarely wasted any movement – they were attuned to saving every drop of liquid in their systems by strict disciplinary regimens that served as a code for their lives. The beasts in front of them were highly active, running in and out of the rubble or remaining in one location and hopping up and down in some eerie sort of dance.

The other thing that puzzled him was that there were many of the beasts moving in and about the strongest parts of the energy vortex -- something even he did not have the skill to do. Then it all came together – "Be extremely wary," he warned the others, "they have found a way to use the vortex to enhance their physical abilities. They are energized in some way by it…" He didn't have time to say more; a howl from many voices drowned him out. The chatts launched their attack.

Thistle drew power to her quickly, sending a massive fire attack into the front right flank of the creatures as they scrambled rapidly toward their protective hollow. Her companions braced for the assault.

Jared and the three elves brought their bows forward when they saw the milling creatures. As the creatures rushed forward, they each got off one shot, that was all. The chatts were amazingly fast.

As her companions dropped their bows and retrieved the swords, Thistle managed to get off another fire blast into the creatures' other flank. The two magical attacks cut swaths through their ranks, reducing the mass of charging beasts by two-thirds or more; but the chatts outside the compass of the blasts and even the wounded ones, almost seemed to fly forward. They were upon them in a matter of seconds. Though Thistle's magic had blunted the initial charge, more and more of them were emerging from the ruins and scrabbling into the fight. Within seconds, Sart's group found themselves in a desperate battle for their lives.

As they were slightly forward of the others, Elanar and Niet took the first attacks. However, the chatts who had made it through the gauntlet of the two fireballs quickly swarmed at them.

Jared found himself leapt at by two of the creatures a second after the first ones had been engaged by Niet. His sword flashed, and his first stroke was deadly, severing the creature's head with one blow to the neck; but the second was clawing at him before he could use a backstroke to cut it down. He thought, By-the-gods, they are quick, as he stabbed upward as hard as he could with the knife in his left hand. The beast kept clawing at him until he brought the sword hilt crunching into its skull. By that time two others were at him. The others of their party were equally frantically engaged.

Thistle, who was high enough above the ground to avoid the first of the scrambling creatures, began to pick off those still coming into the fray with small bolts of intense light. This probably saved all of their lives, as they were all quickly almost overwhelmed by the fierceness and speed of their opponents. She was able to give them a brief respite, enough so they could deal with the beasts with which they were already engaged.

Jared's hilt slam had wounded the second of the chatts badly enough that it had fallen at his feet. It scrabbled at him with its claws, while still engaged with three others. He was using all his ability and knowledge of close-in fighting just to survive. He parried sharp claws and fanged bites, stabbed, pushed, slashed, butted, twisted, and ducked. Yet, he had several scrapes to his torso and legs in a short period of time.

The others were faring similarly. Elanar had killed two with powerful slashes of his long blade; then he was literally swarmed over, fighting desperately, more with his knife and the butt of his sword than with the long heavy blade. Niet, in bear form, proved invaluable. His powerful claws crushed the head or chest of the beasts he hit; and the force of his blows sent the bodies flying far to the side, leaving him space to swipe again and again. His hide also proved tough to penetrate by claw or fang; and though the chatts were all around him slashing and biting, he would pivot from one side to another sweeping them off his side and back. He was the only one of their group who was able to wade forward to join Thistle in keeping more of the beasts from attacking the others.

It took Allin and Joelin a few seconds to understand the true nature of an all-out brawl. There was no formality or code to this fighting; you killed or you died. In those few seconds, they took some dreadful wounds. Allin was down on one knee, still slashing gamely, his left arm dangling at his side. Joelin was barely staying on his feet, wavering under the attack of three of the beasts.

Sart, slower as a fighter, and hence more vulnerable to the quickness of the chatts, was yet a powerfully built man. When he brought his mace into play and got a good swing at one of the creatures, the heavy-headed weapon would crush through any defense they attempted, smashing arms, bones, skulls, and rib cages. He received numerous claw scrapes, yet since he slept in his voluminous robes and chainmail shirt, they rarely struck anything except cloth and the metal beneath,. Unfortunately, all the others had slept in their tunics and night shirts. Their leather armor lay in bundles near the pack mules. Their wounds, though rarely deep, were mounting steadily.

The turning point of the battle came when things were beginning to appear hopeless. More of the chatts were pouring in from the west; and even Thistle, who was still helping the others by rhythmically downing beasts with bolts of energy to give each of them more freedom to fight back, had to break away by paying attention to the few that were now scrabbling up toward her on the boulder. Niet was also being pressed backward by more than a dozen of the creatures.

Having dispatched the two chatts closest to climbing her roost, Thistle suddenly straightened, pointed into the sky and yelled, "Pluere!" A moment later the heavens opened, and a deluge of rain swept over all of them, attacker and defender alike. Thistle slumped down to her knees.

The chatts, unaccustomed to rainfall and large amounts of water, stopped fighting and looked fearfully up into the sky. Then, as if by signal, they sprinted away, heading back up the slope toward the manor. Within a few seconds, they had all disappeared.

Aftermath

They all stood dumbly, weapons in hand and dripping blood, their own blood. In that length of time, the rain stopped as suddenly as it had started.

Jared and Sart were the first to move. Jared had seen Thistle collapse, and in spite of his own wounds, he ran toward the boulder. Sart dropped his mace and looked toward Niet, who growled that he was fine. The cleric, seeing Elanar down, quickly headed over to the elf.

Thistle smiled weakly at Jared as he came up. "Help the others," she said. "I'm fine. Just a bit tired." Then she saw his wounds, "Gods, Jared, you're bleeding badly." She pushed herself up. Turning further toward him, she began to attend to his cuts.

About their camp, those hale enough were helping their comrades. Joelin was tending to Allin, trying to staunch the flow of blood from several deep wounds. Sart was working on Elanar's many scrapes. Meanwhile, Niet had lumbered forward about ten paces from where the focus of the fight had been. He was sitting on his haunches looking to the west, keeping watch to see if the beasts would launch another attack. Though some were dancing about inside the manor, they did not seem inclined to renew their attack; and even these finally left the site. Those the great bear-man could see kept looking upward, as if afraid another deluge would descend from the heavens.

It was some time before Sart, with help from those who could, had tended all their wounds. Thankfully, the chatts appeared to have abandoned their attack completely now. Sart's herbs, tinctures, potions, and healing powers had them all feeling considerably better, though they would be sore and stiff for days to come. Elanar was weak, having lost a considerable amount of blood; but the others were up and about.

When all were out of immediate danger, Elanar, pushing up from Allin's further ministrations suddenly asked, "Where is Motuk?"

Everyone looked up from what they were doing. They all quickly realized that he had been missing from the outset of Niet's alarm.

It didn't take them long to find his body, about a hundred paces to the east. He must have left their campsite in the pre-dawn, either for a stroll or to relieve himself. He had been brutally assaulted on his way back to their encampment. The chatts had torn him apart. He hadn't even taken his utility knife with him.

With Niet keeping watch, they spent that day recovering and preparing a grave in the rocks for their comrade. It was a subdued group. This was the first time the elves had been engaged in a hand-to-hand, close-quarters battle. It served to make them deeply cognizant that they, too, were mortal beings. As all warriors who eventually find themselves in a life-and-death battle discover, the skills and practice they have been through only teaches one so much – experience on the edge is a far better educator.

A day later, after spending the morning searching about the ruins for anything that might be of interest, and finding nothing that would cause them to stay, they said goodbye to Motuk with a prayer service led by Sart at the cairn they had built. As the sun was approaching its zenith, the companions began the trek back to Aube.

The chatts had never reappeared. Sart did not know for sure; he guessed that the shock of a person being able to produce water at will registered more with them as a concept of immense power than the firestorm that Thistle had unleashed when they had first attacked.

It had been a desperate thought on Thistle's part, hoping that the rain would distract them long enough for all of them to regroup, thus giving her time to bring other magic to bear. What she hadn't counted on was the immense personal energy it took her to conjure the brief deluge, literally out of thin air. She had pushed her strength envelope a bit too much. She had never tried a conjuring on that large a scale before. Her drawing of small amounts of water when fooling around with Alicia in their apartments had been simple enough, as there had been water vapor aplenty in the atmosphere about the castle. This incantation had taken considerably more concentration than that. There was far less moisture available in the immediate desert environs. She was pleased that it had worked, and quickly; but she made a mental note to do a bit more experimenting with this type of energy use. She also was determined to speak with Meligance more about true creation – making things from the energy available to her, not just gathering "materials" from what was close at hand.

They rode slowly, keeping careful watch for any sign of bandits or other creatures. They were still a formidable party, and all they saw on their return were the wild animals of the hills. They continued to search for the bandits' hidey holes, and discovered several; after brief skirmishes, the thieves would surrender. Sart and Niet would then encourage them to mend their ways and send them off eastward with only a utility knife and small amounts of food and water.

As summer was ending, they were back in Aube where Sart intended to take a week's pause to regroup, resupply, rest, and perhaps recruit a few more adventurers, before heading further west on the last part of their quest.

Moving Out Again

Ge-or and Stradryk had gotten lucky. A merchant, desperate to get his goods to market before his competitors, was willing to brave the last heat of the summer and the extra expense to haul more water to cross the desert. He was happy to hire on two experienced fighters for a good wage. They left Anada a week before summer's end and headed west and north.

It was rough going. As soon as they left the hills, the heat and dryness hit them. Thankfully, for the first week and a half, the worst of the winds were blocked by the tall mountains of the north Beu' range. Even so, by the time they were skirting the western-most fringe of the Bendir plains heading north, the biting northwest winds were driving the sand almost directly into their faces. They were forced to bundle up in heavy white robes and wear face masks most of the days' rides.

After three weeks prodding doggedly ahead, they finally began to notice a slight change in the winds. Instead of the dry, driving force of the gales that constantly shifted the dunes from one day to the next, often obliterating the well-travelled pathway north, they began to feel a cool, steady breeze rolling off the foothills and mountains of the southern Beze range. It was fall. The men, horses, and mules sensed the change, and their pace quickened.

Nine days later they saw a welcome sight from a high dune looking to the north – the outline of the frontier town of Aube.

***

Sart managed to hire on two new companions for the final part of their quest, which was to lead them north and west skirting the edge of the Beze range. Except for a bit of residual stiffness, everyone else was well-rested and healed of their wounds. They were all anxious to be back on the road. The cleric drew them together at the Prancing Unicorn to make final plans.

"Please welcome our new comrades." Sart made the introductions. "First, Stential, stout dwarf fighter of no small renown to his people." A short broad dwarf, with wicked double-bladed axe and ruddy complexion, rose from his seat on a bench in front, turned and bowed low to all. Thistle and Jared had met him when Sart was interviewing candidates. They both had immediately liked the easy-going fellow.

"And also, Lilith, an initiate of Luna on only her second quest after receiving her clerical robes." A pale young lady with flaxen hair and a slight frame stood, smiled at everyone, and made a curtsy to Sart. She was the protégé of Sart's good friend, Zara, who was one of the more powerful Moon clerics in the north country.

Thistle did have some reservations about taking the fledgling cleric on, as she was from the east and city born, with little practical field experience; but Sart wanted another healer on board and no others had been available. He was also partial to clerics from his church's sister religion. Those of the Earth and the Moon were closely aligned. He would serve as her mentor on the quest.

"We are heading north and west on the morrow. I plan to move into the foothills almost immediately. Though I was tempted to go north to Aelfric first and head west from there on the old road, it is prime Qa-ryk country; and there is even greater evil further along that path. While the going will be slow, we are less likely to run into roving patrols of Qa-ryks if we hug the mountains. We will have to be wary of goblin lairs, keeping clear of them when we camp. At times we will also skirt sections of the pine forests habituated by gzks; yet we are a strong party, and they are unlikely to bother us.

"My aim is to return to the ruins of Kan's stronghold. I have found some information that leads me to believe there may be powerful artifacts still hidden within the depths of the dungeons beneath the ruins. Our goal will be to begin an exploration of the underground labyrinths I believe to be there. I do not know what we will find; my hope is to delve as far and deep as we can before the first snows threatens. Any questions or concerns?"

"How does dungeon fighting differ from other forms of fighting?" Elanar asked. "How can we prepare to face what we will come across in the depths?"

"A good question you broach to be sure, Elanar, and one we shall discuss at more length along the way, as some of us have more experience in deep, dark places. For now," Sart gestured toward the dwarf and glanced at Jared and Thistle, "let me say this: we will be deep beneath the earth in a place where evil dwelt and prospered for many years. Though I do not know what we may run into in that evil lair, it is where Kan bred the first of the Qa-ryks, using goblins or gzks, and ogres as stock. Qa-ryks do not like deep places, so it is unlikely we will meet them below. Whether any of the goblins and ogres remain, I do not know. Be assured, however, dungeons and deep places beneath the earth tend to attract nasty creatures. We will need to be well-prepared and cautious at all times.

"I do not expect to encounter the undead – ghosts, ghouls, skels, and the like – this was not a part of Kan's general magic. That is not to say that these types of undead did not in some way find their way into those dark hallways since his death. We are well-prepared for them with potions, holy water, and the power of two priests. I will also speak on these matters more as we ride westward. Stential, any recommendations specific to dungeon fighting?"

Stential nodded toward Sart, for giving him the honor of speaking first. Dwarves were ever polite and formal as to protocols.

"I have only brief experience in underground fighting," Stential said, "but the quarters are invariably close. We will be in corridors or rooms, and rarely a large chamber, so hone your short swords, knives, and axes, whatever is your preference for close-in fighting. Also, though it is oft difficult to bring them to bear in tight spaces, bring shortbows. They may be of use in certain arenas below ground.

"One other thing is worth mentioning – the oft quoted phrase, which to adventurers is our most fundamental truth, is 'Back to Back.' It comes as much from dungeon fighting as anywhere else. In a confined space, your best defense against long odds is to stand Back to Back, protecting yourself and your comrade. Think on it, for it may mean your life." He bowed low and sat.

"All good advice," Sart said. "We will speak more of the types of creatures we may face, forms of attack and defense against each, and the best battle-order. Let us hope that the dungeons have remained empty and undisturbed since we were last there. Still, it is wise to be prepared.

"Any thoughts on the use of magic in such environs, Wizardess?" Sart bowed toward the Thistle.

She stood, bowing to Sart; then she turned to encompass the group. "Only this, remember that you have a powerful mage with you. If I give a command, it is because your safety and the safety of this group may be in jeopardy. Obey instantly, as I may have little time to do what I must do to counteract what is happening. Also remember," she gestured to Sart, "that our esteemed cleric is the most experienced here. When there is time, even I will defer to his judgment and his decisions."

"Thank you, Wizardess. It is just so. There are many types of creatures we may meet and almost as many ways to fight them. A stout blade may work in most instances, but be of little use against other foes, which leads me back to what our stout dwarf said a minute ago – 'Back to Back.' Ultimately, we all rely on each other. A split-second decision may save someone's life. Make it, if it serves. Always let others know what you intend if there is time. Any questions or concerns from anyone?"

There were none. Jared glanced about the room assessing the mood. He noted that there was a bit of tension, both from the excitement of starting out again and from the uncertainty of any new venture. Everyone, however, appeared comfortable with moving ahead. The elves, newly blooded to close-in fighting, would be solid in a scuffle, though they were not fond of being underground for long periods. Stential was well-experienced and would, by the look of him, be a stalwart companion in a close fight. Lilith was the only question in terms of experience; yet her jaw was set determinedly while they talked, and she had listened carefully to all that had been said since hiring on. She seemed to dote on Sart. It spoke to her resolve that she had already taken on the responsibilities of checking on the healing progress of their most recent wounds. She showed the mien for adventure in the way she carried herself and in the strength he sensed in her gaze.

"Meet here at dawn," Sart said, when no one spoke up. "Baggage will already be stowed and we will leave at once."

"No, I have not received any word from your brother, Jared," Sart answered the half-elf's question as they prepared to leave the next morn. "I have left another note with the tavern owner here. If he and Stradryk make it north in time, perhaps they will follow. It would be good to have their swords with us. As you know, we travel into dangerous country; the Qa-ryks are on the rise again."

"Have you heard anything from Rux?"

"Aye, though his last contact was long in reaching me. The Qa-ryks are ever more active. The rangers are pressed to keep things under control in the west. Still, Xur stands stronger than ever. It will be good to see old friends."

"We stop there?"

"Hopefully on the return. I would spend a day or more with Rux and share information."

"It would be good to see him again, as well as others we got to know there."

"Many are back. The lifestyle grows on those who weather the first few years in that wilderness posting."

***

166

"What in nine planes were those things?" It was at least the tenth time Aberon had asked the question of himself; this time he said it aloud, though none of his battered band of priests believed it was a question he wanted them to answer.

The mission had been a partial success. He had retrieved "the item," the one critical artifact that would give him the power to depose the One. From the brief glimpse he had whilst scrambling to get out of there, it seemed there were many artifacts still left under Kan's fortress, and enough gold and silver to fund several armies. But with those *things* swarming about the place, he wasn't likely to return anytime soon. They had been impossible to fight, even with his best magic and the powers of all those with him. If they had stayed even a few moments more, they would have all been dead. Teleportation was a useful skill, that was certain.

What was most curious was that he had been able to retrieve the artifact at all. It was right where his source had suggested it might be. Yet, no sooner had he picked it up from the floor in front of the pedestal upon which it had likely rested, than they had been swarmed over.

The creatures, whatever unearthly things they were, had come at them from out of the ether itself. These were no fiends of the Nine Planes, nor imps or demons, at least none that he had ever encountered before in his transmigration to other worlds. In spite of their best offensive and defensive magic, there had been nothing that worked against them. Even his most powerful energy field had not kept them at bay. It was as if the creatures could instantly teleport through anything. To make matters worse, Aberon had only got brief glimpses of them when they struck; then the things would be gone in a flash and others would strike. It had been a one-sided battle, until they all had managed to escape.

Now he knew why and how Kan had fallen. It had indeed been from the inside, yet it had nothing to do with Qa-ryks. That was simply another of the ludicrous notions that the past five Great Ones had accepted, which, of course, had influenced how they handled the large beasts. No, Kan had created another entity altogether; and even with the power he had in his grasp, he had not been able to control these fiends. These fell creatures appeared unaffected by magic - - perhaps they were magical themselves. He hadn't stayed around long enough to figure that out.

Small wonder that he and his priests had failed in controlling them: three of his best druids dead and all others were wounded. Two he supposed he would have to put out of their misery as soon as they were well away from the mountain.

"By-the-demons-of-the-Nine-Planes-of-Hell, what had that fool created?" he said under his breath as they descended the rock-strewn slope.

Well, there was nothing for it now; he had other business to attend to. It was time to put this device into play, though he knew it would take him some time to realize its true potential. First, he would learn to wield what he had found. Once he understood that, he would deal with the rest of his brethren, consolidate his position, and set the stage for conquest.

Finally, a-horse, Aberon spurred his mount ahead of the others, gesturing for them to follow. He would stop later to deal with what must be dealt with.

***

Sart's group moved slowly west and north and then west again, traveling high up in the foothills over rough ground to avoid contact with wandering Qa-ryk patrols. Even so, on two occasions they had to hunker down amongst the rocks when Niet warned them of beasts passing below.

They also had to be wary of goblin holes. The creatures often had well-hidden entrances amongst the high hills. In the mountains, small caves could lead to a labyrinthine network of tunnels, oft connected to old dwarven mines. It fell to Jared and the elves to comb the area about where they intended to camp for any evidence of the beasts. They would move on to another site if they found a suspicious cavity or hiding hole leading inward that showed signs of recent usage. Sart and Stential warned them to avoid exploring crevices to any depth, because if they were occupied by goblins, they could be swarmed over quickly. A single warrior had little chance against a mass attack of the clawed and fanged fiends, no matter how skilled he might be.

The first frost was covering their cloaks when they woke at dawn at the end of their fourth week out from Aube. Jared knew they were getting close to their destination. He began to recognize the formations of the southern peaks as they continued to move westward. How he and Thistle had changed since those days when they had first been together. She had been a simple country girl who had no conception of the power she carried within her; and he had been a young half-elf, not quite come of age, thrust into the world by an awful attack that had destroyed his family and former life. Almost five years later, they were back in the vicinity where so much of their lives had turned completely about for both of them.

168

In some ways, he was loath to return to where that early quest had reached its culmination. He clearly remembered the feeling of overpowering evil he had felt upon descending into the depths of Kan's shattered fortress. Neither he, nor Thistle, he guessed, relished the idea of descending those dark stairs again.

As they got closer to the destroyed fortress, Sart told Jared and Thistle that he had been back down into those depths not long ago with Ge-or and others. There he had sought with more prayers, blessings, and holy water to further neutralize the malevolence of the ebon altar he had smote and left broken.

While exploring the dungeons, their group had also discovered that there were many unexplored passageways below the destroyed palace. Sart was determined to root out what he could. The malevolence that permeated the walls of the dungeons of Kan had not been mitigated much by their previous efforts. His recent research suggested that Kan had amassed an amazing array of powerful artifacts. Sart knew that leaving deadly artifacts for the Black Druids to claim could be devastating to the kingdom. Garnering such powerful items, should they prove useful in the hands of those aligned with the good, might give them the edge they needed in finally defeating this resolute enemy.

Having volunteered for the first watch that evening, Jared and Thistle stayed up long after dinner. While they sat their post, they talked about their misgivings regarding a return to the depths of Kan's dungeons. Their first venture there had been when they were young and inexperienced, thrust into an adventure together that they had not sought. They did understand Sart's logic, as well as his compulsion, to pursue this quest to its end point. There was much that potentially could be gained by searching the dungeons if they had not already been despoiled.

Finally, when Elanar and Stential relieved them, they snuggled together on their bed of sweet-smelling pine boughs and drifted into a fitful sleep. In a few days, they would face what they had to face.

Adventure Beckons; Darkness Falls

Only minutes after he and Stradryk had stepped into the Prancing Unicorn, Ge-or was given Sart's note detailing their planned route through the hills to Kan's palace. Over mugs of cold, refreshing ale, they decided to follow as soon as they could re-provision and trade for mountain-bred horses and pack mules. They hoped they would be able to catch Sart's party within the month if they pressed hard. Based on the innkeep's information, they knew the cleric had a nine-day head start.

It had been awhile since they had been on a quest like this. Both Stradryk and Ge-or were looking forward to the freedom of the north country with no obligations to merchants, miners, or sea captains. From what Sart had penned, he potentially expected to find "substantial bounty" in the dungeons. It might be just what Ge-or needed to garner all the remaining supplies and equipment he wanted to finish his personal quest after the great red dragon.

They left early on the second morning after having arrived in Aube. For two weeks they pushed as quickly as possible through the hills, hoping to gain on the cleric's party. From what he had gathered from Sart's note, the cleric was leading a good-sized group. He felt confident that he and Stradryk would eventually catch up to them in the hill country. Ge-or knew where they were going. Once they had moved northward around the hills and westward, he was on much the same route that they had used on his first trek out to the old monastery they searched with Sart a few years before. Only this time, he planned to stay to the south against the mountains and not visit the Borean stronghold they had rested in on that excursion.

He and Stradryk were three weeks on the road when he estimated that there were only about three days traveling left to the ruins. He knew they had made up considerable ground on Sart's party by the signs he read at the campsites they had come across; on the other hand, the cleric's group was still a couple of days ahead and likely drawing near to the destroyed mountainside. They would have to join them underground when they arrived.

***

Sart, Jared, Thistle, and Elanar explored the pathway up to the mountain entrance carefully, leaving the others at the base. It was obvious that a party of some size had been there recently and left in a hurry. Many stones and pebbles had recently been dislodged and scattered by feet and hooves. Strangely, there were bits and pieces of torn clothing, detritus from saddlebags that had been left open, and even the occasional dried splatters of blood on the rocks – more as they went higher and higher.

After exploring up to the dungeon's entrance, they retreated back to the base of the mount for the evening to make camp. Sart was concerned by the signs that told of what had obviously been a hastily departing group. He was not, however, dissuaded from his mission. He thought it was quite possible that a mining party or a party of inexpert adventurers had come upon the place and decided to explore. They had obviously met some sort of resistance and fled. He felt confident in the power that he, Thistle, and Lilith could wield, and in the strength and prowess of Niet and their fighters. It was a formidable group. He set plans for the next day.

"Niet will guard the entrance. He should be able to sense anything coming up the hidden path. He will likely be able to dissuade most creatures should he need to, as well as offer us warning at the same time. His growl, as you have all witnessed, carries and penetrates. Thistle and I will lead the rest downward. I want to start at the lowest level, for that may be where Kan secreted his most valuable items. Jared and Elanar, follow close behind, then Lilith and Stential, and Allin and Joelin, you will bring up the rear.

"Everyone stay about ten paces apart, especially when we are halted by a door or some other blockage. When all appears well, we will motion everyone ahead. What we saw today on the pathway up to the cave tells us that there is still danger in this place, and I know not what form that may take. So, we will be very cautious at every juncture.

"Remember Thistle's caution from weeks ago: if she or I give a command, obey instantly. We will never do so lightly, and it will always be with everyone's safety in mind. Hence, 'Duck!' or 'Get down!' mean, 'Now!' Do so instantly. 'Run!' and other like directives mean you don't have time to think, only react. Elsewise, watch each other's backs and help out wherever and whenever you can.

"We will start as the sun rises tomorrow. I plan to be down in the depths only while it is light." Sart gestured upward. "Evil gains strength at night, so we will camp above ground away from this dread hole as far as we may."

"Have you any ideas about what may have chased this other group out?" Stential asked. "From what we have seen, they left hastily; and some had been wounded."

"Nay," Sart shook his head. "There is not enough left to ferret that out. Jared and the elves are fine scouts, and they could find nothing definitive. Even Niet's nose could tell us nothing else. And trust me, he has a fine nose."

There was a growl from the darkness behind them, and everyone laughed. Sart was pleased. They were nervous about the morrow, yet in fine fettle. They would do well in spite of their inexperience in the depths.

It was the middle of the night when Thistle woke, surprised, but not shocked to find Yolk lying on her chest, staring at her with his big yellow eyes. She hugged him close and whispered, "I am so glad you are back with me. I have missed you so." The creature closed his eyes as if to say, "Me, too." He shuffled his way to his familiar place beneath her cloak on the center of her lower chest and stomach. Thistle slept as soundly as if the angst of the past few days had been swept away.

In the morning, Thistle told Jared about Yolk's return. He smiled and kissed her, rubbing the ovietti's head under her cloak. "Good. It makes me feel better that he is here. We may need all the help we can muster. I hope Ge-or and the half-gzk are coming as well."

"I do, too, Jared. I still have misgivings about this. Perhaps it is my bad memories of this horrid place; I could sense the evil of it as we approached the entrance. There is yet some power there, and it is not wholesome."

Jared agreed. "I feel something, as well. Unwholesome is a good word for it. I don't feel the power; I do feel ill at ease and, well, uncomfortable – almost greasy, as if I had not bathed."

Thistle touched his face. "Stay safe, my love. I am glad that Yolk is here. He gives me more confidence, and that is a good thing."

***

Ge-or and Stradryk were on the trail only about two hours when the Qa-ryks hit them. The two adventurers had just moved into a bit of an open space on the rocky path they were following. The beasts came at them from above and on every side. Ge-or's elf sense gave him a second's warning, yet it was not enough for them to get out of the spot they were in. He signaled Stradryk so that they were able to draw swords and bring their small bucklers around to the fore an instant before the beasts launched their attack. This saved them from the buoas that flew at the outset of the fight. They both caught one on their shields, and Ge-or managed to deflect another with his sword. Unfortunately, two cut Stradryk's horse from under him, slicing into the animal's throat and flank.

Stradryk leapt off his dying steed as it sank to the ground. Ge-or, realizing he could not fight effectively on horseback in the narrow confines of the small gap in the rock, slid off his steed's rear and let his animal fight with her sharp hooves.

As the beasts came on, Ge-or estimated they were up against at least ten; and the Qa-ryks also had the advantage in position. He cursed their incautious haste; they had been far too unwary, pushing too hard to catch up to Sart's party. If he hadn't been so busy fighting, he might have spent more time chastising himself for his foolishness.

He and Stradryk fought defensively at first, until they were able to maneuver into a position where they were Back to Back. The Qa-ryks were forced to come at them head on. Stradryk was a solid short-swordsman. Though smaller in stature than Ge-or, he was quick and could hold his own in a close-quarters fight. Initially, he was able to keep the three beasts trying to claw him at bay, while his partner was dealing with three others.

Ge-or managed to gut one immediately to his front with a lightening side-stroke of his keen blade. He was also able to quickly inflict several deep wounds on the other two beasts. Using all the skills and tricks his father had taught him, and with Stradryk's scrappy fighting, they were standing up well in the all-out brawl. The half-gzk had been inflicting a fair amount of damage, too; on the other hand the beasts outweighed him by thrice. Slowly they were using their bulk to press him back toward Ge-or.

Ge-or could see no way out beyond fighting clear; so he redoubled his efforts, chancing that he would get somewhat free before he was completely winded. He spun and cut through the guards of the beasts closest to him, inflicting serious wounds to both as he pressed his attack. Ge-or's flailing horse had managed to do some minor damage; but more importantly, she had kept three more Qa-ryks at bay. As the fight continued, a brash young Qa-ryk leapt to its back and brought her down with a bite to its neck.

It was at that instant that Ge-or heard Stradryk gasp. A second later, Ge-or's partner stumbled back into him. Spinning to his left and ducking low, Ge-or managed to bring himself around with his back to a boulder, into a position where he could possibly help the half-gzk.

He immediately saw that Stradryk was in a bad way. Qa-ryk claws had racked him across his chest, ripping his reinforced leather armor, leaving the half-gzk's ribs exposed. Another blow had ripped off his helm, tearing through to his cheek bone and his face and neck were bleeding profusely from deep gashes.

Suddenly, something inside Ge-or appeared to explode. The sight of his friend and companion crumbled on the stone path with a beast clawing at his form, attempting to bite his neck, drove like a fiery bolt into the center of his being. It was as if all the battles and death he had witnessed erupted at once in his chest. Roaring loudly, he raised his sword and charged at the beast holding Stradryk. With a heavy strike, Ge-or severed the Qa-ryk's head at mid-neck; then he continued to push forward into the midst of the others, whirling like a maelstrom, his blade inflicting wounds at every swipe.

The young Qa-ryks had never experienced a half-elven warrior in full battle fury, and they suddenly broke and ran. Scrambling back over the rocks whence they had emerged, they were gone in seconds, leaving seven of their brethren splayed in death upon the bloody floor of the trail.

Ge-or, still energized by his battle rage, stood looking about. Other emotions suddenly flooding his conscious, he drove his blade into the dirt at his feet and knelt to aid Stradryk. His friend was in bad shape. Ge-or pulled him up and managed to staunch the blood from the worst of his wounds, but he knew he was not going to be able to save him. The half-gzk's right lung and liver were pierced through, and he had lost a lot of blood.

As he held his head in his lap, Stradryk opened his eyes and tried to smile up at Ge-or. He made an effort to speak, but his energy was fading fast. Ge-or leaned down so he could hear his friend's last words. "I am sorry… I must confess… a crime. Have Sart… pray for me." He stopped, swallowed, and spoke again. "Raped a woman in my youth… son… in Aelfric, at… the sanatorium. Please see to him… for me… friend."

Tears began to slide down Ge-or's face. "It is done."

Stradryk motioned with his hand. "Tell Sart this… ask for my forgiveness… I am so sorry." His head slumped sideways. Ge-or heard the death rattle come up in his friend's chest. That was all the half-elf knew for a long time.

Into the Darkness

Sart led them down to a last platform above the room where the Altar of Kan had been destroyed. Leaving the remainder of the group there, he and Thistle took a quick look around the altar chamber. It was as Sart had left it on his last visit. Nothing had been disturbed.

Climbing back up to the rest of the group, Sart gestured for Jared to unspike the door that led to the west. It opened inward, and though the aura of evil still lingered throughout the whole dungeon, Sart did not sense anything specifically malevolent about the room beyond. He entered first, his rood held before him. He was followed closely by Thistle, who had conjured a ball of light so they would not have to carry torches, though they had them available should they need them.

The chamber they entered was a long, low cavern stretching into the distance. It appeared to be completely empty. There wasn't even any detritus lying about. It was almost as if someone had purposefully cleaned the place before abandoning it. At the far end was another door, which when opened led into another similar chamber.

Sart led the way again, followed by Thistle, Jared and Elanar. They left Lilith, Stential, Allin, and Joelin in the previous room with another conjured ball of light floating up toward the ceiling of the grotto. They also found the ne room empty.

Following the same procedure, they moved from room to room through half a dozen chambers all of the same basic shape and size, leading ever westward. They were all as empty as the first. Finally, they found themselves in what appeared to be a dead-end room. After a thorough search, Stential discovered a secret door set in the long wall to the north. With a nudge of magic from Thistle, the door opened; and they found themselves looking into a similar chamber, this one with a door leading back to the east.

They worked their way through a series of rooms eastward until they had been through another six; then a door leading north led to what appeared to be the same pattern of rooms leading back to the west. These doubled back to the east in a similar pattern of six rooms and again to the west. This last time, they came upon a double set of doors, which led from further west.

Drawing everyone into a semi-circle, Sart motioned for Thistle to open the doors from ten paces away with her magic. The panels swung inward at her command. With the light from the bright ball she conjured, they could all see that this room was perfectly round in shape. Set in the center was a large, rectangular stone pedestal. Sart did not have to tell them that the place exuded evil. It wafted out at them in a flood as soon as the doors were open, and it continued to pulse from the room in waves.

Sart gestured for the others to stay back while he and Thistle moved slowly and carefully ahead into the chamber. They circled the large pedestal at a distance. When nothing happened, they went up to examine it more closely. After about ten minutes, they came back to the others. Thistle closed the doors behind.

There was an audible sigh from the group once the doors were shut. It was as if a great malevolence had suddenly been stifled, though they all could still feel the slight pulse of it coming through the closed doorway. They backed further away to the far side of the chamber.

"There was evil in that room and quite recently, I would hazard," Sart said. "Some artifact of great malice abided there for a time. It obviously has been removed; but as you all noticed, its residual effect is still quite strong. I am afraid we are too late to keep that evil device, whatever it was, out of our enemy's hands. Aberon has been here. I could sense his aura about the altar. That may have been his party's leavings we saw on the path to the entrance. They encountered something, if not here, then elsewhere in these depths.

"Our work on this level is done. The place reflects what was housed in it; over time that will dissipate. Come, enough of this for one day. Let us wend our way back up and out. We will have an early supper. The sun and cool air will help refresh our spirits after such an assault to our senses."

They had no difficulties retracing their steps through the maze of rooms and saw nothing to indicate that there were creatures of any kind in the dungeons below the destroyed fortress of the evil magic-user. It was a relief to emerge from the depths, and the extra rest above ground that afternoon was welcome

Guest

Ge-or woke slowly, his head throbbing. For some reason, his wrists and legs were strangely immobile. It took him awhile to clear his head enough to realize that he had been captured and was trussed up in some way. The beasts he had frightened away must have returned quickly. At least one had come up behind him and walloped him while he was focused on his fallen partner.

Opening his eyes slowly, Ge-or tried to appraise his position. He was tied to a stockade wall of log stakes, his legs and arms spread apart. It appeared that he was in some sort of compound, as there were thick pine posts, pointed at the top and about eight feet high, thrust in the ground in a large circle enclosing wood and mud huts. He could see maybe a half dozen Qa-ryks within his field of vision – some of them obviously larger, and hence older and more experienced, than the ones that had ambushed him and Stradryk.

He had been conscious for only about five minutes when a large brute came up, grabbed his face in its paw, and shook him. Ge-or reacted by opening his eyes wide and glaring at the creature.

The thing roared. Within seconds, another half dozen Qa-ryks came from the huts or from about the compound to join the ones he had already seen. Their prisoner was awake. The party was about to get started.

The first day of his torture was in some ways the worst for Ge-or. He was helpless -- a situation that he decided that if he lived through it, he would never put himself in again. Yet he was relatively unscathed. The beasts had an ideal victim -- someone they could play with for a long time.

For the first couple of hours, the Qa-ryks took turns clouting him about the head and body, burning him with points of small sticks taken from the campfire; or the young ones would pretend to bite his neck with their sharp fangs in what appeared to be a ritualistic enactment of what they would do when they bit their first victim in battle.

In the late afternoon, the beasts changed their approach. They seemed to enjoy gambling, because they would each take turns throwing an odd assortment of sticks into a pile on the ground. The winner would get to approach the prisoner and rake him with his claws. This was done in such a way that they used only the tip of their long three-to-four-inch nails to slice ever so slightly into his flesh. Unfortunately for Ge-or, their claws had a venom or toxin on them that caused excruciating pain as it was left in the shallow wound. Each winner would get one scratch, and the monitor would make sure that the current victor didn't exceed his limit or go too deep. If the scratch was even a bit too deep or too long, the perpetrator would receive a clout from the watcher and be out of the competition for a while.

After a couple of hours of this, it got to the point where Ge-or's muscles would involuntarily twitch as the next winner came forward and would reach out with its claw. Though the beasts could not really smile with their fanged, broad mouths, they seemed to be enjoying his agony immensely. There were many coarse grunts, growls, and shouts, as well as a great stomping of their feet when a scratch elicited a more violent reaction from their victim.

This game went on the rest of the day and into the night, until there did not seem to be any area of Ge-or's body that was not aflame with pain. Ge-or would not give them the pleasure of screaming. He fainted several times, only to be doused awake with water and given enough of a sip of that precious liquid to keep him going for another long spell. He was so thirsty that he faked fainting several times, and opened his mouth wide when they tossed the water at him, gulping what he could when it hit his face.

When they finally tired of their games and curled up about the compound or in the huts to sleep, they left Ge-or hanging from the stockade where he dozed off fitfully from exhaustion. The irritant, however, continued to work; and he would jerk awake to renewed agony almost as soon as his head drooped.

***

The sun was fully up and rising above the hills before Sart led his party back up the mountainside to the entrance to the dungeons. Encouraged that they had not met any evil creatures the previous day, the cleric and the others were a bit more relaxed, yet still cautious. Wanting to take every precaution they could, Sart made sure the doors that had been spiked on their previous day's trip to the dungeons were still securely nailed shut before going to the next level. This took some time, but he still felt an element of unease about what they had discovered on the path leading up to the entrance.

They began their exploration as they had the day before. Upon entering the first room, a twin of the one immediately below, they followed the same cautious exploration course of action. The layout of this level appeared to be an exact duplicate of the other, so they worked their way through the connected rooms slowly, examining each thoroughly before moving to the next. After several hours underground, they were once again facing a set of double doors leading to the west.

The aura here was less pervasively evil; and though Sart and Thistle had each moved within five paces of the two doors, they could not feel the pulse of malevolence that had come at them at this point on the level below. Still, the cleric had everyone stand back while Thistle opened the door with her power.

Conjuring another bright sphere of light, she sent it ahead of her into the room; then she and Sart inched toward the doors. It wasn't until they were at the threshold and the light had moved inward and up toward the ceiling that they could see that this chamber had a massive raised stone dais in the center. This appeared to be piled high with a scattered arrangement of weapons, armor, jars, vases, tomes, and many other miscellaneous items. They could also see a dozen or more chests arranged and spaced evenly along the walls of the circular room. The chests were similar to common travelling cases, with a half-rounded top, and sturdy, slat-supported sides; however, each had an intricate locking mechanism on the front.

Sart had taken his first step forward into the room, when their entire group was hit from every direction nearly instantaneously. It was as if out of the ether itself a swarm of dark creatures, swift and deadly, struck at them. Within a couple of seconds, they had all sustained cuts that appeared to be inflicted by raking claws or fangs. Whatever was attacking them moved so quickly that they could not fix on a particular creature.

The fighters in the group drew weapons and shields and tried to move to the fore to form a semi-circle of protection about the others; but they could scarcely move because they were being hit so fast, one attack following another. Thistle set herself with her legs spread wide, ignoring the immediacy of the fight, and went on both the attack and the defensive. She created a large bubble that encircled the entire group that should have kept out all forms of attack, magical and conventional. If it did anything at all, it only slowed the strikes they were taking. Once that was in place, she sent an expanding ball of energy into the treasure room in front of her, which she quickly followed up with a blast of fire. These two attacks exploded one right after another; yet, in spite of all, the attacks by the indeterminate creatures continued.

The fighters of the group had continued to move forward, albeit slowly, forming a semi-circle facing outward that anchored off of Sart and Thistle. They swung at the flurries of black motion that continued to appear and disappear; unfortunately, their efforts had little effect. Within a few seconds, they were frantically swatting at the air with their weapons trying to hit something, while keeping their small bucklers raised close to their faces to ward off the stinging sharp attacks that continued to rake them.

Lilith and Sart tried to use their clerical power to force back whatever it was that was coming at them. Failing in that, Sart, followed by the young priestess, tried to assist the others.

Nothing they tried worked, except that Jared thought he had heard a muffled scream when his sword had managed to bite into something for an instant. Even though the bright light above illuminated everything in the room, they got only fleeting glimpses of their opponents – nothing clear enough to understand what they were up against. A black mass erupted suddenly from the air about them, struck, and disappeared so quickly that they did not have time to focus on what it was, much less strike it with a weapon.

It was less than two minutes into the battle when they realized how desperate the situation was. Lilith went down under a flurry of strikes; and when Allin tried to protect her, he, too, was swarmed over and went down as well. Sart, his face grim, switched to his mace and was swinging wildly, trying to push through to their two fallen companions. Yet, even that movement proved to be difficult. He kept running into forms, and then lurching forward when they disappeared an instant later. At each step, he was attacked anew.

Thistle had also been badly scraped in places, yet she continued to try various magical attacks and defenses. Finally, understanding what must be happening, she suddenly dematerialized, folding into the ether where she stood. Suddenly, there were some eerie screams erupting from the air about them. A moment later, she reappeared, next to Sart.

"Together," she yelled. "Everyone together over there." She pointed to the wall next to the door where Elanar, Stential, and Joelin were trying to keep the things at bay. "Bring the others and stay in a tight group." She was shouting, while gesticulating in the air and clutching her chest. "I will be gone again for an instant. When I return, be ready." With that, she disappeared again.

Jared, seeing Thistle disappear for the second time, screamed at his helplessness against the creatures. He redoubled his efforts to strike at whatever was assailing them. He kept his body, buckler, and weapon between the frenzied attacks of their opponents and Sart's and Stential's efforts to drag the two downed comrades into the small circle that had formed against the wall. His blade seemed to bite several times into solid flesh as he spun into one of the faster sword-forms his father had taught him, yet more often than not it simply swished through the air. He gamely continued to swing, moving as fast as he ever had in his life. He knew he should trust his wife to be able to take care of herself, but he was desperately worried that she would not return from where she had gone.

A long moment later, when all were finally in a tight semi-circle together with backs to the wall, there was a distant boom that sounded as if it had come from another room. This was immediately followed by a great many howls and screams emerging from the ether about them. An instant after that, Thistle appeared right next to Sart. She gestured expansively, and suddenly they were all standing in the bright sunlight next to their camp. Three dark bodies hurtled out of the air, twisted about as they fell, and landed screaming on the rocks; seconds later they lay still. Thistle slipped to the ground in front of the tight group, exhausted from her efforts.

***

Ge-or was woken from a stupor by a bucket of muddy liquid thrown on his head. He managed to wet his mouth with what trickled down; unfortunately. it did nothing to slack his thirst.

Awake again, the Qa-ryks started in with a new game. The rules seemed complicated; still, the general idea was that whatever beast won the privilege was allowed to throw a buoa at Ge-or from ten paces away. The ideal throw placed the buoa so precisely that it touched Ge-or's skin when it stuck in the stockade logs, yet did not cut him. It didn't seem to matter what part of the body they aimed at, except the head and neck were off limits. Ge-or guessed they didn't want an errant throw to kill their victim or render him unconscious before they had all their fun.

Unfortunately, the young pups were not as accurate as their elders and their blades often cut into Ge-or's legs, arms, and sides. Most of these were superficial; nevertheless, a number were deep enough that a great roaring would ensue, and the youngster would receive a clout from one of the elders. A thick viscous mud and grass mixture would be slapped into the wound to staunch the flow of blood. They obviously did not want their victim to bleed out too quickly either. The game would resume.

Through the long hours that day, Ge-or lost a lot of blood. He knew that if he were to survive this torture, he would have to find a means to escape or at least make the effort and die in the attempt. Though he kept his head down, preferring not to watch the beasts have their fun, he was not as beaten and lethargic as he was pretending to be. Over the course of the day, some of the errant buoas had caught parts of the ropes binding his hands and legs. Dusk was settling in when he knew he would have to take his chance. The rope binding his right arm had recently been completely severed and the other ropes at least partially cut through, except for the one binding his left wrist.

Throughout the afternoon he had tried to use times when the beasts were distracted by their roaring and other antics to get some blood flowing into his stiff limbs and hands. Any movement was painful; but he forced himself to flex his fingers, wrists, toes, ankles, and other muscle groups as much as possible. He had been moderately successful; he believed he would be able to move, at least a bit, when the time came.

Since this patrol had only six buoas, Ge-or decided to make an attempt at escape as soon as the final blade of one set was launched at him. The game had progressed now to a stage where the Qa-ryks were purposefully throwing the blades so they cut partly into his flesh. When five of the blades were imbedded in the wood and cutting into his thighs and side, Ge-or tensed himself to move. Just as the sixth blade was launched, Ge-or twisted to the side away from where it flew, grabbed one of the circular disks from the stockade, yanked it out, and with as much power and accuracy as he could manage, he launched it at the leader of the clan. As stiff as he was, he was happy he managed any sort of throw at all. The blade wobbled in the air and went wide, sailing past the beast's ear, finding a mark in one of the younger pups behind.

Ge-or immediately pulled another blade, used it to cut through the bonds on his left wrist, and threw again at the leader's chest. The blade flew true this time and buried deep. Ripping the remaining buoas from the stockade as fast as he could, and not caring that he was further damaging himself in the process, Ge-or kept throwing them, trying to work his legs and muscles as it did so. With the last blade in the air, and the beasts starting to react, he turned and jumped up, grabbing the top of the stockade logs with his hands. Using the strength of desperation, he hauled himself over.

After that, pure panic gave him the strength to move. He stumbled forward through the woods, not thinking anything except that he needed to get away. He had no weapons or clothes, was weakened by the loss of blood and the long ordeal, and only had his anger and mental reserves to go on. He went into the gathering darkness, lurching and staggering up the slope with the compound behind.

His one real piece of luck was that the gates to the compound were on the opposite side to where he had been hung. It would take the pursuit a few minutes to come around to pick up his trail. Ge-or didn't know how many of the beasts he had managed to put out of commission. He believed he had killed the leader and hoped that there would be some further indecision about going after him as a result.

He was maybe two hundred yards from the compound when he heard the first of the beasts roar as it picked up his trail. Qa-ryks were slow afoot. If he had been whole, Ge-or could easily have outdistanced them to start with; but they were also indefatigable, and he was not. Ge-or had perhaps issued these pups the worst kind of insult – he had escaped capture. They would not give up the pursuit, no matter how long it took; and they were masterful trackers, their noses as competent as a good hound's.

A few paces further, Ge-or splashed into a stream. Desperately thirsty, he wanted to dive in and drink his fill; instead he turned downstream, to the north, and continued to lumber ahead. He knew that this tactic would not delay the beasts for long, yet he hoped that it would slow them enough that he could drink further down the hill.

It was full dark when he finally sank to his knees and put his face in the water. He drank and drank, paused, listened, and drank some more. He could hear the howls. He guessed they were now a half a league behind. Gulping air, he sat back into the stream and let the water slosh over his shoulders and pour around his back. It helped ease some of the pain, though he knew the wounds would need caring. Already many of the scrape marks were oozing pus and the tissue was swollen. He rested for five minutes, relishing the coolness of the stream. He knew by the sounds of the pursuit coming down the hill that he had to move ahead. He did not know where the stream led; he figured as long as it went down, it would be best to stay with it. He would need to stop and drink as often as possible to replenish the fluids he had lost.

Alive

Jared was first to come out of the daze of being teleported. He saw Thistle slip to the ground and started to go to her side. After only two steps, he slipped to one knee, grabbing his side as a sudden sharp pain stabbed through him. His hand came away wet with his own blood. He swayed dizzily on one knee and tried to call to Sart, no words came out.

The cleric, perhaps the least wounded because of his heavy robes and the chain mail shirt, shook his head once; then he looked about, taking in the whole scene while trying to assess their situation and condition. Lilith and Allin were lying crumpled on the ground, in much the same position as they had been lying when he and Elanar had dragged them together in the dungeon. He saw Thistle on the ground, too, but sensed she was all right. Her magical aura was strong and she was beginning to move. Though she had obviously spent great personal energy to teleport their whole group out of the depths, with Yolk's assistance it had been possible for her to succeed. Sart had been teleported several times before on adventures with Meligance. He knew the spell was draining.

Finally, he saw Jared sliding to one knee as the half-elf started toward her. At the same time, he noted that Stential was standing rigidly at the far side of the close-knit group, looking like he was in shock. Elanar, starting to move from where he had 'landed,' seemed to be the only one who was capable of helping.

"Stay there, Jared," Sart said, taking a step toward the prostrate forms of the two downed adventurers. "Thistle will be all right. She knew what she was doing. Elanar, check everyone and staunch any heavy bleeding, yourself included. I will be around in a moment." He knelt next to Lilith's form and felt for a pulse.

As Sart began his work, Thistle pushed herself up and looked around. A bit wobbly, she went toward Jared, kneeling next to him to check his wounds.

None of them had escaped injury. Only Sart and Stential had come out of the fray with minor scrapes, and both had been wearing chain mail. All the others had deep gash wounds about their bodies, mostly their arms and legs, anywhere that leather armor did not fully protect them. It took the cleric only a minute to realize that he could not help either Lilith or Allin. They had sustained many deep gashes and succumbed to the loss of blood. He left them where they lay and went to tend the others.

Thistle, he knew, could tend to most wounds; so as soon as he had his medical kit, he passed over to her what she would need to sew up, salve, and bandage the worst of Jared's slashes. Stential, also, had a good bit of experience binding wounds. He helped with the deep cuts on Elanar's upper back and left shoulder.

Luckily the cleric had only taken a few gashes to his legs and one to his cheek. Stential had lost a big chunk of his beard on the right side of his face, when claws had raked a shallow gash across his chin, otherwise he was fine. Jared had received numerous gashes, the worst a deep cut across his right side that had ripped through his leather armor and nearly penetrated to his liver. Thistle, too, had received numerous shallow cuts about her arms and legs – nothing incapacitating, yet painful nonetheless. Her ability to move about magically had saved her the worst of the clawings.

It was a half hour before Sart was satisfied that they were all out of danger. He passed around an elixir that not only eased the pain a bit, it took the chill out of their bones. It would help speed the recovery of their wounds as well.

As a final measure, after all had been cared for physically, Sart borrowed the pendant from Jared and, going deep within, used it to help ensure that their wounds would heal safely and quickly.

Though they were all despondent at the deaths of their companions, the elves especially devastated by the loss of their long-time friend, there were still things they had to consider while still so close to Kan's dungeons.

It was after all were out of danger, that Thistle and Sart went over to examine the bodies of the creatures that had somehow come up out of the dungeon with them when she had cast the teleportation incantation. They were followed closely by the others.

"Goblins or gzks, or very like both," Stential said, poking one with the handle of his double-bladed axe, "with wings; and there's something wrong about them."

"The coloring is wrong for either species," Jared added. "These are almost completely black. Not like the greys of the goblins nor the grey-green-brown of gzks. And look, their eyes are red, not orange."

"Aye, it is more than that; they are… twisted, or something."

"I think I can explain," Thistle said softly. She had been standing behind Jared with her hand lightly on his left shoulder. They all turned to look at her. She moved up next to the creature they had been examining.

"Obviously they are an aberration," she said. "Some abomination created by Kan would be my guess. They can fly, as we could sense when they were coming at us from all directions, even above. Worse, they don't exist fully in this plane. Somehow," she paused to think of the best way to explain what she had discovered and what had allowed her to strike back at the creatures. "Somehow they have the ability to actually shift at will from this plane to another closely aligned to this one. It is not uncommon for diametrically opposite planes to exist next to each other, as if to balance each other out in the cosmos. Thus they can move from one to the other instantaneously. The reason we could not see them, except for fleeting glimpses, is because they were only truly in our world, our plane, for short instances – enough time to strike and teleport back to their own plane. When you saw me disappear, I was trying to duplicate within my own body the vibrational world the creatures came from so that I could attack them there. It took me a while to match it. When I did, I could see them much more clearly. They are horrid." Thistle paused, passing her right hand over her face, as if to wipe out a dire image of what she had seen.

She grimaced. "They appear much as you see them here. Their bodies are quite lean and muscular; and they are very quick, darting back and forth and 'in and out' from one dimension to the other in a blink of an eye. Luckily for what I was attempting, they spend much more time in their own dimension than in ours. I was able to blast them with energy and destroy enough to give us the needed time for me to teleport all of us here. I do not think I did much damage to the full mass of the creatures. There were hundreds, maybe thousands of them milling about in their own space.

"These three teleported here with us purely by chance; they were within the parameters of my energy, within our plane, when I initiated the spell. What you see here is what I believe would happen to them if they remained in our world more than a few minutes. It would kill them, as it did these, because their bodies cannot adjust to our vibrational level fully. They are not magical; at least they cannot actually wield magic. What they do, their ability to move from one plane to another, has been bred into them."

Thistle looked at the others to see if they had more questions. Sart spoke up. "It explains much about what likely happened to Kan. He created or bred these creatures in some way and then could not control them. He was destroyed by his own evil. It was not the Qa-ryks who ruined him, as many have long thought."

Thistle nodded. "Yes, I came to the same conclusion. Another key point, and I think we have some evidence to support this as well, is that sunlight is hazardous to them, or perhaps, even deadly. The world they live in is dark and dire." She pondered this for a minute. "Perhaps, there is a reason someone destroyed the palace, leaving only the one opening. The question is who? There may have been more at work here than any of us ken. There is much that we may never know about what Kan was about and what led to his downfall." Her voice trailed off.

They all sat looking at the crumpled creatures, thinking in their own way about the frantic battle that they had fought with the things less than an hour before. It was several minutes before Sart broke the silence. He said sadly, "Come. Let us move away from this place and find another campsite to rest until the morrow, when we will build cairns for our fallen. Stential, call to Niet. We will need him if anything else comes our way. Dark will come soon enough, and I would like to find a safer place further away to rest this night."

Pursuit

Ge-or kept moving, staying in the middle of the watercourse as he loped downward. It was an old mountain stream, and the rocks underfoot were well worn with age. He was able to keep a fair pace without further damaging himself. On several occasions, after the moon had risen and he could see his surroundings in its crescent light, he took a short jog to one side or the other. He did this to try to confound the pursuit as well as to search for anything he might use as a weapon.

If he had even a small knife, he would be in better shape than he was now. A trained woodsman could survive for a long time with a knife. He had nothing, and during the dark he would not be able to find the flint rock he would need to make one. On his third jog to the side, he managed to find a heavy hardwood branch, about two inches thick, and five feet long. It had enough resilience and strength to serve as some form of defense. It wouldn't help much against Qa-ryks, yet it made him feel better to have something to hand.

He continued downward, until he sensed he was nearing the lowlands. Moving a bit more cautiously, he discovered that the stream narrowed through a gorge, plunging downward about six feet in a small waterfall where it emptied into a medium-sized lake. Taking a chance that the water would be deep enough, Ge-or tossed his staff over, and dove from the top of the falls into the water beneath. He surfaced about twenty yards into a small lake, recovered the staff, and swam northeast toward the outline of the shoreline, which was barely visible in the moonlight.

Once ashore, he headed due east. He wasn't sure, though he sensed that the Qa-ryk compound had not been far from the ambush site, perhaps a few hours or, at most, a half day's "stomp" of the big beasts to the north and west. He hoped he might be able to come up and around, back to the place where he and Stradryk had fought the beasts. Perhaps he could find some shreds of clothing and hopefully a weapon or two.

He had thought about taking one of the buoas with him, but he had quickly nixed the idea. To carry one of the sharp spiral blades with nothing to place it in would have been hazardous. Plus, he reasoned that if the last of the weapons had even slowed one more of the beasts from following him, he might stand a better chance of actually escaping.

It was midnight when his exhaustion, weakness, and wounds began to catch up with him. He had distanced himself enough from the Qa-ryks that he could no longer hear their howls. He knew they would find him in spite of all the false paths and tricks that he threw in their way. Finally, unable to go on, Ge-or climbed a broad oak and settled onto a large branch to try to rest.

He woke perhaps an hour later dazed and disoriented. After a few minutes, he realized he was feverish. There was little he could do for that. He could again hear the howls of the beasts coming from the west, less than a league back he guessed. He swung himself out of the tree and turned to face south. He hoped that his keen sense of direction was still with him. He set himself into an easy, painful lope along the side of the hills.

Daybreak found Ge-or struggling amongst the now rocky slopes of the foothills. His fever had gotten worse. Half the time he wasn't able to focus enough to know where he was going; nonetheless, something inside him drove him upward. It was nearing mid-day when he located the site of the ambush. He found little left there. Stradryk's body had been torn in pieces. Though it was difficult to face searching the area, he managed to find a small knife that had been tied to the gzk's inner thigh. It wasn't much; nevertheless, the five-inch blade was sharp and true. As he had expected, their horses had been dismembered and hauled off as food. The other weapons were nowhere to be found. He knew that Qa-ryks only occasionally used weapons other than buoas; still, they knew enough to trade or sell them to the gzks or chatts.

Their two backpacks had also been shredded. Despite a thorough search, Ge-or found little that was usable. He was able to tie enough odds and ends of clothing together to make himself a type of loincloth. He wanted to bury the remains of his friend, but Ge-or knew he could not take the time. The beasts on his trail had closed the gap slowly all day. He would have to move on.

He also knew that he could not go on much further. He was past drained. Though he had found several other small streams along the route, he always felt thirsty in spite of drinking his fill at each. He felt he had two choices: to head eastward along the route he and Stradryk had taken, or to head north and east toward Xur. Either meant days of travel, yet he could not see anything else for it. He could not fight the beasts, he didn't have time to make or set traps, and there was no succor in the form of a homestead or farm within several days' flight.

He doggedly set off to the east along the path through the foothills. He could decide later to either move north toward Xur if he lasted that long, or to continue east. He would see how he held up.

***

The next morn, Sart's group found a crevice in the rocks where they could lay their comrades, so they could build a cairn over their bodies. They worked as quickly as possible. This was the heart of Qa-ryk country, and Sart did not want to stay in the wilds longer than was necessary without additional assistance. They would head east and then north to Xur where they could receive the help they needed. They could stay there for several weeks as long as they left before the snows settled in.

After a modest ceremony for their fallen comrades, where each said a few words, Sart led a blessing over the site. Both Elanar and Joelin were in shock over the loss of their fellow elf. They had witnessed the death of friends during the first of the Qa-ryk wars; they had been youngsters, and had all fought as archers, above the hand-to-hand fighting. This was close and personal, and it hit them both hard. After the brief rites, Sart drew the two aside and spent some time offering his support, while the others prepared everything for their journey.

The sun was high when they finally set out along the path eastward. Their horses were in good shape, having been hobbled among sweet grass at the base of the destroyed palace, so they were able to ride and doze in the saddle. The going would be slower than he would like. Sart knew they would make that up and more by riding well into the night. He, too, was devastated by the loss of Lilith; yet he was ever the cleric. He would bring these others through, until they could reach additional help at Xur.

***

It was near dusk when they came across the ambush battleground. Though the body was in terrible condition, Sart recognized that it must have been Stradryk from the various scraps of material and equipment strewn about and the part of his face that had been left intact. Without saying anything to the others, he asked Stential and Joelin to help him bury the body of the half-gzk. He set Jared and Elanar to read the signs of the fray.

"Ge-or and his friend?" Jared asked Sart, when they had all gathered again. He hoped he was wrong, but all the signs pointed to an ambush and battle of two fighters against a large patrol of Qa-ryks.

Sart nodded.

Frowning deeply, Jared said, "From what I can read here, Ge-or survived after a bloody fight. It looks like he was badly wounded or knocked unconscious, for he was dragged away. Somehow, he must have escaped and returned here subsequently, perhaps even this morning. He is alive, or was; and he went east

190

after searching the area. The Qa-ryks are back on his trail." Jared was now pacing back and forth before the others. He stopped, turned toward Sart, and shouted, "We must go after them!"

Elanar, having read the signs himself, was confirming all Jared said with a nod of his head. There was a gleam in his eye; he wanted as much as Jared to fight something. The loss of his elven friend weighed on him.

"We," Sart gestured to all in the group, "cannot go after him. You are all weak, and a chase through these hills will undo much of the healing work I have done. A battle with Qa-ryks would make things worse. You must head northeast and make for Xur."

"We must make for Xur? What about you?" Jared questioned him, his tone sounding harsher than he meant. He was angry at the cleric's words, even angrier because he knew Sart was right. They were far from whole. Except for Niet, none of them were capable of fighting a patrol of the fell beasts. Though he would heal faster than the others because of the pendant he carried, Jared knew he was far from top form. It would be several days before he was.

Sart raised his palms, to calm Jared. "Listen. Niet is whole, and I have only a bit of stiffness remaining from my cuts. When alone, Niet is fast afoot. He can catch the beasts and engage them while I go after your brother. Our horses are fresh enough. I can make better time on my own in the pursuit."

"I…"

"Sart is right, Jared," Thistle broke in, taking his arm in her hands. "You, we, are in no shape to fight. It will be days before I regain most of my core energy and power. The teleportation took most of what I had in me. If it weren't for Yolk, I might not have gotten us out. I…" She stopped, knowing she had made her point.

Jared passed his hand over his face, grimacing. He knew she and Sart were right. He felt awful and his side was already throbbing from the jostling it had received during the long day's trek. He would not be much good in a fight for a while, and he knew the others were in similar shape.

Elanar bowed his head, feeling as if he had just lost another battle. But he knew that the cleric spoke true. He could barely lift his right arm above his waist. He would be of little use in a melee.

"Do not despair," Sart said, his face set in a grim mask. He knew better than the others how difficult the next few days would be now, yet he hoped against hope that he would find Ge-or before he was finished off by the Qa-ryks. "The beasts will be spread out as they track. Niet can move as silently as any and more quickly. He can pick them off as he comes upon them. Once I find your brother, and I will find him, we will come to Xur if at all feasible. If not, we will head east to Aelfric." Sart rose as he spoke. He was already moving toward his mount, gesturing for Niet to go ahead. "If we are not there within the week, plan on heading back to Aelfric when you are sound. We will try to meet up there." He swung his bulk into the saddle. "Ride all night if you can and onward during the day. Push through to Xur. There you will find succor, and you will be able to rest and heal in peace. By all the signs, the Qa-ryks are out for blooding. It would be best to get there as soon as feasible and without confrontation. May the gods protect all of you!" Sart made the sign for Gaia in the air to bless them; then he spurred his horse up the trail to the east.

Poor Timing

Ge-or kept lumbering ahead. He had abandoned the trail awhile back as his feet were starting to crack and bleed from the rough going. He aimed for the evergreen-forested slopes and plunged into the coolness with the soft pine needles underfoot. By nightfall, he didn't even know what direction he was going, only that the howling of the Qa-ryks was getting closer every hour. He just could not keep up a steady pace. By midnight he was delirious; and though he thought he kept moving, he would suddenly rouse as if from a stupor and find that he had fallen to the soft cushion of the forest floor. He didn't know how long he had been out each time, but he would pick himself up and struggle further into the darkness away from the noise behind. Somewhere in the night he lost his staff; the knife he had tied to a thong at his waist. It still hung there. He knew that he would not be able to put up much of a fight if they caught up to him.

If he had been half alert, he would have discerned a different tenor to some of the howls late that night and into the next morning, including a few yelps coming near dawn. Somehow, he had managed to continue ever ahead when he was cognizant enough to know what he was doing. What direction 'ahead' was he couldn't have told anyone. He focused only on a sense of getting away from the danger behind.

The sun was cresting the hills to his front and left when his strength finally gave out. He had been a remarkably fit and toned warrior. The past five to six years of adventuring in all types of climes and terrains, plus his zealous approach to keeping his fighting skills honed, had created a hardened and tough fighter out of the young half-elf that had set out from Thiele. A lesser man would have collapsed hours into such a flight, considering the torture and wounds he had suffered. He finally reached his limit of endurance on the slope of a high grassy hill. He tumbled down for a long time before his body came to rest in a hollow near a large pine tree, against the boot of a large man who had moved into his path to further block his fall.

***

Niet had easily followed the path the Qa-ryks took after their victim. He barely needed to change his ground-eating-all-four-strides to catch their scent. Sart, who had spent time with the man-bear in the wilds, knew enough to give him his lead and to simply follow.

Before sunrise the were-bear caught the hindmost of the Qa-ryks. Focused as they were on the chase and strung-out in a long line, the rest didn't notice that two of their brethren were missing until the great bear lurched out of the trees into the flank of three who were lumbering ahead together. As grey threads of dawn were beginning to penetrate the forest, the were-bear charged into their midst, his great hairy arms swinging from side to side, the deadly claws ripping through hide and flesh with each swipe.

A short battle ensued. However, with the advantage of surprise, Niet was virtually unstoppable. He crushed the skull of the first of his opponents with one swing. The second managed to rear back into a fighting pose before the great bear ripped his claws across its chest, disemboweling him with his other paw. The third, a young pup, understanding the futility of staying and fighting, took off as quickly as his heavy legs would allow, down-slope and westward. The other three Qa-ryks that were up ahead heard the change in the cries of their patrol-mates and turned back. Once they saw the large bear coming toward them, they also turned and retreated down the slope.

Sart, only a half league behind Niet, caught up with him as the great were-bear turned about and headed down-slope to begin his chase of the fleeing Qa-ryks. The cleric waved as he passed, knowing that the were-bear would take care of the few remaining. Niet could make thrice the speed of the slow slogging beasts. He would catch each in turn and dispose of it.

Sart had come around the side of the hill when he caught sight of Ge-or lumbering above at the crest, swaying like he was drunk as he struggled ahead. The great man had run an incredible distance since leaving the ambush site; but as Sart watched, he saw him straighten, look out at the rising sun, and topple forward down the steep grassy slope. Sart spurred his horse to try to intercept Ge-or before he fell to the rocks below.

As chance would have it, Sart had just dismounted and come around a big pine tree when Ge-or's body, slowing as the slant of the hill lessened, tumbled into the hollow between the tree's roots. Sart was appalled by what he saw.

The half-elven warrior's entire body was covered with a mass of swollen long red pustules oozing yellowish-green matter. There were deeper cuts all along both his sides, legs, and arms. Some looked to have been cauterized with a burning brand and others to have been smeared with some pitch-like mud mixture. Ge-or's face and neck, spared whatever had damaged the rest of the body, were red and swollen, likely from the whipping of branches as he fled through the forest. Even the soles of his feet were almost in shreds, with mixtures of pine needles, sap, and dirt filling in the gaps where the skin had split open.

Sart knelt and immediately took a vial from his cloak. Taking Ge-or's head in his hands, he tilted it back, forced open his lips, and poured the entire contents into the half-elf's mouth. For an instant, Ge-or opened his eyes, swallowed, and then his head lolled sideways.

For the next two hours, the cleric ministered to the fallen warrior. More than once he wished he had borrowed the healing pendant from Jared; yet Sart had been too concerned with going after Ge-or to plan clearly, and perhaps it was best kept in the young lad's hands. Jared had taken grievous wounds himself.

Tired as he was from helping with everyone in their party and from the long ride through the night, Sart found deep reserves of strength to tend to the worst of Ge-or's wounds, using his healing powers to the limit of his own endurance. After that, with no more energy to give without rejuvenating, he dealt with what he could physically.

Of most concern was the fever and infection that the half-elf was fighting. Sart had medicines – tinctures, salves, potions, and herbal pastes he had mixed himself – that he knew were efficacious against wounds of this type. He also had herbal teas and medicines that could help with infection, but he had never seen anyone so completely ravaged by so many wounds and the contagion that followed. After resting for a half hour, he found a nearby stream at the bottom of the hill. He managed to pull the half-elf down to it. He bathed Ge-or's entire body, carefully cleaning out every cut and scrape. Finally he applied all the medicine he had.

It was nearing nightfall; and Sart had managed a few hours of fitful sleep, cradling Ge-or in his arms, when Niet came back looking pleased with himself. He grunted at Sart upon seeing Ge-or and looked sadly at his mentor.

"Yes, he is in a bad way, my friend. We will have to take extraordinary measures to see him through this. Are you capable of another full night and day of it, and perhaps several more? You will have to draw him on a sling behind."

"I go," Niet rumbled.

"Good. Let's get one made quickly. We will make for Aelfric. It is the closest place where we will find another competent cleric. Xur will not do. It is lucky that he covered so much ground to the north and east in his flight."

***

Four and a half days later, a large hairy man carried a shroud-wrapped body into an apothecary shop in the middle of Aelfric, followed by a well-known figure in those parts. The alchemist moon cleric, Zara, standing behind the counter came around immediately from where he was mixing a tincture to look at Sart's bundle. He frowned when he lifted the covering and saw how bad a shape the half-elf was in. He nodded and directed Niet to the back room.

Three days later, Sart, Zara, and their charge were on the road east and south to Efsted. Niet, uncomfortable in human form, had left the day before for the hills west of town to await Sart's next need of him.

Sart was taking no chances with Ge-or's condition. He and Zara would spend the long journey doing all they could to maintain the delicate balance of healing energy that had brought Ge-or back from death's door to the edge of survival.

Sart knew of a place along the coast that would be able to assist with Ge-or's further healing, and then care for the fallen warrior over the long months it would take for him to recuperate – but only if they were well paid. He would take care of the cost with money from the king's treasury; he doubted the king or any of his upper ministers would ever know.

***

After over a week recuperating in Xur, Jared and Elanar led their small band eastward toward Aelfric. An escort of Rux's Rangers accompanied them through the worst of the Qa-ryk range. They arrived at the border town as the first snow began to drift from the sky.

Sart had left a note for them with a local tavern keeper. In it, he let them know that Ge-or was alive, though in bad shape. And that he and Zara were personally taking him to a healing emporium in the southeast where he would receive the best of care. Sart had left word that he had heard from both Leonis and Meligance that Elanar, Joelin, Thistle, and Jared should head back to Borea with all speed. Stential, having received a sum Sart had left for him for his participation in the quest, decided to remain in Aelfric looking for additional work.

A-Barding We Will Go

Five weeks later, they were back in Borea for the winter. Thankfully, they all were given a long week to simply relax and shake off the residual effects of their adventure before they were required to assume other duties. Jared, Elanar, and Joelin settled into Bard Hall. For now, Thistle decided to return to her rooms at the palace. Three days after returning, the newlyweds began a search for suitable lodging in the city.

The first snow of the season was beginning to blanket Borea when Jared, Thistle, and Elanar were called to a special meeting at Bard Hall with Leonis. Sart, who had finally returned from the south, greeted them with great hugs as they entered the grandmaster's study. Though he had kept them informed through Meligance of Ge-or's condition, he nodded to Jared after their embrace. "He is improving, slowly. I will speak of his condition more after this meeting. There are a few concerns we should discuss."

Just then, Meligance came in, looking ever regal and in control. She nodded graciously to each. When all had settled, the White Wizardess held the floor.

"My condolences to you all for the loss of cherished companions." Meligance bowed toward Elanar, to acknowledge his deep loss of a longtime friend and comrade. "I also congratulate all of you on the completion of a difficult, but successful venture. Both Leonis and I are more than pleased with your efforts and personal growth.

"Thistle and Jared, we also wish to offer our sincere joy at your marriage. Before we get to the business at hand, we three have conspired to give you a small gift as a token of our esteem and caring. Leonis…"

Leonis stood and took a large silken-wrapped package from the stand set next to the table around which they were seated. "It is a trifle from us and from your good friends who are currently afield. They will return to wish you well themselves." He handed the package to Thistle.

The two unwrapped it together and found a red leather, gold-embossed, newly bound tome entitled, "The Folksongs of the North, as Gathered by Karenna and Simon-Nathan the XI of Borea." Opening the book past the title page, they could see Karenna's fine hand on the first of the vellum manuscript pages. The first song in the book was the madrigal, entitled "Love is the Joy of Springtime."

"It is beautiful," Jared managed to stammer out. Thistle, with tears in her eyes, added, "We will always treasure it. Thank you."

A few minutes later, after they had a chance to admire the fine volume, Meligance brought them all back to focus on the future. "What you have all shared about your recent experiences in the west has caused a great deal of consternation to those few who have been given privilege to the information. This portends a great many things that could have an impact on the empire over the course of the next few years. I have held council with the king and a few of his inner circle of advisors that I trust will keep this news secret.

"First, there is ample evidence that some powerful evil artifact resided in the dungeon beneath Kan's fortress for all the years since his defeat. We know he had the Black Diamond. What has become of it? That, we do not know. Though we have a few ideas, there is far too much about Kan and what happened to him that we do not ken. We also know that the Black Druids have derived some of their power from that dark place. For years they used Kan's altar for their own devices. There are other evils growing in the west as well. Whether these are under the influence of the Black Druids or others, we do not know. Darkness grows in the south, closer to Aelfric and Aube than ever before. Mostly we have only the rumors of evil spreading slowly out from a center south and east of Xur. We must trace what few threads we have by searching the archives throughout the kingdom. Little has been preserved from Kan's era, yet we must try and find out what we can. This will be both Sart's and my primary focus in the months to come.

"Secondly, the abominations you faced in the dungeon are a serious threat not only to the kingdom, but to the entire world of living creatures. If these beasts – perhaps we should call them demons, for they seem to resemble nightmarish creatures of our imaginations – should figure out a way to survive above ground or expand their range underground, there could be widespread devastation. We will need to learn how to fight these things and to rid our world of them.

"Finally, by all accounts coming in from the west, the Qa-ryks are active again and continuing to expand their range. Rux has reported many more clans filtering eastward, and he has had to draw in his patrols closer to Xur to keep them safe. For whatever reason, the Black Druids have drawn back and allowed the beasts to proliferate and return to their clannish roots. They are no threat to Xur, for the stronghold can withstand a major force; nevertheless, they will become a danger to every farm, hamlet, and village west of the King's Wall, including the coastal villages, and perhaps even border towns like Aelfric and Aube.

"Hence," Meligance nodded toward the three sitting opposite their elders at the rectangular table, "we need eyes, ears, and power in the west." She gestured toward Leonis and Sart. "We have discussed this for many hours and have decided that the three of you should continue your education at Xur." Meligance paused to let that information sink in.

Jared blinked several times as if he hadn't heard the Wizardess correctly. He had longed to return to the wilderness outpost at some point in his educational experiences that would lead to his becoming a Bard, yet he had not thought to request it this early in his Apprenticeship. Thistle took Jared's hand and squeezed it. He knew she had wanted to return to Xur as well. Elanar shook his head as if he had heard something altogether unbelievable.

Meligance went on. "Please understand that this is a choice. We do not dictate that you accept such a difficult assignment. Think carefully, for it will be two years or more before you return to the east. In that time, Sart and I hope to find some answers so that another incursion into Kan's dungeons may be possible." Meligance paused again and looked at each of them in turn.

It was Thistle who stood and spoke first. "I will accept this post if Jared is willing. On this recent quest, I realized how much I have to learn; and experience is what I need more than anything. I come from the west; and the life-style, while it will be a change from all I have enjoyed at the palace under your tutelage, milady," she nodded a grateful bow toward her mentor, "will be more to my liking, because it is part of my roots."

Jared stood while she was talking, putting his arm around her waist as she finished. "I, too, relish a chance to go back to the west. There is something in me that speaks of adventure and action. The life suits. I would be honored to be part of Rux's Demons." He referred to the original appellation he had heard in reference to the "bandits" that occupied the stronghold in the center of Qa-ryk country. "But I must defer to Elanar and his decision, as he would be my mentor. I understand the placement is not typical of one elevated to Bard."

Elanar stood and bowed to each person at the table ending with Meligance. He looked her in the eye. "I am honored by this posting. There are many reasons for me to remain in Borea, and it will be difficult to leave; yet I know I can learn much in the field. There were difficulties and losses that were hard to bear on our recent quest, yet I have realized that I long to be where the action is. I have come to understand that the life I led in Moulanes with my former brethren – one filled with peace, solitude, and beauty, one that I have for years longed to return to – is only half of a life. For me, born and raised there, I had no ken of what lay beyond.

"For too many years I resisted anything that infringed on the quietus within me. Now I understand something I did not before. Because of friends like Jared, Thistle, Sart, and the others I have spent long hours with on the trail, I see that life is so much more than meditation and exclusivity. I have also come to understand that peace within comes at a cost sometimes – it is so much more valuable when one has something to contrast it to.

"I accept as well. It will be a great honor to work further with the friends and companions I have come to trust and care for. It will be an honor to serve." He bowed low; then he sat, as did Thistle and Jared.

"Good. It is decided. There is only one key caveat – your mission is to observe and report. No one," Meligance paused for emphasis, "is to return to the dungeons beneath Kan's palace. At least, not until we know more. The danger is too great. However, I will promise this – when the time comes to revisit those depths, you three will be offered the opportunity to be part of that quest. Am I understood?"

They each nodded as Meligance's eyes locked on theirs.

"Good, I will leave you in the hands of our dear cleric to discuss details. Though we would wish that you could all leave immediately, the winter is nigh upon us; and the western hills and passes will be covered in snow. Each of you will be assigned study tasks over the next months. You will ride west as spring approaches." Meligance rose; everyone followed suit. She bowed slightly to Leonis and Sart and nodded to the three adventurers across from her. She swept, elegantly as always, from the room.

In spite of being busy with new studies and other efforts, once Karenna and Simon-Nathan returned to Borea they managed to pull together one weekend in which to have a party to celebrate Thistle and Jared's marriage. Simon-the-Elder wanted to throw a massive affair; in the end, they settled for a joyous weekend at the merchant's large mansion, where they rejoiced with their good friends and indulged in good wine, good food, and of course, good music.

Jared was given advanced instruction in Bard Lore, as Sart had spoken to Leonis about the healing he had done in the Bendir camp. He discovered that much of what he was learning crossed over into work with semi or pseudo-religious overtones. While there was ample evidence that music was a powerful contributor to mood and even could facilitate healing, when one took it to the next level, there seemed to be a gray area that spoke to "natural talent" rather than a learned skill or ability. He was told that he would be able to study this even further when he returned following his Apprenticeship.

Thistle concentrated on her work with vibrational frequencies and her ability to shift to other planes. She worked specifically on understanding her capabilities while she was in a parallel realm. Meligance finally had to warn her that too much of such work held other risks, including becoming infatuated with the sense of power it gave you, as well as other reasons that she would have to discover on her own. Thereafter, Thistle backed off and spent time practicing many of the skills and techniques that had become part of her repertoire. The experiences of their recent adventure taught her that to fully understand her power, limitations, abilities, and skills, she would need to push herself until everything she did could be done almost without thinking.

Elanar continued the required studies of a newly anointed Bard. There were classes and tutoring on politics and intrigue, teaching, clandestine communications, and so on. His head was spinning when they finally took to the road, and his saddlebags were stuffed with additional required readings.

They received regular updates about Ge-or's condition from the south, the last being a note written by Ge-or himself. The missive had been short and in an almost child-like scribble. Sart delivered it himself, having gone down to see him on a circuitous route to Aelfric. Ge-or's note simply said that he was recovering, and that he was sorry and sad to have missed connecting with them. Sart, when queried, had to admit he had to force Ge-or to write something. His mood varied so much from day to day that the cleric was seriously concerned for his full recovery.

*****

Ge-or was fuming. He hated being cooped up, even though it was for his own good. It had taken long months for his entire body to overcome the ill effects of the poisons and toxins running rampant from the many infections he had suffered. He had numerous clerical healings, swallowed far too many doses of potions, herbal teas, and the like, and had a myriad of tinctures, salves, and pastes smeared on his body – all in the guise of his recovery and health. He supposed, since Sart was at the root of everything they did to him, that it was indeed for his own good; yet he was tired of it all.

Worst of all was the persisting weakness. For three months, he could not get out of bed. He actually counted himself lucky that he had been delirious much of the first two months. Even after that, it had been a major trial, with the help of two strong assistants, to use the bedpan or to make it three steps to a chair with support, where he would sit for long hours looking out at the sea.

Now that he was improving, and he could walk the ten paces to sit outside, he recognized that his full recovery would take many more months. It would be a full year or more to recover even a semblance of his former strength and prowess. It was frustrating to him, a person who liked to always be doing, always be active, always be into something.

He had taken to reading – something that he had been taught by his mother, but had never spent much time at. Unfortunately, even that was becoming too mundane. Sart had brought him books, as had the nursing staff: on weaponry, siege engines, war strategy, types of armor, defensive and offensive strategies for fighting creatures of all types – some no longer found in Borea -- plants, herbs, husbandry, philosophy and religion, sailing, even cooking, and many other topics. He read them all, more for something to do than for any enthusiasm he had for any of the topics.

He pushed himself physically, too, as much as the healers, nurses, and attendants would allow. There was always someone about. It was part of the service. Still, his heart wasn't really in it; and while everyone was kind to him, their interest in him was always superficial, or so he felt. He was so weak and helpless that some days all he would do was sit and doze at the window. After a long while, lethargy took hold; and though Ge-or still went through the motions of repairing his body, something inside had shut down.

***

It was early in the spring when Thistle, Jared, and Elanar met Sart and Niet in Aelfric for the trek westward. "I am a bit worried, Jared," Sart said as they rode west. "Your brother was always so full of fight before. And while he says he wants to get back to where he was before this happened, and he appears to make an effort, there is something missing. He won't talk about it, even to me. He has shut the doors in his mind to what happened whilst he was captured. I think it drags at him."

"Perhaps Thistle and I should visit him. Before, it seemed that we would have only been a further burden, interrupting the work of the healers there. Now that he is out of bed and alert, wouldn't our presence help?"

"I had wondered about suggesting exactly this to Meligance and delay this riding to Xur, yet, I do not think he would wish to be seen this way. He puts up with me because I have seen him since the very beginning, at the worst of it. I think he is embarrassed by his condition, greatly embarrassed.

"There is something else that drags at him now that his wounds are mostly healed. I do not see the life, the fight he had. Much of the time, he stares into space and frowns. It is hard to get him to respond to anything you say; and when he does, it is mostly with grunts."

"Yes, I can understand that side of my brother. He was ever stubborn and would hold things close to his chest. He is in good hands? In the right place?"

"For the present. I do have plans to move him to a recovery home for fighters – perhaps to Aelfric, maybe elsewhere. There at least he will be able to get a sense of the west and all that he loves about being in the field. Maybe it will be the tonic he needs. That move, however, is still months away. He needs to recover his physical strength enough to get around on his own. He works his body, yet I see no joy in it. He used to love to spend hours at the blocks or sparring."

"You said he has money?"

"Aye, a decent sum with the moneylenders in Aelfric. He left some equipment there as well. He lost all he had with him to the Qa-ryks, including quality leather armor, a fine blade, and other equipment. He will need to regroup. The dragon and your father's sword still burn in his breast or did before this happened. Perhaps, if I can reawaken that sense of duty and honor in him, he will bounce back."

"It seems so long ago now that we lost so much. You are right; the dragon may be the focus he needs to regain his sense of self and purpose."

Sart's face was set in a deep frown. He was silent for a while. Finally, he managed a slight smile. "Fear not, Jared; I will find a way to get him back on the trail. We will need his like before long. He is the finest warrior I have ever seen. Your father trained you both well."

"Aye."

The two let the conversation lapse as they rode on toward the sunset. For Jared, a new life beckoned out in the wilds, a life with his young wife. For Sart, it was another trek to be returned from so that he could start yet another. For both, there appeared to be a larger purpose that drove them; yet, if one had asked, today they would have had trouble putting it into words.

***

Upon arriving in Aelfric on his return from Xur, Sart's next mission was something he had promised Ge-or. It was one thing that Sart felt would help ease a bit of the burden the half-elf was carrying regarding the death of his partner and his own capture. He visited a sanatorium there and spoke at some length with the director. The place was one of the most well-run he had ever seen. It was clean, the clientele was well cared for, and though furnishings and amenities were sparse, no one was suffering ill treatment.

Sart went to several moneylenders and set up withdrawal accounts based on information that he had received from Ge-or. Finally, he returned to the facility and met with the director once more. Stradryk had asked Ge-or to ensure that his son, who Sart discovered was named Ardryk, would be taken care of for the rest of his life. Sart examined the half-gzk's ample bank accounts and determined that not only could the funds help keep the disabled boy in good stead, with careful planning and use of the interest and part of the principle, the whole facility could be upgraded. Ge-or wanted to donate his own remaining funds to the cause as well. Sart managed to convince him to hold on to half of his monies, so he could reequip himself when he was ready. Sart had promised to make a donation himself to equal the difference.

When he was satisfied that all was in good order, he sent word to Ge-or, promising to check in on the young lad every time he was in the border town. Finally, when all had been done to his satisfaction, he rode north and east to Borea to return to his work with Meligance.

Recovery

He took long walks on the beach with no purpose in mind except to walk. He also did all they told him to do relevant to his recovery, but no more. Often the nurses would look out and see a lonely skiff far offshore. It would be Ge-or fishing. The fresh striped bass, cod, blue fish, and tuna he brought in, depending on what was running, were all appreciated by the cooking staff. Yet, it concerned everyone that when he came in, he would lay his catch down without a comment or a smile and return to his room and his piles of books.

He did not engage anyone. Even when asked direct questions, he would typically nod or shake his head, or if it required, give one or two-word grunting responses. He went through all the motions of living – his body responding as it should, or as he willed it to – with no emotion in anything he did.

By mid-summer the healers pronounced him whole in body. He had even returned to some degree of fitness with his many walking and fishing excursions. Otherwise, he avoided the workout yard and all weapons, even though they were available if he wanted to make the effort to return to fighting trim.

Sart, visiting at the end of one of his quests to the south, talked with the staff about moving him that fall. He listened carefully to their concerns about Ge-or's mental and emotional health; nevertheless, he was not convinced that staying in the seaside sanatorium was best for Ge-or now that his body was sound. He decided to bring the case up with Meligance.

***

"He is cured? No residual effects of the toxins?"

"I examined him carefully myself. I went within and scanned him with my power. Everything appears to be functioning as it should. He has taken to long walks and rowing about the bay in a small skiff. He is fit, trim, and tanned, yet has no interest in getting back into fighting shape.

"He doesn't react to anything: news, others' emotions, jokes, even talk of women. I tried to interest him in what his brother was up to; he only nodded."

"Women?" Meligance asked, raising her eyebrows. "Though in some ways I am loathe to suggest it, that may be an avenue to pursue. Will the clinic allow female companionship for the patient's health?"

"Wives, girl-friends, no others. They are picky about such things; but with what we pay them, rules could be stretched or even broken."

"Does, or did, Ge-or have anyone special?"

"He has had many lovers; I know of two that he spent a good bit of time with. One has disappeared since; the other is the young illusionist, Katelyn."

"Yes, I remember her. Studied with Hasfust. She has some talent. What do you think?"

"It is an idea. I had not considered talking with her."

"Do so. If she is willing to go see him, maybe it will be just the tonic he needs."

***

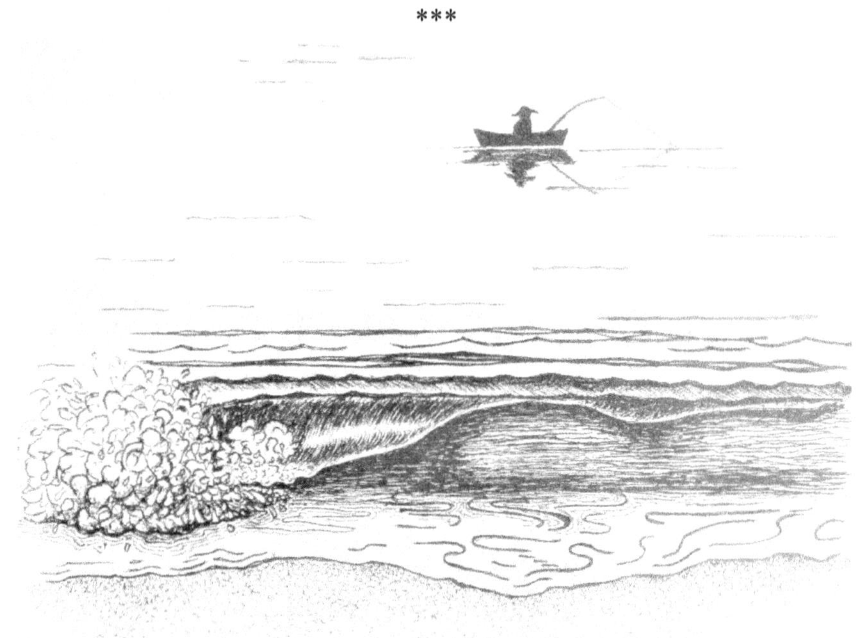

"I am sorry, Sart. He acted genuinely glad to see me, or at least he said so. But there was no life in him. We talked… well, mostly I talked, and he listened. We spent several days walking on the beach, reading together, sitting; yet he never was truly interested in anything we talked about. It was as if it was all right for me to be there, yet it didn't really matter one way or another."

"And?"

Katelyn blushed. "I made the effort. At first I tried to be coy and suggestive; he did not respond. He did not want to be touched. He would brush off my hand. Finally, I got pretty blatant about what I wanted. He would turn away. Frankly, it was embarrassing."

"I'm sorry. It was important to try."

Tears came to Katelyn's eyes. "I care for him, Sart. He was always kind and generous to me and… and gentle in spite of his strength. I would go back if you ask me; however, I don't think it will help. He is lost to me right now."

Sart put his arms on her shoulders and drew her into a fatherly hug. "He will come around, my child; do not be too distressed. There is life in him yet, I can sense it when I am with him. Something smolders beneath the surface. We need to find the right catalyst to bring it forth."

Xur

Thistle, Jared, Elanar, and Alicia settled in to the rigors of the western outpost. Thistle had been especially surprised when her handmaiden had insisted on going with her. She had explained the difficulties they would face and the long time they would likely be away; still, Alicia had wanted to remain with her mistress.

At Xur Thistle insisted that "Alli" take her place amongst the other inhabitants. Alicia readily acclimated to the differences in their life and in her relationship to Thistle. Her mentor agreeing readily to her former handmaiden's shy request to begin using her birth name. Xur was a place of equals. Alicia quickly made friends and became involved in many facets of the workings of the fort. She was especially fascinated with weaving, since visiting the museum dedicated to the craft in Borea; and it turned out she was talented at bringing flax and wool through the many processes until it was ready for the loom. Before a year was out, she was considered the key person to ask about anything associated with the production of cloth and clothing for the inhabitants.

Elanar and Jared both took on the duties of Barding. Elanar was a great teller of epic tales, which became a once-a-week evening's entertainment when neither he nor Jared were singing. And at least a couple evenings a week, Jared would take the front and improvise on portative harp, lute, and even the beautiful Anu gifted him from the Slivs.

Though he was not strictly in the employ of the Army of Borea, later that year Jared was promoted to vice-commander and master-at-arms of the regiment. His new duties included overseeing the weapons training of all the inhabitants of the fort. He was busier than ever, but so was Thistle.

Jared still found time to practice his improvisations and his love of entwining the old music with the new harmonies at the root. As he set his fingers to the strings of his lute or lyre, he found new ways to twist the melodies and chordal structures to produce a particular feeling, a mood, or a balance whenever it was needed.

Now, instead of changing guards on a bi-weekly basis, Rux sent a strong patrol out for four-week stints at the ruins. There they built a reinforced redoubt out of the granite rocks lying about the base of the mountain. Thistle, Jared, and Elanar became key figures in leading these regular expeditions.

Elanar focused more and more on his work as a leader and fighter. He had taken to heart Jared's knowledge of all things related to weapons, and he worked hard to practice at every opportunity to gain further expertise. And though he missed Simon-Nathan's sister, Athena, of whom he had grown quite fond, Elanar seemed to have finally found a life experience that spoke to his soul.

Since the attack on the fort years before, which Sart, Thistle, and Jared had been involved in, Rux had requested and received a magic-user. Domast helped to add another dimension to the garrison's defenses and also its offensive capabilities. Unfortunately, the fellow was a middle-aged curmudgeon who did not fit in well with the easy-going populace of Xur. He became even more withdrawn and obstinate when Thistle showed up. He instantly recognized how much more power she wielded than he. Having failed to gain Wizard status years before, he was immediately jealous of her position.

Thistle tried to befriend him and even offered to work with him on improving his skills; he actually turned his back on her, an act that might have warranted him a warm backside from a bolt of power had he dared to try such a thing with Meligance. As it was, he refused to speak with any of the new arrivals. He performed his duties as directed by Rux, yet otherwise kept to himself. Thistle and Jared regretted that they could not gain his trust and friendship, and eventually they let him be.

With the new worries associated with Kan's dungeons, Meligance wanted a mage or cleric present at the ruins continuously. Thus, it fell to Thistle, Domast, and a young priest named Fafher, who had joined the fort the previous fall, to be co-leaders of the expeditions. They would be able to sense any change in the magical aura surrounding the place, and most importantly witness whether the "nightshades," as Elanar had come to call the goblinesque creatures, ever came forth.

Very little was ever mundane or routine in the wilderness. They all became acclimated to their duties and made the most of the situation as it presented itself. Everyone pitched in with almost everything; and in spite of the heavy workloads, there was always time for relaxation, music, games, and storytelling.

Thistle was pleasantly surprised when her former handmaiden began spending time with a young soldier, new to the fort. She and Brandir were often seen together at evenings' entertainments.

The young Wizardess continued her examination of the world of energy and magic associated with different planes or vibrational levels. She discovered that if she refocused immediately when moving into another plane or realm, most of her magical power and abilities were still available to her. Of particular importance was that the same use of energy in her plane often acted differently in another. Thus, the fire of her world might be a relatively benign occurrence, and hence no threat, to the inhabitants of a parallel plane. However, wherever she went, energy was still energy, and that served as the foundation for what she could understand within another plane and what she could do there.

Thistle became adept at knowing how to shift from this world to a specific plane nearby by controlling her vibrational frequency precisely. More importantly, she explored what type of protection she might need on another plane, as changing her own frequency did not necessarily mean she adapted completely to a new environment which might very well be hazardous to her form. She came to realize that most of the time it was far safer to be only partially in sync with another plane's vibrations, because it kept the adverse effects of a dire place predominantly at bay; yet, she could still observe and learn while in a semi-material state. It was much like when she became invisible in her own world.

Most importantly, she came to better understand the vastness of the universe and the incomprehensible nature of energy itself. Infinity seemed too limited a word to describe all she understood to be possible. She realized that in spite of her ability to connect and work with vast amounts of energy, she knew little about how it really worked at the deepest levels. Several times, she went as deep as she had the time one tress of her hair had turned prematurely white. She did not attempt to interact with the what she thought of as obverse energy – energy directly opposite of, and hence dangerous, to their world; but she spent a good bit of time observing its nature.

What came to influence her magic, and helped her expand her capabilities more than anything, was her realization that she had finally found one of the things she had been seeking for some time. It came in the form of an old, giant, black walnut tree that stood at one of the crossroads leading to Kan's ruins. They had often passed the majestic tree; nevertheless, on this one eve, as she and Jared were heading out for a four-week stint at the redoubt, she stopped, suddenly drawn to it.

"That one!" she said to Jared, as they looked up into the array of branches. She pointed above to a branch that thrust out from the main core of the tree toward them. "Stand back and watch."

Using her magic, she excised the branch from the tree, tracing the threads of its power into its heart and gently pulling out each fiber until she held the one-and-a-half-inch thick, five-foot long branch in her hand. With a deft use of magic, she drew in the tendrils she had drawn from the heart end and folded them in on themselves until they formed a knot at the one end of the staff. As they began to curl in upon themselves, she took something from the pouch at her side and placed it amongst the enfolding wood. It was a large blue sapphire, given to her by Meligance for just such a purpose.

When she was done, she smiled at Jared and raised the wood above her head, brandishing it for the entire astounded patrol to see. "The Wizardess has her staff!"

It had been a dreary night over a year before when Meligance had called Thistle to her studio and instructed her on finding and preparing a staff. She had specified two key components to Thistle's search. "Find a tree that speaks to you. When you have pulled forth a branch from its center, blend this stone into its heart strands. It is called a dragon's eye. I have saved it for many years for an apprentice, should I take one on. The sapphire speaks to you, Thistle. It is your color and your fire.

"As you know, gemstones can hold immense concentrations of energy. Once you have selected and created your staff, it will be a lifelong quest to build into it that which will be most useful to you as a mage. Different stones hold different forms of energy, different foci. You will discover that as you proceed.

"You will also find that the wood itself will provide its own source of power, and an extra, different, storage medium as well. It does not hold as much power as a gemstone, but it will support and add to what you mold it into. Different woods act in different ways, too; that is why you must find the right tree. Let it draw you in; then you will know."

"As you may have noticed, child, my staff has a diamond – the purest form of energy manifested as matter. My staff is oak – a thing of strength and resilience. The sapphire also holds pure energy, with different leanings. Discover its truths and understand the wood you choose. If you pay attention, you will ken its value and quality."

Jared would have sworn that her eyes shown with a slightly different light from that day forth. There was a blue fire deep within them that merged with her natural green, which was somehow deeper and brighter than ever.

A major event at Xur that spring was the marriage of Alicia to Brandir. It was a beautiful ceremony at a beautiful time of year and a joyous time, especially for Thistle. Handmaiden no more, Alicia was now a confident woman who had made her home in the wilderness fort. She grew into the role of managing the handling and weaving of all types of cloth, and the quality of clothing produced at the fort rose exponentially as a result of her efforts. With her young soldier, they made Xur their home and hoped to start a family.

Jared and Thistle, Elanar, and Alicia's tenure at Xur stretched on with little changing except the seasons. As in any wilderness village or outpost, there was always much to do. They fell into the difficult work of surviving the vagaries of weather and the ever-present dangers of being deep within Qa-ryk lands.

It wasn't until the fall that Sart finally decided to yank Ge-or from the "all too comfortable" surrounds of the sea-coast sanatorium and bring him west. Ge-or did not protest or even react to Sart's proposal to move him to a fighters' recovery house in Aelfric. He simply went along as he was requested. It was the healers and nurses of the establishment that were reluctant to let him go. Sart, however, did not feel as if they truly had the great warrior's recovery in mind as the primary reason – he was an ideal patient who caused few problems; and they were drawing in large sums of money for his care.

Not that the facility in Aelfric would be much less expensive. That was not the issue for Sart. He wanted to try to stimulate Ge-or into snapping out of his lethargy. He hoped that being amongst other recovering fighters, adventurers, and soldiers would somehow give Ge-or the impetus to at least pick up a sword again and make an effort on his own behalf. He was not altogether sure it would work.

Sart tried hard on the three-week ride north and west to engage Ge-or in any sort of conversation. Ge-or simply followed along, did what he was told, nodded or shook his head at questions, but was not interested in anything. Even more curiously, though Sart made them available, he wanted nothing to do with weapons. The only thing he carried was a utility knife, which he used for eating or other tasks he was given by the cleric.

***

The Fighter's Retreat was an old manor set on the northeast side of Aelfric that had been specifically designed for convalescing warriors. It had seen better days, yet was still a solid stone building with semi-comfortable rooms. The most important feature was that it had a full-blown workout and sparring facility, both outdoors, which included a shooting range, and indoor rooms for sparring and working out in the winter.

Ge-or and Sart were given the full tour by the master-at-arms. Ge-or showed no interest in what was available. When he was shown his room, he put his few belongings in the small closet, set his saddlebags, half filled with books, on the dressing table, and sat on the edge of the bed looking out toward the hills from his single window. He didn't even say goodbye to Sart.

There were no scheduled activities or requirements at the Fighter's Retreat, so Ge-or was free to do as he pleased. Sart received reports from the master-at-arms that the "big fella" seemed content to read, wander about town,

213

and end his days sitting in the Blue Bell tavern across the way. There he would sit by himself, drink ale for several hours, and eventually find his way back to his room. "In-his-cups, but not excessively drunk," was the official report.

He stayed away from the workout areas. However, even in the worst weather, he continued to wander about the town. He ate when meals were provided, or when he got the notion that it was time. Nothing else penetrated his shell.

It was midwinter when something happened that not even Sart could have thought to plan. It was the evening of an especially crisp day; Ge-or had diverted slightly from his regular routine by ordering hot rum instead of the local brew. He was well into his second mug when a small, lithe figure, dressed in a hooded grey cloak, slipped onto the bench across the table from him. Ge-or looked up over the lip of his tankard at the little man and mumbled, "Mine." He waved with his hand for the fellow to leave.

The small man stayed where he was. He pushed his hood back, revealing a roundish face, a small wisp of a reddish goatee of a beard, and bright red, shoulder-length hair. He smiled at Ge-or; and pulling a dagger from somewhere about the folds of his cloak, he begin playing with it, twirling it about his fingers.

It took Ge-or a minute; when he finally focused on the blade his eyes suddenly displayed more alertness and interest than they had in many a month. "Hey, that's mine," he accused the sea-elf, for he could see that the man in front of him was at least partially of that heritage. The words came out in a half-croak, as if his voice was rusty from not having been used. In fact, it was the first time in over a year that he had spoken three words consecutively.

"Was yours," the man across from him retorted, smiling brightly. "Finders-Keepers!" Ge-or now recognized the subtle differences in the man's appearance that suggested he was of mixed breed, most especially, that he was small for a man, yet tall for a sea-elf.

"You stole it." Something in Ge-or was awakening further. He half-rose, growling as he did so.

The half sea-elf waved him down and plunked the dagger onto the table with a quick flip of his wrist. The blade stuck in the wood, in the exact center of the table. Ge-or reached for it; the sea-elf-kin waved him back with his hand, still grinning impishly. Ge-or glowered at him but sat back down and stared hard into the other fellow's eyes.

"You have to earn it back."

"I'm not interested. I'll take it." Ge-or reached out again with his hand; half-way to the blade he stopped, noticing that the fellow now held a ring he recognized in his fingers.

Ge-or exploded at seeing his mother's ring in the other's hands. He roared loudly, pushing up from the table so quickly that his bench tipped over behind him. He reached out again for the blade, intent on skewering the small man in front of him and gathering back the one possession that he had never let anyone else handle, which, until a short while ago, he had believed was still on his left little finger.

As fast as Ge-or was, he was out of practice. The little man had the dagger in hand and up against Ge-or's throat in a trice. Ge-or growled, glaring at the fellow, but he knew he was bested. His antagonist was good, and from what he had witnessed, not only a thief – likely a master at that dubious trade and profession. He might even be an assassin. Ge-or stood without moving, waiting for an opening.

"Sit!" The thief withdrew the blade and pointed at Ge-or's bench with it. He waited while his opponent reset it and settled back, still glaring at the part sea-elf.

"My name is Slyn," the small man began. "The ring you can have back now. I can see it has some import to you. The dagger I keep until… well, let us discuss that." He spun the ring onto the table so that it twirled toward Ge-or. The big man snatched it up, examined it carefully, and when satisfied, slipped it back onto his little finger. Slyn sat back down across from Ge-or and again twirled the blade dexterously with his fingers.

"I am a Master Thief by profession, as you may have surmised. Please understand, I do not trek with the rabble around here. I am an independent, shall we say. I, like you," he pointed the blade at Ge-or's chest, "have been on an adventure or two. They are more hazardous, perhaps, yet more fun than pilfering from wine merchants or dandies." He cleared his throat more as an affectation than for need. He wanted to be sure he had Ge-or's attention.

"I'll be blunt. I need a partner for another venture. I chose you."

"Not interested," Ge-or growled. He kept his eyes glued to the half-elf's.

"That we shall see. You seek to conquer an old red, I hear."

Ge-or was surprised to hear that the thief knew of his quest, and at that moment something deep within his being opened back up and became accessible to his consciousness. He thought, Who had spoken of his search? That meddler Sart? Or… Ordrake? Or… Well, there were any number who knew. He had not kept it much of a secret.

"I can help," Slyn continued. "Together we can retrieve your father's sword and become quite rich in the bargain. From what I hear, dragons love things bright and beautiful, gold, jewels, and the like. First, another little quest so we can garner enough wealth to equip for going after the beast. Here's the deal…" Slyn lay the dagger down in front of him, point to the side, and spread his hands on the table.

"I will return in two months. If you are fit – back to fighting prowess by that time – you may have your dagger back. Then I will consider taking you on this little adventure I have in mind. If all goes according to plan, we will net some quality goods in the haul. We will have what we need for the main thrust – the pursuit of your dragon.

"You need not agree now. Be ready when I return, and I will take that as your answer. If not, well, I suspect you will have no use for this anyway." He picked up Ge-or's knife and deftly pocketed the blade somewhere beneath his cloak. He stood. "Don't try to find me. I will find you. Two months. You have a great deal of work to do. You have become soft and slow." He left as quietly as he had come, slipping from the tavern. Ge-or sat there for a long while, stunned.

The next day Ge-or was outside at the blocks in spite of the frigid temperatures.

He changed his routine after that in several other ways as well. He never again went back to the Blue Bell, though he occasionally wandered into the south and west of Aelfric to his old haunt, the Druid's Hut. He also made it a point to visit Stradryk's son at least once a week.

Life Is Tough

Ge-or discovered how much he had lost in the intervening months since he had been ill. In spite of his long walks, regular fishing trips in the small skiff, and the work he had done physically in the sanatorium under the guidance of the staff, he was nowhere close to being in fighting shape. Yet something had woken in him; and now there was a deep burning in his gut that drove him into the yard every day, twice a day, in spite of sore and aching muscles, the blisters that were reluctant to turn into calluses, and the stiffness of joints long unused.

He was well into his third week of exercise when he discovered, through a discussion with the master-at-arms, that there was a massage parlor down the street that catered to just such a need as his. They were not "purveyors of sin," as the devoutly religious ex-soldier referred to the other types of massages available in the border town. However, the burly man said they could be quite good for aches and sore muscles.

Ge-or went to the place reluctantly. Once there, he spent an hour in agony under the ministrations of a diminutive lady who appeared to enjoy inflicting pain. When he discovered the next day how much freer he felt while working the blocks, he went again a few days later. From that point on, he included regular visits there as part of his routine.

He worked out on his own for a full month before seeking out sparring partners. Even off his feed, Ge-or was better than the best of the fighters housed at the manor; so he engaged the master-at-arms, who, although well past his prime, had been a competent swordsman in the King's Guard. Thrice a week they would spend an hour together working with swords, bucklers, and knives. It was another form of tonic that Ge-or needed desperately – engaging another being.

Sart came for a visit as the spring thaw was starting in earnest. Ge-or was greatly embarrassed to see him; however, he swallowed his pride and begged the cleric's forgiveness.

"There is no need, my friend. You were gravely ill, both in body and soul. I am simply glad to see that you have turned the corner."

"I cannot thank you and Niet enough, or the other priest who..."

"Zara," Sart said. "He is a Moon cleric, as well as an alchemist and a close comrade of mine."

"Please thank him for me. I could not have gone further. You both brought me back."

"Truly, my good half-elf, I have never seen anyone with wounds as grievous as you had survive, even with healing and competent medical help. You have an amazing constitution and a powerful will. Else you would not have made it.

"Would you care to talk about your experiences? It would be good to unburden your soul."

Ge-or's face darkened and he bowed his head. He sat still for such a long time, that Sart began to worry that he had pushed too hard and sent him back into whatever space he had been in for so long. After a few minutes, the great warrior took a deep breath, raised his head and shook it. "I am not ready. The memories are too fresh."

Sart nodded, placing his hand on Ge-or's shoulder. "In due time, then. Come, let us have a couple of ales together. I must be off on the morrow; duties call."

The two spent the evening together and stayed well into the night talking of many things. Ge-or told Sart that he remembered everything during his convalescence, describing what had seemed like a long dream he had been in. He had not been able to break out of the haze and had not had any great reason, or so he felt at the time, to make an effort to do so. He asked the cleric to apologize to Katelyn for him and to tell her that he hoped they would meet again. At that, Sart blushed, deeply chagrinned at having arranged the whole debacle.

They also spoke of Jared and his wife and the posting he had received to Xur. Ge-or was sad that he had once again missed his brother. He resolved to stop by the frontier outpost when he next set out for the west on his quest for his father's sword.

Finally, as Sart indicated he would need to leave soon, Ge-or asked him about the thief who had come to him.

"Nay, I have not met him, Ge-or, though he has a reputation in these parts to be sure. He is one of the best of that maligned profession, or so I have been told. He doesn't truck with the organized elements in Aelfric ruled by..."

"Spyder?" Ge-or interrupted Sart.

"Aye. A nasty sort, he is. I see you have been versed on..."

"Stradryk taught me such things when we first met. I..." Ge-or interrupted again, but stopped suddenly.

This time Sart knew enough to let Ge-or continue or not. When he didn't, Sart went on. "Some here might even consider it an honor to have Slyn steal from them, as it indicates that they have become wealthy enough to warrant his attention. He is, by reputation, an honest thief, Ge-or, if there is one. That is, he believes in honor amongst his friends and allies. You could do worse for a partner. It is interesting that he came to you.”

“He spoke of the dragon and the treasure the beast guards.”

“Aye, it is true that dragons have great treasures, or so the old lore tells us. Slyn could have quite a comfortable living without so much danger involved. There must be something more, perhaps a specific item?”

“He mentioned none.”

“Nor would he. He would need to get to know you and trust you. You will find that the best of the independent thieves are loyal to a fault, but one needs to earn that loyalty.”

“You think I should go with him?”

“Did he mention the goal?”

“Nay, nor where.”

“True to form. Certainly, hear him out, Ge-or. If you feel comfortable and well enough, go. It would be good for you to get back out in the field, and perhaps it is time you got your father’s sword back after all. We will need power weapons in the hands of fine warriors before too long.”

Ge-or raised his eyebrows at that; however, Sart was already standing up to leave. “Well met, old friend. I am glad to see you on the mend.” He laughed. “Back to Back!”

“Aye, Back to Back!” Ge-or returned. As Sart waved goodbye once more from the tavern door, he added, “Always, old friend.”

Slyn

Slyn showed up exactly two months from when he had first approached Ge-or. This time he came to the manor yard where the half-elf was engaged in a sparring bout with two hefty fighters. He could see they were greatly overmatched in skill by Ge-or, yet they were gamely trying to keep him at bay. The thief waited patiently for them to finish their practice.

"Well met, again."

"I am not ready," Ge-or growled, seeing his dagger sticking from Slyn's belt.

"I can see that. However, it will take us a month or more to get to where I wish to go. There will be another fighter along you can spar with on the way."

"Where is it we go?"

"We head south and west. I will tell you more on the morrow when we meet."

"Who else?"

"You will meet her tomorrow."

"Her?"

"Patience. Have you gear? Weapons? A horse?"

"Nay, and not much coin left to purchase anything."

"I figured as much. I will put together what you need for the trek. Get yourself a sword and some leather armor. Here…" He tossed the sheath and dagger to Ge-or, and a leather purse that clanked as Ge-or caught it.

Ge-or caught the dagger deftly and immediately stuck it in his belt. He bounced the bag in his other hand. "Now I need not have truck with you."

"You will. You are an honorable man, else I would not have bothered with you. Dawn tomorrow, at the Druid's Hut. Use what you have and that. It will not buy you a fine blade; it will get you something you can use."

Ge-or showed up an hour before dawn and waited. More than anything he was curious, but he was also beginning to feel that underlying tension and excitement that was part of the beginning of an adventure into the unknown. It was a good feeling to have again. He wanted to relish it as long as he could. It helped him feel he was alive.

Slyn and a young lady showed up about a half hour later. The woman was lithe, of medium height, with short blond hair, and a pleasing, yet stoic face. Ge-or could see she moved as a fighter would move – there was power there that

221

waited to be unleashed. She bowed low when she came up to Ge-or. "I am honored to meet you, half-elf. Your reputation grows by the day. I am Elise, formerly from the south."

Ge-or bowed back, surprised at how soft her voice was. It belied the hardness that he sensed in her. "The honor is mine, maiden. It will be my pleasure to cross swords with you."

She bowed again. Slyn, a bemused look on his boyish face, interrupted the formalities. "Come. The horses are stabled to the side. All is ready. We ride south, then west at Aube."

Slyn had outfitted them with all the basic necessities for an adventure. They had three pack mules that carried the bulk of their gear and food. Elise rode a young grey mare, frisky and swift-looking, that fit her frame well. The half sea-elf rode on a sturdy pony that looked like it had seen many a day in the wilds. He had purchased Ge-or a solid, old stallion, who was well-trained. The horse, which Ge-or dubbed Fresh Start, reminded him of the mare he had purchased for his first trek to the west with Stradryk.

It was a bittersweet moment for him, for his dead friend often crossed his thoughts. While he stroked the stallion's mane, he remembered their first meeting and a wave of sadness threatened to drag him deep within again. A light hand on his shoulder caused him to jerk up. Elise stood next to him. She said nothing and removed her hand when he looked at her.

They rode slowly that first day, heading due south along the trade trail. Slyn told them that in a week or so, after staying the night in the border town of Aube, they would turn west along a trail that led to an old trading post. From there, they would head south around the hills. He would detail the rest of the quest when they stopped that night.

It was over the campfire that evening that Slyn laid out their destination and goal. "We go to an old property set in the western hills near Chaac Kata. If you have not heard of it, it is in the heart of chatt country now. There is a small castle, long abandoned, that has likely been ravaged many a time by beasts and treasure-seekers, but..." Slyn smiled his wispy smile, while producing a weathered piece of parchment from his tunic. "I have a map."

"A map? You mean a treasure map?" Ge-or asked. "By-the-gods, Slyn, have you fallen for this old a ruse?" He stared across at the thief as if he were addled.

Slyn waved him off. "Nay, good fighter. Perhaps you have heard of claims like this before. This, I believe, is indeed the real thing. Give me a minute to explain. I acquired this map from an old man who was soon to die with no kin, or so he said; and it would have been a shame to leave this prize to the greedy proprietors of the home in which he was kept.

"This old fellow had been an adventurer in his younger days and was with a party that went west to raid an estate soon after it had been abandoned as a result of the Qa-ryk Wars. According to his account, they found considerable treasure in the old castle, but could only transport about half of it back with them. The rest they buried nearby. Subsequently, though some of the party later tried, the place became overrun with chatts; and none of them ever made it there and back. Most of the original group died trying. The man I talked with had barely escaped from their last venture, and only because he was at the rear of the party when they were attacked. He was the last of the original party. He never tried again."

"You found all of this out, how?" Ge-or asked, still skeptical.

"I sat with the old fellow for many a day prying it out of him with well-timed rum toddies. He was, after initial reluctance, happy to talk of his youthful days. He knew he wasn't long for this world, and it gave him pleasure to recall his adventures. Luckily, he had a fondness for drink. After a time, he told me of the map, for he knew he would never go out and find the treasure they had left. It is sort of ironic when you think about it. He actually ended up giving it to a real thief, albeit one who did befriend him in his final days."

"You believe this to be the truth?" Ge-or looked down at the darkened parchment that Slyn had passed over to him. Ge-or groaned when he saw it. It looked much like the types of maps one could buy in any dark alley in Aelfric from a fellow "who knew someone who had done something, and knew so and so, and..." To make matters even worse, there was actually a large "X" on it in red ink, marking "the spot."

Slyn noted Ge-or's disdainful look. "Truly, Ge-or, I do not know why he would have lied. He was telling the tale of his life, to a person who was willing to listen and, in a sense, pay for it."

"Well, I guess I have naught better to do for the nonce," Ge-or snorted, handing the map to Elise. "I shall continue to be skeptical until I see the color of gold."

"So be it. You will see."

In quiet discussions with the young fighter-maiden during their long days on the trail, Ge-or learned that Elise was a rogue warrior with better than a quarter of her birthright from the Slivs of the Great Plains. Her grandsire, she had been told, a young lord of the plainspeople, had been banned from his clan because of his tendency to oft bed women outside the tribes. Her mother had been one of the results of his liaisons with a young maiden from Baarth. Though she spoke angrily of the Plains Riders and

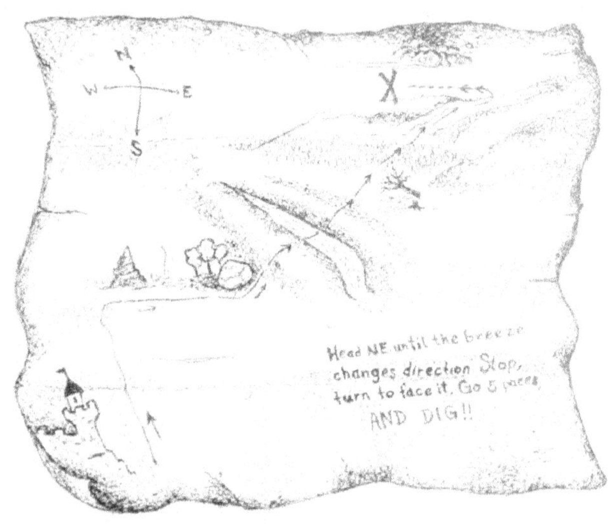

their closed, male-dominated culture, she was proud of her heritage from the perspective of her fighting abilities.

Ge-or soon discovered that she was actually quite adept at fighting with a wide range of weapons. Her favorites were somewhat heavier and shorter versions of the Sliv blades used by the horsemen and horsewomen of the plains. The two blades, dagger and sword, were lighter than the typical short sword and dagger of the day and had some characteristics of the Sliv weapons – being flared slightly toward the point, with a blood-groove the length of the blade. She had designed them herself and had them crafted by a dwarven smith in the south. She was skilled at using the knife-sword combination. Ge-or learned some new moves and techniques from her during their practices. Though his father had spoken of the long slim blades of the horse people, he had not had versions to hand to train his sons in their use.

Ge-or and Elise sparred every day as they moved south, then west, and finally south again along the foothills around the Horn of the Beze range, and after rounding the hills, back up the other side. Elise was quick and tough, but she could not match Ge-or's strength. They both learned from each other. Ge-or found that she was an ideal partner for him as he brought his flexibility and prowess back to top form. She was in tip-top shape and could give him a thorough workout. Ge-or had never seen a woman who had honed her body to such an extent. She was tougher than most male fighters with whom he had worked out. Elise also drew him into her regular morning exercises and long runs, so that he was working all parts of his body.

Though there was an attraction between them, neither made a move to bring it to fruition. Ge-or stayed a bit distant, still struggling with the emotions of his immediate past, not particularly keen to open himself further emotionally. Elise was not shy, yet she seemed reluctant to make the first move. All in all, the three of them related as all adventurers do – with a camaraderie and joint effort that spoke to the task at hand. There was purpose to all they did, and everyone pitched in according to their abilities and needs. They settled into a comfortable relationship without having to speak of responsibilities or duties.

When they made the turn around the Horn, they began to encounter strong winds and blowing sand. As they moved into the eastern foothills along old mule paths, the rocks helped block the pervasive flying grit. They also were better protected there from any potential chatt attack. Elise, who had spent a fair amount of her time bordering the plains and the desert, told them that the wiry creatures often buried themselves partially in the sand, blending so well with their mottled yellowish-brown skin that they could erupt upon unwary bands of travelers in well-designed ambushes. To an extent, the rocks prevented this tactic, thus minimizing the chance of a surprise attack. The large boulders and narrow confines of the low hills also allowed them better defensive postures should they be attacked. Unfortunately, the paths through the hills were irregular and choosing this route slowed their pace considerably.

Water was far scarcer on this side of the mountains, so they had filled up all their skins from the streams on the western slopes before making the crossing. Every third day or so they would find a trickle coming down off the upper hills. They would stop long enough to replenish their store. In between these tiny oases, they carefully rationed what they had with them.

They were almost five weeks out from Aube when they turned westward once more, following the curve of the steep southern edge of the mid-Beze range. In another week's time, they reached the small castle that had overlooked a spread-out estate. According to Slyn, they were less than a half a day's ride from

Chaac Kata, a ghost town that had once been a booming trading center for mining parties coming down from the mountains.

River Run, as the delta's valley was known, had been the primary provider of food in the form of corn, wheat, vegetables, cattle, and lamb for both Chaac Kata and the mining parties. It was the only lush area on this side of the mountains. The fertile land was fed by many rivulets coming off the high peaks to the north. The river was now more of a large, shallow delta that fed into the sands and disappeared. The rich soil along its banks was arable with a fairly long growing season, protected as it was from the north and northwest winds. For many years, it had provided sustenance for those that lived in the area.

That first evening at River Run they explored the ruins of the castle and outbuildings. After ensuring that several of the smaller rooms with intact slate roofs were easily defendable, they settled in for the evening. They had been lucky so far. On the rare occasions they had seen fleeting glimpses of creatures scurrying amongst the foothills, they had not been attacked.

In spite of their position being easily defensible, they set watches -- Ge-or receiving the last. He set himself toward the back of one of the chambers and slept soundly on the bed of pine boughs he had fashioned.

The light of early morning was peeking up over the distant hills to the east when Elise passed Ge-or, who was now on watch, motioning to him that she was heading outside the castle proper, where they had set up a protected spot for a latrine in an old guard enclosure. The small room still had three of its walls relatively intact so it would serve for some privacy.

Ge-or nodded, then stood, stretching. In doing so, he brought his sword, which had been lying across his legs, to hand. He stepped a few feet out into what had been the entry hall to the citadel. There he had a better view of anything coming from below, though he could not see past the guardhouse walls some forty yards to his right.

Several minutes later, he began to feel that it had been longer than necessary that Elise had gone out of sight. He moved forward about ten more paces until he was outside the mostly crumbled main wall. Looking south, he saw a movement out of the corner of his eye, and a second later, another. He tried to remember whether Elise had been carrying any weapon with her when she had gone past him. He had seen a utility dagger stuck in her belt, yet he couldn't remember seeing her carrying her sword.

Sheathing his own sword in his back scabbard, Ge-or bent down and picked up his bow and drew an arrow from the quiver next to it. Nocking it to the string, he half drew as he moved down and around to the south to get into a better position to see the outhouse without fully disturbing Elise should she still be inside. He whistled shrilly to alert both her and Slyn that he was moving and concerned.

The sun was not up, but the lighting was good enough. He only had to take a couple of steps when he saw two thin, gangly, goblin-like creatures crouching over a form that was half lying and half-sitting amongst the broken rocks. The chatts looked like mottled yellowish, light-brown, sinewy cousins of the deep, earth-dwelling grey goblins. This was the first time Ge-or had gotten a good look at one. As he continued to sidle down the slope, he took in everything he could of their appearance and posture. Their fangs were shorter than gzks and goblins; their claws – long, thick, and yellow – appeared ideal for digging or ripping; and their small ears, squished nose, and yellow eyes gave them an eerie, devilish look. They appeared to favor staying in a slight crouch to standing fully erect. They appeared thin, muscular, and fast. One of the creatures was pawing at Elise's clothing; the other was holding her dagger to her throat with its right claw. It was staring directly at Ge-or. They appeared to be waiting to see what he would do.

As Ge-or continued to move sideways in an arc to get in a better position for a shot, he scanned to both sides to see whether any more of the creatures were set in ambush about the area.

Elise appeared to be unconscious; but Ge-or could not see any blood on her, on the beast's claws, or on the rocks nearby. The one pawing her suddenly straightened and stared at Ge-or as well. The other pressed the sharp blade inward. Ge-or saw a thin line of blood trickle down where the beast had made a shallow cut. It was a warning.

He stopped, bow still half drawn. Slyn had appeared like a shadow, sliding through the rocks behind the two creatures, moving stealthily closer. Ge-or came to full drawn, hoping to keep the chatts' attention toward him, and praying that they would not react yet.

The situation was untenable from every perspective – a slight jerk of the blade inward would cut through Elise's jugular. The beasts obviously knew what they were about as far as killing was concerned. Though Slyn was getting close, the risk was too great that even if Ge-or's arrow struck cleanly in the chatt's chest or neck, the knife could penetrate and Elise would be dead.

Sighting along the bow, Ge-or formulated a plan. For a long instant, he hesitated. He had not killed, fought, or wielded any weapon in anger since his escape from torture at the hands of the Qa-ryks. Their delight in his pain, his vulnerability, his torment came welling up from within and he nearly coughed in anguish. Just as quickly, that waft of emotion was replaced by the hopelessness of knowing that a creature could be so pervasively evil as to enjoy hurting another, doing atrocities to another entity no matter how different, relishing their victim's agony, and reveling in the prolongation of pain. If the situation had been any different, he might have doubled over in agony as that feeling ravaged through his chest and gut. In the same instant, or certainly following quickly upon it, another emotion rose up from the depth of who he was. This had nothing to do with pain, anger, evil, or angst. It had much more to do with honor, truth about his nature as a human being and as a warrior, a deep caring for life and goodness, and a sense of rightness. In that instant, his eye focused, the bow shifted slightly as he drew aim on the only hope he saw, and he released the arrow.

The shaft flew true. The tip of the arrow hit the knife handle below where it met the shaft of the blade. The hilt was punched toward the chatt; the force driving the blade out away from Elise's jugular and toward the right. The knife did cut her neck, not deeply – slicing more to the front and side, where it would do the least damage. Diverted by the hilt of the blade, the arrow buried itself at a downward angle into the chatt's shoulder. The beast screamed, dropped the blade, and fell backward from the force of the blow. Slyn was on the second of the beasts in an instant and slit its throat. Then, before Ge-or had a chance to take two steps forward, Slyn buried his knife to the hilt in the wounded one's chest.

Elise was all right, only stunned by the blow she had received from behind when she had exited the privy. The knife wound was bleeding a good bit; yet once bound with an herb poultice, it would heal well enough. She was feeling incredibly foolish with the large knot on her head, but with no permanent damage except to her pride. Nothing further was said about the incident. Slyn did clap Ge-or on the shoulder as they made their way back to their quarters as if to say, "That was impressive."

Ge-or didn't respond; he was back. And though he hadn't realized it until that instant a few minutes before, when he had struggled with all those emotions; he knew that there had been considerable doubt as to whether he would have ever fought or killed another being again. His honor to a fellow comrade, and his caring for Elise as a fighter and as a person, had brought him full circle. He was back; he was a warrior again.

Seek and You Will Unearth

Making sure they stayed within sight of each other thereafter, they set about following the so-called treasure map from its origin, the northeast corner of the citadel, to its end, the "Big Red X," as Ge-or jokingly referred to the hopeful resting place of the cache. He still thought it looked remarkably like any of several maps he had seen hawked by dubious characters in Aelfric. Slyn, however, insisted on its authenticity, so Ge-or went along with the game plan.

To be sure they missed none of the distances or clues, they set markers at each juncture they came to and re-paced every leg. The map led them north and east from the outer castle wall, sometimes offering distances in paces, at other times referring to some landmark off in the distance. Most of these were readily seen: a jutting point of rock, a large boulder, a passage through a narrow channel in a deep dry wash. A couple – a large oak that had fallen and mostly rotted away, and an outcropping shaped like an eagle's head – they had to find through careful study of the area. Elise spotted the downed trunk of the tree, and Slyn managed to puzzle out that a rockslide had destroyed what must have been the eagle formation.

Finally, as the sun was beginning to head to the west, they found themselves on the opposite side of the flat delta area, staring up the side of a high hill, with the final note on the map a cryptic, "head northeast until the breeze changes direction, stop, turn to face it, go five paces, and dig."

Slyn attempted this first and came back a quarter hour later shaking his head. "I noticed nothing. The wind is from the west as usual. Perhaps it has to be a stronger wind?"

Next, Elise tried, and she, too, came back with a puzzled look on her face. "I noticed changes to the breeze; but they were erratic, nothing definitive enough to walk toward, except the steady westerly flow."

Ge-or looked at both his partners and an idea hit him. "How tall was this fellow?"

Slyn raised his eyebrows. He, of course, was short by any human standard; and though Elise was tall for a woman, she came barely above Ge-or's shoulder. "He was tall, taller than you in his prime; I would imagine he had shrunk a bit."

"Allow me," Ge-or smiled. He set off along the same path they had trod.

He stopped abruptly after about two hundred paces. Something had changed. He spun around took two paces back – a west wind in his hair. He turned again and took two steps. The wind definitely shifted and was blowing from the south. Two more steps and he felt the westerly breeze again. Moving back to the spot where he had noticed the change, he set a couple of stones in a pile, and then stood and looked around. He saw the reason for the shift. He had been in a dry wash for about twenty paces; but at this point there was a rise in the ground, as if the water during a storm had plowed out two channels instead of one. When he stepped up and reached the peak of the division, exactly at that point there was a break in the walls of the wash that caused the wind to whistle through and change direction momentarily. He went back to the others.

Within minutes of digging at "the spot," Ge-or's shovel hit something solid. On Slyn's instructions they cleaned carefully around the area, lest they spring some type of trap. Their efforts revealed a curved top to a large, sturdy case. Examining it carefully, Slyn discovered poison needle devices embedded on each side of the ornate brass-work. The master thief quickly disarmed it, using his picking skill to open the heavy iron lock. Not long thereafter, they were staring into the open maw of – literally a treasure chest. It was filled with hundreds of gold and silver pieces; a few large, quality gems; handfuls of smaller, lesser-quality stones; and a great many miscellaneous pieces of gem-encrusted wear – from cups, to bracers, to gaudy jewelry, to tableware.

It took them two days to pack it all out and settle it on the mules before they were ready to head back to Aelfric. They put some of the weightier coinage in their own saddlebags, so as not to overburden the pack animals. The whole time Slyn was whistling cheery tunes, and Ge-or was smiling to himself. The little fellow had been right.

That first evening on the trail as they were preparing their campsite, Ge-or poked Slyn in the shoulder. "I saw you left that nice jeweled goblet in the chest."

Slyn grinned impishly. "Well, I have this great map I can sell. If someone actually makes the effort, I believe they should find something."

Ge-or chuckled. Thieves, he mused. Truly, he liked the little man. He had been true to his word so far, and he could find far worse companions to be with in a pinch.

It was a week later, as they neared the Horn, when Elise came to Ge-or in the night. He was surprised, yet pleased. Ge-or had not wanted to press the issue, though she had shyly begun to sit closer to him when they were in camp, or ride protectively closer, as if her rescue from the chatts had increased her concern for him. He let her make the choice.

He was pleasantly surprised to discover how soft and supple she was in his arms. He had imagined that she would be hard but flexible, as she was lean and wiry when they sparred together. However, her strength and resilience melted into him when she let down her guard.

From that point on, the two spent their nights together. Often, they simply lay close, enjoying each other's company. It was a tonic Ge-or needed, perhaps more than anything else, now that he was back from the depths of the despair he had sunk to.

Two days later, rounding the far side of the Horn and keeping close to the hills, they were surprised to see what appeared to be a small caravan coming at them from the east. It was comprised of fourteen horses and the figures of cloth-covered men leading the animals.

It did not take them long to realize that there was something wrong with the whole scene. It was the height of summer; and no caravans, particularly one this small, would be traveling this far to the south, much less heading due west. Plus, there did not appear to be any pack animals amongst the unsaddled horses, so it was not an exploration party. Deciding to be cautious, they scrambled into the nearest opening in the rocky hills and drew their own animals into a small canyon. There they waited for the column to come closer. The procession looked like it would pass right beneath them if they held their ground.

When the group got closer, they could see that the figures leading the horses were small in stature in comparison to humans; they were easily dwarfed by the large plains stallions and mares. They were hurrying across the sands away from what appeared to be a large cloud of dust and dirt following them at a league or more behind.

"Chatts," Slyn whispered, drawing his shortbow forward. "They have cut out some horseflesh from a Bendir herd. Look!" He pointed southwest. Ge-or and Elise could see a mass of movement coming up off the sands toward the Horn. It looked like a hundred or more of the desert creatures were coming to aid their comrades.

Chatts loved horseflesh even more than Qa-ryks. The Slivs waged a continuous war against the wily creatures all along the western border of the Great Plains, where the dry-lands began and eventually blended into the vast Great Desert beyond. Ge-or could tell that if the line of horses and chatts made it past their position, the elves who were chasing would lose them to the small army of chatts coming up from the south. "Ambush these?" he asked Slyn and Elise.

His two companions agreed, so they began to work their way further south to the tip of the Horn, leaving the pack animals and their horses where they were. They scampered downward until they were at the foot of the hills, amongst a pile of boulders from which they could each get an open shooting lane. If the chatts leading the horses continued in their strung-out straight line, they would pass immediately below the three adventurers.

The waiting seemed interminable. While they watched they could begin to make out the charge of about a dozen Slivs on their steeds coming hard from the east, as well as the milling of the bodies of the large mass of chatts coming up from the south and west. Ge-or guessed, based on the speed of the three groups, that the small caravan would pass them in only a few minutes and reach the safety of the sands and their comrades in maybe fifteen. The Slivs were easily twenty minutes out, even if they could maintain their current pace. Ge-or knew that once the hard-packed sand and earth became shifting dunes of loose particles, it would slow the Slivs down considerably. Horses and ponies, even if specially shod, did not maneuver well in loose sand. The agile chatts would have the advantage there, especially in swarming numbers.

Using a complicated series of gestures, Slyn indicated that he would step out and block the "shortcut," a narrow trail leading through the base of the Horn, for which the chatts appeared to be headed. If they went that way, they would get to the other side via a narrow canyon much more quickly than if they deviated further to the south. Ge-or signaled back that he understood; however, he resolved to discuss hand signals with the thief at another time. If they were to continue to work together, they would want to know precisely what each was "saying" to the other.

The chatts were only about thirty yards below them when Ge-or caught Slyn's signal to shoot. Ge-or spun around the boulder he was behind; Elise doing the same on the opposite side. They both shot smoothly as their arrows came to bear. Slyn also released his shaft. The first three chatts fell, each pierced through the heart. The three horses they were leading, freed by the downing of their handlers, leapt forward, only to be met by Slyn waving a large white rag in their faces. They stopped, rearing back and jarring into each other, trying to turn away from the menace to their front. Meanwhile, Ge-or and Elise each loosed two more arrows, after which the big half-elf leapt down from above to further confuse the animals. He hoped to help Slyn drive them back from where they had come.

Ge-or drew his sword from his back scabbard as he leapt in amongst the horses, while Elise released one more arrow before turning back as prearranged to gather their own horses and pack animals. Charging forward amongst the frightened animals, Ge-or downed two more chatts with hard blows that cut down through their shoulders to their mid-sections. He decapitated two others who, in spite of the arrows in their bodies, were scrambling up to fight. He didn't turn to see what Slyn was doing, trusting that he was following their plan and would be close behind. When he drew up next to one of the large stallions, he grabbed its mane in his left fist. Using his right for leverage, blade still to hand, he heaved himself up onto the broad back. Driving his heels into its flank, he forced the horse around and forward. Following the drive of the stallion, the other horses nearby came around and headed east as well.

Somehow during the next moments of the melee, Ge-or managed to fend off two chatts who leapt at him. He speared another who had jumped up on his back with a thrust under his armpit with his sword. By then, the horses had cleared the opening of the canyon and were heading back east across the hard-packed soil. After another minute, Ge-or was able to turn and see Elise closing from the northwest. Slyn was riding a mare behind and herding the last of the horses to the east. He could not see any of the chatts still on their feet.

As the horses began to slow from their mad rush out of the canyon, Ge-or pulled on the reins of his big stallion and eased him back, turning it to the left with his knee. Elise and the pack mules gamely following, nevertheless were rapidly losing ground to the free horses. Behind, the chatts coming from the west had scrabbled amongst the rocks of the ambush; they had stopped there. The desert creatures had no wish to fight a well-armed Sliv patrol on solid ground.

Slyn also pulled back on his mare as the Slivs approached. They let the small herd settle into an easy walk. The Slivs to their front were now close enough that they could see the horse elves' long dark hair flowing behind as they raced across the packed sand and earth.

Elise was coming up with their horses and mules, when the Sliv riders eased back their mounts and couched their lances as they rode up. They looked stern and ready for action, not understanding what had transpired. Sheathing his sword, Ge-or raised his hand, palm outward. He said in the ancient tongue, "Hail and well-met, riders of the plains. Your horses are safe and the chatts who took them have been killed. Please," he gestured to the horses, "with our good will."

The tallest of the Slivs placed his open hand on the center of his chest. "You honor us, elf-kin. You have done us a great service this day." He nodded a bow to each of them from the seat of his magnificent white stallion. "Will you accompany us to our camp, so we may have the pleasure of your company for our evening repast?"

"It would be our honor," Ge-or responded. He returned the gesture and the bow.

Through the course of the evening, Ge-or once again learned that his brother's reputation had preceded him. When the Slivs heard that Ge-or was formerly from Thiele, they asked him if he had known another half-elf named Jared. Because of their rescue of the Slivs' horses, and because the Slivs seemed to have an almost reverential awe of Jared's prowess as a musician and healer, they were treated royally.

After a celebratory banquet, they spent the night with the Slivs. The next day they chose to ride eastward with them for three days, following the grazing herd until they intersected with the north road to Aube. In parting, the Slivs gifted each of them fine steeds. It was a magnanimous gesture, and Ge-or felt it was far too great a gift for what they had done. He knew, though, that it would be rude to refuse; so he selected a fine young, broad-backed stallion, whose name was Oesing, Bringer of the Wind. Elise picked a beautiful piebald mare, named Windflare, which suited her temperament. Slyn selected a spirited pony, which he chose to name Breath of the Sea, as the Slivs not only raised the swift, high-spirited plains horses, but also many other equine breeds.

These were truly princely gifts, and they were honored to receive them. On inspiration, Ge-or took a perfectly matched pearl necklace that had been in the treasure chest. He broke the string holding the large pearls and gave one to each of the twelve riders who had been with the original band when they had freed the horses. He also gave one to Elise and Slyn and kept one for himself. He threw the last into the tall grasses beside the path – "For the gods." The gesture appeared to please the Slivs.

Three and a half weeks later they rode back into Aelfric, tired yet happy, with enough wealth to stay in the Druids Hut with the best of food and rooms for a well-deserved rest. With careful bargaining of the gems and jewelry, they would have more than enough to outfit all of them for further adventures.

Though Ge-or and Slyn offered, Elise declined the opportunity to join their quest after the dragon. She chose to return to the south, so she could set up her mother and brother in comfort for once. They wished her well and hoped that someday they would ride together again.

***

Sart continued to garner information from his order's acolytes in the field. For some reason he had yet to fathom completely, the evil in the west had gone to ground. Everything that came in through his network suggested that nothing was happening. There was no longer an evil power focused on the east as there had been for many years.

There was, however, some undercurrent – found only in small pieces of information – that hinted at a change in control and structure in the evil forces he sought. Something had driven the Black Druids further west. There was some trace of another evil, or more than one, growing and threatening the status quo. As a result, the Qa-ryks had been left to themselves to grow and expand according to their nature, not because they were being controlled.

Sart wondered and pondered, knowing that he would need to go back into the field himself to see the truth in why things were changing and to discover what forces were at play in the west, perhaps deeper into the west than he had ever gone.

A month later, after a brief sojourn at Xur, where he caught up with his friends, the earth cleric was hugging the north slope of the Beze mountains, heading west. His companion, a huge bear of a man, led the way. They were following a trail, the hint of a trail left by Aberon. Sart WAS sure of that.

Dragon Hunting

The first winter back from their treasure hunt to Chaac Kata, Ge-or and Slyn spent in acquiring the best equipment they could find. Ge-or purchased a quality dwarven-made sword that suited his arm-length and was forged of the finest steel. He also found an expensive, exceptionally made, elven yew longbow that suited his draw-length. It was so powerful that even Ge-or had to raise his workout standard to be able to easily draw it back. He practiced with it for many long hours that winter to be sure he could pull it in an instant and bring it to his eye in one smooth motion.

They each had a full suit of armor made of the braided swamp grass cloth he and Stradryk had brought up from the south, attached to the inside of light leather, including bracers, vambraces, full jacket, gauntlets, gorget, and leg pieces. He instructed the leather workers to sew the swamp grass cloth between two layers of fine supple leather, leaving one end open on each piece so that the inner fibers could be soaked with water. It was a slow and costly process that took several months; in the end, he and Slyn had somewhat bulky, flexible suits that provided extra protection against fire and heat. These were reinforced with stiffer, thick leather pieces at important protective points of the body, without losing much of their ability to move freely.

Finally, they had their helms lined with the swamp cloth and had mid-garments, meant to be worn over their undergarments but under the leather armor, made from the swamp grass, too. Ge-or also spent several weeks making a large rectangular wooden shield to which he tacked layers of the finely woven grasses on both sides for added protection.

During this time of preparation and the adventures that followed, Slyn and Ge-or became close as only partners who have shared extreme hardship can be. They devised a coded language of hand gestures, with elements of the thieves' unique jargon and Old Elvish included, so that they could communicate with each other with little chance of being understood by any passersby. It proved useful in many a situation, as the two of them had a proclivity for finding trouble. They also got to know each other's quirks, accepting how they differed, as well as enjoying the many things they had in common.

Slyn proved to be an incomparable companion. He was loyal, honest in only the way a master thief could be honest – to one's friends and one's commitments – and he was superb at his trade. Though he was fairly quiet, he complemented Ge-or's reserved nature. What communications they had with each other served them both well. When in their cups, they oft shared tales from their lives and told stories gleaned from other sources; however, neither would have ever accused the other of being a conversationalist. They got along well.

Another thing became apparent to both of them as they made preparations for going after the dragon – Ge-or was developing a reputation. As Slyn was well known in southwest Borea as a masterful thief who preferred his independence to joining various nefarious groups of bandits and pickpockets, Ge-or's reputation as an extraordinary weaponsman began to spread as well.

Though Ge-or neither participated in his renown, nor really understood how it had happened, he had become not only a person who might be sought for his talent, but also a target for those wishing to enhance their own reputation. He and Slyn, therefore, discovered that they needed to watch their backs more and more as they went about their daily lives in the border towns like Aelfric and Aube. It was with extra watchfulness that they finally prepared to seek the dragon who had destroyed Ge-or's village and killed his father.

Finally, in the late fall, Slyn and Ge-or set out with laden mules for the north and west. They were only a half league from Aelfric, riding easily along the rocky landscape that led up into the hills, when they were saw movement ahead. Slyn signaled Ge-or to be alert, though the big man, too, was already checking to make sure his weapons were loose in their sheaths. They were not expecting any trouble so close to the border town; so each was only wearing a medium weight leather jerkin and had a minimum of weapons to hand, which in Slyn's case might mean about a dozen hidden about his person.

Acting at ease, they rode ahead waiting to see what developed. They knew that it was highly unlikely to be Qa-ryks, as they were rarely found this close to Aelfric, and were also unlikely to be discovered so easily. Qa-ryks preferred to ambush their prey.

As they neared where they had seen the movement, a hulk of a man, swarthy from years in the sun and well-used by both nature and struggle, stepped out from behind a large rock onto the broad road. He certainly looked formidable. His belt, backpack, and even leather leggings were bristling with weapons; his face and bare powerful arms were a mass of scars; and he bulked more than even Ge-or in the midriff and legs.

"Hail," Slyn offered pleasantly.

The man grunted, "Want him." He drew his sword as he spoke and pointed it at Ge-or.

Ge-or, preferring to take his partner's lighter approach, said, "Here I am. How can I serve, sir?"

"I'm Mastiff, and I challenge you to fight. You will die." He drew a two-bladed, throwing axe from his weapons belt with his left hand, and started swaying from side to side, brandishing his weapons as if he were going to charge Ge-or while the half-elf was still astride his plains-bred mount.

Slyn glanced over at Ge-or with a bemused look on his face, more interested in seeing how his partner would react than worried by the threat.

Ge-or sat for a minute, eyeing his potential adversary; finally, he shrugged and swung his leg over Oesing sliding to the ground. He did not draw his sword, though he did take a long step ahead to distance himself from Slyn.

"I would advise against such a plan, sir," Slyn answered, giving Ge-or more time to assess his potential opponent. "You obviously have experience, and a certain strength about you; but I doubt you have the training of my good friend here. Stand down, and he will not hurt you."

As he was talking, a long throwing blade appeared suddenly in Slyn's left hand. He, too, slid down from his mount, pushing the pony to the side so he was also clear of the equines should it come to a fight. From what they had noticed earlier, there were at least two other brigands amongst the rock., Slyn started to slide slowly to the south.

Ge-or, standing at ease with his sword now resting lightly on his right shoulder, still tried to dissuade the other fellow. He drew his belt knife as he spoke.

"Let us choose another course to see who is the better man – a brief contest, blade to blade. No one hurt, and we continue on our own business."

"Kill now!" Mastiff pushed off into a lumbering charge.

At that same moment, three arrows flew from the rocks aimed at Ge-or, two from the south and one from the north. Two hit Ge-or as he set himself to meet the brute's attack: one in the side of his shoulder where the leather padding was doubled, and the other low in his left side. Both penetrated, though the shoulder strike was only a small puncture wound; the other was deep enough to make Ge-or grunt and turn slightly. Dropping the belt knife, he yanked out the arrow before Mastiff reached him, else the sharp point would cut him more while he moved about.

Slyn reacted before the first arrow was half-way to its target. Launching the throwing knife as he broke into a low run, he was drawing another as he reached the rocks. His first blade struck the archer full in the left side, deep into his armpit. The man spun sideways, back into a boulder and slid down, blood beginning to leak from his lips as Slyn leapt past. He had the other man in his grasp with blade to chin before he could do anything else. Turning about quickly to scan the other side of the road, Slyn could see the other brigand raise his arms above his head. They were empty.

Both Ge-or and Slyn were astounded that even lowly brigands as these would stoop so low as to attack in so base a manner. The law of the adventurer was one thing, "Back to Back" meaning a great deal to men like these two adventurers. There was also honor amongst fighters, even thieves, that spoke to a level, righteous match when challenging someone to a duel or fight.

Ge-or, for his part, had been willing to quickly disarm the lout setting this challenge, without attempting to injure. That was until the arrows came at him. He had to act quickly. Mastiff was almost onto him when he threw the arrow to the ground. Sliding slightly to his left, Ge-or brought his dwarven blade down in a small swipe to his right; he drew another knife while Mastiff's attention focused on the movement of the sword.

Mastiff came in low, with body and blade. Maybe good for a small, lithe man like Slyn, not so much for a huge man who needed to be fast; a high attack would have been smarter.

Ge-or easily side-stepped the man's lunge, letting the bandit's bulk send him across Ge-or's two weapons. He held his knife in such a way as to block Mastiff's sword thrust had the bastard been quick enough to adjust it. Instead, the sharp blade slid across the ruffian's shoulder just below the leather jerkin on his bare arm. As his blade sliced a broad, deep wound across Mastiff's muscle, Ge-or thought: another scar this brute can show to the ladies.

Mastiff's momentum carried him right across the dwarven blade at stomach level. The jerkin did stay some of the strike, but it was so sharp that it opened his belly enough that his guts partially slipped out on his right side. Dropping blade and axe, he grasped his side. Cursing, he stumbled ahead until he sank to his knees on the path.

Minutes later, after searching the three men, Slyn and Ge-or left them to fend for themselves, sans weapons. If they were lucky, Mastiff might make it back to Aelfric to a healer. There, Ge-or hoped, they would pass the word that it would be unwise for others to try the same.

For his part, Ge-or was angry. Not so much at these bunglers, as for the arrow wound that caused them to reverse course and head back to town themselves. Unfortunately, his wound resulted in a high fever; and by the time Zara gave him clearance to continue westward, the snow was beginning to cover the nearby hills. They would have to try again in the spring.

What the two adventurers had hoped for didn't happen. Though they were infrequent, Ge-or received enough challenges over the next six months that he longed to head back into the west as soon as spring arrived. Unfortunately, even after careful preparation, including leaving surreptitiously in the wee hours, it was not to be. This time it wasn't brigands, or a fighter wanting to enhance his reputation, that caused them to miss their planned stop at Xur and continuation westward. It was the expansion of Qa-ryks eastward.

The beasts had been left to their own devices the past few years, unrestricted by spells that kept their activities in check. Thus, the clans had continued to increase in number. The young beasts were always willing to start a new tribe and gain a reputation by fighting amongst themselves and any who dared move into their territory. This is what Ge-or and Slyn ran into head-first that next spring.

After far too many ambushes avoided, skirmishes fought with roaming bands of youngsters, and two of their pack mules lost, the two adventurers gave up the effort only twenty leagues into the west from Aelfric. Weary and blooded more times than they cared to acknowledge, the two adventurers made it back to the Druid's Hut before the first frost of the fall. They resolved to head west again the next spring, on a different route.

It took them several more starts and a number of other adventures before Ge-or and Slyn found themselves in the late fall far to the west after hiring out a small ship to take them to the dock at Thiele. From there, the trip south and west had not been easy; thankfully, for the most part, they had been able to avoid the larger concentrations of Qa-ryks. Finally, on a sharply cold day, they were staring up at Dragon's Peak – the mountain where Fis had his sanctuary. They had found the now-overgrown, but still solid, trapping cabin that Stradryk had built and he and Ge-or had used years before. The two spent their first week cleaning it of debris from the small animals that had used it since. They settled in for a winter of observing the big red on its occasional excursions for food, seeking routes up to its lair, and generally making plans for how they might succeed in bringing the dragon down.

Slyn, who was as quiet and sneaky as any small person could be, took it upon himself to do most of the scouting on the mountain. He could slip silently and unobtrusively through almost any terrain. Ge-or would oft watch his partner set out for another climb, expecting to see him until he was well up the side of the long upward slope. Within a minute of leaving the cabin, however, he would disappear into the shadows of the trees. Ge-or would not set eyes on him, no matter how carefully he watched, until he emerged virtually next to him hours later. It was disquieting at first to have Slyn sneak in like that, though Ge-or eventually got to feel comfortable with his partner's talents.

While Slyn was away, Ge-or would study the grounds about the base of the mountain, occasionally taking axe to hand. One tree at a time, he adjusted the terrain to accommodate his vision of a potential battle with the dragon. He also spent many hours fashioning fine arrows that were wider in diameter than normal shafts, and therefore stronger, so that they could handle the powerful elven bow. He had shot many shafts from the bow and had several shatter – certainly not a pleasant experience, and potentially very hazardous. He did not want to have anything go wrong when confronting the beast.

By the time winter was starting to wane, they had formulated a plan. Slyn had discovered several potential routes to the dragon's lair that were easier (for him), faster, and more surreptitious than anything Ge-or had explored years before. Then again, the thief could climb virtually any surface. Two of the three proved impossible for Ge-or to even think of tackling. Still, it was Slyn who needed to be able to get up to Fis's den and back without being discovered. Ge-or planned to be ostentatious about his approach once the full plan was launched.

They talked at some length about the appropriate time in which to make their attempt. Slyn argued for either spring or autumn to take advantage of the best weather for the ascent and descent. Ge-or felt that the coldest part of the winter might prove the best. It could serve as another ward from the intense heat the beast could produce. He had seen the liquid fire pour from the dragon's mouth and what it could do to flesh and material. Ultimately, because of several considerations, Ge-or won out. Thus, through the spring, a long hot summer, and the next fall, the two of them continued to refine their plan, hone their skills, and keep watch on the mountain.

It was somewhere near the Yule or shortly thereafter when they at long last readied themselves for the final phase of the plan. Slyn disappeared for two days heading up the slope of the mountain. While he waited for his partner, Ge-

or checked and rechecked everything, practicing his maneuvers under the protection of a large grove of trees. When Slyn finally returned, materializing out of the morning haze, Ge-or nodded at his partner. That evening he readied his weapons. The next morning, he headed west and south toward the mountain and finally up. More than ten years after the destruction of his village, his oath was about to be put to the test.

Dragon Fighting

There was an extra reason for celebration at Xur this Yule season. Two babes had been born to Alicia and her young knight, Brandir; and Jared and Thistle were named godparents. The two girls, Cynara and Carlina, named after two types of thistles common to the region, were healthy and strong. Both parents and godparents were overjoyed. Since births in the enclave were uncommon, almost everyone else became honorary godparents. There was certainly no lack of people who would watch the babes if duty called the parents away.

The past years had been good for the bastion. There had been only a few disturbances at the redoubt below Kan's Mountain, and none of these had involved black priests, druids, or magic users. A couple of young Qa-ryk patrols had sought to blood themselves by assaulting the small fort. One group had been beaten back by a shower of arrows from Jared's well-trained troops. The other patrol was fried into oblivion when they made the mistake of interrupting Thistle's magical work while she was on duty there.

Time at Xur was always filled with doings. Since there were changes in shifts during the spring and fall, Jared had new fodder for his demanding training regimen. To help him, Brandir had taken over assistant duties when Elanar was away on scouting patrols. Alicia's husband had taken to the finer points of archery and was an excellent all-around weaponsman. Even Alicia, encouraged by both, had learned to shoot a shortbow.

Thistle continued to spend time learning about alternate realms and how she could function magically within them. As Meligance had suggested, the work was tiring. Since it was all trial and error, with a good bit of caution and intelligence thrown in, progress was slow.

She was also able to focus on developing her staff, especially during the long hours in the field at the redoubt. She added energy to "the blue," as she thought of the bright sapphire, now embedded in the head of dense walnut. It was a large stone, yet not ostentatious, with an overall deep blue color and cool feel. When she looked into its depths, it now seemed somehow a bit murky despite its dramatic, perfect cut -- as if the energy Thistle imbued into it churned about, waiting for release.

Thistle also worked with the fibers of the walnut to imbue special qualities that reflected her overall approach to magic and to life. When she worked on the staff, she felt like she was creating an entity, a living thing. She knew, though the wood was long separated from sustenance, that deep within there was a type of life – or the potential for life – in its energy.

Elanar had become a co-swords-master with Jared, but his real joy was being afield. He spent as much time as he could on patrol. He had a good sense of everything that was capable of impacting his troops. Rux made him an unofficial captain of the Borean Army, as Elanar had become one of the finest officers and leaders he had available.

All in all, they prospered and grew. Jared and Thistle had become life partners in the truest sense, mellowing into a comfortable and loving relationship that belied the intensity of their life at Xur. Alicia had grown ever more independent, and Thistle loved to watch her now-confident former handmaiden at work with the looms and with the people she directed as Mistress of Weaving.

Recently they had received word from Leonis and Meligance that in the spring they would be called back to Borea. They loved their life here, but Jared's Apprenticeship was near its end. He was required by tradition to return to Bard Hall for more training.

Although Thistle and Meligance communicated on a regular basis via energy spheres, the White Wizardess was anxious for her protégé to return and begin her work helping with the training of young mages – those who would have the capabilities and skills to help with the defense of the empire. Thistle knew that there were still some gaps in her training and of her overall knowledge and understanding of magic, so it was time to return to her mentor's guidance.

Elanar received a letter encouraging him to stay at Xur for a bit longer to help train Jared's replacement. Leonis promised to send another apprentice out with either the spring or fall caravan. Alicia and her husband had chosen to sign on for another tour of duty in the wild. She and Thistle had a good cry together when they realized that after such a long time their lives would finally diverge. Alicia now had a full life independent of her former mistress. The parting would be one of friends saying goodbye and promising to get together again as soon as possible.

***

Ge-or had a great deal on his mind as he struggled up the slope toward the dragon's lair. He was feeling a bit trapped and uncomfortable inside the bulky combination of armor and "swamp clothing" that he wore. And though he was confident in his ability to fight in spite of the bulk, as he had practiced long hours in full gear, he hadn't fully considered how awkward it might be climbing the mountain in the snow and ice with all his gear – including the heavy rectangular shield, sword, dagger, bow and arrows, and water skin. Coming down, he knew, would not be a problem; much of this would be used and discarded by that time. As he continued to struggle upward, he laughed to himself at how they had planned that part of the venture.

More than anything he hoped the beast would not attack him whilst he was climbing. That could be devastating. He and Slyn had discussed that possibility; however, their only recourse at that point would be to try to escape by whatever means they could. He trusted the old beast would stay in his lair. Based on all the lore he had heard about dragons, they did not like to be disturbed. Fis would be loath to budge from his rest, particularly in the wintertime after filling his belly.

Since avarice was a well-known trait of the beasts, Ge-or felt that the dragon would first and foremost want to protect his treasure trove. Slyn would be hidden from sight, so Fis would not know the whereabouts of the second intruder. Perhaps this would give him another reason to stay guarding his riches. There was no doubt in either of their minds that the red dragon knew they were there, and that he likely knew what they were about. They were counting on his over-confidence and arrogance as part of being able to pull off the full plan.

At the forefront of Ge-or's mind was the clear picture of the red dragon swooping in on the square at Thiele to annihilate everything in the path of its terrible breath. He had managed to suppress this image for many years, now it helped him refocus on his pledge to destroy the beast. The dragon had shown no regard for the lives he had destroyed. As a result, the higher Ge-or climbed, the more anger rose in his gorge.

Now, they were here and as prepared as they would ever be. As he trudged upward, Ge-or realized there was no turning back. He hoped that their plan was solid. Slyn had done the first part; now it was his turn. The wily half sea-elf would play other roles as the attack developed.

Ge-or had also pledged that if he survived this, he would do his best to seek out his brother. They had been close while growing up, and though they had squabbles and fights as all siblings do, Ge-or had been "the big brother," and Jared had always looked up to him. Now they were both men. They had talked to Sart and others about each other and knew something of the other's exploits. Still, Ge-or wanted to see the man his brother had become. As he continued climbing, he realized that he had not made nearly enough of an effort to find Jared; and that disturbed him.

Another question that nagged at him as he climbed was when to drink Sart's fire-resistant potion. He and Stradryk had gotten two vials of the precious liquid when they had gone south in pursuit of fire lizards. They had never had cause to use them. Before the trek that resulted in Stradryk's death and Ge-or's torture, they had stored those, the swamp cloth, and other items unnecessary for the dragon quest at a storage house in Aube. He and Slyn had brought the two vials with them.

Unfortunately, he was unsure whether they would have any potency left at all after this many years, or whether perhaps their usefulness would be enhanced by the wait and further blending of the alchemical and herbal ingredients. It had been so long ago that Sart had described them to him that he couldn't remember whether he needed to drink the concoction twenty-four hours in advance, twelve hours, or a half-hour; and he also had no conception how long the effect might last.

Ge-or knew he was taking a big chance in using the stuff at all. Sart had spoken of side-effects – cold chills, sweating, tinnitus, tetany, and the like. Would these be severe enough to trouble him? Would they be worse now that the potion was so old? Or would they be weakened as the potion's effectiveness might be weakened?

He and Slyn had decided that whatever might happen, they did not dare toss aside something that had the potential to mitigate in any way the effects of the dragon's breath. Ge-or hoped to protect himself in a variety of ways, but he doubted that he could completely avoid the heat from the beast's fire. He knew that for their plan to be successful he would have to survive that flame at least once, probably twice, before he would get in a strike that might kill the beast.

They had both decided to take the potion. Ge-or would wait until he was at the edge of the beast's lair following the arduous climb upward. He wanted to be at full strength and have a chance to catch his breath before he took something that might affect his constitution and composure. Slyn would wait until Ge-or emerged from the cave to down his. If the beast followed, and Ge-or made it safely down the mountain to implement part three of their plan, he hoped the liquid's effects would have kicked in by then.

It was nearing mid-day and the sun was bright and high in the sky when Ge-or reached the ledge that led into the dragon's cavern. He had not made any pretense at going quietly, and he hoped that the dragon was well aware that someone was daring to approach his lair. He wanted his father's bane to be overly confident before he hit him with a full dose of reality – a reality that said you, too, are vulnerable.

Stepping into the shadow of the cave's walls, Ge-or found a broad stone and took a seat. He took the large water-skin from off his back and poured the contents on both sides of the shield and inside his jerkin, leather leggings, and everywhere that he could reach without removing any of his garments. The swamp grass was much more effective as a barrier to heat when it was wet, though Ge-or surmised it was probably quite damp in places from his sweat after climbing to this point.

Drinking the last of the water, he discarded the skin and sat quietly. Pushing the many thoughts out of his mind he had on the climb up, he now drew inward to focus. It was, when he had the time, the way he prepared for any trial he might face. He cleared his mind, released the tension from his body, took some deep breaths with his eyes closed, and allowed himself to feel who he was – a powerful, honed warrior.

Finally, feeling relaxed and focused, Ge-or pried the waxed top off the vial and downed the fire resistance potion in one gulp. He stood and waited for ten long minutes, counting off each second to see if there would be any untoward effects from the liquid. After about five minutes, he did notice some tingling in his hands and feet; and a chill swept through him thrice, that was all. Satisfied at last that he had done all he could to prepare, Ge-or turned and stepped into the darkness ahead.

Slyn had, upon his numerous treks up and down the mountain, created a fairly accurate map of the cave entrance and the dragon's lair; though there were several parts of the inner cavern that he had not been able to investigate without the risk of being detected by the beast. Ge-or had memorized the map and listened carefully to Slyn about every detail. He knew where large boulders stood, at which junctures the cave would jut to the right or left or up or down, and he knew what to expect underfoot.

The passage was well worn with centuries of the beast going in and out – the entire length smooth and nearly debris free. It was only at the end, as the pathway opened into the large cavern, that he would have to be careful with rubble underfoot. According to Slyn, there was a section near the beast's lair that looked like Fis used it to sharpen his claws. Ge-or planned to edge around that on the way in and try to leap across it in two bounds on the way out.

Slyn had also given him another tidbit of valuable information. Whatever liquid fire burned in the beast's belly created light. Dragons, or at least red dragons, glowed in dark places. This was important. It meant Ge-or would not have to carry a torch. Both his hands would be free, and he knew he needed every advantage he could get.

One thing that Ordrake had told them had eased Ge-or's mind a good bit. Although dragons were powerful and deadly, they did not typically use magic; nor, as far as the old wizard used the term, were they inherently magical. They were highly intelligent, could talk, and sometimes seemed able to create magical effects; they did not wield magic or energy as a mage or wizard could. He suggested that Ge-or ignore odd bits of folklore and focus on what the beast could do physically.

Another important detail, pertaining to Ge-or's escape following phase one of their plan, was that the cave and cave mouth were small enough that the dragon would have to scrabble through. Fis would not be able to launch in the air and fly to the outside. He was more alert than he had ever been before; and he strode forward, confident now that the beast would not attack him until he was well within the lair. Every sense radiated outward; he was absorbing minute details of his environs as he went forward.

Ge-or was surprised to note that though Slyn had believed the cave worn by centuries of use, and indeed that may have been partially the cause, the walls had actually been melted to a glass-like material by the heat of the beast's breath. For ease of egress, the dragon had seared the walls until they were so smooth and iron-hard that he could pass through with no impediment from any stone, pebble, protrusion, or defect. Thankfully, Ge-or's heavy leather boots found a purchase and he felt that he would have no problem running along the length of the tunnel when he had to.

He also noted the height and width of the walls and memorized the route he wanted to take on his way out, one that would afford him the most protection should Fis decide to breathe while Ge-or was retreating.

When he got to the place where the cave began to widen, about a hundred and fifty paces in from the ledge, the light behind had dimmed to virtually nothing. Nonetheless, a warm reddish glow had begun to emerge to his fore. He stepped further in, pausing at the edge of the broken rock in front of him as he caught sight of the top of Fis's back.

Just as he stopped, the great head lifted up. Fis stared in his direction. "Ge-or of Thiele. I have been expecting you."

Ge-or was surprised, upon hearing Fis address him. He was also a bit shocked that the damned beast knew his name. Well, he thought, taking another deep breath, he had a shock in store for the dragon as well.

"You are a fool then, for I have come to kill you." Ge-or spoke calmly. His initial aim was to enrage the beast while staying perfectly in control himself. If the dragon wanted to banter with him, he would make it work to his advantage. The angrier he could get Fis, the better for their plan. He did not want the dragon in full control.

"Hah! Yes, that is, I suppose, noble and brave of you. However, my valiant half-elf, you are the foolish one. Look about you. There are hundreds here who have tried over the centuries. I do not think you match even half of these, for many were the best of another age."

Ge-or could see that the dragon was not idly boasting. Half its bulk was resting on the skulls and bones of what must have been many a fine warrior. The other half, and he was tempted to focus on it, but he didn't, was a bed of treasure that Fis's front end was lying upon.

Rather than waste precious time, Ge-or decided to sidle sideways whilst they talked, in order to avoid the worst of the torn rock to his front. Fis continued to try to lure him into doing something rash.

"The great hero, your father, died under my breath. It shall be the same for you. I will not honor you by saving your bones. I will burn you to ash; and after, perhaps I will go after your brother."

Ge-or was surprised again. This beast was being informed, by whom? That dark priest, Aberon? Ge-or did not take the bait. He was too focused on what he was doing and what he and Slyn had planned. He aimed to keep their strategy at the forefront of his consciousness. He was quite willing to bait the dragon back. "You will try; yet in the end, I will have you, worm. Oh, great Fis, you are not the only one informed. You think I waited so many years for this day because I was afraid? Nay, it was because I wanted to be sure you didn't stand a chance."

At this, the dragon shifted slightly, pushing his front end up off the treasure pile and lowering his head to stare at Ge-or, who was once again approaching as if unafraid of the monstrous beast in front of him.

"In truth, I have had few chances to banter with an idiot warrior for some scores of years now. I am growing bored of this conversation; and though it was amusing for a while, I would like to get more rest. Come a bit closer, and we will get this over with."

Fis puffed out slightly, creating a small burst of flame, as if to check to see that all was working properly. It was also probably meant to strike some fear into the foolishly brave half-elf, now striding confidently deep into his lair. "You will pay dearly for your arrogance, fool. I have watched you whilst you were watching me. You do not have the weapons to strike me down. I am impregnable to all except magical weapons of the best quality. The dwarven sword you carry is a nice trinket, to be sure, yet it is nothing to me. Only a weapon like your father's sword could harm one as old as I. It is one of the reasons I wished to own it."

"And because that blade was used to kill your sire?"

At that, Fis rose up even more on his forelegs. He emitted a low growl. "You should watch your tongue, half-elf. Else I will roast you slowly and eat you whilst you are still alive.

"You are getting soft and unobservant in your old age, beast. I came for my father's sword; I also came to kill you. One task is complete; the other is before us."

At Ge-or's words, Fis reared up to full height and glanced down at the treasure pile beneath his frame. Then he let loose a mighty roar that hurt Ge-or's ears as it roiled around the cavern. At that moment, Ge-or reached behind his back and drew out a blade that flared into a cold blue flame as it swept upward. He yelled loudly, "Are you looking for something, beast?"

Fis roared again and shook out his wings. He jumped forward and nearly let loose with his breath; however, he was acutely aware, as Ge-or had learned also, that a dragon can only breathe flames so many times before his store of liquid fire needed to be recouped. He crouched about thirty paces in front of Ge-or and waited, for the half-elf did not seem afraid, and that was troubling. It would do to be cautious a bit longer and try to assess what defenses and offenses his opponent might have.

Ge-or, following his planned motions, resheathed the blade. He set the heavy shield down in front of him, balanced on a long spike at its back so it would stay upright. Finally, he brought his elven bow forward.

Dragons are keen-eyed, and Fis was studying Ge-or carefully. The half-elf obviously had on leather armor, an armor that was strangely bulky – perhaps layered. This was not a particular concern because he knew his breath could sear through many layers of such protection. Metal armor was even better as its occupant would roast quite nicely when the metal heated up. The half-elf before him had obviously figured that out. However, there was something about the shield that drew his attention – there was some sort of material attached on the outside that was dripping wet. It looked like a woven fabric made of leaves or something similar. It did not look particularly formidable, so he decided he would hold nothing back when he did decide to let loose.

Meanwhile, Ge-or had nocked an arrow, which had not gone unnoticed by Fis. Arrows were generally of little threat, even in the hands of a good archer. Dragons, especially in their youth, had vulnerable spots on their hides – most notably their bellies, underneath their throat, and their leg pits. Fis was old, ancient by any standards, and over the centuries the protective scales all over his body had become thicker, heavier, and harder with age. There was little damage that a bow, even a powerful longbow, could do to him. Still, he eyed Ge-or and waited.

In a single smooth motion that was faster than most humans could follow, Ge-or suddenly raised the bow and shot. Fis was surprised at the quickness with which the half-elf moved; he had only seen this kind of speed in true elves; still, he was not concerned. The force of the arrow might create a minor sting as it shattered against his scales, nothing more.

That was how he felt the instant before the heavy point and shaft hit home at the joint of his right front shoulder. It had been many, many long years since Fis had felt so much pain – pain inflicted by a humanoid of any breeding. The arrow did not penetrate; it hit at a very sensitive juncture, perfectly aimed at the right spot. The compression of the point on his scaled body hit a nerve causing a slicing, stabbing pain that echoed down his leg and left him unable to lift it for a couple of seconds. He roared again, this time swinging his head up and glaring into the half-elf's eyes.

Ge-or had taken that moment to set another arrow to the powerful bow and to draw back once again with incredible agility and speed. This arrow flew straight and true as Fis opened his mouth and let loose with the howl of pain and rage. The point punctured his tongue and lodged in the roof of his mouth. This time Fis did breathe. He let go with a full blast of flame.

As soon as the second arrow was on its way, Ge-or dropped the bow to his side and knelt behind the shield. He pressed his head into the mid-top of the swamp webbing on the inside and covered his face with his arm and elbow. The flame shot all around him, and he felt it. If he had thought at the time to describe the sensation, it was as if he had stuck his whole body into a blacksmith's kiln for an instant, pulling it out in the nick of time to avoid a blistering or charring of the flesh. It was hot; thankfully, it was also short-lived.

As soon as the flame blast subsided, he was on his feet. Leaving the now badly charred shield, he also left the bow where it had fallen and sprinted for the cave entrance. He took a long leap into the pile of rocks, slipped, almost fell, managed to gain a purchase with his boot and leapt again, clearing the last of the rubble and landing on solid ground behind.

Another minor tidbit from dragon lore that Ge-or had managed to pry out of Ordrake, drove him to run as fast as his encumbrance would allow. It took the beasts a bit of time to recover their ability to breathe fire following a blast – but didn't take long.

Ge-or sped ahead to the mouth of the cave, half-expecting another blast to hit him from behind. Yet he heard and felt nothing.

Fis was beyond angry. This elf-kin was proving to be a major nuisance. The blast of fire had incinerated what was left of the arrow, so that was not a concern. His mouth, however, did hurt and his shoulder still pained him. It was time to finish this. He raised his wings, flapped twice, launching himself toward the cave's tunnel. Ge-or might gain the outside; but once Fis was in the air, he would have the advantage, sword or no sword. If the half-elf was foolish enough to bar his way in the cave, well, Fis had more fire and other tricks as well.

The Great Druid

On another mountain in the same range, not many leagues from where a battle to the death was taking place high above the forest, a gaunt, ascetic figure in black was enjoying the fruits of a hard won, and certainly long-awaited, victory.

What a wonderful way to celebrate the Yule-tide.

Aberon had cause to feel good. Two, Three, and Four were subdued and caged; and here at his feet groveled the One. At last the power is all mine! He kicked at the head of the once Great Druid. The bloodied face lolled to the other side, away from him.

Ignoring the unconscious man, he walked over to the open window and looked out over his domain.

It was frozen now, it almost always was; the view nonetheless was magnificent. Atop the highest of the Impassable Mountains stood the stronghold of the Black Druids, or as he liked to think of their collected might, the Creed of Pain.

Pain was such a luxury. It was too bad more people didn't think so. Pain kept one aware of one's life force and how precious it was to have and to keep for oneself. Most of the fools out there, the Boreans, whatever their ilk, gave that up much too easily. A bit of pain, real pain, once in a while kept one alert. It reminded you not to take softness and ease for granted. If you truly understood its value, pain could be a part of the very pinnacle of pleasure.

Pain was even more of a luxury to give, to inflict on others. He felt great satisfaction when he would see it written across the face of a victim – especially a victim who had no reason to understand why he or she had fallen from their mundane life into a hell that made no sense to them. You could see it in their faces: "What did I do to deserve this?" or "Why me?" The pleasure of hearing them beseech their gods sent thrills up and down his spine. For some reason, they always hoped someone would come for them, rescue them. In the end, it was just pain. To see their despair and hopelessness – that was even more of a juicy treat for his heart. He reveled in it; it was a release on the best of days and a tonic on the worst.

It was pain, true pain, that the creature on the floor behind him would soon suffer. He meant to keep the next three below him in place. They would have their uses, because they did wield considerable power. Unfortunately for them, they had been no match for the power he had been imbued with when the

Altar of Kan had broken. And then added to, after recovering Kan's Sceptre from the dungeons above his Altar.

After escaping those horrific winged beasts -- set, he had to assume, to guard the thing -- it had taken him over two years to probe the power and secrets implanted in the device. He discovered that the vital energy he had acquired when Kan's altar had split, spoke directly to the power in his Sceptre. Once he had deciphered how to wield and control all that Kan had imbued into it, he had understood what true power was. And that was only a mote of what he would eventually wield. When his full plans came to fruition, he would have it all. He wouldn't make the same mistakes that idiot had either. He would use the power for what it had been meant for – destruction, not self-preservation. Kan had been a fool.

His only real trial had been to subdue Two, Three, and Four without hurting them. He needed them if his plans over the next decade or so could come to fruition.

The One? Well his agony and death would serve as a warning to any who would even begin to think to oppose him. The Great Druid had been so arrogant, so demanding, so belittling during Aberon's tenure as an acolyte, priest, and eventually as a groveling initiate at the meanest level of druidic lore. There was a debt to be paid back to this one. He meant to have a good bit of fun ensuring that the debt was paid in full. It had felt immeasurably good to walk into the great hall, whisk away the defeated "Great One's" staff with a flick of the Sceptre of Kan, and send him crashing into his own altar with a wave of Aberon's hand. The astonishment and disbelief on Number One's face was almost payback enough – but not quite.

It was time to start the festivities. Aberon turned back toward the center of the hall. With a gesture to the nine monks standing along the wall with their heads bowed, he indicated that he wanted the former Great One placed upon the altar. He ordered them to bring the Three up from the dungeons.

He took his time. Time was a true luxury now. Soon enough they would be busy regathering the diverse clans of Qa-ryks and building all the other forces he intended to use to crush the kingdom; for now, he could play for a bit.

He had planned for ten days of it. Ten days from the winter solstice to the beginning of the New Year. An appropriate length of time to torture a "great" man, he thought. Originally, he had considered a week; however, that seemed too short for any number of reasons, most importantly that the Three, and all the other druids and priests of the Black Keep, would be able to witness what might lay in store for them should they make the mistake of causing Aberon even a modicum of distress. He wanted them to know what failure would mean, what any form of disobedience would bring, and what kind of power their master could wield.

While he worked, his victim screamed and writhed, Aberon stayed perfectly calm. Depending on his audience, he would actually discuss plans, or talk about the new structure of the Black Druids, or detail the incantations and devices they would need to use to corral the Qa-ryk horde. He knew that the emotional ambivalence toward what he was doing would strike even more fear into the hearts and souls of these men he intended to rule with an iron will and an iron hand.

The overall structure of the Black Druids would remain the same – it was tradition. However, the true power structure would be vastly different. Aberon would lead the "Nine," and there would no longer be challenges to the reign of "the One." His rule would be absolute, and their purpose would be to obey – not question – obey. He would be "the One," "the Great One," "the Great Druid."

He was starting the eighth day of the torture when he got the idea to have his chosen help with the final torments. It would give them something to do instead of standing around cringing. It would also be good for them to get their feet wet a bit. There was nothing like in-house training to warm the blood. It would help him solidify his position; and perhaps even more importantly, it would be the perfect means of setting them apart from all the others who thought to rise to power. He would have more fun, too, because he would be able to focus exclusively on the old man's pain. Let others be involved in creating it; he would sit back and enjoy.

***

Aberon had planned well. The Great Druid expired at the twelfth hour of the tenth day. He was there in all his glory to bask in and receive the former strength of his counterpart. It had been a grueling last twenty-four hours. The incantations he needed to cast to ensure that little was lost in the transfer of power had drained him. This was one time when he could not use the power of the Sceptre of Kan. This was about enhancing his inner strength; everything about the Sceptre was centered in the gathering and use of energy from without.

If his minions had not been afeared of him before this final transformation, the obvious power that radiated from his body as the energy flowed into him when the former Great Druid died would be a reminder. They all threw themselves on the floor at his feet when he stepped forth from the altar and moved to the center of the hall. Though he couldn't see himself fully, he knew that his whole body was a dark void wreathed in a dreadful deep red light that coruscated about him, as if he had stepped from the depths of hell. Now it was time! Now it was *his* time!

Death in the Wilds

Ge-or drew a thick leather roll of hide from his back as he sprinted toward the cave mouth. The triple-layered set of skins had been painstakingly sewn together by him and Slyn. Between the three hides they had layered some soft cloth, brought with them for just such a purpose. They had tested it on short hillsides covered with snow and ice. Right now he was hoping that it would work as they had planned and hold up on the long plunge down the mountainside.

Surprised that he hadn't heard or felt the dragon in pursuit, Ge-or made the last slight curve to the right and headed up the slope to the entrance. When he burst through the opening into the bright sunlight, he slowed a bit and jogged to the easternmost part of the ledge. There he dove over the side, headfirst; and though he followed no particular religion, he whispered a few words of prayer to the gods.

This route down the side of the mountain had been one that Slyn had thoroughly explored. It was too steep and had too few handholds for Ge-or to use going up, but it had been an ideal path for Slyn to take up and down while planning his theft of the sword. Now that the mountainside was covered with ice and snow, they both had felt it might function as a type of chute for Ge-or to slide down on, and hopefully end up somewhere near the bottom.

Before the snow, Slyn had made every effort to brush aside any loose gravel or remove larger impediments to a straight shot down the slope. Unfortunately, there were still a few obstacles along the way. Ge-or firmly gripped the stout wooden staff that had been sewn into one end of the sled, as he shot down the mountain. He knew he had only limited ability to steer the thing. For that reason, he and his partner had been over the route verbally a hundred times. His partner had even drawn him a rough map of where the obstructions were. There was no way, however, for him to be completely prepared without actually having been up and down the path many times.

As the ground sped beneath him, Ge-or steeled himself for the first and most dangerous of the hazards in front of him. This part of the slope was the steepest, and he was moving at a very fast rate of speed when he finally caught sight of the boulder jutting out from his right directly into the center of his straight-line route downward. He barely had time to react, and the roar from above as the dragon reached the cave mouth caused him to flinch and lean a bit too far to the left.

He shot past the boulder, barely brushing it with his right thigh; but his over-tilt caused him to come mostly off the leather sled. He found himself careening downward with his body at an angle to the leather and with only his shoulders and part of the right side of his chest actually on the device. He held on.

Above him, another roar erupted as Fis leapt into the sky. The dragon was surprised upon emerging from his den not to see the half-elf directly in front of him, or at least scrambling down the slope on the path that the damned black priest had always used. Once he was in the air he took in the whole picture. His foe was nothing if not resourceful. Twisting his body sideways, Fis gave a great heave with his wings and dove downward, paralleling the slope and coming at his enemy from behind. He would meet the fool at the bottom.

Within a couple of seconds, having no chance to readjust himself, Ge-or hit the next impediments. Slyn had described in detail a set of three "slight ditches" that, "unless they had completely filled with ice and snow, might present difficulties." Had Ge-or been fully on the sled it might have helped; as it was, when he hit the first "ditch" he had the breath knocked out of him. Before he had time to recover, he hit the second; and that one, a long dip followed by another heavy hit on the far side, caused him to lose his grip with his right hand. He flopped sideways, tried to keep a hold of the sled with his left, when he hit the third hollow and rolled sideways. He then glanced off a small boulder, which caused him to lose the breath he was taking. Tumbling and rolling to the left far off the chosen route, Ge-or continued down the slope.

This unplanned development probably saved his life because, though they had hoped and tried to calculate the dragon's speed, Fis had already swept past Ge-or, flipped over on his tail, and aimed a blast of fire so that the half-elf would slide right into it. The blast hit exactly the spot that Fis had intended, only Ge-or was tumbling sideways at the time and didn't even notice or feel the intense explosion of heat as ice and snow turned to steam, and the power of the dragon's breath melted the stone of the mountain beneath.

The well-padded half-elf, sustaining many a bump and bruise, continued downward on an altogether different pathway. Later, Ge-or would have sworn that he had hit every rock and boulder on the mountainside in his uncontrolled tumble. He covered more than two-thirds of the rest of the distance to the bottom before the slope eased and he was able to manage some sort of control to his descent. By this time, Fis, who was even more furious at having wasted another breath, had come around and was watching the erratic plunge while formulating another strategy. He didn't want to use another blast unless he was sure his victim would be directly in the path of the center of the flame. That, he knew, was something that the half-elf could not survive, regardless of what protection he had. The shield he had made had protected him once. This next time, unless he materialized one with magic, Ge-or would be at his mercy.

As the slope gentled, Ge-or managed to spin himself about and get his butt under him so that he could stay relatively upright and continue the slide. Unfortunately, having completely lost the path, he continued to hit things. Finally, realizing that he couldn't stand up to much more pounding, he pushed his feet out and down. With his heavy boots pressing into whatever they could find any traction against, he finally came to a stop.

As he slowed, Ge-or tried to orient himself. He could see the dragon circling off to his right at about a hundred paces. Strangely, the beast seemed to be waiting to see what Ge-or would do next. Ge-or quickly calculated that he had tumbled to the left well over a hundred paces from the planned route, and he was still some hundred paces shy of the bottom where he had hoped to end up. The disadvantage was that he had that distance to cover before he could implement the next part of the plan. The advantage, as it turned out, was that Slyn was in the woods on that side. The half sea-elf would be within close bow range of Fis if the dragon dove over to attack Ge-or.

Doing the only thing he could, Ge-or got to his feet and started loping down the slope, taking huge leaps from one foot to the next. Luckily, here at the lower elevation, there was little ice and only a dusting of snow.

He tried to keep one eye on Fis; however, most of his concentration had to go to where he was putting his feet. He knew Slyn would be watching what transpired; yet he wasn't sure how much the thief could help, not until he got down near the trees.

Dragons are highly intelligent, and they tend to spend a good part of their lives contemplating esoteric things. Fis had been around a long time; and had he been at the top of his form, he might not have let his anger influence his reactions. It had been almost an age since he had had to pay any attention at all to anything resembling a competent fighter. The few idiots who had come westward for glory in the past hundreds of years, he had the great pleasure to toy with before eating. He couldn't reverse what had already happened in the cave. His mouth still stung, but he was thinking clearly now. He wouldn't let emotions influence what he did next. This half-elf would find out what it meant to disturb his equanimity.

There was nothing like a bit of human or elven flesh to break the monotony of his usual fare of cattle and sheep. He had developed a bit of a taste for it during the dragon wars. True, it was a bit odd to eat the hand that had fed you for centuries, though times changed. He ate what was available, especially if it was delivered to his doorstep freely.

He had considered making a meal of this fellow when he first showed up years ago; the truth was he had grown lazy in his ancient age. It was far too much trouble to bother with swords and armor – the latter tending to give him indigestion. If the half-elf insisted on coming after his father's sword, he had figured he would deal with him in his lair where he had all the advantages, or so he had believed. It had indeed been a long, long time since he had met a fighter who had this one's skills, temperament, and forethought. Ah well, now that he was awake and focused, he would make short shrift of this thorn in his side.

So, instead of diving down to intercept the running half-elf, Fis circled and watched. He would not waste another breath until he had Ge-or cornered, and there was a great deal of open space between the half-elf and the protective forest. Not that the trees would stop Fis either; it would make his task a bit more difficult if the warrior got under cover.

Puzzled that the dragon did not swoop in and try to attack, Ge-or continued his plunge. He was nearing the flat leading toward the forested area where he and Slyn had laid out the next part of their plan, when the dragon finally put its tail down and began to turn. Continuing to run, Ge-or now reached over his shoulder and drew his father's sword.

Slyn was watching. Dropping the short pole he was holding, he drew his bow off his shoulder and nocked an arrow. He was a good shot, almost as good as Ge-or; but his bow was not in the same league as the powerful elven weapon Ge-or had used. At best, he hoped he could distract the red long enough for Ge-or to clear the trap they had laid.

Fis was determined to intercept the half-elf before he could get to cover. Surprisingly, even though the trees to Ge-or's left were closest, the half-elf was sprinting toward an open space in the wood. Fis had just turned, to come at the half-elf from behind, when he felt something smack into the side of the head. He growled and looked to the left. He could make out the thief that had partnered with Ge-or. The sea-elf was setting another arrow to string. Pests, he thought. His mind automatically registered the force of the arrow strike; and in an instant, he knew that whatever weapon the thief was using was not powerful enough to do him any damage. He continued his dive.

Slyn, for his part, cursed his shot. It had been caught by the waft of wind from the movement of the dragon's wings and thrown off course by several inches. Taking aim again and trying to calculate windage, speed of the dragon, and any other effects that might alter the arrow's flight path, he released again.

This time the arrow flew true and struck Fis in his left eye. It did no damage, as dragons have two eyelids – the inner one a semi-transparent, faceted membrane that allowed them to see during battle – yet he did feel the pointed hit. It made him involuntarily blink with his outer lid and in turn shut down his depth perception for an instant. That caused him to swoop up slightly from his dive.

As Fis made a remarkable spinning-looping turn in the air to re-orient his attack, Ge-or continued to run ahead. Slyn dropped his bow and stepped back behind the tree, once again picking up the broad pole he had let go of only seconds before.

It was close. Fis was extremely agile. In fact, dragons actually became more flexible with age. The young pups were the ones who had succumbed first in the dragon wars, not only because their scales had not fully matured; but because they could not maneuver as well in mid-air.

Ge-or had barely crossed the imaginary line of their trap when Fis came in low some thirty paces behind, opening his mouth to breathe.

The situation seemed ideal for the dragon. Ge-or had entered a small opening cut from the woods and was vulnerable to the dragon's fire blast from every side. The thief had disappeared. Fis had chosen to ignore him anyway, now that he knew where he was. Another arrow would not disturb him; he knew about that possibility now.

Ge-or had learned another important key to how dragons attacked when he had reviewed in his mind Fis's final attack on Thiele. It had not been difficult to do, since the image was burned into his memory. When he had studied the burn path, it was obvious that the beast had to have come in quite low, for the ground was scorched in a long narrow corridor. Whether all dragons attacked this way from the air, or only Fis, Ge-or wasn't sure. What he had seen was the dragon dive, come in low, above ground level, and angle his breath so it would burn the longest possible swath through its target. He was counting on Fis doing exactly that again.

Timing was critical. As Ge-or crossed the trap line, Slyn pulled with all his might on the staff in his hands. This caused a rope and vine netting to spring up across the clearing anchored at the far end to a broad oak tree.

Fis saw two things that registered in his mind as problematic as he prepared to breathe; unfortunately, he did not have time to think them through since he was committed to the attack and the fire roiling up from within. The first was that the clearing had been altered slightly. There were trees down. If he had the time, he would have been able to think back and search his memory and tell exactly how many and where they had been. The second was that there was something on the ground that didn't quite fit in, though it was partially covered with snow, lying some yards ahead.

As soon as Ge-or was seven steps past the laid-out stretch of netting, he put on the brakes, spun around, and dropped to one knee. Then, as the netting began to come up, he drove himself up and forward, the bright flaming-blue blade of his father's sword held by his side.

At the same instant, Fis saw the netting rise. He flared his wings a bit to brake slightly and raise himself. It was an automatic response, which is all that Slyn and Ge-or had intended to happen. The netting was not high enough to entangle the dragon, unless by some miracle the dragon caught a dragging talon in it; but they had figured correctly that it was virtually impossible not to react when something was moving up toward you. Instinct took over and you tried to avoid whatever it was – like bringing your arm or hands up to block a bright flash.

Even though he pulled back and somewhat up from the netting, Fis's forward motion continued. He was focused enough that he was able to regroup and bring his head down to re-aim the breath strike at the half-elf. Yet with the dragon's forward momentum and Ge-or's pounding legs driving him back toward the beast, they came together much sooner than Fis had expected. He was used to his enemies fleeing his attacks, not purposefully coming at him.

As the dragon flared his wings, Ge-or had the opening he needed. One, two, and a third step closer, and he pushed off, lunging upward and driving the blade to the length of his reach. Ge-or's powerful thrust carried him up in the air on an angle that increased his reach an extra four feet or more. His lunge and Fis's continued motion forward caused the flaming blade to plunge deep into the dragon at the base of its neck above the chest. The magical blade, made of the finest steel, honed to the keenest edge, and magically imbued with extraordinary killing potential, cut through scales, skin, and flesh. Ge-or followed the thrust through, driving the blade out the other side before gravity carried him downward.

Fis, his breath at the full impulse phase of the strike, could not stop either his momentum or the blast. What occurred next was something that Ge-or and Slyn would never talk about except to Sart and close kin, because it seemed almost completely incomprehensible. Ge-or kept his right hand wrapped around the hilt of the sword and with his own forward motion and that of the dragon's, the blade slid, cutting downward into the beast's breastplate and opening a gaping wound. As Ge-or fell, he rolled to his right, drawing the now unencumbered sword with him, trying to get free of where the dragon might come down. He spun onto his back and saw liquid fire pour through the cut, which had the effect of incinerating the dragon's exposed flesh as it passed. Fis howled in pain, flapped frantically with his wings, and then did a complete somersault, finally crashing into the ground, falling into his own pool of fire. He thrashed several times and lay still.

For a long time, Ge-or lay where he had come to rest, only feet from Fis's ruin, staring at the dragon as if he expected the beast to rise up and continue his attack. Slyn came out from behind the tree, where he had hidden when the fire first burst forth, and stared as well. Though the dragon had looked huge with its wingspread bearing down on them, laying in a motionless mound right in front of them Fis was immense – something truly out of dreams and legends.

When nothing happened, Ge-or finally pushed himself up, keeping his father's sword in hand. It was at this point that he began to notice the many aches and pains that he had acquired in the last – could it have only been about twenty minutes? Besides numerous bumps and bruises, he realized that even with all the protection he had, including the fire-resistant potion of Sart's, he hadn't escaped burns completely. Where the armor had been thinnest, he could now feel the heat of reddened flesh. Yet, his focus was still on the beast. He wanted to be sure Fis was dead, so he sidled around until he was facing the huge head. Fis's maw was open revealing rows of large, very sharp teeth. Ge-or stepped forward, swept the sword out and up and drove the point down through the skull and into the dragon's brain. Fis did not move.

Ge-or desired for nothing more than to rest for a day or more, yet he knew that the next three days would be critical to taking full advantage of all this great beast had to offer. The treasure would have to wait. As much as both he and Slyn wanted to search the beast's trove, there were far more time-pressured matters to attend to.

Slyn came out from the trees fully now and stood slightly back from Ge-or, admiring the massive creature. He was still hesitant to approach closer. Ge-or gestured for him to come ahead; and as he did so, Slyn brought several large vials from underneath his cloak and handed them to his partner.

Ge-or raised the sword once more, and this time neatly sliced a line across Fis's throat at a point where he could hold one of the vials underneath the vein and collect whatever blood oozed out. He had to massage the neck a bit in order to get enough to fill the two glass containers. Finally satisfied, he handed them back to Slyn, who stoppered them. Later, they would seal these with melted wax; for now, it would do. Dragon's blood was worth ten-thousand weight in gold to alchemists and mages alike. Whether the stories were true, and few lived now that would know except the elder elven mages, dragon's blood was reputed to have amazing powers both in incantations and in affecting dramatic results in chemical reactions.

While his partner took the two precious vials of blood back to the cabin, Ge-or set about gutting the dragon. Fis had fallen in such a way that most of his lower underbelly was exposed. First, Ge-or inserted his blade as far down the belly as he could; and with it angled sharply, he slid it up toward the beast's left forearm, which was resting below the lowest part of the breastplate. While another knife or sword would probably not have even penetrated the tough flesh of the dragon, much less cut through scales and membrane, Fisbane, newly named now in Ge-or's mind, cut easily upward through all. The magical blade of the elves passed on to Manfred had inherited a new owner. By the time Ge-or had exposed the full gut sack by cutting through any membrane that remained, Slyn was back with several other large, heavy glass containers and a pile of supple leather gloves.

Ge-or wiped the sword as clean as he could with a piece of leather his partner had brought back with him for that purpose. He then took off his thick leather gauntlets, the swamp-grass reinforced jerkin, and the other bulky accoutrements. He put on one of the other pairs of gloves so he could begin the truly dirty work ahead. The two adventurers had poured through numerous manuscripts about dragons over the past two winters while waiting for the next spring's attempt, but they had not read anything about how to go about retrieving the many parts of a dragon that would be useful or valuable. There was plenty written about how important the spleen was to alchemists, or how the heart should be preserved and dried to be used in potions, and so forth; however, no one had mentioned whether working with a dragon's flesh, guts, blood, and so forth was caustic or dangerous in any way. They had decided to err on the sensible side and had prepared thirty pairs of long leather gloves while they waited their next opportunity to head west for the beast. They would wear them while they labored over and around Fis's carcass.

Using two long poles, Ge-or and Slyn with great effort managed to slide the bulk of Fis's guts out of the cavity and onto the ground. There, Ge-or carefully proceeded to identify those organs and parts they wished to preserve. The stomachs – there were five in a dragon – were set aside. The fire sac, something they wanted to deal with later, was cut out and tied off using part of the tube that stretched upward toward the throat. This they placed carefully far off on top of a pile of snow and ice where they hoped it would remain safe. The intestines were pushed out of the way. Then, one after another, Ge-or located and removed the spleen, heart, pancreas, liver, and gall bladder. As he set each of these aside, Slyn cleaned them with snow, wrapped each carefully in leather, and placed them in large heavy cloth sacks designed for transport. Finally, he took them to an icehouse they had prepared where they would be left until it was time to head east in the early spring.

With the organs preserved the best they could, Ge-or and Slyn turned their attention to the fire sac. It had been warm, not hot, when they had removed it from the mass of innards. Luckily, at least as far as they were concerned, it was mostly empty. The final blast from Fis had been more of an eruption of fluid following Ge-or's strike than a true breath blast. The liquid fire had flowed unchecked from the long slit down its throat bursting into flame as it coruscated outward. They guessed the final death throes of the beast had further emptied the pouch.

The leathery membrane obviously could withstand a caustic substance. Though the sac now only measured a few feet in diameter, Ge-or understood that, when full, it stretched out to several yards. The first order of business was to carefully empty the remaining liquid. Sart, who was a fairly adept alchemist himself, had poured through many manuscripts and given them some advice on how to attempt to preserve the liquid, which "seems to ignite when exposed to the air." Ge-or and Slyn were a bit reluctant to make the attempt; but Sart was keen on trying to preserve at least a small amount of the liquid, so he could experiment with it and see its properties.

The cleric had designed a device with a carefully carved conical bone spout that could be inserted into the end of the tubing membrane leading from the sac. The other end would be inserted into a large vial lined with wax to preserve the seal on that end. He had instructed Slyn, "Stretch the tubing membrane over the spout and tip the sac upward, pressing to push the contents into the jar. If you ensure that the membrane is flush to all sides of the cone, there should be no leakage." The tricky part would be sealing the vial once the liquid had been transferred, before it could explode.

"Fill the jar completely. Then slip the stopper on as quickly as possible," was the best advice Sart could give. They hoped it would be good enough. The cleric could not offer them an answer to their question as to whether the liquid fire would explode when exposed to whatever air was in the vial. He "hoped it would not be enough to set off a reaction." Yet, he had also suggested that they cool down the sac as much as possible, as "temperature often affects a chemical interaction." It was a small consolation; but Sart had been so helpful to them and such an influence on Ge-or's adventuring life, that he felt obligated to make the attempt. In addition, as Ge-or had recently witnessed, when Fis breathed, the liquid effusing from his mouth did not completely ignite until it was clear of his muzzle. The effect of air on the liquid was not immediate.

Once all the pieces were in place for the transfer, Ge-or lifted the sac in both his arms high enough that whatever liquid remained would flow down toward the heavy glass vial they had set upright on the ground, wedged in by ice and snow. Once all was in position, Slyn signaled Ge-or and he raised the sac enough to straighten out the remaining tubing. As Slyn watched carefully, a greenish-yellow, thick-looking liquid streamed down into the vial. The thief, who was closest to the danger zone of the liquid transfer, had placed pine boughs along the ground for five paces off to the side in case he needed extra traction to make his escape should the liquid explode.

Shortly, the large vial was filled. The most difficult part of the process remained. Slyn packed more snow around the jar – now filled up to the edge of the neck – while Ge-or lowered the sack until the curve of the tubing closed off what little remained in the pouch. After a couple more minutes of waiting for the liquid to further cool, Slyn nodded that he was ready. He held the stopper in his right hand and reached out with his left to disengage the snout from the vial. He was fast. Probably as fast as anyone could be, for his profession demanded that type of dexterity. It was less than an instant – Ge-or could not even tell that it had taken place – and the stopper was in place. There was no explosion.

Slyn sat back and looked up at Ge-or, wiping his brow. "That was one of the bravest things I have ever done."

"And no one will ever sing about it."

"Aye."

Ge-or grinned, setting the sac back down. He had read nothing about the taking of or possible use of the fire sac in all the literature he and Slyn had poured through. He figured, however, that it might prove useful to someone, so he was determined to see if the large bladder-like organ could be put to good use. Having his partner stand aside he reached out, pierced the pouch with his sword, and jumped back. There was a sharp hissing sound as whatever gas inside escaped and then a poof of smoke came from the hole, and nothing more.

Stepping ahead again, Ge-or used his blade to slice the length of the organ and pushed with the tip to open it more to the air. There was another brief flare of smoke. He poked at it with the blade several more times; when nothing further happened, he went closer and made a perpendicular slit to the first one. The sac flopped open and drew in even more. He flipped it over with the tip of the sword and let it lie in the snow.

The light was beginning to fade, so he reached out to help his partner to his feet. "Enough for today, we will continue this work on the morrow."

That evening, for the first time since he had been a young lad, Ge-or examined his father's sword carefully. It wasn't a long blade by fighting standards. It was probably originally designed for battle in many different environs, from horseback, to dragon-back, to tight melee. It was lighter and shorter than the bastard sword or the long sword preferred by men in a pitched fight. Fisbane – he liked the new appellation – was weighted toward the hilt, perfectly balanced for his muscled frame, the blade a bit over twenty-seven inches. It had two wide grooves running its length, molded into it to save weight, with a strong, smooth center ridge that gave the sword its strength. As with many elven weapons, it was tapered for a good length of the blade. It was a sword that could be used effectively, whether to slash, stab, bash with the hilt or guard, or use one-and-a-half-handed when additional power was desired. There was nothing ostentatious about it except that it had an elegant beauty to its overall design. The hilt and guard were inlaid with gold and silver, only as bespoke the gentle grace of the blade itself, heightening the beauty of the flow of the whole weapon. There were no marks on it to indicate its makers or its history. The blade spoke for itself. It was a weapon crafted by the best, for the best.

Though it did not need it, Ge-or spent a half hour with his finest whetstone, caressing the edge. When he finally put the sword in the back scabbard he had made for it, it truly felt like his own. There was a lingering heaviness in his heart, for he would rather have received it from his father when he had come of age than by killing the dragon.

Sitting around their warm hearth, Slyn and Ge-or quietly talked about the battle. They spoke of their fears and successes, and mostly about the magnificent beast they had killed. Dragons had once been revered in their world; yet, through far too many permutations of fate, they had become enemies. In reverence for the ancient dragon and because killing was something neither Ge-or or Slyn reveled in, they decided never to speak on all that had transpired beneath this mountain to any others except Sart. They would let those who felt the need to speak and sing about great adventures use their imaginations, which, in the final analysis, was likely what they would do anyway.

When they came back to the death site the next morning, everything was as they had left it. Lying upon the snow, the fire sac skin had contracted tremendously as it cooled, until there was less than a three-foot wide square of the material. Yet, when Ge-or picked it up in his gloved hands, he found it was pliable and malleable, albeit now over an inch thick. If he pulled on it, it stretched easily, but immediately went back to its current form when he released the tension.

After a bit of debate, he and Slyn decided to treat the sac like they would treat any leather. Ge-or cut the membrane into one-foot squares. Then using willow stretchers, the two of them took each square and slowly pulled it out to the full length of the frames they had built. Though Ge-or expected the material to stretch a good bit, because the bladder had obviously been much larger inside the dragon when filled with liquid, he was really surprised when each square easily stretched to a pelt thrice the footage on a side.

Even more surprising is that when they went to inspect the bladder pelts a week later, they had not lost any of their malleability and were still soft and flexible. They didn't appear to have lost any moisture whatsoever. Weeks after that, when they finally began to gather everything to leave camp, the squares, when removed from the stretchers, returned to the one foot a side and one-inch-thick dimension they had held originally after being cut. Ge-or decided he would let Sart and Ordrake puzzle the mechanics and makeup of the fire sac pieces at their leisure.

***

That first day following Fis's death, and well into the next day, they spent occupied in preserving all that they could of the great beast. The weather turned even colder, so they did not have to worry about putrefaction setting in. The huge mound of flesh would take a long time to cool down and to freeze solid; thankfully, the cold would at least delay the inevitable.

While Ge-or worked for two days cutting off all the skin he could reach, Slyn worked at removing the dragon's many teeth and claws. These were valuable, more as talismans, than anything else, though some magic-users and clerics claimed they had certain powers that facilitated this or that spell, healing, or protection. These would also be proof that they had killed the beast, for it would be a tale eventually told in a thousand different ways, all of them having little to do with the truth.

On the third day following Fis's death, both Ge-or and Slyn began the tedious job of cutting the scales from the skin of the beast. Each scale, unlike those of a fish, was attached to the hide by hundreds of heavy thread-like hairs. These were extremely tough to cut through with a normal blade, yet easy enough for Fisbane. Much of the time, Slyn would simply pry up a scale so Ge-or could slice it off. To ease the tedium, sometimes they would work side by side. Slyn would slice away with his carefully honed blade, taking ten times as long to remove a single scale as Ge-or. After a few scales, he would have to re-sharpen his knife.

For the sake of preserving the hide, they had to cut through the upper part of the scale as closely as possible to where it attached to the skin without cutting through the pelt. Ge-or had to be especially careful because the magical blade made no differentiation on what it cut through.

Dragons had thousands of scales, so the task seemed unending. Finally, after another half day of it, Ge-or suggested that they take a break and visit Fis's lair the next day. Slyn was hopeful that the dragon might have other magical bladed weapons in its stash that would make his part in the process more productive. When they settled in that night, they were about half done and looking forward to the next day's exploration.

Power!

Aberon was steeped in power. It was an amazing thing to feel this much energy flow through him, to know that if he needed to call for it, he merely needed to focus and draw it forth. And if that were not enough, he had Kan's Sceptre, which gave him a much wider sphere of influence and control. Sometimes, he felt like he could whisk across the great distance separating him from the Borean capital, so he could destroy the place from within. Well, he knew he still had limitations, and there were those with power there as well. He would be cautious until he had the completed artifact in his hands. No one would be able to stand against him. Why risk himself, when he would soon have thousands upon thousands of minions to do his will?

His nine chosen were in place and in such awe of him that he had no worries at all that they would even think of rebelling. He had sent them forth to gather acolytes. It was time for the true training to begin.

Unfortunately, there was no real way to speed up that process: test, retest, get rid of the useless ones, test again. The truth about magic and the druidic powers he and his fellow druids called upon was that one either had it innately or one didn't. If a person did, then they had to determine how much was there and whether that person was capable of learning to use it. For every ten souls they brought to the Black Keep, one or two managed to survive a year of training. After that, the odds increased dramatically that they would succeed at some level; however, they still lost some of those who had the talent but lacked the will or the focus.

He wanted a hundred or more trained druids: priests who could wield devastating magic, others who could lead battalions of Qa-ryks with their incantations, and still others who would set protective webs about all that he coveted here. He did not want to just win this war; he wanted to smash all opposition in his path.

True, many would die. That was a small thing, really. He did not connect with his underlings. Honor, duty, loyalty, and especially anything remotely associated with sentimental feeling were useless for the work he planned. Instead, he drove them all through fear. He let them know on every level how fear was a marvelous thing to behold, to sense, to revel in.

Aberon licked his lips. Perhaps this would be a good time to have another taste of it. To relish the fear he could create and manipulate with his power. There were a few of the new recruits who needed chastisement. It might be fun to make a bit of a party of it. No sense in everything being so serious.

He stood up from his seat on the massive ebon throne, stepped down from the dais, and beckoned for the Nine with a flick of his fingers. He licked his lips again. At that, the Nine bowed low. They knew this mood. There was blood coming, and they wanted to ensure it wasn't theirs.

Aberon smiled.

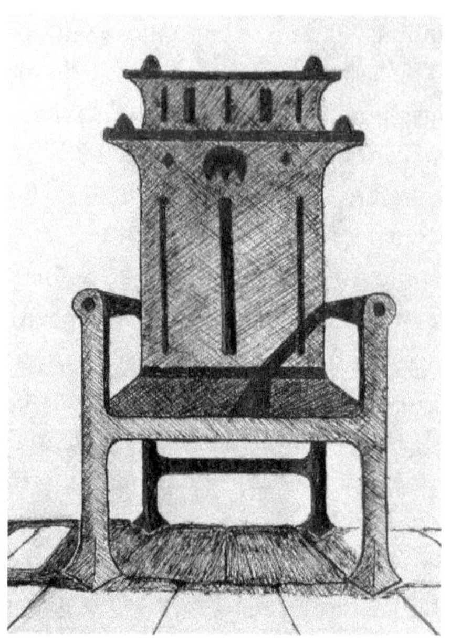

Treasure Enough to Please a Dwarf

"Ancient reds can be a bit quirky when it comes to treasure." Or so Ordrake had told them one day when he was reminiscing. "Don't expect to find a great horde; that's for the younger pups. They'll collect anything bright and shiny for their beds. The great reds, well, they get picky after a few dozen centuries. Don't like carting all that extra weight around with 'em when they change dens. You'll see what I mean. Don't know about ol' Fis. He's been around for a long, long time. From the early years of the elves is my guess. He's probably gotten downright persnickety about his trove.

"Well, there's nothing for it. Bring me back a bit of his blood, some of his organs if you can manage it, a few baubles and we'll be square. Oh… and maybe a bit of the heart. It might give me a kick start for my next hundred years."

The old fellow had been a wealth of information, but it took a good bit of cajoling to get it out of him. Still, Ge-or had enjoyed his visits there; and Slyn had gotten to know the wizard better himself. They owed him a good deal, and they intended to pay the debt and more.

***

Slyn had been up to Fis's lair several dozen times. From the dragon's last feeding before winter had set in, up until Slyn set out to steal the sword before the Yule, he crept up the long slope thrice a week. Part of their plan had been to catch Fis sleeping contentedly on his pile of riches with a fat belly – anything to give them the slightest edge. Slyn and Ge-or hoped that with a full stomach, Fis would be less likely to wake and take notice of the thief's preparations for making off with the blade. Ge-or knew well enough to leave this part to his partner. When it came to stealth, Ge-or's bulk made him like an ox in a dry goods shop.

His partner had crawled over a fair part of the old one's treasure mound and had a good sense of what the beast coveted. Much of the main mound, where Fis rested his rump and stomach with tail curled about, was primarily composed of piles of bones, armor, and weapons. His front end and head, however, lay upon a long slope of high-quality gems, gold, silver, and jewelry. The only true oddities strewn amongst the entire hoard were pieces of what must have been fine furniture, exquisitely built and carved of the finest and richest woods. The dragon's bulk, unfortunately, had squashed and splintered most of the pieces, until they were simply pretty pieces of smashed sculpted wood lying about amidst all the glitter. Also scattered amongst the mass of valuables were many a large shard of reflective glass from mirrors he must have admired and desired at one time. Here, too, his bulk had wreaked havoc on the fragile items.

Over those weeks of exploration, Slyn had aptly fulfilled his appellation of "Master Thief." His whole purpose had been to locate the sword, figure a way to remove it from its position in the mass of treasure, and get it away without Fis knowing. They had waited until after one of Fis's rare flights out to eat. Luckily, the old dragon was too lazy to stir himself on a regular basis; and he would only rouse when he was truly hungry, fly to the east after a fat bullock or two, or perhaps a half dozen sheep, and circle back to once again crawl onto his trove to doze. Even then, Slyn decided that he would stay away a full week after Fis had downed his catch before he attempted his first reconnoitering of the treasure. He wanted the beast well into his deep dream state by the time he broached the entrance to the cavern.

It took him eight days to plan and execute the safest route to the edge of the treasure, another week to survey the extent of the pile and to locate the blade. He spent nearly four weeks working his way back and forth from the edge of the massive pile to the blade and back again. The sword was sticking partially out of the apex of a mound of treasure halfway down Fis's long neck. It was a foot and a half away from the nearest bend, but luckily his head was tilted away toward the far wall. Slyn was able to silently sneak up to the blade without ever actually being within the dragon's line of sight.

Once in the cave and perched off to the side of the mound, Slyn would sit for hours watching the dragon breathe. He studied every movement, eye flutter, and flick of its tail. When Slyn finally got close enough to work on getting the sword out, one major roll or change of position and he would either be discovered or squashed. He wanted to know how the dragon slept and what to expect.

Whether it was because Fis was so old or simply because that was the way dragons slept, he rarely moved much at all. When he did, it was usually a tilting of the head slightly, followed by a small eruption of smoke from his nostrils. Slyn thought of it as the dragon letting off pressure or steam from its gut. His most frightening moment was when he was working to get the blade free. One of these small explosions happened when he was only a foot from Fis's neck. He almost lost his balance, wavering on the balls of his feet. When he finally regained his composure, it was all he could do to wend his way back to the mouth of the cave, where he stood taking long deep breaths. He was drenched in sweat and decided he had had enough for that day.

The most difficult part of the whole venture was freeing the blade one piece of treasure at a time, so that he would eventually be able to slide it out without disturbing anything, not even the smallest gold or silver coin. It was tedious work. The blade was entirely surrounded by gems, coinage, and other bits of treasure. Luckily, most of the hilt was exposed already. Slyn knew he had to clear it entirely of any debris before he would have any chance of sliding the blade up and out.

If patience was ever a virtue, Slyn was truly a saint during those long hours he stood braced against pieces of treasure while he worked the blade free. Sometimes he would spend a whole hour working one or two coins, or a shard of glass or bit of wood out. Each piece had to be laid carefully down somewhere nearby without making the slightest of sounds. All of which was accomplished while he stood within arm's reach of the breathing giant.

For the master thief, it was tedious, yet rewarding, work. His ability to move silently in any environs, his amazing dexterity with his fingers and feet, and his keen eyesight gave him the edge he needed. One thing that was most difficult for him, which almost proved to be his downfall, was his innate need to pilfer things. Leaving behind all the wondrous glittery objects each time he left the cave was hard to bear. A dozen times he had the overpowering urge to reach out and pick up a fine ruby or diamond, or a beautifully wrought necklace of silver and jade. Each time he was able to struggle with that inner part of himself and finally resist. The two adventurers weren't sure whether the old dragon would notice if anything was taken, but their mission was specific. They didn't want to risk even the slightest chance of rousing the beast until the elven blade was in hand.

Both Slyn and Ge-or had discussed at length the thief's approach to acquiring the blade. One of Ge-or's questions from the start had been, "Can you do this without disturbing anything else?" Slyn promised he could and would; and he was, if nothing else "an honest thief." His word was his truth. So he left all else undisturbed in spite of his leanings.

Now that the beast was dead, the treasure beckoned. With much of the immediate and essential work on the dragon's carcass completed, Slyn could at long last fulfill that fundamental part of his nature – greed.

He and Ge-or had built a makeshift sled of a lightweight framework of willow wands and stretched deer hides. Empty, it was easy enough to drag up the long slope to Fis's lair; and full, they hoped they could tilt it over the edge, using a long rope to slide it down to the base of the mountain. From there they could use the mules to pull it to the cabin.

The first thing that Ge-or retrieved was the fine elven bow he had dropped behind the shield as he sprinted from the dragon's lair with Fis on his tail. The bow, made of the finest layered yew and reinforced with outstanding craftsmanship, was unscathed, though the gut had been burned away with only small pieces of it left hanging on each nock.

Treasure is treasure and seeing a huge mound of it will warm the heart of any adventurer. For a long time, Ge-or and Slyn stood in front of the expanse holding their torches high to take in the whole effect. They both knew it was unlikely that they would ever see the like of it again.

Finally, Slyn took a couple of steps forward and stabbed the butt of his long torch shaft into the nearest pile of coins and jewelry. Satisfied, he swung a large sack off his back and gestured to Ge-or. "Have at it, partner, you have earned this."

Ge-or smiled. He moved to Slyn's left eight paces before jamming his torch in a like manner into an area where bones, coins, gemstones, and armor were freely mixed. His primary interest in the hoard was to find the best armor and weapons he could.

Nearly every source they had consulted during their research, including Ordrake himself, had specifically mentioned the fondness dragons had for things magical and for the weapons and accoutrements preferred by the best warriors. This was not so much because dragons coveted these odd assortments of gear, or for their magic either; it was primarily motivated by the desire to get the stuff out of circulation so it couldn't be used against them. Prior to the wars between the elves and dragons, the winged beasts' troves were much smaller and were comprised mostly of gems and gold.

While Slyn, who had a good eye and knowledge of gemstones, jewelry, and the most valuable of old currencies, sifted through the fore-pile where Fis's head and shoulders had rested, Ge-or began a search of the aft-mound. Here massive quantities of humanoid bones had miscellaneous pieces of armor and weapons and other detritus mixed in.

They worked carefully and thoroughly. They were not rushed as they did not plan to leave the cabin area until the first of the spring thaw. Ge-or decided the best approach would be to sift through the rubble of bones with a comprehensive plan in mind. He marked off a yard square area in his head and began to toss aside everything that was of little interest. Before long he had a small pile of equipment and a few weapons near his feet, and a much larger pile of bones, broken wood, mirror shards, and the like growing off to his left.

He had moved into his second square yard of dragon debris when Slyn stopped him as he set a large helm onto the pile near his feet. "Whoa, Ge-or! Pick that helm up again."

Ge-or looked at him questioningly; in response, his partner motioned with his hands for him to lift it again.

Ge-or picked up the helm and turned it over in his hands, seeing nothing of particular note about the heavy pot-like headpiece.

"Draw your sword."

"Why?" This was even more puzzling to Ge-or, because there were no enemies near that he could see. Once again Slyn mimicked what he wanted Ge-or to do. He had come to trust Slyn explicitly – it was a type of professional trust they had built between them over the past few years; and it had served them well in a variety of tight places. Reaching over his back, he slid the blade out from its scabbard. He held it out in front. He noticed right away that it was glowing a shallow red all along the blade. Curious, he moved the blade closer to the helm and the color immediately deepened; and when he touched the helm with the edge, the blade became a deep magenta.

"Try the pile," Slyn gestured.

Ge-or put the helm down and aimed the blade downward toward the mix of miscellaneous weapons and armor pieces at his feet. As he moved it across the pile, he noticed its color move from neutral, to various shades of red or blue depending on its position relevant to a specific item.

Slyn dropped his sack and moved over near Ge-or. He motioned for Ge-or to step back; then he picked an item at random from the pile of armor and weapons, a bracer, and held it toward the tip of Fisbane. The blade remained neutral. One by one Slyn lifted different items and held them toward the sword blade. After a few minutes, they could see that the sword responded with a reddish glow to a few items, a bluish glow for others; yet for most items it retained its natural sheen.

"Magic, I'll warrant," Slyn said, placing a small dagger back down. "That last one was painful to hold. Did you notice the deep red gleam to your sword?"

Ge-or nodded.

"Dark magic, evil, or both, I'll bet. The bluish items have a cool feel… Good magic?"

Ge-or shrugged his shoulders. "Can't say. I only handled the blade once in my youth. Our father let my brother and I look at it one evening when he was a bit in his cups. At that point, it was obvious he planned for it to be mine when we came of age. Jared was much smaller in build than I was. Manfred always kept it in its scabbard above the mantel of the fireplace. Even when we went on patrols to drive away gzks who had wandered too close for comfort to our village, he never took it with him, preferring a short sword he had crafted himself. The only time I saw him wield it was during his last fight. I remember it shining a bright blue that day. You could see it above all the smoke in the midst of the melee. It flamed the same way when I drew it to fight Fis, though it does not seem to flame if one brings it forth elsewise."

"Perhaps it responds to emotions as well, and the heart or motivation of the wielder determines its color? Hence the response to magic – good or ill?"

"It will be useful with the sorting. I will need to go through this pile again and separate all this into three piles, not one."

"Perhaps it will help with gemstones and jewelry that have been magicked as well?"

"Aye, if you are right. Well, that can wait until we are in camp."

Slyn smiled brightly. "Good. Let's proceed." Their task had taken on a new dimension.

Their first day's work on the treasure trove yielded several large sacks of gems, jewelry, and coin, as well as a small pile of what Ge-or had determined were high quality armor pieces and a couple of weapons. He had left a good bit behind – anything that the sword responded to with a reddish glow they set aside. They also left a medium-sized pile of armor and weapons of lesser manufacture. They were more than pleased as they lowered the nearly full sled-cart down the slope of the mountain.

From that day on, they alternated working on the trove and carefully working the dragon hide. Slyn found a magic dagger that registered a deep blue when it was touched by Fisbane. It was almost as if he had expected to find it. Ge-or also found one that when touched by Fisbane registered a deep blue. By its look, it was obviously a fine elven and dwarven crafted blade. He decided to keep it as a partner to Fisbane.

Slyn used the magicked blade he had taken to accelerate their work on the scales. It still took them several more long days of work to finish. Once the pelt was clean of scales, they set to work drying, salting, and stretching it, so it would be preserved until they could get it to the tanners. Stradryk had built his cabin not far from a salt lick, both because of its ability to draw game and for the salt needed to dry and preserve hides. Ge-or and Slyn now used it to help them prepare the dragon remains.

Their days were tedious but rewarding. Each day spent in the dragon's lair yielded more treasures and artifacts from amongst the bones and debris. Slyn was able to bring out a couple of nice-sized sacks filled with the best of the gems and coins every day they worked on the trove.

It took them two weeks to paw through the entire mound once. At that point, they were satisfied that they had gotten everything of any interest weapon and armor-wise; and they felt fairly confident that Slyn had garnered most of the best of the rest. What remained still made a substantial mound. Both Slyn and Ge-or were content to leave it for others to find. There was no feasible way to move all of it down the mountain into some hidden storage place, nor could they take it with them. The truth was, they probably could only take about a third of the sacks and equipment that they had already gleaned from the trove back with them to Aelfric. The rest they would have to secret away. This work occupied them for another two weeks.

They decided against an elaborate scheme to hide their cache. They both remembered "the map" and its complicated maze of directions and points that had led to the treasure chest they had found at the "big red X." They used only two points of reference, both which they assumed would be there for some time to come. They buried their treasure wrapped carefully in furs mid-way between a direct line from the northwest corner of their trapping cabin to a large boulder that looked to have fallen off the mountain many years before. It was a sole sentinel in the forested area and could be seen from half a league away. Just to make sure, in case the hut burned down, Slyn and Ge-or both paced off the distance from the boulder to the center of the hole they had dug and marked the angle by using the crown star from the King's Constellation as a guide.

Burying treasure is a good bit of work. They spent days digging, chopping roots, and moving stones large enough that the task required Ge-or's great strength to heave them up and out of the hole. It wasn't so much that they wanted to bury their horde deep, but that there was so much of it that they needed a fairly massive hole, several yards deep and several yards in circumference.

The only other items they finally decided to bring down and bury were the pile of weapons, armor, and miscellaneous items that elicited a distinctive reddish tinge from Fisbane. These they did not want to deal with again, nor did they wish to leave them in the open, available to potential enemies. They chose a remote location, difficult to get to, and dug another deep hole, piled rocks atop the mound of items, and covered it all with dirt and finally a blanket of moss and pine needles.

The smell of spring was on the breeze when they finally headed out of camp for the north and east. A somewhat rudely-constructed sled, filled almost to overflowing with dragon hide and a variety of weapons and armor from the hoard, was being pulled by the two sturdiest mules. The other two were laden down with sacks of gems, jewelry, and coinage, all carefully selected by Slyn.

Ge-or had spent considerable time and effort sorting through the weapons and armor they had brought down from the lair. He had made some hard choices, finally settling on bringing a non-magical set of the finest megas-metal plate; a full chain mail shirt of the same materials, manufacture, and quality; and a small assortment of other items that would fetch a high price in the markets. Of weapons, he took only the best of the best: elven and dwarven-wrought daggers (several of which he and Slyn appropriated for their own use) were already stored about their persons; a couple of magicked blades and swords; one fine blade that Slyn especially had his eye on that elicited a deep blue tinge by Fisbane; and a fine magicked mace as a gift for the cleric. They also took one bag full of miscellaneous items that Fisbane also identified with a blue glow. These Ge-or felt might be of interest to either Sart or Ordrake, or perhaps other mages. They included a small crystal orb, several wands and small staves, a decrepit-looking blue floppy cap, which was perfect for Ordrake, a puzzle box, and other knickknacks. All in all, it was quite the haul. Even without the mass of items they had buried, they were rich beyond anything they had ever imagined.

Riding Forth

Though they had months to prepare, Thistle and Jared's departure from Xur in late spring was difficult. They had come to feel a part of the community and had made many good friends. They would be leaving behind people they had grown close to. It was especially difficult for Thistle to say goodbye to Alicia, Brandir, and the twin girls. Her former handmaiden had made a good life with her family in this wilderness community, independent of Thistle. Still, the two young women had shared a great deal of their formative years together.

Elanar would stay until the fall caravan and replacements arrived. This would give him the opportunity to train the newly arrived Journeyman Bard and his apprentice. After that, Elanar would head back to Borea for an appointment at Bard Hall as an instructor in swordsmanship and "Bardsmanship: The Weaving of Tales, News, and Politics," a new course for Apprentice Bards heading out on their first assignments.

Rux, too, was sad to see the couple leave. Jared had been instrumental in raising the combat level, particularly the archery skills, of his men; and the young Apprentice Bard was a popular entertainer. The major had leaned on both him and Elanar over the past year in leading patrols and taking charge of the redoubt at Kan's Mountain. And though Thistle had rarely overtly used her magic, the mere threat of having such a powerful magic wielder at Xur and in the field had likely discouraged many an attack. It was for this reason that she and Jared were leaving under the cover of early morning darkness and fog, hidden deep within the caravan headed east. Rux wanted to keep the illusion for as long as possible that the two of them were still stationed at the wilderness fort.

Meligance had sent another young mage out to work with Domast -- not so much to fill Thistle's shoes, for the girl to gain field experience. The training of young mages was becoming a priority for the kingdom's defenses. The young Wizardess would become involved in that process in the near future.

There was a great celebration the evening that the replacement caravan reached Xur. Jared and Elanar performed together one last time with supporting roles from the two new arrivals. There were many laughs, a good bit of drunken revelry, and finally, many tears shed as friends said goodbye.

Two mornings later, when there was only a glimmer of light in the eastern sky, the wagons and former residents of Xur rode out of the gates heading south and finally east along the now well-worn cart path. Unlike the days when

Jared and Thistle were first introduced to the outpost with Sart, Rux's men and women no longer tried to hide their identities under the guise of robbers and thieves. They still preferred to dress in tough mountain clothing that wore far better in the rugged country, rather than garb and uniforms of the Borean military.

***

Slyn and Ge-or reached the new Borean outpost at Thiele several weeks after having departed the western cabin site. They had moved slowly and cautiously through the wilderness country and had been surprised to see so much Qa-ryk activity this far to the north and west. One small, young-looking patrol threatened to come at them. However, when Ge-or raised Fisbane and charged at them upon Oesing, the blade flashing blue with a hint of crimson in the setting sun, they thought better of it and fled. Otherwise, their trek to the outpost had been uneventful.

They had considered heading in a more south-easterly direction and making a long stop at Xur, where Ge-or hoped to meet up with his brother at long last. But with the overloaded sled and mules, it made more sense to stick to where the ground was still hard from the permafrost and where the sled could glide relatively smoothly. The terrain was no less difficult whichever route they took. As it was, they had to take a circuitous route using old cart paths and animal trails. Even then, they occasionally had to portage the gear and treasure over rough spots or deeper streambeds.

Once at Thiele, they planned to take the eastern road to Permis and there hail a boat eastward, which would save them considerable effort in moving their cargo. They would hopefully buy passage on a supply ship once the northern bays were free of ice, debark in the capital, sell some of the gear and treasure to purchase a large wagon, and finally head back to Aelfric where they planned to have the dragon leather, armor, and other items dealt with as quickly as possible.

The outpost commander told them he expected a supply boat any day. The weather had been balmy for over a week, and much of the ice along the coast was already out of the bays and coves. Weary from their long trek out of the wilds, Ge-or and Slyn jumped at the chance to set sail for the capital without having to cart their booty further. The return voyage of the ship would be direct, having already off-loaded goods at each village port and picked up furs from the winter harvests on the outbound trip.

At Thiele, Ge-or was moved by the monument that had been built in remembrance of the town and battle. He stood for a long time under its shadow in the center of the former town square and reminisced about his youth, the battle that had cost the lives of his father and so many other friends and acquaintances, and the awful day he had spent gathering the remains to give them a respectful burial at sea. He struggled to keep his emotions at bay and was finally able to push the pain away with a flare of anger at the dragon and the Qa-ryks that had cost him so much. That night he drank far too much of the "military brew" he and Slyn were offered by the resident soldiers. His partner understood. At the last they carried him to his bunk to sleep it off.

Little did Ge-or know that once again he would miss a chance to connect with his brother. It was only a day after they set sail that Jared and Thistle rode into the coastal town of Permis to spend two weeks with her family, friends, and the few survivors from Thiele who had now been completely assimilated into the village. A week after Ge-or and Slyn had taken ship, Thistle and Jared rode westward together to visit Thiele themselves.

Jared, too, had a strong emotional reaction when he returned to the site where so much had happened and so many had died, where he had suddenly been thrust into manhood and the life of a wanderer. He was overcome by the swirling emotions surrounding the losses, his meeting Thistle, the many trials and battles they had been through, and his acceptance at Bard Hall that had now brought him full circle. He sank to one knee and cried softly when he approached the monument. Thistle laid her hand on his shoulder, understanding the depth of what he felt, having shared in much of it herself.

They found out from the young lieutenant who commanded the garrison that Ge-or had been there only a week before – bringing news that he had slain the dragon. The commander showed Jared a claw from the beast that the stout warrior had set into the monument there by laboriously cutting a place for it and gluing it in with pitch. Thistle, with Jared's permission, used her energy to fuse the claw into the stone, thus making it a permanent part of the memorial to all who had given their lives there.

***

Sart, who had only recently returned from the far west, had been anxiously awaiting word about Ge-or and Slyn's quest. He was overjoyed to see the two crusty adventurers wander into the Druid's Hut as spring was beginning to favor summer. The three sat and drank well into the night telling tales and jokes as only those who have faced death and returned can do.

It was late that first night together that Ge-or asked Sart what he had been up to. Strangely the usually loquacious cleric said only that he had been "seeking more information about Aberon," and nothing more. Ge-or, well in his cups, let the question drop.

During their first week back in Aelfric, Ge-or and Slyn disbursed all the various parts of the dragon they had preserved to both Ordrake and Sart, as well as giving (upon the cleric's recommendation) samples to other alchemists and priests for further study. It had been a long time since anyone had slain one of the great beasts, and the lore and myth surrounding what could be gleaned and used from them was sketchy at best. Both Slyn and Ge-or hoped that the materials would be of use to whomever received them. Except for keeping some of the claws, the teeth, and most of the skin, they had no wish to retain anything else associated with the carcass.

Ordrake was beyond thrilled to have "such interesting offal." Neither Slyn nor Ge-or had ever seen the fellow so lively and appreciative. He promised that he would make the best use of everything; and the old Wizard told the two that if he figured out a way to put the squares cut from the fire sac to good use, he would let them know.

Sart, though he accepted only some of the dragon's blood and the vial of liquid-fire, was more interested in hearing how the two had accomplished their amazing task. The three spent a week of eves chatting over mugs of rum and ale catching up. He was also appreciative of the magical mace they had brought out from the treasure trove. He promised them that when he returned to the capital, he would spend the effort and time to discover the nature of the other magically-imbued items they had brought out with them.

Slyn and Ge-or simply relaxed for once. The long years Ge-or had spent preparing for the quest had been draining in many ways; and though his current partner had only been a part of the quest over the past several years, the two of them had put their all into the venture. It was good to take a few weeks off from any sort of travail. Beyond wealthy, they returned, as was their wont, to the Druid's Hut. However, now they stayed in the best private room and ate the best cuts of meat almost every night for dinner.

Jared and Thistle arrived back in the capital late one spring morning, with the scent of cherry blossoms wafting through the air as they rode through the main gate. It was a strange feeling for both of them to ride the familiar streets up toward the palace. This city, which had been their reality for four years, now seemed a distant memory. They had grown accustomed to living the adventurous life of the outpost and a more rigorous existence in the wilds. The streets were bustling with the beginning of a new week; and Jared felt like he had stepped back into a dream, where no one was quite as awake and as alert as they should be if they wanted to survive. It all was so completely mundane. These people did not have to worry whether their sword was honed to a keen edge, their bow-string waxed properly, or if the evening's meal would be predicated on whether or not a hunter brought back a hind, braces of rabbits and squirrels, or a young boar.

They first rode to Bard Hall. Jared wanted to check in with Leonis and determine what options he and Thistle had now that they were married. He knew there were apartments available to married apprentices and journeyman, but he had never seen them; and neither he nor Thistle had any great desire to live at the palace, though she was certain that would also be an option.

At the gilded gates, Jared sang the appropriate answer to the question posed by the keeper. He bowed and smiled when the young fellow asked if he needed any further help. "Does Leonis keep the same quarters?"

The boy raised his eyebrows. He had never heard anyone so young use the grandmaster's name without the honorific title. "Aye, three doors past the fountain on the left."

"My thanks." Jared bowed again. He and Thistle went in.

A few moments later, a familiar deep-booming voice rumbled as they approached the appropriate doorway. "No need to knock, you two. Come in and welcome back."

Jared grinned as he pulled the door open and held it for Thistle. He whispered, "See, I told you. There is magic about him."

"I heard that." Leonis beamed as they entered. "Not magic, my young Bardling, just a bit of subterfuge. Must keep the sluggards on their toes – not that you ever fit that category. A successful venture then?"

Jared smiled as he helped Thistle sit in one of the chairs Leonis had indicated. He knew that the grandmaster was in various ways kept well-informed of what his students and Bards were up to throughout the kingdom. He took a seat himself and looked across the table at his mentor. Leonis was much the same. Perhaps a new wrinkle or two, but he looked hale. Jared did not know how old he was; he had been the head of Bard Hall nigh unto forty years, and typically one was "venerable" before one was ever considered for the position. "I believe we have fulfilled our commissions, sir. It is a brave crew out there amidst all that danger, and it is a different life as well. I am not sure how easy it will be to readjust. We have come to enjoy sleeping under the stars with the scent of the woods in the air."

"Good, good. I understand. I used to do a good bit of roaming in my younger days myself. It's good for the constitution. Still like to walk, yet I rarely get out of the city anymore. Well, soon enough you will likely be back in the field; there is more to learn. There is always more to learn.

"And you my dear? My apologies, I did not intend to ignore you." Leonis nodded toward Thistle.

She smiled and nodded a "Thanks" to Leonis for his deference. "I am well. As you know we were both north-coast bred; and though the softness of the palace has its temptations, Xur was a wondrous place to spend our first years as husband and wife."

"Ah, yes. My sincere congratulations again. Ah… that reminds me, I have something for you both."

"It is not necessary, sir," Jared began to say. Leonis waved him to silence.

"Nay, it is not from me. This is from your brother."

"My brother?"

"Truly. He came through here not a month or so ago and knocked on our gate." Leonis chuckled as he handed a package wrapped in a beautiful silk cloth across to Jared. "Surprised me, too. I know you had mentioned him a few times when we used to have our chats, but I never expected the chap to show up at my doorstep. The fellow doesn't have a musical note in him, does he?"

Jared grinned. Ge-or had never had much success carrying a tune or playing an instrument. He couldn't even bang a drum in rhythm. Holding the package, he said, "He didn't quite get the musical response correct?"

"I couldn't quite tell if he even tried. There did seem to be a change in pitch when he managed to rasp out, 'I wish to see the director of Bard Hall.' Hah! I haven't been called that in a good space."

"You were at the gate?"

"Aye. I like to keep my hand in once in a while. Like when you first came here. That was mostly chance, you know?"

"Was it?" Jared raised his eyebrows and smiled.

"Harumpf…"

Jared decided to shift the conversation and tell Leonis why they had stopped by. "We were wondering what options we might have for quarters while we are both assigned here in the city."

"Yes, well, open the package, and that might help you decide. Your brother asked what he could leave you for a wedding present. He hoped, and I as well, that we did not presume too much."

Jared held the package out to Thistle. She untied the bow and opened the first layer of silk. Laying on top were two oddly shaped objects that it took Jared a second to understand. He took in a sharp breath and looked up into Thistle's eyes, then over at Leonis, "The dragon's teeth?"

"Yes, he has slain the beast – an amazing feat in this day and age."

A look of recognition dawned on Thistle's face, for lying on the soft cloth were two of the largest teeth she had ever seen; and though neither of them had ever seen a dragon's tooth before, it was obvious now that's what they were.

"He wanted you to know that he had at long last fulfilled his pledge and quest."

"There is more," Thistle said, starting to unwrap another fold of the cloth.

Jared picked up one of the teeth and admired it while Thistle unwrapped the next layer. They both gasped when they saw the size and quality of the seven large blue gemstones lying on top of the silk. "Sapphires?"

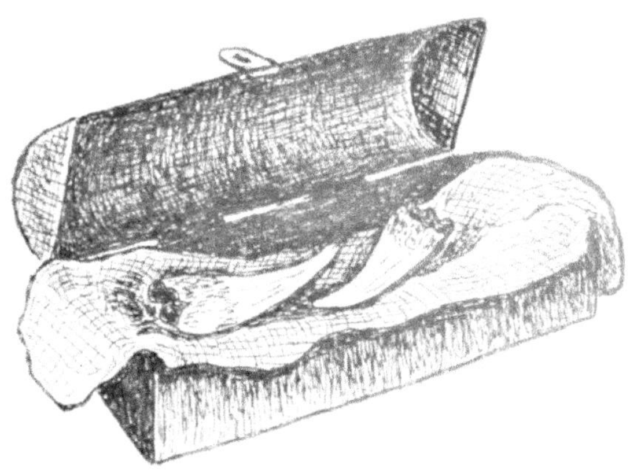

"Truly, and of exceptionally fine quality, I might add," Leonis said. "The great red, as dragons are wont to, had a treasure trove. He wanted you to have these. He gave a like quantity of fine rubies to the Hall – a royal gift, which will be put to good use. Your brother is a generous man."

Jared was dazed, yet there was still something else wrapped in the silk. He gestured for Thistle to take the gems. He unwrapped the rest of the bundle. After a bit of tugging, he finally held in his hand a piece of newly scribed vellum scroll. He unrolled it and held it out so he and Thistle could read the official looking script together.

This time Thistle gasped and a tear came to her eye as she continued to read. "It is a deed to a house, Jared. Your brother has bought us a house here in the city."

"And," Leonis said, passing a key ring with several keys attached to Jared, "it is located about halfway between here and the palace. If I am not mistaken, I believe that should take care of your immediate concerns.

"As a small token to add to this generosity of your brother, the Music Masters and I have conspired to loan you a virginal so that you may have musical soirees in your quarters, should you wish to entertain." Leonis' eyes sparkled, because he and they knew that fine wine and good food were the grandmaster's foremost weaknesses. "Unfortunately, it is only a loan; and when you both return to the road, we will abscond with it, I'm afraid."

"It is much appreciated." Jared stood and bowed. "When we are settled, you will be the first to know."

"Yes, well, please forgive me, for I hate to rush you both; the rest of the day beckons to all. Meligance wishes to see you, young lady; and there is always work to be done. On the morrow, Jared, bright and early we will get you back into the swing of things here at the Hall."

"As you wish, Grandmaster," Jared said, still too stunned by his brother's largess and the Leonis's openness to offer a more elegant and clever repartee as they left.

When he experienced the "jump" to Meligance's studio, Jared almost lost the quick lunch they had grabbed at a street vendor. It was the first time he had ever been asked to come to where Thistle had spent so much of her years of training.

The White Wizardess stood and bowed when they approached her. "My congratulations on your success in the west. I am truly happy for you both. Rux is really pleased with your work; and so am I, and Leonis as well." Meligance came around the table, and much to both Jared and Thistle's surprise, she gave them each a quick hug and kiss on the cheek before returning to her place behind the desk.

"As you know, Jared, Thistle and I have touched base regularly; so there is not much we need to discuss in regard to your efforts at Xur. There is a great deal now to explore together and to prepare for. Eventually, you will both be involved in great happenings. Events and doings that will impact whether the kingdom will survive the threats it faces from within and without.

"War is coming. There are ever new rumblings from the west. There is still time, yet there are forces on the move that few ken; and even fewer care to do anything about." She looked downward with a distinct look of disdain.

Even Jared understood that glance. Though the old king, once a strong and capable ruler, still held sway, his courtiers and only son paid more attention to the niceties of court life than to the business of the kingdom. Far too often, the revenues that came in from across the realm were spent on frivolities and not on building a capable army.

"You are both back safely, and there is much for all of us to learn and do.

"Jared," Meligance nodded to him, "your duties and education will largely be at Bard Hall these next years; however, I may also call upon you at times. Sart has told me much of your potential. Please know that if I can help you in any way, you have only to ask. However, I will always defer to Leonis' sage advice in regard to what is best for you, and, of course, as it relates to Thistle as well.

"As to you, Thistle, there is more for us to discover together if you so choose. There are still insights I can give you from my own work and experimentation; but in most ways now, we will work together as equals. The most pressing need is for us to train others. That will be both rewarding and frustrating for both of us. Talent comes in many guises, rarely, very rarely, as powerfully as it is in you and me. Our patience will be tried again and again. For the sake of the kingdom, it is paramount that we succeed.

"As you know, I have been working these three years you have been at Xur on training those mages and witches who already possessed a certain degree of skill in various aspects of the magical arts. Now, you and I will direct our attention to new recruits. I have put a call out across the kingdom for any with talent and innate ability. We shall see what we shall see – expect to work hard."

Thistle bowed low to her former mistress and mentor. "I am still at your command, mum. Though you suggest my power is equal to yours, my experience is not. I know there is much that I can still learn from you. I am open to all."

Meligance chuckled. "Ah, you and I are still too formal together. That will change as we get more comfortable with each other. Know this, my child – for so you still seem to me, more because of our age differences than anything else – you are innately more gifted than I, and you are already more powerful."

Thistle opened her mouth to protest; Meligance waved her to silence. "It is important for you to understand this, Thistle. Our tasks in the coming years will diverge because you will be able to handle things that I cannot. There will be choices to make and battles to be fought. You and I must wisely select what we shall face, or we may fail before we start. It is always shrewd to know your limitations; it is equally unwise to not trust what you are capable of, to underestimate yourself.

"Now, both of you go and get settled in your house. Jared, I had hoped to meet your brother while he was here, but the opportunity did not present itself. Sart thinks the world of him, and that is enough for me. Perhaps someday our paths will cross. I am glad you are all safe."

Settling In

During the first summer back from his Apprenticeship, Jared discovered that not all of Barding was to his liking. Bards were considered to be the true historians of the kingdom; and in spite of the lays, florid romance poems, and grandiose epics they told and sang, extensive records were kept at Bard Hall of anything that was determined to be of import to the kingdom and potentially to its history. Thus, he spent days upon days writing down everything from his adventures in the west that might be considered historically or politically relevant.

Once he had completed this task, at least to his satisfaction, his writings were examined by a resident historian. Following this review, he spent weeks being quizzed about virtually everything he had set down on paper and a great deal he had not. Then he was required to go back and "fill-in-the-gaps."

After another two weeks of what he was beginning to feel was a pedantic waste of his time, the process repeated itself, until he was pacing the floors on the weekends, voicing his frustrations to an equally tired and equally frustrated Thistle.

Part of their frustration was simply getting used to living in a city again. They had both grown accustomed to wide open spaces, sleeping under the canopy of the heavens, and trekking about the forests and hills around Xur. Here, though the two-story stone house Ge-or had purchased for them was ideal, they felt hemmed in and restless. Their "yard" was the fifteen feet of vegetation, of an indeterminate nature, between the main street and their front steps. In the back, their wall literally abutted the house behind; and to the sides there was only two feet of space, which in Borea was a luxury, as most houses shared walls on both sides.

They took to going on long walks every evening, often outside the main gates, in spite of warnings that it was a bad area. When they could, they would ride in the countryside on the weekends, giving themselves and their plains-bred horses a well-needed stretch.

"Ge-or's house," as Jared liked to refer to their ample abode, was a lovely cottage of six rooms – large by any country standard, but "cute and cozy" within the city. It had been sparsely furnished when they moved in; however, with their allowances from Bard Hall and the palace, as well as other monies they had saved, they filled in the gaps until they felt at home.

It had been quite humbling when they had first opened the door to their house and realized how few possessions they actually had. Virtually everything they owned, except for a number of items that Thistle still had at the castle, was either in the backpacks they had slung off their shoulders, or the saddlebags sitting on their horses outside. They had looked at each other, stared about empty living area, and laughed.

Money-wise they were quite comfortable. Thistle could have asked for anything, and it would have been given to her. However, living back in the west, where everyone pitched in with everything, had reminded her that she didn't need that much to be happy. Meligance did insist that she take on a new chambermaid, paid for by palace funds. She wanted Thistle to focus on other things than caring for a house. Though neither of them really wanted anyone, she and Jared finally agreed to take on a daygirl, who would help with the cleaning and cooking, but not see specifically to their personal needs.

They settled into this new life, neither feeling completely comfortable. The stability of new lives as students had been exactly what they needed when they were at a loss as to what to do with their lives. Now that they had tasted the open road again, the wide-open spaces were never far from their thoughts.

Thistle likewise had to give to Meligance a detailed report of her work. Luckily, since they had maintained regular contact, this meant only a couple of days of filling her in with more specifics about her experiences, especially her work delving into alternate realms.

Her focus, unlike her husband's, was facing a summer of testing candidates for Apprenticeship in the magical arts –specifically the art of offensive and defensive "spell-casting."

As Meligance had previously suggested to her, many witches, magic-users, and adepts simply used an innate sense of power, without any conception of where that energy came from or how to garner it from without to further enhance their prowess. Most often these types of "magicians" coupled their "spells" with outlandish verbalizations, formulaic or just plain weird gestures, and other forms of rigmarole. It was almost impossible for Thistle to believe that these had somehow become associated with the end result, which was a simple manipulation of the environment in some form or another with energy.

Thus, the removal of a wart might be accompanied by a completely useless poultice and a string of nonsense syllables, while the witch waved her hands in some strange pattern above the person's offending member. In actual fact, she was using her inborn magical energy to remove the physical growth itself. Or the levitation of a common object, like a chair, might include a freakish gaze, a thrusting gesture, and a vocalization that sounded somewhat between a cow.mooing and a chicken squawking as if it were about to lose its head. Again, the truth was much simpler – the magic-user was simply lifting the chair with his or her own power.

When Meligance opened the doors to all adepts for training, their first task during the summer and early fall was to assess whether the hundreds of savants who presented themselves at the palace actually had any potential to help Borea in the war to come. Initially, Thistle wanted to toss them all out on their ears. It was incredibly frustrating to observe the antics and gyrations they went through when she knew how foolish these displays were. Even when she explained to them what was taking place, including a demonstration where she accomplished the same "trick" without even raising a finger or an eyebrow, they looked at her with completely blank expressions.

It took Meligance several lengthy lectures to convince her protégé that she needed to find as many as possible who had a "modicum of talent and inner power." She reminded her former apprentice that she, too, had once thought of her power as "indigestion." At that, Thistle had begun to giggle; and the two had fallen into a fit of laughing that anyone who might have observed, if they could have penetrated the White Wizardesses' studio, would have certainly believed the hope for Borea was already lost.

After that, Thistle tried to be more patient. In the end, as the first frosts were covering the streets and the ice in the fountains was beginning to freeze over at night, they still had only a score of potential candidates and another group that "might" have a modicum of talent.

At the beginning of the fall semester, Jared was finally released from historical duties to begin his final studies before he would be anointed as a Journeyman Bard. His courses were to include "The Art of Music," "Music and Healing," "Lore II," and "Advanced Musicianship." In addition, he was to serve as Assistant Master of Archery with Selim and Assistant to the Master of Short Sword. He was further encouraged to practice his weaponry in any other areas in which he deemed he was "lacking or needed further instruction."

It was during the week before classes began that Karenna and Simon-Nathan came back from their latest jaunt to the villages along the northern coastline. They were brimming with news. The four of them met at the Green Horse and spent the better part of two whole weekend afternoons telling each other of their adventures.

It was only after their first round of ales that Simon-Nathan spilled the news that he and Karenna were expecting their first child.

"By-the-gods, truly?" Jared asked.

Karenna blushed and nodded. Simon-Nathan took her hand and beamed. "She is expecting sometime in March, we think. Father is overjoyed, and Mother starts crying every time she sees Karenna."

"We are so, so happy for you," Thistle said, flushing herself, but not out of embarrassment.

Jared noticed and took her hand under the table and gave it a tight squeeze. He knew she was truly happy for them, yet deep within there was a hurt and an emotional scar that would never quite go away. He would tell Simon-Nathan at a more appropriate time of what had happened out on the Bendir plains.

"And that's not all our news," Karenna said, noticing with her woman's intuition that there was some tension that had suddenly arisen across the table from her and Simon-Nathan. "Simon graduated last spring and I will graduate this spring, assuming all goes well."

"Which it will, of course," Simon-Nathan said, beaming at his wife.

"We have been given permission to write a joint dissertation of our work on the northern folk songs for our Senior Mastership!"

"Two-three more years, maybe four," Simon-Nathan bubbled. "It's been so much fun working together, and we have both been given courses to teach as well. I believe you will have Karenna for Advanced Musicianship, Jared."

"Truly?" Jared looked at Karenna, wondering immediately whether that would be a concern for any of them.

Simon-Nathan looked as happy and ebullient as ever. He and Karenna both nodded a "Yes." Thistle gave him a squeeze with her hand this time.

One other surprise happened during the party at Simon-Nathan-the-Elder's house celebrating Karenna's pregnancy: Elanar, who had recently returned from Xur, proposed to Athena. In the midst of the celebration, he stood, knelt down, blushed a deep red, and asked for her hand. Ever a bit shy, all she could say for a few moments was, "Don't do this to me. Don't do this to me," over and over. But in the end, she happily accepted. It was a wondrous time for all of them.

The Art of Healing

Jared was a bit perplexed. It was nearing the Yule, and while his courses had been interesting and not particularly taxing – well, except for the modern theory section of Advanced Musicianship, which he had Karenna and Simon-Nathan to help him through – he hadn't felt like he had learned anything of particular import from his "Art of Music" or "Music and Healing" classes. These two courses seemed only to encompass a broad perspective of what he had been able to discover on his own.

His "Art of Music" class essentially focused on how music moved people and – depending on the type of music, the melody, the style, rhythm, harmonization, flow, and even tuning of the instruments, as well as what scales were used – how it could influence in one direction or another. He and Elanar had used this knowledge and a feel for the music in many ways when they had toured the eastern seaboard towns. They had even used it surreptitiously at Xur as a means to calm frayed nerves, or heighten a celebration, or cast a certain mood. Except for learning a few new tunes associated with basic mood swings, Jared didn't feel like he was learning anything more than common knowledge thrust at him day after day in class.

Likewise, the "Music and Healing" class seemed only to touch on a broad sense of music having the ability to influence one's health and one's recovery from accident or illness. They were given logical explanations, supported by a variety of studies that eminent Bards had conducted, that explained why a certain style or musical effect might assuage one's anxiety, or how another style might encourage faster healing, and so on. There was nothing that spoke to the depths of the healing experience that he had in some way created that long, long night out on the Bendir plains.

Finally, he chose to bother Leonis with his concerns. The grandmaster was spirited as usual. "Well, my boy, I was wondering when you might show up on my doorstep. Couldn't even leave me alone for one semester?"

Jared smiled broadly. "Your reverence, I have no idea of to what you are referring."

"Then you truly are confused, and there is naught I can do for you."

Jared bowed with a flourishing of his hands. "Just a simple question, Grandmaster. Nothing to trouble, I'm sure."

"Well, I guess you must out with it, for I'll get no peace until you do. What is on your mind this time?"

"'Music and Healing,' I do not see the purpose of this class. It does not speak to what I have experienced myself."

"Ah, yes. Well, my young pup, you are… shall we say… gifted." Leonis gestured for Jared to sit. He himself perched on the end of a high practice chair facing him. "By the way, I read your report of your travels – interesting, quite interesting. I also spoke with Rux. Did you know he was back from Xur and in town for the winter?"

Jared nodded. He and Thistle had met with the commander of the outpost one evening to get caught up with the doings at Xur.

"He sang your praises and… ahem… the truth is, I would appoint you early to your Journeymanship and get you back in the field. However, as we have discussed before, there is 'tradition' to deal with." Leonis caught Jared's eye, then raised an eyebrow as if to say that what he was about to tell Jared was definitely out of the ordinary.

"Jared, you are gifted in a way that few Bards are. There is an amazing array of talents that go into making a Bard, and few of the men we accept here make it through the twenty or more years of study and work that leads to their being anointed. Elanar, as a case in point, spent thirty-five years here with us; and he might never have made it, if it weren't for his relationship with you. There are even fewer who have the talent that you exhibited out there on the Bendir Plains – perhaps one in scores of years, sometimes once in a century do we see such a gift. Please note, for this is important, young sir, none of us would have guessed that you had it either. It was the experience you had that brought it out of you.

"If you are patient, and I urge you to be, next year in the advanced Healing and Music section, they will speak on exactly what you are now questioning me about. Even then, it will be as if they are only talking about a potential or possibility. The truth is, Jared, we haven't had a truly gifted musical healer in my lifetime; and I, as you know, am no spring bunny." Leonis smiled and placed his hand on Jared's shoulder.

"This, I think, is one of those things that cannot be taught – like perfect pitch. You either have it, like you and I do, or you don't. Believe me, we have even experimented with trying to teach perfect pitch to babes fresh out of the womb, by producing the purest note on an instrument and saying its name. We have also tried the same throughout their childhood – doesn't seem to help. We can train good relative pitch, even excellent pitch, but… Well, I digress.

"What I am trying to say, Jared, is that you will be on your own with this. Next year, or the next, depending on whether I can sway the council, I will try to gain permission for you to read those archives we have relating to this gift. Typically, we do not allow access to these until one has finished their Journeymanship and is scheduled to be anointed. In your case, perhaps, we can make an exception. I will work on it." He winked.

"Still," Leonis clapped Jared on the shoulder and stood, which Jared knew meant the conversation was almost over. "There is much you can learn from every experience and every class. Pay attention, for it might be in the minutiae that succor comes in exigent circumstances." Leonis chuckled. "Sorry, I have always liked, shall we say, 'musical' words. Go, my young Bardling. It is always a pleasure to talk with you in spite of what I might grouse about. My door is open."

Jared bowed and turned to go. Leonis added before he got to the door, "Remember – Honor, Duty, Truth, Wisdom, Healing, and Joy. There is a reason that Joy is last on that list, my boy."

"Yes, Grandmaster."

Jared would ponder Leonis' final statement for some time to come.

"But mum, they don't get the simplest things, the most basic ideas."

"I know, child. Believe me, I know." Meligance smiled grimly. She, too, was frustrated. It was beyond difficult to understand, much less teach, those far less competent than oneself.

The White Wizardess had, to everyone's astonishment, descended from her tower and personally taken on the education of the new trainees -- something she had never done. Now, with matters of the kingdom's survival pressing, she could no longer delegate this responsibility to others.

There were few enough truly competent mages about the kingdom these days; and the best of these were too old to be charging out into the field, fighting major battles against dark priests, demons, and the like.

When the elves, a race that had more of a penchant for magic than all the others on Gaia, had reclused themselves in their southern enclave, it seemed to have sapped the energy from the heart of all that was magical in the kingdom. Part of the reason, Meligance knew, was that the elves had long been the leaders in helping those with the gift understand their power, develop it, and polish it. The kingdom's magic school and the mages that ran it had been a poor second effort. That institution rarely produced anyone of sufficient quality to pass the Wizard or Wizardess examinations and challenges. Talent was being wasted. Meligance had always far too many other concerns and duties to try to infuse a more rigorous and dynamic approach to the old school. Now, she didn't have a choice. They would need competent mages – and soon.

The two of them, both Wizardesses in their own right, had each taken on nineteen of the candidates they had tested and accepted as apprentices. The first month of trying to work with them had been frustrating for both women. Unfortunately, they were the best of those that had presented themselves.

"It is time to weed out the chaff, Thistle," Meligance continued. "They will be disappointed. There are sixteen, from your reports and mine, who will never make the level we need. We will place them with various masters elsewhere. They may eventually prove of some service in the fringe use of our arts. There are at least a couple of these who might prove adept at illusions, and so on…"

Meligance paused for such a long moment that Thistle said, "Yes, mum?"

"I have been thinking back on that day when you first came to me, when I proved to you that you had power."

"Yes?"

"Can you remember the trials you went through during those early weeks? Clearly?"

"Yes, mum."

"That is where we must start with our new adepts. We must take them through that process, the experimental process that led you to understanding the foundation of magic, power, and the use of energy."

"How?"

"Slowly, Thistle, very slowly. You were, are, unbelievably gifted. Once I gave you a starting point, you took off. Think of our new young charges, and a few not so young, as having a minute part of your gift and far less of your insight. We have to both force this on them in one sense and coddle them in another. Only understand that it will take them far longer to ken all that you did. We will have to break what you may have accomplished in a day into parts, stages. It may take weeks, more likely months, to bring them along a path that took you a day. You will need to describe every nuance of your experiences. Relive it in your mind and find a way to explain it to them in bits and pieces. I think it will be less frustrating for both of us if we can see any sort of understanding and advancement. So far, we have been butting our heads into a brick wall.

"Starting tomorrow, we will join the remaining adepts into one large group. Then we will hold half-day sessions where you will be the primary instructor. Start from the beginning, from that moment I had you go within to find your core energy. Use the energy balls, as I did with you. I will be there and pay close attention myself. If I have an insight, I will add it; however, this initial training will be yours, Thistle. My training and experiences are too far in the past to recall in any detail. Perhaps we will find a new way of teaching magic. We *need* to find that path."

"There is news from Sart?" Thistle asked, jumping off the hint in Meligance's words that they had spoken.

"Yes," Meligance frowned. "Things are getting worse. He has sensed a new power growing in the west. The Black Ones are better organized and they have been enhanced magically in some way. He believes that another artifact from Kan's dungeons was taken by the group that entered there before you. It now has been placed in play. There is still time, a few years, perhaps a decade, no more. If... if we were ready now, it might be the most opportune time to strike. The king is old, and the son is weak, a drunkard, and a playboy. The armies have been brought in to protect manors and palaces, not the western borders. We have to do what we can to prepare for the storm."

Meligance looked into Thistle's eyes. "We do not yet understand what we are up against. If it is as Sart fears, there is reason for caution, and for action as well. A move in the wrong direction might devastate our chances; but a success… well, that is what he is working on right now. He delves deep within the archives for knowledge, any hints that will tell him what was, so we can have a chance at understanding what may be.

"Of utmost importance, as we discussed several times previously, is that you both eventually return to the dungeons below Kan's ruined palace. That is where the keys may lie to understanding some of this. To do that, we need to know how to fight the winged creatures you encountered there. That is what you and I will work on when we have the time. After the Yule, we will set our schedule accordingly."

"There are other aspects of magic I would ask you of, milady."

"Truly! It is a never-ending study for the likes of you and I. Be patient, my child. Let us get these young ones on the path; then we will have more time for our own work."

"Yes, mum."

Making the Most of Your Money

Though they would have preferred warmer climes, perhaps even a jaunt to Athalia, the settlement furthest south along the Borean seacoast, Ge-or and Slyn had chosen to remain in Aelfric this winter. They wanted to oversee all phases of the processes needed to turn the dragon hide into supple, fire-resistant leather that they would be able to wear for decades to come in their adventuring.

They had enough wealth in what they had brought back to retire from any kind of work at all. Yet that was not who a true adventurer was at heart. The money was simply a means to an end. Part of that "end," right now, was to equip themselves with the best available. It would be expensive.

Slyn was spending some of his new-found wealth on equipment relevant to his profession: goods, poisons, and weapons that would make any of his ilk extremely envious. He even spent a fair amount of coinage to spend time with some of the eldest and best master thieves and assassins available in the border town. It was hard work to encourage them to come out of retirement to regale him with their wisdom and methods. Good drink and bribes always worked when avarice was in one's blood.

Ge-or, for his part, was having the megas-metal plate armor that he had taken from the hoard reworked to his own design. It had not come close to fitting him anyway, and he wanted to garner the most benefit defensively from the expensive metal while maintaining as much flexibility as possible.

Pure megas-metal, or titium, as the alchemists and metalworkers referred to it, when alloyed with steel became a light weight and resilient metal. It could fend off most weapons, even when wielded by the best of hands. Plate armor, lighter in weight when made of the expensive ore, was still quite restrictive in form. Ge-or's advantage in battle was not only his tremendous strength; it was also in the elven agility he had inherited from his mother. He was having the solid plate pieces cut into small disks, which he was going to have made into something akin to a combination of the designs of scale mail and chain mail. He spent the whole first part of the winter working with the best smith and armorer in the town to come up with a final design.

Though they had expected the dragon hide to present problems for the tanners and leatherworkers, the process was considerably more difficult and time-consuming than either Ge-or or Slyn would have thought, and hence quite expensive. Thankfully, there were still tomes available that spoke to the appropriate procedures relevant to turning dragon skin into supple armor. The

302

tanner they chose for the task, among the finest in the kingdom, was willing to make the effort, if he had coin in hand to devote his workers to the year-long tanning process. It took a good bit of gold upfront to convince them to proceed. They ended up paying yet more coin when they were unhappy with the suppleness and flexibility of what the tanner produced initially. The work dragged on.

They were not unhappy with the master tanner. They visited his evil-smelling establishment set off in the hills south of Aelfric often enough to know that he dedicated himself and most of his skilled workers to processing the dragon leather. It was for him and his business a matter of professional pride and reputation to have worked with dragon hide, for there were no other tanners left alive outside of a few elves in Moulanes, and maybe a couple of elder dwarves/gnomes far south in the southern mountains, who could brag of such a feat. However, the hide was difficult to deal with; and it took the men a long time and many months working it over and over again to bring it to the fine flexible weight and form that Slyn and Ge-or wanted.

Once the dragon leather was supple enough and ready to be made into garments, it would take more money and a good bit more time, perhaps another full year, to have it sewn into the under-armor garments they required, including full-length pants, full-armed jerkins, gloves, and linings for helms and shields should they ever require them.

Thus, they bided their time in the border town. Having rented a small, comfortable cottage near the southwestern edge of town, they settled in for the winter.

***

He was overjoyed that Ge-or had been able to salvage so much from Fis's carcass. Once he and Ordrake had the various organs, bits and pieces, the vials of blood, and the container of the liquid fire in hand, the two sat down for several weeks, discussing the nature and use of such rare items. Eventually they came to terms with a division of the "goods," with Ge-or and Slyn's blessing, on how best to put them to use for the benefit of their own knowledge, experiments, and hopefully to the benefit of the kingdom.

The greatest puzzle to all, mage, cleric, alchemist, and leatherworker, had been the thick, pliable one-foot squares Ge-or had cut from the fire sac. Finally, placing three of the squares in storage, Ge-or had left Ordrake, the master tanner, and each of the alchemists that Sart recommended a piece to work with. He hoped that some use for the rubbery wedges could be found.

Returning to the capital at the end of the summer, Sart reported to Meligance of the ominous rumors coming from the west. Though they both had suspicions of what artifact or artifacts had been placed in play, there were long gaps in the history and lore from the early days of Kan's absconding with the Black Diamond, leading up to his eventual destruction from within. Sart was determined to ferret out all that he could from the archives of both the kingdom and, if Leonis would grant him permission, the vaults at Bard Hall – a place few, other than full Bards, had ever been allowed access to.

The Power of Pain

Aberon was enjoying himself. He held up the bleeding finger-piece into the light with the tongs and watched the last drips of blood fall onto the granite pavement. Who would have believed that each and every joint of the human body could be luxuriously pulled apart one segmented body part at a time? All it took was a couple of pairs of good-gripping tongs and a colleague willing to hold the other end firmly.

The screaming fellow he was currently working on had made the dire mistake of failing his druidic tests for a third time. Now he was being made an example of. Well, Aberon mused, the fellow had been a bit of a tenuous candidate from the outset. He was prone to gluttony, which was not something Aberon, who was if anything severely ascetic, was fond of; and he had also been a bit lazy. Now he was paying the price for his sloth.

This newly devised torture kept his victims alive and mostly fully aware of what was happening for the whole process. It was a macabre, garish spectacle that no one would ever forget. Which, after all, *was* the point, wasn't it? A lesson for the others to be sure – there would be no more lolling about when there were things to be learned and things to be done.

He was quite bloody when he finished. As he stood under the flowing water of the ice-cold stream to cleanse himself, he considered once again the magic he was having the Nine bring into play. The Qa-ryks were now fully under his sway. In the interest of keeping things on an even keel, he had given strict orders for his brethren to keep each extended clan apart. The unification process would take place only when each family group had grown to the extent that he could field an army of the beasts numbering in the tens of thousands. That would take a few years, perhaps a bit shy of a decade. Then he would be ready to strike.

At that point, he hoped all the other pieces to his plan would have fallen into place. There were delicate negotiations that needed to happen; and even more importantly, there were the plans beyond the plans that would bring all that he coveted into full play. Patience, he thought. I will need to be patient. In the meantime, he would take pleasure in the small things. Perhaps a bit of tea would be nice?

The Art of Teaching

For a long time, Thistle considered how best to approach the trainees as they started the next phase of their training. As Meligance had oft used with her, she decided a demonstration might prove the most powerful motivator, as well as a lead-in to the lesson that would follow. She spent almost the entire night before this first combined class in a meditative pose, reflecting on the minutiae of her own experiences, those first weeks she had worked with "Blinkie." It all seemed like a dream she had a long time ago; however, her memories were clear on the processes she had used to gain focus and to understand her own personal energy, as well as how to "gather" energy from the world around her. These were the keys she hoped would help her students make the leap to being able to wield and control true offensive and defensive magic.

Meligance was a known quantity to the students; she was admired and feared. Her reputation as a powerful Wizardess and the most powerful mage in the kingdom held all of them in awe. Thistle was considered a force as well, because she had been the only person ever chosen to apprentice with Meligance. Yet she was entirely unproven. She intended to demonstrate a bit of herself so that the apprentice magic-users would pay attention as readily to her as to the White Wizardess.

She took them out to the courtyard below Meligance's study where she herself had spent countless hours practicing her skills and focus. Arranging them in a semi-circle, with Meligance at one end, Thistle, without saying a word, spun around, drew her hand up into the air as if to grasp something, and then threw her fingers out toward the wall opposite. There was a flash of light, followed by a massive burst of flame that shook the stonework.

It had the desired effect; most of the students' mouths dropped open. Thistle did not give them time to think. She gestured to Meligance and her mentor made a similar gesture and sent a bolt of pure energy crashing into the wall. While sparks danced about the stonework, Thistle turned back and said, "All of you have the potential to do that, and more. It is why you are here. Meligance and I have sensed the power within you.

"Note! And this is perhaps the most important thing I will tell you — there are no words, or gestures, or machinations you have to say or go through to use pure energy or mold it to your use. Sometimes we do use single words or phrases to help our focus. They are unnecessary. Watch again."

This time she didn't even raise her hand; and a bolt of fire flew, approximately chest high, across the yard and exploded into the wall. She raised her hand to gain their attention. "When we use words or gestures, they are simply a means to help us draw a focus and focal point to the magic, to the use of pure energy. Again!"

This time Thistle used the same gesture as before, combined with the word for fire from High Elvish, "Igneo." A flash erupted from her hand, and again a massive fireball exploded into the wall.

"That, the gesture I use to focus the gathering of energy and the word, sets in my mind the result I want. It makes it much easier to focus and create virtually instantaneously what I want with my power and with the power I garner from the ether. It took me many, many long hours of practice to reach a point where I can do this as I will, with a simple gesture and only a single word to help me focus.

"Starting today, you are going to find your own power within and learn to focus it. As your ability to bring your inner energy into play grows, you will also learn to gather and focus energy from what is all around you. However!" Thistle paused to emphasize what she was about to say. "You will all need to give up these outlandish notions that intricate gestures, alchemical processes, complex verbiage, and other irrelevant actions are necessary for magic. They are not. Watch again."

She turned one last time and yelled loudly, "Poppycock," wildly gesticulating in the air at the same time. What emerged from her hand was the exact same "spell" of fire she had just "thrown."

She let the residual sparks and flame disperse before she gestured for all of them to sit on the stonework benches set behind them. Then she had Meligance join her, and the two of them quickly created several dozen small brightly lit balls of colored energy. They tossed one to each of the students.

"Focus inside now and try to follow the thread of the energy that is helping you control the ball into your center. Focus…"

It was not easy, and it still took a tremendous amount of patience; yet slowly, day by day, week by week, they began to understand and they began to learn. After each class, Meligance and Thistle would sit down together and think through what experience they could provide that would help their students take the next step forward.

***

Jared, on the other hand, was thoroughly enjoying his teaching. He was a natural with the younger students and they loved his patient, careful explanations about everything to do with a bow and how to shoot it. Many of the older and more experienced archers also sought his advice. Each afternoon he would spend an hour on the archery range. Three days a week he taught short sword to advanced students as well, focusing on creative, battle-ready fighting skills. Often those hours would be filled with him demonstrating techniques and sparring with young men who were planning on joining the Borean army as officers. His field experience was an invaluable asset to those who would be soon posted to the frontier or on the King's Wall.

Simon-Nathan showed up when he could get away from his teaching and other duties for both archery practice and short-sword instruction. He was improving his skills; though as he said to Jared one day when they had gone out for a quick drink at the Green Horse tavern, "All I wish is to become competent, just in case."

Jared smiled at his friend's comment. "Not long ago, Leonis told me I should learn as much as I can from my classes, especially the boring ones. He implied that there are always things we can learn that might prove useful down the road. I think he is right, Simon. You have become more than a little competent, and you have gotten in much better shape as a result. I would urge you to continue, even when I am not here. There is something about physical activity, as well as the ability to wield a weapon competently, that gives us much more than a simple skill. For example, you have become more self-confident; and I see that in how you move, your dealings with others, and in your general demeanor."

Simon-Nathan laughed. "You, too, Jared. I see the Bard in you already. We have both grown. Shall we go pick up our ladies for dinner?"

On the two days when Jared was free to choose his own practice regimen, he would often spend time in the "odd" weapons corner. Here were gathered strange forms of "normal" weapons, and a few less-common weapons, that one might face in combat. There were double-bladed knives; sweepingly curved swords and sabers; short, long, and even longer polearms with heads of many shapes and sizes; and so forth. He also got to practice with the buoas of the Qa-ryks, the tapered sword and dagger of the Sliv lords and maidens, and the heavy hammers of the dwarves and gnomes.

His goal was not necessarily to become adept with any of them; it was to understand their capabilities, how to defend against them, as well as how to facilitate his own strikes against them, should he have to face these wielded by an enemy in a fight.

All in all, working in the yard was his favorite time of the day. He stuck with his classes and tried his best to glean what he could from them, as Leonis had suggested; but for the most part he found them uninspiring and of no great import, from his perspective, to his knowledge base.

Of Other Curiosities

Spring was in the air when Thistle finally got around to spending time with Meligance that was not associated with the developing apprentice magic-users and dealing with their many problems. During what free time she had, she continued her work of shifting frequencies into alternate, closely allied planes, trying to ken as much as possible. It was difficult and time-consuming work because she had to maintain an incredible focus and control, always being alert for the unexpected. She knew even the most closely associated planes held hazards that one could not fully appreciate until one experienced them.

It was, however, exactly these types of concerns that Thistle wanted to experience. This form of practice would provide her with the knowledge to defend herself in different planes. She was learning to use energy in vastly different ways than she ever used it within her own world. The real key, she had to remind herself, was that energy was energy, no matter what realm she visited; and because of this, it could be coalesced and manipulated. This was the understanding she had been seeking – the ultimate knowledge that would give them the ability to fight the beasts that Kan had somehow bred so they could jump back and forth between two planes. Thistle would need to learn to use energy effectively in other worlds.

"A hard year?" Meligance said wearily, gesturing for Thistle to sit opposite her.

"They are learning at last, draggingly slow, but learning."

"Yes, you spoiled me. There was so much you simply grasped on your own and moved forward with. Working with them is like feeding a baby in its first months."

"Well," Thistle smiled, "perhaps they have reached the toddler stage now."

"Indeed! Progress is progress… You wished to talk of other magic use?" Meligance asked.

"Truly, I am curious, always. I think you instilled that in me or awakened it." Thistle smiled at her mentor.

"That is a good thing. Then I did my job. Ask away; I will share what I know."

"Can we use magic to heal? It is something I have pondered and even asked Sart about. He hemmed and hawed and told me to ask you."

"Heal in the sense that a priest or cleric does?" Meligance frowned. "Perhaps. It is not impossible, certainly. As you have learned, our use of energy is different from that of a priest's use of power. Clerics garner and build their personal energy, which they somehow reinforce by connecting with alternate sources – as in Sart's case, the earth, Gaia herself. Others draw energy and power from the sun, druids from the moon and earth, and so on. It is different, yet the same. Their relationship with those sources somehow is more personal – established as a result of their deep beliefs.

"From the way he has described it to me, they do not understand or use energy as we do. It is more a general sense of manipulating the energy that is part of them and of other things – a feeling, a flow they connect with. They can use the power within to heal or use it in other ways as well. Remember the fire Aberon brought down upon you?"

Thistle nodded. It had been the distant connection with Meligance through Yolk that had helped her survive that powerful attack.

"I imagine he was using his druidic powers for that strike, though he may also have studied magic. Clerics can do more than heal, but that is oft their focus. Sart rarely uses his powers elsewise, though he can. I have seen him do so, and to devastating effect.

"You may know that there are those who have followed both paths: the use of magic, and the power of the earth or sky or another source. One who comes to mind was named Ixus. He was a powerful cleric who also delved into magic later in his life. Most typically that is the way of it; some clerics eventually decide to explore the magical realm. Priests already know energy – personal energy and how to focus it. However, it is quite rare for magic users to become clerics. Or perhaps a better way to phrase it – to seek a healing process for their use of energy. The few I have known who have tried, found it confusing to their inner control and focus. As I said, it is the same, yet different.

"Thistle, Sart will also tell you that healing can come about naturally, as well as through other means. Your Jared has experienced this. Music is a powerful force; and there have been a few, a very few, who could twist its power in such a profound way that healing energy becomes a part of the effect of what they produce musically.

"Another means of healing, Thistle, which all magic users are certainly capable of learning and facilitating, is practical medicine, which includes the closing and binding of wounds, herbal and alchemical concoctions, and the like. Incorporating magic is a matter of using energy directly in those pursuits. It is more of a facilitation, a manipulation of elements that may hasten the use of what is already available. It is not true 'healing,' in the sense of stopping and curing a disease or the healing over of a wound – things clerics and priests can do with their inner power and focus. It is also not placing one's hands on another and calling upon one's inner strength and power to heal an organ or cure a dreadful illness. That takes a singular focus and ability which I do not understand. Does this help?"

"I could bind together the edges of a wound if I delved deep enough and was able to connect with the energy of the flesh?"

"Certainly. Again, that is the pure manipulation of the fundamental elements of energy. And, you would expend a tremendous amount of effort to do such a thing."

"Yes. I imagine it would be quite difficult. It is akin to creating water from energy, rather than drawing it to me from the air all about," Thistle said.

"Exactly."

"I thought as much. True healing would be a diversion from what we typically focus on, and I would imagine it would take considerable personal energy and time to make the simplest of efforts from what you have said."

"All true. What else, child?"

"What of raising of the dead? I have heard tales that clerics have done this?"

"Aha! Now we get to the crux of it! Again, this is probably a better question for our dear Sart. I will tell you what I know.

"Death… is death. There seems to be a point at which we pass over, or go beyond this world and any hope of returning to our current form and the world it is in. The moment when this transition takes place is what has been debated for centuries by priests, clerics, and the wise. Some think it happens as the last breath is taken, others not until some time after that, and still others even hours or days later. Sart is of the mind that a return to life is still possible if one can catch the... well, soul, I suppose is the best word to use – the essence of a person – before it passes over or into whatever comes next. He believes that this may be possible after the earliest stages of physical 'death.' He thinks, and he does feel strongly about this and he has some experience with it as well, that the soul begins to leave the body immediately when all life functions cease. That is, unless it is literally pulled back or called back by another force."

"There are those who can facilitate this 'calling back?'" Thistle asked.

"Yes, or maybe I should say, perhaps. Sart has taken part in these types of healings. However, they were always immediately at the cusp of death. As you phrased it – 'The raising of the dead.'

"Speak with him. As you know he loves to share his ideas and insights. This is one arena that we magic-users do not attempt to deal with – the soul – whatever it is that makes us unique and alive as beings. That is truly the realm of priests and religions. I suppose if one asks the question of oneself, one must wonder about these things. As Sart believes, I, too, feel there is something about us all that endures."

"Which is?" Thistle asked.

"Most people believe what religions tell us to think. In my case, the truthful answer is, 'I don't know.' My hope – The basic essence of who we are and what we have accomplished? Perhaps this is simply our desire of what endures of our lives. Possibly none of our religions or philosophies understand the truth of it, either."

"A conundrum to ponder?"

"So Sart would likely say; you should speak to him of this as well. Such questions help me to remember to ponder the imponderables." Meligance smiled. "Is there anything else you wish to ask about?"

"Seeing the future; the past?"

"Ah! Now we get to something that is rooted in magic and energy. It is something I have long pondered… But it is more the realm of seers, prognosticators, and the like." Meligance looked slightly amused, yet she said nothing further.

"And? Is it possible? Can we… I learn how to do this?"

"I looked into just this a long time ago – spoke with those I believed had some understanding and connection with such powers."

"And…?"

"You have heard of people feeling like they have been someplace or experienced something before? Or have an image or dream of something that happens later?"

"Yes, we always called it 'before-seeing'."

"And you have heard of foretelling, foreseeing, divination, and the like?"

"Of course, it is a common practice of hamlet hags, witches, and seers, or so I'm told."

"Truly, and do you believe such things are possible?"

"I don't know…" Thistle frowned. "Well, yes. I guess I would have to say I have heard enough and even experienced a few things like this to believe they are conceivable. Yet, I don't understand how."

"Well, another thing you might want to talk with Sart about is his belief that we actually lead many lives, some of them similar to the life we currently lead. There is even supposition that we lead all of these many lives concurrently, and the life we are living is simply the life we are at this moment focusing on."

"So if we could touch another of these many lives, we could see things past, or even possibly in the future?" Thistle asked.

"You have made a leap, my young Wizardess, that took me some time to connect with. 'Before-seeing' may simply be memories we have that are associated with another life. Perhaps this is some of what we experience when we dream. In other words, dreams may be our connection to our other lives – those that are parallel, yet running at different times and with subtle or even dramatic differences relevant to our 'current' life."

"So this is what seers or diviners use to see threads of the future?"

"Maybe. Or perhaps they have the ability, sometimes enhanced through trances, meditation, even medicinal or hallucinogenic plants they take, to see possibilities of what the future might hold. Isn't this what divination really is – the ability of some gifted people to tap into other lives? Any proper seer will tell you that their foretellings are 'What *might* occur.' They are never an absolute."

"Yes," Thistle said. "Now that I think about it, Nagama'a, the witch woman of the Slivs, is a seer who seems to see portents of the future, or, as she says – possibilities – threads of the loom of life that may or may not happen."

"Truly, she is perhaps the greatest of these our world has known, though the elves in Moulanes have their seers as well. I was greatly humbled when I met with her."

"You have spoken with her, too?"

"Many years ago, in my early years as a Wizardess… One of her statements stayed with me, 'We only observe time; we cannot control it.' And all of what we are talking about is wrapped around our understanding of time."

Thistle thought for a long moment, understanding that what Meligance had just said spoke to and expanded into the weighty concept of time. She also realized that she could spend days, months, even a lifetime considering such things. Meligance, though she had not said anything directly about it, was letting her know that such considerations had little to do with magic and energy, but were rooted in another ability or gift neither of them had naturally.

She nodded then and said, "I will think on it… when I have time," and she smiled.

"Good," Meligance smiled, too. And after a few seconds, "Is there anything else?"

"A thousand little things, but our true work beckons. Shall we plan the morrow?"

"In a minute. I have a question for you, Thistle. Where is your staff?"

"At home."

Meligance raised her eyebrows.

"In the closet in our bedroom. I do not typically carry it with me."

"Get it."

"Now?"

Meligance raised her eyebrows again. Thistle turned to leave; her mentor's next words stopped her. "Now, as in 'Now!"

Thistle turned and flushed a bright red at the command. She was embarrassed that she hadn't considered teleporting it to Meligance's chamber. It was the first time in a long time that her mentor had issued her an order. She felt a brief flare of anger, but she pushed it down.

An instant later, she was standing before Meligance with her staff held in both hands across her chest, her eyes downcast.

"May I take it?"

Thistle raised her eyes, surprised by the soft tone of the request. She nodded, and held the staff out; Meligance took it gingerly.

For several minutes, the White Wizardess examined the staff. From its crowned head, with the blue sapphire embedded, she moved her hands across the tendrils of wood until she came to the other end, where Thistle had meticulously folded each thread of wood back in upon itself to create a hard, smooth surface. Finally, Meligance closed her eyes and swept her hands once again along the length, this time ending at the top knot. When she opened them again, she passed the staff back to Thistle.

"I apologize for issuing such a stern command to an equal, but I needed you to understand what I am about to tell you. Your staff is much more than a magicked walking stick, Thistle. It is a badge, a symbol of who you are and the power you carry. It is also a lifeline when in dire need. That is why you will spend hours, days, months, and years imbuing it with every nuance of energy and purpose that you may.

"Carry it always, on every occasion you can, my child. None will be able to ever question your power or position. These two things can be critical to your influence in any given situation. When you are away, in the wild, any situation you are not absolutely sure of, I would recommend that you always keep it close to hand. We are often tested when we least expect it. Here in the city, it is your honor. It separates you from all others. And here, in this palace, where there are so much intrigue and politics at play, that is a good thing. Out there," Meligance gestured grandly to encompass the Borean world, "it can mean life and death. Understand?"

"Yes, ma'am. I am sorry."

"You didn't know." Meligance waved as if it were not so important. She smiled slightly. "It is a wonderful staff. I am proud of what you have already done with it. Continue to mold it to who you are and imbue it with the power you carry. It will serve you well in what lies ahead.

"Now, shall we get back to our teaching responsibilities?"

***

It was also in the spring that Elanar and Athena got married at his small estate on the outskirts of the capital. In spite of Simon-Nathan's wishes to throw his sister and Elanar a grand affair, the two lovebirds decided on a quiet wedding on the banks of a peaceful spring amongst the cherry blossoms blanketing the banks, with only close friends attending. Jared and Thistle had never seen Athena as vibrant and lovely as on her wedding day, and Simon-Nathan was beaming throughout the ceremony and festivities that followed.

A larger reception was held the next day in the capital with key people from the banking and mercantile businesses of Borea invited. Athena, having been taught by one of the great businessmen of the kingdom, knew the value of making friends and keeping them close. Simon-Nathan's father's business was in good hands.

Restlessness

It was more than a year since they had slain the dragon, and Slyn and Ge-or were getting restless. Early in the spring, they decided to ride south to Aube to see if any adventures were in the offing while the remainder of the work on their equipment and leather was being done. It had taken considerable effort on the tanner's part to work the dragon hide to a suppleness that satisfied the two. Now that the skin was in the hands of the tailors and Ge-or's armor was nearly half complete, they felt they did not need to be overseeing the work. What they did need was to give in to their wanderlust.

When they reached that southernmost town, the heat of summer was beginning to sweep across from the west. To their surprise, Aube itself was in an uproar, crowded to overflowing with refugees out of the Beze range. Farmers, ranchers and miners who had been brave enough to re-inhabit abandoned homesteads and digs had been forced out once again by Qa-ryks.

The beasts were back, several large clans; and these had taken back the mountains and hills as far south as the beginning of the Horn. The smart people had fled quickly. The few that had stayed, no matter how brave and stalwart, had been overrun.

After searching the border town for anything of interest, Ge-or and Slyn volunteered to join a strong contingent headed by Zara, the moon cleric who had helped heal Ge-or. He was leading a rescue mission into the foothills to see if any beleaguered families or parties had managed to survive. In two days, they were on the road due west.

***

Three months later, after many skirmishes with the aggressive Qa-ryks, their party dragged back into Aube. They had not accomplished much beyond saving a scant score of survivors from two groups that had holed up in abandoned mines. Though they had decimated several Qa-ryk patrols, there was no shortage of the beasts. The mission, as much a reconnaissance in force as it was a rescue mission, provided valuable information for the kingdom. It also confirmed that the Qa-ryks were once again on the move and taking territory abandoned since the first war.

After a brief respite in Aube, Ge-or and Slyn headed back toward Aelfric to check on their armor and other accoutrements. Satisfied that all well, in the late summer they turned their horses toward Efsted, planning to skirt the Bendir

317

plains. Slyn wanted to head for Panterra where his seafaring family resided. Ge-or had it in mind to turn north to seek out his brother at long last.

***

Jared and Thistle took every advantage of their summer vacation from their duties and responsibilities. They rode north and west with Karenna and Simon-Nathan with their young babe, Simon-Nathan the Twelfth in arms, and also with Athena and Elanar. The four musicians sang for their room and board at small wayside taverns and any hamlet or inn that was willing to take them in. They simply enjoyed the freedom of the road. Their small caravan of horses, a comfortable carriage, and two pack mules was welcomed with open arms once the word was out about the amazing performances they provided the local populaces.

Diligent as ever, Simon-Nathan and Karenna took copious notes on local tunes and musical idioms whenever they heard something new. The two were well into the development and writing of their senior Master's paper but were open to anything that might make their work as comprehensive as possible.

Thistle and Athena, on the outside looking in at all the "work" that the others were involved with, became close friends. Elanar was a bit overprotective of his frail wife; however, she continued to blossom during their meanderings through the beautiful farmlands.

It was the tonic that Jared and Thistle needed to brace themselves for another fall and winter of studies and teaching while being cooped up in the city.

Truth from the Past

Upon reaching Efsted, Ge-or discovered through Sart's network that his brother was galivanting about the countryside until the fall. He and Slyn decided to ride the waves for the last month of the heat, serving as protection against pirates on various merchant vessels. When they returned to Efsted, Slyn headed south to visit his family, and Ge-or turned north to head to the capital.

Jared was free this fall of studies and teaching duties and had been given a special writ from Leonis that allowed him access to one specific restricted area of the archives beneath Bard Hall. While Thistle was busy working with her students on the importance of absolute control of the energy they garnered, Jared finally had something to read and study that he found absolutely fascinating.

Jared spent most of his days deep within the cool vaults below the main Hall complex. He only came up for the two-hour early afternoon sessions in the practice yard where he assisted with archery and short sword and tried to maintain his own fitness. What he discovered in the depths below Bard Hall were reams and reams of carefully preserved parchment that spoke in great detail about the Art of Musical Healing. These had been written by gifted Bards from by-gone eras.

One of the first things he realized as he scanned the collection was that the prevalence of Bards with this special gift seemed to be in an inverse relationship to the present day. A thousand years ago there were at least several "Healing Bards," as they were known in those days. As one progressed further toward the present, there were fewer and fewer, until there were only two mentioned in the past few centuries, and both of those had what was referred to as a "limited gift." Jared made a mental note to ask Leonis about this interesting fact.

Satisfied after a couple of weeks that he had a good perspective from which to start, Jared decided to begin with the writings of the two most recent Bards with "the gift" and work his way back. These first tomes were histories and anecdotes of healing occurrences that the Bards had been a part of. In some ways, they mirrored Jared's own experience, yet on a far smaller scale. Still, he mused, they had not had the pendant either. He wondered whether the gem he now always wore on a sturdy titium chain about his neck had more to do with his expertise or his gift than his own innate ability.

Though the writings were clear, he gleaned little of practical use from these tomes. A few of the Bards mentioned the titles of tunes they played, some of which Jared was familiar with, and a few which had been discussed in his classes in reference to them having a "healing effect." Others he did not recognize, so he copied the titles and made another note to see if any manuscripts existed of the melodies and harmonies.

After a full month of diligent reading and study, he began a massive tome that had been written some four hundred and fifty years before by Staffir of Aragon. The world was a different place that far in the past; and Staffir, from what Jared could tell, was an elven Bard with extraordinary powers of healing. Some elves, he knew, were natural healers. It seemed their communion with the earth and all that grows upon and within it helped them draw on power similar to what Sart claimed his own personal focus revolved around. The cleric had several times mused to Jared and Thistle that he wished he could talk at length with the elves and get permission to study in Moulanes with some of their wisest healers.

As Jared read, he realized that Staffir had an altogether different sort of gift. He seemed to be able to take the music of his day and twist it to serve his purposes when he was within a trance-like state. Then he could produce "waves," as Jared interpreted the old verbiage, "of energy that flowed forth and eased the suffering and ailments" of whole villages or groups of people struck by some calamity or another. Even more importantly, he had written down, after every healing, a detailed description of what he had done, how he had felt, and the tunes he had used, including any variations he could remember.

The problem, and it was a serious one, was that four hundred years ago the notational system for music was in its infancy. Tunes, and even elaborate compositions, were traditionally passed down by rote – one Bard learning from another. The musical staff of Staffir's day consisted of only two lines, ut, or do, and la; and the notation itself was more decorative than accurate. Thus, they served as more of a reminder of how the tune went, than as an absolute depiction of the notes involved. Even less accurate was the rhythmic notation. There was no standard rhythmic notation, much less any indications for the subtleties of the ebb and flow in the music. It was anyone's guess as to what a particular-shaped note or slash across the staff might indicate in relation to tempo and duration. The scales of that period were well established; unfortunately, nothing about the notation indicated which scale or scales had been used, much less what specific notes were being indicated by the marks on the staff.

Jared made a game attempt at deciphering a number of the melodies, but he felt the results were far from satisfactory. It wasn't until he began the next set of tomes, written by another Bard who was of equal stature as a Healing Bard as Staffir, that Jared found a key that might help him understand and work out the melodies of that era. DasPray, frustrated himself by the limits of the current notational system, had devised his own. Unfortunately, he had gone as far to the other side of notational definition as was remotely feasible, by detailing everything to an extent that the mass of characters and devices were virtually indecipherable. His staff alone consisted of twenty-four lines, which Jared thought reflected the notation of intervals smaller than the conventional half step of modern music.

Jared was determined to get at the fundamentals of the music itself. He was not sure whether it would give him any further understanding or inspiration relevant to his own supposed gift; if nothing else it would show him the types of music these early Bards had performed during their healings. Should he truly have a gift for musical healing, he knew his own approach might prove to be completely different – something welling up from within rather than something learned, as it had during the eve when he had saved the children of the plains riders. Or he hoped he might be able to combine what was previously known and practiced with his own innate creativity.

***

Summer was ending and Jared was pacing, waiting for Thistle to return from her work at the palace. They had many times discussed their return to Xur. If they were to do so before winter set in, they would need to make a decision soon. Things had changed for him, and he was worried that she might balk at what he wanted to suggest. "She's back," he said to himself, hearing the door downstairs open. He sat down on a chair next to their bed to wait for her to come up to the second level. But he could not stay put even for the minute it took for her to climb the stairs. He was pacing again when she entered the room.

"Jared?"

"Thistle!" Jared crossed to her and gave her a lingering kiss. He still loved kissing her. Her lips were so soft and inviting that he could lose himself in her; and he almost gave in to the feeling now, because he felt it a preferable choice to what he was about to propose.

He pulled away from her and looked into those equally fascinating green eyes.

"Are you all right, Jared. You seem… nervous."

"I am that. I… I have something to ask of you. It is difficult. In some ways, well, many ways, I feel convinced it is the right thing for me… hopefully for us." He took a step back, blushed, and took her hand again.

Finally, he blurted it out. "I want to stay here another year, Thistle, maybe two. I'm sorry. I know we have talked many times about returning to Xur as soon as possible; however, the study I am doing is… important. If I truly have this gift, I should develop it. I should know all that I can as soon as I can if… if I am to help others with it."

"Truly?" Thistle asked, looking questioningly at him.

"I know. I know, Thistle. I… I don't know what else…"

Thistle raised her hand to stop him, touching his lips with her fingertips. "It is what I want as well, my love. I didn't know how or when to broach it with you."

"You want to stay?"

"Yes, definitely. Our apprentices are at a critical stage. We have years of work with them before they will be ready. Meligance and I have discussed this at some length. I should be here to take on much of this burden; she has other duties and concerns to attend to."

"By-the-gods, Thistle, I am so relieved." Jared lifted her at the waist and spun her around thrice before putting her back down. He drew her in and kissed her again quite thoroughly.

It was awhile before they resumed their discussion.

"I am so relieved, Thistle," Jared said that evening as they sat over a quiet meal their housekeeper had prepared. "You can't imagine how nervous I was about bringing this up. Well, perhaps you can." He reached across and took her hand, softly stroking the top.

"Have you spoken with Leonis?"

"Just today. If you agreed, we were going to set a time to meet and plan the next year. He wants me involved again with teaching and other 'Bardly duties,' whatever that means. The grandmaster had an impish smile on his face, so he has something up his sleeve. He wants me to take some advanced classes -- things I wouldn't normally take until I return from my Journeymanship. I am guessing he does not want my elevation to Bard to be delayed further. He seems anxious that I should move forward as quickly as I can."

"He likes you. You do know that?"

"Aye. I think in many ways we are cut from the same piece of leather."

"Perhaps he is grooming you for something grander."

"By-the-gods, Thistle. Do you think he wants me to be grandmaster some day? He is looking that far in the future?"

"Not so far as you might think, Jared. He wants his legacy continued. Bard Hall needs to find its way out of the Dark Ages. You are as forward-looking as any."

"I suppose, but I do not think I have it in me to be grandmaster. I will be content to become a Bard. That I do think is in my blood." He smiled at his wife. "It is strange to be talking of these things, two country bumpkins not long ago, and now you a Wizardess and me soon to be a Journeyman Bard. I would not have dreamt such a thing a decade ago."

"We have both grown in many ways, my love."

"Truly, yet, I wish we could go back to Xur. I miss being there. I miss the wide-open spaces."

Thistle turned her hand over on top of Jared's and stroked his. "The news is dire out west. The Qa-ryks are multiplying rapidly. Sart told me today that they have returned to the Beze Range and that Ge-or was in some skirmishes there this summer."

"He is all right?" Jared asked, concerned.

"Yes, he is fine. He was coming here, when he heard we were out touring the north. He spent the rest of the summer near Efsted and plans to head to the capital soon. Ge-or asked Sart to pass this message to us." Thistle handed Jared a well-mussed piece of parchment, that had obviously spent more than a little time in one of the good cleric's many pockets.

Jared spread it open and read out loud, "Good brother. Plan to come north soon, three weeks or so before the Equinox. With fair weather, I should be near the capital a fortnight thereafter. Long to see you and meet your bride. Ge-or."

"He is not long on words," Jared laughed.

Thistle laughed, too. "Sart also said, 'Your brother ever finds his way into trouble,' though he has been making good use of the dragon spoils – outfitting himself in dragon-leather armor and fine plate, as well as helping others in need."

"It is hard to believe that the tales surrounding his adventure after the great red beast have become the talk of the kingdom," Jared said. "The Bards have been making a lay of it, though no one seems to know how he actually did slay the beast. I would imagine that my brother finds things like this disconcerting. He is bold and brave, yet there is a shyness in him."

"He has a new adventure planned; did you know that?"

"Sart or Ge-or?"

"Both actually," Thistle smiled. "Sart is planning it. Now that our good cleric is back in the east, he wants to go to Dagger Island. There is an old monastery there; and because he does not know what to expect, he wants some muscle with him. It may be abandoned, or… well, he isn't sure. The monks there were always reclusive; however, no one has heard from them in over a century. Because of its shape and high cliff walls, the waters are dangerous around the isle, so it is not oft visited."

"When will they go?" Jared asked. "Perhaps we could take a week off and ride south with Sart and Ge-or before they embark."

"Before winter sets in. After that, the currents work against ships trying to land there."

"It would be good to see Sart. Is he still here?"

"Nay, he is off again. He came, met with Meligance briefly, and I happened to come in before he left. He rode out this morn. I would like to spend more time with him, too. I always have questions to ask him; his wisdom and wit are far different than Meligance's."

"I know!" Jared grinned. "If I didn't feel compelled to finish my work here, I would volunteer to go with them. Sart said before the winter sets in? There is not much time then."

"I will try to find out when Sart will return. I barely had time to get a hug from him, a few questions. and he was gone. It would be good to know his mind before he leaves on this new venture."

"What does he hope to find on Dagger Isle? Is it not a wild place?"

"Except for the monastery on the eastern Hilt of the dagger, yes," Thistle answered. "It is supposedly a refuge for many beasts. According to Sart, the tip of the Blade is a haven for pirates and buccaneers, nothing more. He wishes to explore the vaults at the monastery. Its archives were once the most extensive in the kingdom, housing even tomes from the First Age. He ever seeks knowledge of the Heart of the World. He sees it as the key to all that lies ahead."

"He has a singular focus."

A Great Loss

"Other Bardly duties," Jared found out, included his first venture into formal classroom teaching. It was expected of those who wished to continue their Bard studies that, before or during their Journeymanship, they would experience the full range of responsibilities that a Bard might be expected to have. "One has to find his niche," Leonis had boomed while clapping Jared soundly on the shoulder. "Nothing like a bit of history to wake one up in the morning."

Jared would make the best of it.

***

Things were not going nearly as quickly as Aberon had hoped. The Nine had returned from extended tours among the clans and the reports were all the same – slower than expected growth rate, smaller litters, and more runts, who were typically destroyed by the dams, in each batch. Overall, they were expanding their numbers and range, though much more slowly than Aberon had hoped. He wanted the beasts to overwhelm the east. To do that they would need far greater numbers than were currently being produced.

His priests had finally gotten them to extend into the Beze range. Once they had grown in sufficient numbers, he would use that entire southeastern spur as a staging area for his invasion. However, this drop in birth-rate and quality of their spawn was bewildering to be sure. Perhaps taking from them their natural tendencies to fight and conquer other clans was somehow affecting their breeding ability.

Maybe he would ease the restrictions, let them have their little spats and conquests as long as they didn't destroy each other. He would have to experiment with the controlling magic and find the right balance. It would delay his plans a year or two; still, he would manage. More time to get all the acolytes, priests, and newly anointed druids in shape for what was to come. He didn't want to take any chances. The more power he had at his disposal when battle was joined, the better.

***

Ge-or never made it to Borea to see his brother. In truth, the great warrior never made it out of the Efsted Dukedom. He had even set out early, hoping the weather would hold off its chill while he headed north. He was only a half league outside the walls of the inner city when he was first accosted.

Thankfully he was well-accoutered, thinking he would take what he needed for when he met up with Sart's group on the coast of the capital city. The first fight was a well-muscled brute, who challenged him shortly after he had made request for an ale at a local tavern.

"Dragonslayer!"

Ge-or groaned as he turned from the bar.

"Outside."

Tired from the long ride through streets and alleyways, Ge-or smiled at the stranger, nodded a bow, and said, "You win." He turned back to the inn keep.

The grizzled man him simply repeated himself, growling, "Outside."

Ge-or shook his head, knowing that he would have to in some way either dissuade or face this mountain of a man. Turning again to the inn keep, Ge-or set a silver-piece on the counter. "Private. Bath. Roast. Three minutes." After which, he followed his challenger through the maze of chairs and tables to the door and outside.

In the early evening light, Ge-or assessed his opponent as they walked to an open space in the courtyard, clear of the many tethered horses. His father had taught him this, too. "Know your opponent – in any way possible!"

Brutus, as Ge-or had already named the beast he followed, was big, massing several stone more than Ge-or. However, it took Ge-or only an instant to understand that the fellow had used his weight and strength his whole life to win fights or control or discourage others. His walk alone spoke volumes. He didn't have the grace of a trained fighter – a grace that came from balance, speed, strength, and 'the dance.' Ge-or was an expert at the dance, as it had been developed as part of all the standard sword and weapons forms. He was even more of an expert because his father and Jared had challenged him to step out of those forms and to develop his own dance. And, except for his brother, Ge-or had never known anyone who was as good as he was at dancing with swords.

The man turning to face Ge-or was wearing heavyweight whole-body leather armor; had two blades in hand, both of equal weight and length; knives in his belt and boots; and a mace hanging on his weapons belt.

Ge-or shrugged, deciding not to even draw Fis-bane. This would be a short brawl. He would react to what the man did next. He knew he would have plenty of time, no matter what the fellow did.

Frustrated that Ge-or was standing there doing nothing, Brutus roared. Raising his short blades above his head, he charged directly at Ge-or.

High position… body charge… one-two… sidestep… step… left dip… spin… slash… drive up… push…

Ge-or's right straight-arm, from a low position to the front-right side of Brutus caught the man full in the throat. With a follow-through push, the man was overbalanced; and he crashed to the dirt and muck of the courtyard. Ge-or stepped across the man's body, leaving him gasping for air. He was tired and wanted to relax.

Seven more challenges in the next four days and Ge-or gave up trying to head north. He hadn't made it very far, and he was quite chagrinned that he once again had failed his brother. Unfortunately, he had to accept the fact that word was out, and the "Dragonslayer" was fair game. Anyone who could wield a weapon wanted to prove themselves against him.

By the time he made it back to the sea-side tavern in Efsted where he and Slyn, and occasionally Sart, would meet, Ge-or was fed up with people recognizing him and either talking to him, touching him, or trying to get him into a fight. Some of the challenges were fair and formal; others were brawls or even ambushes. Ge-or had to be careful. He received only a few nicks and scrapes as a result, yet it seemed only a matter of time before some idiot challenger would get lucky. Thankfully, he only had to seriously wound a couple of cheats who had come at him at night in a dark alley; by then he was fed-up with the whole business. Slyn had been instrumental in helping discourage other similar efforts in the past; but now that Ge-or had slain Fis, his reputation was far greater and more widespread.

Once they connected, he and his partner would decide what to do next. Perhaps this side quest to Dagger Isle was just the thing they both needed to get out of the notoriety of Fis's demise for a while. He motioned to the wench standing nearby – he would write Jared another note.

***

It was late fall when Sart's company finally boarded ship to set sail from Panterra to Dagger Isle. Though Sart had originally planned to take ship from Borea, he was too long afield on his most recent trek and finally met up with his crew and carefully selected band of adventurers in the south. Ge-or and Slyn had taken a fast clipper south when they got news of the change in plans.

Sart was taking two ships – one a fast clipper that would return to Panterra with most of the crew until they were needed in the spring to extract them from the isle, and a larger bulkier sloop to haul them and their gear. Most of the sailors did not want to spend a half year or more on a nearly deserted isle, and certainly not in a monastery.

Not knowing what to expect on the island, the cleric had raised a formidable force. Besides Ge-or and Slyn, the group consisted of Baline, a dwarf Ge-or had met on the trek west with Zara; Katelyn and her brother Ardan, who were both also known to Ge-or; two acolytes from Sart's religion who were to help sift through the archives; and two other fighters from the Southlands. In addition, the sea-elves would be manning the helms of the two ships -- Faldo the clipper and Nolo the sloop -- with small crews on each.

He had selected each one in the contingent with care. Both Slyn and Ge-or were experienced with boats and would help with the day-to-day sailing of the sloop. The same applied to the two acolytes, Fannir and Postulo, who had some experience with smaller sailing vessels. Both of the fighters, Truk and Warph, swarthy warriors of dark skin and powerful build who came from the dry pampas south of Moulanes and west of the Beu' range, also had some sailing experience. These two had spent a good part of the last decade hiring on to caravans and ships, much as Ge-or had done more than a few times. They knew enough to assist with the sailing of the vessels as well.

In addition, Katelyn, Ardan, Ge-or, Slyn, and Baline all read the old language and could help the monks searching the archives. The fighters were all skilled woodsmen and hunters and could help augment their larder over the course of the months they planned to be on the isle. Though information about the island was over a century old, the few sea-elves who had been there all had remarked about the many "extraordinary beasts" that inhabited it, including large deer with massive antlers, "cats" of tremendous size, fierce boars, and other more exotic fare, like brilliantly-colored birds, exotic lizards, huge turtles, and humanoid creatures that lived in the trees.

It was a bright fall day when they put out from shore. The trip would likely be a short one. With the northwesterly winds and the tides favorable, they would raise the western shoreline of Dagger Isle in less than two days. It would take them another day to sail south down the length of the Blade to maneuver around the tip and come up the leeward side. There they would anchor in the only serviceable place on the isle to put in with a large ship, the bay formed by the eastern Hilt. The windward side of the island had granite cliffs and rocky shoals to contend with.

The currents coming off the cross-guard of the dagger were exceedingly complicated and deadly. As they swung around both sides, they created an even more dangerous environment for shipping. Only a slow approach up from the south along the leeward Blade side, close in to shore, would allow a ship to approach the protected cove. It was the primary reason the island had remained virtually uninhabited except for the reclusive monks. In winter, it was impracticable to sail to or from the Isle, as the currents became completely impossible to contend with. Thus, Sart had planned to stay until spring.

The sloop was a bit unwieldy for the task, because the cleric had wanted to bring enough gear and supplies to last until they left. This included two braces of mules to haul goods from the bay to the heights of the monastery, which sat on a large rocky hill on the dagger's Hilt.

Otherwise, for an adventuring party, they were traveling light. Ge-or and Slyn had been tempted to bring along their newly finished dragon leather armor. In the end, they had settled for "their regular leather stuff." Each had brought their weapons of choice, but Sart had urged them to bring only what was necessary. He really didn't expect any battles to be fought. It was generally assumed that there would be no one left alive on the isle after such a long time with no communications from the monks that had been ensconced there. However, until the winter currents set in, there was no point in taking chances. He wanted to have enough strength along that buccaneers would be discouraged from considering their party and ship a target.

They weren't bringing any horses or riding mules either. Ge-or had been reluctant to stable Oesing for this long a time. He had grown fond of taking the sleek warhorse out for rides as often as possible during their sojourn in Aelfric. He had finally relented to leaving him, having thought of an alternative solution. On their trek eastward across the northern Bendir border, he and Slyn had given over their animals to the care of the Slivs and were lent lesser-bred mares to complete their journeys.

***

As hoped, on the second day out they made the isle as the sun set behind them. Nolo eased the larger sloop, Highsail, southward and the clipper, Galewind, settled in behind them. Shortening sail, they spent the evening and night sliding down the western edge of the Blade. By morning, they were nearing the tip and the difficult maneuvering began.

Nolo had to ease the ship southward, past the strong currents that swept off the steep cliffs at the western side of the point of the Blade. There was a short space where a good helmsman could bring the ship around at the right moment to catch the wind and the current as it slid eastwardly for a pace. If one missed it, it would mean another full day tacking back up into the wind to get around the dagger tip because the currents would try to drive the ship further south.

The two ships made the turn precisely and, as the sun rose to its zenith, they cleared the tip of the isle. Swung wide by the current to the east, they had to tack back in close to the leeward shore, before continuing slowly up the far side of the Blade toward the bay. They were making good progress. And though the more cautious Faldo had slipped a bit further back than Nolo would have wanted, he was encouraged that they would be both able to anchor safely before nightfall.

It was as the bowsprit of the Highsail crossed into Dagger Island Bay that things seemed to happen all at once. Nolo, at the helm, suddenly noticed that the steady northwesterly breeze had shifted due west in an instant and had increased dramatically in intensity. Caught by the northern hills of the isle that formed a tunnel for it to blast through, the wind howled across the southern edge of the bay and drove the ship around and eastward. Nolo reacted almost instantly, and a few of his sailors were already in place to reduce the sails; but another power grabbed at the boat from below at the same time.

Whatever forces were at play, the ship spun further to the east and in the dim light of the evening, Nolo saw off the port side what all shipmasters dreaded -- a massive eddy.

From behind, Faldo could see that something was wrong with his sister ship. He could also see what Nolo could not – a huge thunderstorm that had come in from the west over the hills was at least a partial cause for the sudden shift and change in intensity of the wind. He witnessed Nolo gain some control of the Highsail as the rains came and the wind intensified even further. Spinning his own wheel to swing the clipper eastwardly so it would stay clear of the Highsail's way, Faldo finally saw the huge whirlpool that had the bow of the sister ship in its grip. The clipper swung around to the east short of the bay. Caught by the wind, it seemed to fly forward out of harm's way, but also out of helping reach of its sister vessel.

Ge-or, standing next to Nolo at the helm, saw the eddy just as Nolo shouted loudly to shorten sails. Though he was used to the motions of boats, the sudden twisting turn of the sloop caused Ge-or to lurch sideways. Regaining his balance, he headed forward, leaning into the now strong wind. Making his way across the slippery deck, he passed Sart trying to tie Katelyn to the main mast. As he passed the cleric, Ge-or could make out Slyn scrambling up the mizzen rigging. Ardan was trying to follow; unfortunately, the young mage had little experience with ships' rigging.

Knowing by the feel of the vessel that the ship was in trouble, Ge-or caught hold of Ardan and pushed and pulled him to the mast. Grabbing a nearby length of rope, he handed it to the mage and yelled, "Tie yourself… too dangerous to go aloft. I'll go."

Ardan nodded. He already was worn out by his efforts to head into the rigging to help the sailors there.

Ge-or had already turned and virtually slid down the tilted deck to the rigging. Swinging around he set his foot and started up. He only got about halfway when the boat lurched mightily again. Sticking his arm through the ropes, Ge-or grabbed ahold of what he could. Then the rains came.

.

Caught by two essentially opposing forces, Nolo worked the wheel while everyone aboard the Highsail who could clamber into the rigging fought against the gale force wind to go aloft. In spite of their efforts, the heavy ship listed far to the right and slipped further down the vortex of the swirling waters. Knowing that the ship was seriously in danger of being swallowed by the maelstrom, Nolo spun the wheel hard to starboard, hoping to use the force of the spinning water to help drive the ship eastward and up out of the deathtrap. For a moment, it appeared to be working; but another shift of the wind, as the thunderstorm opened its floodgates, pushed down almost directly from above. A sailor screamed as he lost his grip and fell, plunging from the mainmast into the raging whirlpool. There was a loud splintering sound as the mizzen gave way.

Ge-or felt a hard wrench in his shoulder, saw the raging waters coming straight at him, and knew no more.

***

Meligance had summoned both Jared and Thistle to her studio. When they materialized in front of her long table, they immediately knew something was terribly wrong. The White Wizardess had been crying. She stood, but did not speak, only pushed a scrap of parchment across the table to them.

Thistle and Jared read it together. "I am sorry to inform you that the Highsail with all aboard has been lost at sea."

The End

NEXT: Book IV, *The Making of a Bard -- Ciaccona*

Excerpt from Book IV

The Making of a Bard – Ciaccona

Shipwrecked

Ge-or had a funny feeling in his mouth that he couldn't quite explain, and for some reason he was cold. His feet were especially cold. He struggled further into consciousness and wondered. Why is a dog licking my feet? Then he realized, I don't have a dog! It took him a minute to comprehend that he was lying flat on his stomach. He tried to move his arms, so he could push himself up; they seemed inordinately heavy and sluggish. He managed to rise about four inches when a wave of dizziness hit him, and he threw up.

After that rather violent reaction, he was fully awake. A flood of memories hit him in quick succession: ship – storm – whirlpool – holding on and swinging above the deck as the ship spun about – flying through the air – darkness. He sat back on his legs in the wet sand with his head down, trying to clear away the dizziness.

Ge-or slowly assessed his situation: it was still dark, and waves were lapping at his feet; his right arm hurt all along its length, but he could flex it; and thankfully, he didn't think he had any serious injuries. He was alive, unless hell was a dark cold beach. Cautiously, he began to rise; he stopped as his stomach threatened to give way again, settling back on his knees. He decided to slowly ease around so he could sit on the sand to look about without bringing his head up any higher. It was a bit awkward, as his back scabbard was still strapped in place; however, he managed to get turned around. It was comforting to know that Fisbane had come through the disaster with him.

It was night; the sky was now full of stars, and the moon was showing over the hills to his left. Ge-or didn't know how long he had been out. The storm had obviously passed eastward. He was facing what he figured was the opening to the bay on Dagger Isle. As he looked out over the water, he could see a large, deeper dark space directly in his line of sight. For a moment, he thought that he had somehow injured his head and that his eyes were playing tricks on him; then he realized he was staring at the raised stern of the Highsail.

Ge-or was beginning to put more of the events of the last few hours together in his mind, when he heard a distant call above the still howling wind.

333

"Haloo, Haloo, anyone there? Haloo!" He realized it was his partner, Slyn, coming from the north toward where he sat on the beach.

Ge-or raised his hand to wave. Then, realizing how foolish that was, he tried to answer the call. All he managed was a dry croak of something that barely resembled his partner's name. The odd sensation he had in his mouth when he first woke was of sand, much of which he had expelled when he had thrown up; but he could still feel the raspy dryness of it in his mouth and throat. He reached forward, swished his hand in the water, cupped some in his palm, and tried to rinse his mouth out. The cold saltiness helped get the nauseous taste from his mouth as well.

Meanwhile, Slyn had continued to call and was coming closer. Ge-or tried to clap; but his hands were so cold and stiff, that all he got was a wet slapping sound. He rinsed his mouth several more times. Then he managed a louder croak just as his partner materialized out of the dark a hundred paces to his left. "Slyn?"

"Ge-or…Ge-or?" The half-sea-elf broke into a run down the beach, albeit an awkward one. Ge-or could see that he had injured his left leg. His friend was hopping more than he was actually running, taking the brunt of the lope on his right side.

Ge-or managed to get onto his knees as Slyn approached. "By-the-gods, Ge-or, I am glad to see you. Are you alright?" Slyn took Ge-or's left arm and helped him ease up onto his feet.

"I'm alive. You're injured?"

"A strain, nothing serious."

"Others?"

"Sart is up there," Slyn pointed to the north, "at the bend in the bay. He is unconscious, though breathing. Truk is searching the north beach along the hilt. We found Warph, dead on the beach, and two of the crew's bodies in the water up there as well. Truk has got a large splinter of wood in his side; still, he can move. Of the others, we are searching. You are the first one I've seen coming south."

"Have you searched the ship?"

"Nay. The currents are strong, and I can't swim with this leg. Truk isn't in any shape to swim either. He shouldn't even be moving; yet he insisted on helping me search for survivors. Do you think you can go?"

"I don't know. I think I might, if I can get my head clear enough. My right arm is sore – a rope burn, maybe? The last thing I remember was having it wrapped around some rigging. I will have to try. Katelyn tied herself to the mainmast, and I believe Ardan was by the mizzen when I last saw him."

"Nolo strapped himself to the helm," Slyn said. "That's the last I saw before I was swept overboard."

"Can you tell how much of the ship is above water?"

"The stern sits high as you can see. The bow appears wedged down into the sand. I tried to wade out to her, but it got deep quickly. The currents are still strong, though I believe the whirlpool has either dissipated or moved to the south."

Ge-or took a tentative step forward in the water, then another. "In a minute, I will try," he said, flexing his right shoulder and arm. "Can you rouse Sart? We will need him soon enough, I'll warrant."

"I tried once, to no avail. Do you know where he stored his medical kit on board? Maybe that will help?"

"He stayed in one of the aft cabins, next to the captain's. I will look once I am out there." Ge-or took a couple more steps until he was up to his thighs. Glancing back, he turned, undid the large buckle at his chest, and pulled his back scabbard off. He handed his sword to Slyn.

Slyn knew its value. He had been the one who had taken the blade from under the dragon's nose. Ge-or took two more steps forward, until the water was lapping at his lower chest. He could sense the agitation of a strong undertow now, and he better understood Slyn's hesitation to swim with a game leg.

"Ready?"

"Yes." And with that, Ge-or plunged headfirst into the swirling waters. Slyn watched his powerful strokes for a minute. Satisfied his partner would be all right, he turned south again to resume his search for survivors.

Ge-or was a strong swimmer; but these waters were frigid, and the currents as bizarre as any he had ever encountered. Every few strokes it felt like he was battling a new dimension as the waters twisted about him. He plowed ahead, trying to let the exercise and the cold bring him to full alertness. The ship was maybe a couple of hundred paces out.

He reached the port side of the stern, swam to the left, found a dangling rope, and used it to haul himself upward. Grasping the rail, he pulled himself over onto the steeply slanted deck. He was surprised by what he saw. Fully a third of the front end of the ship was gone, ripped off by whatever demonic force the eddy and storm winds had brought together to doom the vessel. The whole section of the ship that included the bowsprit and foremast was missing. When he turned slightly, he saw that Katelyn was still tied to the mainmast. Her head was hanging down. Ge-or did not want to speculate as to whether she was alive or dead.

The light was dim, the moon only in quarter phase. As Ge-or watched, he thought he saw her move, her shoulders rising and falling slightly. Grabbing the rail, he began to pull himself up the slippery deck. Using the plethora of rigging hanging from the mast and lying about the deck for support, he made his way over to the mainmast.

"Katelyn?"

The illusionist raised her head, staring blankly for a few seconds; finally, recognition came to her. "Ge-or?"

Ge-or could see that she had been crying. As he touched her arm, she burst into tears. "Oh, Ge-or, he's gone. My brother is gone."

Author's Note

On Writing *The Chronicles of Borea*

In 1979-1980, I wrote the first book of *The Chronicles of Borea,* entitled *IXUS* (now the fifth book). At that time I sent this work out to a variety of publishers because it was still possible to do so. The book made it to several senior editors, from whom I received personal suggestions and comments re: revisions. Many of these were instrumental in the rewrites and the direction the series would go.

The idea of a Prequel to *IXUS* crept into the picture fairly early. I eventually wrote a short novel entitled *The Making of a Bard*, for my young son. Then, with my professional life taking up more of my time, I put this manuscript aside, and only sporadically returned to fiction over the next several decades.

Many years later, I envisioned expanding and finishing the *Chronicles.* From the early 2000s, I completely revised and expanded *IXUS – Corrente* several times; and *The Making of a Bard* was extended into a series of four complete works: *Preludio; Gigue; Siciliana; and Ciaccona.* The initial drafts of the final two books of this series -- *Civil War Threatens - Tempo di Borea;* and *The Great War - Grande Finale,* were completed in 2011. A novella, entitled *The Hunter's Mark*, was completed in 2022 and now serves as an introduction to the series.

As a musician and avid Sword and Sorcery fan, this series was a natural for me. I think my love of this genre really solidified when I read T.H. White's *The Once and Future King*, Tolkien, Lloyd Alexander, and others, and also when I was introduced to *Dungeons and Dragons* © -- Thank you, Gary Gygax and Dave Arneson, MYRIP.

I owe a great deal to all of these "mentors" and many other figures in this arena, and thus, have paid them homage by referring indirectly to their work. As an example: Tolkien's orcs have become a mainstay of gaming for a creature with certain characteristics. However, as it was pointed out to me by a senior editor of a famous publishing house, they are uniquely Tolkien. So as a nod to the Dean of this genre, I have twisted this type of creature to my own usage with "goblin" (used fairly synonymously with "orc" by Tolkien) as a beginning reference point. My goblins, gzks, and chatts are creatures who are from the same heritage, but were mutated by their environs – I have chatts of the desert, goblins of the caves, and gzks of the evergreen forests.

I also like to play games with titles, names, sayings, and words in general. Therefore, I began placing many references within my writings for fun. This probably started when I picked names for the characters in *IXUS*. Some of these are fairly obvious if your background includes the information to decipher them, e.g. Lassus is a Bard named in *The Making of the Bard, Book I* – Orlando di Lasso, or di Lassus, is a Renaissance musician (16th century). Others are more elusive and personal, e.g. Aelfric (a town in my kingdom) was a dwarf character of a librarian (thanks, Carol) in one of my early *Dungeons and Dragons* groups (as well as a real abbot and writer). I hope you will have some fun finding the hundreds of subtle underpinnings and references within these books.

As a musician, I like the <u>sound</u> of words, so I tend to play around with that a good bit in my manuscripts – note the opening to Book I -- *"Kla-a-ng, Kla-a-ng!" The deep pitch resound of the village bell echoed across the scattered boulders of the high hills...* The question is, "How would you <u>translate</u> 'Kla-a-ng' into sound?" What you hear in your head tends to be very personal. Throughout the series, I have considered the sounds of words as I write.

Truly, for my readers. my sincerest wish is that my writing is first and foremost enjoyable.

May your life be filled with the wonder and joy of words and sounds.

Joe Koob

About the Author

Dr. Koob is a former college music educator, having taught: – Violin, Viola, Cello, Bass; Music Courses; Interdisciplinary advanced seminars; and conducted University-Civic Symphonies for many years. He has performed in symphony orchestras throughout the United States and Europe.

Dr. Koob served in the United States Air Force during Vietnam as a C-141 Starlifter Navigator.

Education: Bachelor of Music – DePauw Univ; Master's Degree in Violin – Montclair State Univ; Master's Degree in Counseling, Northern State Univ; and Doctorate in Education – Univ. of Illinois.

Writing Awards: ***The Making of a Bard – Gigue, Book II*** of the ***Chronicles of Borea***, Winner of a **Kirkus Star**, 2023, *Kirkus Reviews*. ***A Perfect Day – Guide for a Better Life***: **Winner – Best Book Non-fiction,** Oklahoma Writers Federation, and **Certificate of Merit**, ***Writer's Digest*** Self-Published Book Awards. Winner Various Local and Regional Writing Competitions

His background includes work as an Executive Coach and Motivational Speaker; Author of Music Educational Software, Music Texts, Manuals, and Adjudicated Articles; as well as many books and articles on "Understanding and Working with Difficult People." Other interests include bicycling, woodworking, painting, reading, archery hunting, fishing, and more. Joe is happily married and has two grown children. He divides his time between FL and MI.

Website: **chroniclesofborea.com**

Blog: chroniclesofboreabooks.wordpress.com